THE STANDING STONE
The Challenge of the Master

A True-Life N

GW00746523

MARGARET DILLSAVER

OM FULL MOON ENTERPRISES

HARRIMAN, NEW YORK

Om Full Moon Enterprises
PO Box 78
Harriman, NY 10926

omfullmoonenterprises@gmail.com
www.omfullmoonenterprises.com

Cover picture by the author.

Design, Layout, and Typesetting by Alexander Becker
www.alexanderbecker.net

Manufactured in the United States of America

1 3 5 7 9 10 8 6 4 2

Library of Congress Control Number: 2013906330

ISBN-13: 978-0615800028
ISBN-10: 0615800025

FIRST EDITION

Dedicated to my Guru

Shri Brahmananda Sarasvati (Ramamurti S. Mishra, M.D.)

ACKNOWLEDGEMENTS

Ramamurti S. Mishra, M.D., founder of Ananda Ashram in Monroe, New York, also known as Shri Brahmananda Sarasvati, is the teacher, the Guru, who made an impact on my life that is beyond the scope of acknowledging with words. But I have tried. It is to him that this book is dedicated and it is about him that I write. Hopefully the reader will feel the amazing power of his presence and teachings.* Although he has departed his physical form, his dynamic energy continues to touch all who visit the Ashram or who have any direct connection to him.

Two friends were part of the halcyon days of the book's evolution. The debt I owe to them is lovingly acknowledged here and I hope they know they have my eternal gratitude. One provided the table and chair upon which the beginning and end of the book were written and can never be repaid for his great kindness to this American during her trips to England. He is George Elworthy. His gracious friendship was so deeply appreciated during the intense creative process that produced the manuscript. It was with George that I shared an evening toast on the day the first draft was finished. The other is Paul Samoilys, a provocative force throughout the writing. Without his presence in my life, the book would never have been written. Five of his letters to me are reprinted in Part II with his wholehearted permission. I am grateful for his approval of their usage in the book. This valuable contribution to the drama of the story is truly eloquent and beautiful. Few are the people we meet in our lives with whom we feel an immediate connection. As the reader will soon understand, Paul will forever have a special place in my heart.

---

* More about Shri Brahmananda Sarasvati can be found on the Ananda Ashram website at www.anandaashram.org.

For the sake of storytelling, most of the names have been changed, including those of the two friends mentioned above and a few of those mentioned below. However, I did not change the name of the Guru. In the story, just once he is introduced as Ramamurti S. Mishra, M.D., but otherwise he is referred to as "Guruji." His spiritual name of Shri Brahmananda Sarasvati was not so much in use at that time in the mid-1980s, and so I did not disclose it in the book.

One other name also was not changed. Nhoj (John Davey) kindly reviewed excerpts concerning the character based on him and consented to the use of his nickname. And he fortunately made sure that a particular joke used in the book was written correctly.

There are those who had an influence on this manuscript either directly or indirectly and to them I give my sincerest thanks: Dr. Mary Tasch, Pandit Banarsi, Angela Lazzaro, Dr. S. Lee Hays (my chiropractor in Oklahoma), Dr. Majid Ali (my physician in New Jersey) and Dr. Vasant Lad (the renowned Ayurvedic doctor who encouraged me to pursue publishing this work). The financial support of my parents in the 1980s, without which the concentrated focus needed for the writing would have been impossible, will forever be thankfully remembered. I am especially grateful to Dr. George F. Leone for his thoughtful and critical review of the manuscript at its early stage. I also thank my dear friend, Maria Sucheta Geer, whose timely assistance allowed me to begin the final editing, and my sister, Katharine Dillsaver, for catching errors and raising pertinent questions during her careful read-through of the manuscript in 2010. And I thank Joan Golley for introducing me to Haidakhandi Babaji's teachings. His beautiful eighteen-line message is presented in three installments, serving as epigraphs to the book's three parts. I thank Margaret DeVivo (Babaji.net) for kindly granting permission to use it.

The blessings that were bestowed by Baba Shivarudra Balayogi, Yogi Karve and Professor and Mrs. Ram Karan Sharma for

ACKNOWLEDGEMENTS

the success of this endeavor are gratefully acknowledged and were humbly received.

I don't know if an author can ever adequately thank an editor. Removing the myriad of mistakes, "adjusting" awkward phrasing, providing just the right word, keeping the text stylistically correct, and making it clear where rewriting is needed, an editor helps transform a work into something publishable. I firmly believe that it was providence that brought me Anna Knutson. The story about my Guru called for an editor who understood and appreciated his spiritual message. Formerly on staff at the ashram in 2010, Anna returned in 2012 after her trip to India and we connected when "by chance" I found out she was an editor by profession. I am awed by the amazing job she did.

I gratefully acknowledge the Baba Bhagavandas Publication Trust (BBPT) for giving permission to reprint Chapter Five from the *Fundamentals of Yoga: A Handbook of Theory, Practice and Application* by Ramamurti S. Mishra, M.D., (Shri Brahmananda Sarasvati), and to reproduce excerpts from Dr. Mishra's "Keynote Speech" given at the Second European Conference on Universal Brotherhood in Copenhagen, Denmark, July 1985; as well as transcriptions from several of his audio recordings. Radha Gaines and Bharati E. Balmes, both trustees of the BBPT, gave generously of their time in reviewing the manuscript at its later stage. As Anna, my wonderful editor, departed for a nine-month world tour, the final copy editing fell to Radha Gaines who brilliantly caught additional errors that I'm extremely grateful will forever remain unpublished. And her gentle alerts helped me recognize areas that needed to be smoother. Having this last critical review was a great gift. Also, Bharati Balmes was always solicitous in addressing my many questions. If there are any remaining errors in the book, the responsibility is solely mine.

A guiding hand was also needed in establishing the special agreement with the Baba Bhagavandas Publication Trust, wherein it was mutually agreed that a significant portion of the proceeds of each book sold would go to the BBPT, to be dedicated specifically for their support of the International Schools of East-West Unity, Inc., at Ananda Ashram and/or for an endowment. I thank Ron Cohen, Esq. of Cohen, LaBarbera & Landrigan, LLP for giving such guidance.

The cover picture was taken at Ananda Ashram on the summer solstice of 2012 by the author. But without the great help of Kutturu Radhika Charka with Adobe Photoshop, the picture would never have become the prototype for my book cover. For her kind assistance I am deeply grateful. I am also indebted to Kenneth J. Hatton for giving permission to reprint one of his graphics from a 1997 paper presented at the SUNY Institute of Technology. Nick Grimmer, Director of Alumni Affairs at SUNY Institute of Technology in Utica was kind enough to help put me in contact with Mr. Hatton. They both went out of their way to respond to my queries and for that I am very grateful.

In making the "final strokes" on the manuscript, I had wonderful exchanges with Bernie Davis, DaEl Walker, Roy Eugene Davis, Dava Sobel, Paul Devereux, Paul Screeton, Joy Palazzola, Father Benedict at St. Vladimir's Seminary, Connie Moore at NASA, Helen Wilson at Guardian News and Media Limited, Anna Meyer and Camille Apodaca at PARS International, Klaus Steeg at OSHO International, Yessenia Santos at Simon & Schuster, Inc. and Niki Stavrou at Kazantzakis Publications Ltd. Their kindness will not be forgotten.

In reading James Altucher's article, "Why Every Entrepreneur Should Self-Publish a Book," which my dear sister emailed to me, I discovered the name of Alexander Becker. It was with great excitement that I received Alexander's response to my query, stating that he would be willing to do the layout, typesetting and formatting for my book. His reassuring responses to all my questions relieved my trepidation in approaching self-publishing. He also masterfully transformed the book cover. I have a cyberspace basketful of gratitude to Alexander,

ACKNOWLEDGEMENTS

whom I hope one day to meet in person, for all that he did to give a professional presentation to the book.

And finally, I must also thank a very mystical teacher who came into my life in 2004 during my stay in Pune, India. I very much feel that Shri Brahmananda Sarasvati guided me to her. Her name is Dolano.*

* More about Dolano can be found on her website at www.dolano.com or www.myspace.com/dolanosatsang or www.friendsofdolano.org

PREFACE

I wrote this book, events from my life, not as a memoir but as though it was a work of fiction. It was the only way I could write it. It is told from the perspective of a narrator who has spent an afternoon in dialogue with the protagonist, a young woman who has studied with a Master. Without thinking of it as someone's personal saga, I wanted the reader to identify with the journey of exploring the unknown of the unmanifest world. But the details and descriptions given are exactly as I experienced them. Throughout the book, I have capitalized the words Guru and Master instead of following grammatical convention, because I so strongly felt to honor those who have shown us the way.

Deepak Chopra writes in *The Third Jesus*, "Jesus is pressing the disciples to move swiftly onto the spiritual path if they want to outpace illusion."[1] I loved that expression, "to outpace illusion," the illusion of all our suffering, misery, insecurity, anxiety created as we blindly grope for the meaning in our lives. The good news is that the "reality" of our lives is fictional or illusory in nature, defined as it is by time and space, and to realize this, all we have to do is shift our awareness. "But shift our awareness to what?" you might ask.

Osho writes in *The Dhammapada: The Way of the Buddha*, "One of the most important things to be understood about man is that man is asleep. [...] You sleep in the night, you sleep in the day; from birth to death you go on changing your patterns of sleep, but you never really awake. Just by opening the eyes don't befool yourself that you are awake. Unless your inner eyes open, unless your inside becomes full of light, unless you can see yourself, who you are, don't think that you are awake. [...] Hence Buddha's insistence...and not only Gautama the

Buddha but all the buddhas have insisted on only one thing: Awake! Continuously, for centuries, their whole teaching can be contained in a single word: Be *awake!* And they have been devising methods, strategies, they have been creating contexts and spaces, and energy fields in which you can be shocked into awareness. Yes, unless you are shocked, shaken to your very foundations, you will not awaken."[2]

This awakening is a spiritual awakening. It is a shift to something beyond relativity, beyond the body and sense organs, beyond the mind, to the path of enlightenment, to God-consciousness. To make this shift, it helps very much to have a Guru, a Master. In this book, I write about my experiences with a Master, the man I have called "Guruji." Yes, in this story, you will see the strategies, the amazing "context and spaces" he created to shake me to my very foundations. The words Guruji speaks in the book are direct quotes, many recorded by the hand of this author while in his presence. His message is real. I hope I have done it justice. His name is Shri Brahmananda Sarasvati, Dr. Ramamurti S. Mishra.

There is one word that stands out when investigating the world beyond relativity. The word is "paradox." Mystery is wrapped in its very meaning—defined by the American Heritage Dictionary as "a seemingly contradictory statement that may nonetheless be true." To see the trueness requires the courage to leap into the unknown. And for this to be possible, a willingness and deep yearning is absolutely needed. Then the unknown can become known. Shri Brahmananda Sarasvati wanted us to leap.

If we use our mind, we can arrive at logical conclusions, or form praiseworthy opinions, but really we cannot *know* anything on the spiritual path. The wonderfully radical Zen Master Dolano profoundly summarized it this way in a discourse during her Intensive Satsang in Pune, India: "It is all so different from what we hear, what we read, what we understand. It is all so different. In the end you will be surprised. You read a sentence after you have the right vision; you laugh. You say,

'My God, the words are right, but what I understood at that time was definitely not like that.'"[3] This is the paradox. This is the challenge facing any Master: to help remove the paradoxical shroud creating the illusion of our separation from the realm beyond relativity. When this illusion vanishes, then we know the truth that our natural state is divine.

PART I

~

ICKWELL

Love and serve all humanity.
Assist everyone.
Be happy, be courteous.
Be a dynamo of irrepressible joy.
Recognize God and goodness in every face.
There is no saint without a past and no sinner without a future.

Excerpt of Message from Haidakhandi Babaji
www.babaji.net

See epigraphs of Part II and Part III for continuation of message.
Reprinted with permission.

ONE

~

She could not have been more than four or five at the time. She sat on the couch in the living room. It was early evening. She does not remember where her parents or her sister were; she remembers only that she was alone. But this was not unusual. She often spent solitary hours bouncing on the couch, sitting and rocking rhythmically. It was not a good habit, but one that was marginally tolerated in the family. She loved to bounce. Although there was a rocking chair in the room and she also had her own small one, she favored the couch, to the chagrin of her parents. More than once they'd had to reattach the back cushion buttons. But in the adult rocker her feet could not reach the floor and it was tiring to keep it rocking. The child's rocker tended to slide backward with each rock and required readjustment of seven feet forward after only ten minutes of rocking, which was a nuisance. She was most comfortable on the couch, with her feet barely hanging over the edge of the cushion. It was ideal. It had a tall back with good padding. But what she liked best was that it was across from the stereo.

She rarely bounced without music. She had learned quite early, as children often do, how to turn on and off the console stereo and record player. Looking back, her parents were lenient in allowing her to do this since they were strict about her touching other things in the house. She was grateful for their leniency since it gave her great pleasure to stack several classical records onto the tall silver post, balancing them above the black turntable, each to drop down in its own time.

The stereo had a tiny amber light at the bottom of the console which lit up when the stereo was on and glowed beautifully in the dark. She had passed many long hours sitting and staring directly at that light, bouncing rhythmically to violins and flutes exquisitely orchestrated by great composers. Even now, many years later, she can see that golden light and hear the strains of music, which included Tchaikovsky's *Symphony No. 5 in E minor (opus 64), Swan Lake, The Nutcracker* and Borodin's *String Quartet No. 2.*

The sun had almost set. The room had a hazy glow through the drapes which had already been pulled. She stopped bouncing and slid down so her feet touched the carpet, still half sitting on the edge of the couch. Then it came as a wave. She sensed it coming but did not know what it was. She began to feel as though every object in the room had a sharp edge to it... the orange pillow on the chair, the coffee table in front of her, even the lighting and the air in the room had a sharpness about it. She didn't move except to slowly turn her head. Then the sensation changed and everything took on a different feeling, as though things were flowing together in soft, gentle curves. She even felt her body was melting as the strange sensation moved across her skin. She liked this feeling better than the sharpness.

She remembers thinking, "Sharp edges, no edges. I must never forget."

The feeling passed away. She does not recall having been frightened or concerned, nor thinking there was a need to tell anyone about it. But even if she had wanted to tell someone, how to put it into words that they could understand? This is actually the first time she has spoken of the experience, and even in telling me, she was not sure she could adequately describe it, as though the words did not exist which could possibly recount what had happened. Imagine a young child trying to describe such feelings. An adult would have thought it a wonderful creation of the child's imagination or would have been at a total loss to give any explanation for it. This she seemed inherently to know and so had remained quiet about it until now, decades later.

The experience repeated itself only once after that, when she was eight. This time she was sitting in a rocking chair starring blankly into space. Music was playing. It was afternoon, about four-thirty. She'd come home from school and plopped down for a "rock" before going back outside. Rocking had become like a friend, giving her comfort and a quiet moment to mull over ideas or just daydream about anyone or anything. This day was not unlike any other. Nothing extraordinary had been on her mind. Then, she once more noticed that strange feeling. She watched it. Things around her began to take on a different quality.

She thought, "At last, it has come again."

But the thought alone seemed to interfere, and the feeling did not last nearly as long as the time before. Again, something in her body felt different. The odd sensation soon went away and she continued rocking slowly.

Elizabeth Susan Dolman did not relate these experiences to me to necessarily imply that she was a child out of the ordinary. The point was that these experiences brought to her an awareness that reality was not always clearly definable, that there possibly did exist something beyond "normal" perception. She was sure of this since none of her senses had been able to explain to her what she had felt. Although only occurring twice in her childhood, she never forgot these moments of strange sensations.

A major turning point in her life came when she was sixteen years old and her sociology teacher inquired of the class, "Who believes in God?"

In that split second she asked herself rapidly ten times over, "Do I or don't I? Do I or don't I?"

Confronting her skepticism, she raised her hand with those negating the existence of a divine being. But it left her with an unsettled feeling. Not being indoctrinated in any formal religious teachings, she did not know where to seek the real answer. Baptized Episcopalian, her family had left the church when she was six years old, the reasons for which she didn't explain to me. But she had some vague memories of her churchgoing days; dutifully singing "Onward Christian soldiers marching as to war..." while sitting in a high-ceilinged room looking out colorful stained-glass windows; reading in her Sunday School book stories which were nice like any other story but with no other greater meaning.

The question of the existence of a God preyed on her mind, although by outward appearances one would not have guessed that there was anything deeply disturbing her. But the disturbance surfaced at seventeen in the form of a severe depression. This was a time in her life when she should have been happy and satisfied. She had successfully completed her junior year of high school and it was a lovely summer August.

Her mother assumed Elizabeth's gloomy outlook was a sign that a change in surroundings was needed. Concerned that the depression was lasting so long—almost three weeks by her estimation—she proposed that her daughter visit a country retreat. It was one that she herself had visited a few years earlier. It must be said that this was no ordinary retreat. It was an ashram. Her mother had discovered it through an interest in yoga and had been very impressed with the books she had read by its founder, a man of unusual character. "This man," Elizabeth had said to me, "will hereafter be referred to as 'Guruji.'"

Still assuming that it was summer doldrums from which her daughter was suffering and not a deep anxiety about life's meaning and purpose, Mrs. Dolman had dropped Elizabeth at the doorstep of the ashram. Here Elizabeth was to meet her spiritual teacher. She had known of this man since she was seven, when her mother had begun reading excerpts from his books to her and her sister. Elizabeth had herself started reading one of his books when she was fifteen, but had only gotten as far as the first few chapters. It was not that she had lost interest but that there had suddenly been too much to assimilate to go any further. The last chapter she had read was Chapter Five, entitled "Rules for Practice of Yoga." She had stopped there because of the instruction at the end of the chapter which stated: "Now you have finished this fifth lesson. Close your eyes and recall all the rules. Consider them. Read the lesson again, close your eyes, and remember it. Do this until you remember the lesson by heart."[4] It had taken her two years before she could claim she'd even come close to memorizing it, because to memorize it, it had to be put into practice. These were the rules that had begun to guide her life from that point on:

1. Keep before the mind the fact that you have firmly decided to reform your life and to transform your conscious and subconscious mind into superconscious mind.

2. Enrich yourself with every possible truth and renounce untruth and prejudice as soon as possible.

3. Every mental and physical condition is in accordance with the judgment of supreme consciousness and supreme nature. The child may weep if an operation is needed but parents decide to do the operation to save the child. In the same way, you are unhappy and full of anxiety, but this operation on your mind is permitted by nature to save you from destruction. Even death is nothing but the greatest operation; after this operation, old age is removed and the Self is incarnated again as a child. Ponder over it and be free from all cares of body and mind.

4. An unhappy and restless mind cannot concentrate. Make every possible effort to make your mind happy and peaceful. The standard of admission in Yoga is a peaceful and happy mind.

5. Increase the atmosphere of expectancy and remove melancholy from the mind.

6. Believe in yourself and in your mind, and that you will obtain the supreme state.

7. If you fail to obtain some positive results in your practice, do not lose confidence. Owing to your inexperience, you are not yet able to recognize the positive higher changes in your mind. You may have the traditional habit of looking at the back of your mind.

8. Make it a habit to stand as a witness in every mental activity. Thus, you will save yourself from being the agency of mind and become the guide to your mind as an instructor. Don't play with your mind as if you were a servant and an agent. If you do so, you will face calamity.

9. Truth in speech, simplicity in manner, and firmness of mind are infallible divine instruments to certain success.

10. You must concentrate your mental waves with utter and complete confidence in yourself and in the nature in you and around you, which have manifested innumerable suns, stars, and planets.

11. Don't be nervous; a nervous attitude may interfere with your performance.

12. Know this: Mental and natural powers are looking to you to give you something that you have never seen before. They want to enrich you with divine and eternal powers. Eternal forces are serving you constantly, whether you know it or not. Before birth and after death, where no material things can go with you, these natural forces are serving you. Wherever you go, they are there before you.

13. Remember, you can do anything and everything that has been done by any great Yogi or Saint in human history. By your performance you can become a son of God, and by the highest performance you can become one with God. Nothing is impossible to the mind.

14. One wave of the mind is always skeptical of everything. Do not consider this wave as an ordinary one. Try to solve it in

a right way through your instructor and practice; otherwise skepticism will wreck your performance. Here or hereafter there is no success or happiness for the skeptical. Always, from the beginning of your practice, it will try to create doubt and suspicion in your practice, but after a few days of practice these mental waves will be the first to applaud your success in concentration. These mental waves of skepticism at first refuse to recognize anything. They recognize facts: nothing but facts. No philosophy, no religion, no gods or God is recognized by these waves. They recognize only direct experience. Therefore, to conquer these waves, practice constantly. They recognize your successful experimentation. When these waves perceive directly the eternal electromagnetic current of supreme consciousness, they recognize your feat and become your fast friend. When you have mastered your skeptical nature and obtained the right method of autosuggestion (*dhyāna*), you will have powerful mental waves in your favor. Now those waves which are weaker and still present in your mind cannot disturb you because you have seen the truth. Now you are not only the master of your mind, but you are going to become the master of all material minds.

15. Practice of Yoga will open the third eye in you, which is called "Yoga *dṛiṣṭi*," "*divya dṛiṣṭi*, " or "divine eye."

16. Demand complete silence from your material mind and command it completely. When you achieve this control, nothing can disturb your practice.

17. Do your practice seriously. If you do it lightly, you may lose faith, confidence and enthusiasm in yourself.

18. When you see any extraordinary vision, feel no fear; otherwise you may have a nervous breakdown, or you may harbor fear of ghosts or of death in your mind. No harm can befall you. Go into deepest experimentation. Place your body in a comfortable position and soon you will magnetize your body. Your mind will soon be enlightened.

19. There is one other peculiar disturbing wave of the mind: the wave of arrogance. In practice you obtain success, and success sometimes brings conceit, and conceit brings hypocrisy. Be careful. Do not harbor this wave in your mind, as it may ruin you. You are not doing anything that has not been done previously by Yogis. It is not you but supreme consciousness and nature that want to present you before the world for the service of all living beings. Be careful not to become arrogant and conceited. Respect all more than yourself.

20. A proper and clear-cut suggestion is important to your mind. If you do not start distinct and powerful autosuggestion, your mind will start its own suggestion to you, and you will be governed by your mind. By powerful autosuggestion govern your mind, but do not let yourself be governed by your material mind."[5]

Standing under a tree on the ashram, Elizabeth saw a man in an orange robe in the distance walking across the grass toward a large white house. She had known that this was Guruji. She stood silently and watched him pass. She remembers the moment so clearly because, in a sense, at that moment her life would take a whole new direction, because it was this man who would help her come to understand the dimension into which she had only but glimpsed during those first few years of her life. For she knew it was an altered state of consciousness that she had experienced, sitting after long periods of time gazing at that amber light or at that point in space, a meditative technique she would soon learn was called *trāṭakam*. The feelings she'd had then she would now begin to comprehend. And oddly they were related to the question of God which had so filled her with doubt, wonder, and confusion during the past year. It would almost seem as though the very great desire to understand this question had brought her to someone who could show her the answer.

But the answer would come in the form of training and discipline, and its full assimilation would in fact require a lifetime's effort. She had kept a respectful distance from the man in orange, a former medical doctor and East Indian. Her first visit to the ashram lasted for twelve days. And over the course of the first few days, her depression had lifted and she had become aware of a lighter feeling inside.

ℰ * * * ℭ

She next told me of an odd occurrence that took place during one of her first meditations with this teacher. It was a group meditation held outdoors on the grass. Everyone had been deeply relaxing, lying on their backs, and Guruji had been leading a guided meditation. To give me an idea of what that was like, she played just a few minutes of an audio recording. Guruji's voice was deep and resonant: "Enter into your own form. Tell your thinking mind to go into sleep and feel directly the pulsation...within you. Feel it. Feel your form like the blue sky—pulsation of your life, dynamic vibration of *prāṇa*, cosmic energy. Feel this body is your cosmic television, with which the total universe is communicating and expressing. There are seven bodies, one after the other within: physical; etheric, pure vibration, the body of meridians; astral, the body of mutual pulsation and projection; mental, the universe of pure light and sensation; the body of individual consciousness and cosmic consciousness, joined together; and the body of blue sky. Now transcend the seven bodies and seven *chakras:** crown *chakra* in the head; third eye; *vishuddhi chakra* in the neck; heart *chakra* in the chest; solar plexus in the navel region of the abdomen; *svādhiṣṭhāna* and *mūlādhāra*... Your real form is present everywhere in the space. Feel it... Feel every part of the body submerged in the blue sky, dynamic vibration and pulsation."[6]

Just like this he had guided them that day, and she said that when Guruji spoke of the heart *chakra* as she lay there in the grass, she had suddenly felt as though someone was reaching inside her chest and trying to pull her out.

---

* energy centers

She described it to me: "I had heard of 'out-of-body' experiences and couldn't help wondering at the time if this was what was about to happen. But I cannot say that I was out 'there' somewhere looking down on my own body and everyone else's, watching, as is described by people who have near-death experiences. No, I did not get all the way out. I was somewhere in between. There were no visions behind my closed eyes, only that very strange sensation over my heart. Then suddenly I heard Guruji saying something about coming back into the physical form.

"My mind was saying, 'No, no, just a few more minutes.' But already I could feel I was back. I sat up and immediately had an enormous surge of energy, unlike any burst of energy I had ever felt.

"I thought out loud, 'I just feel like running.'

"The man next to me turned and said with amusement, 'Well, run.'

"That was enough. I stood up and took off running at top speed across the grassy slope behind the white house. For just a moment, I felt like I was flying. I didn't want to stop but my mind began to shout, 'Sharp gravel ahead, sharp gravel ahead. Better stop now. Now!' So I did stop, just inches from the gravel road.

"Another voice in me started chiding, 'What a fool you were to stop. You were flying, anyway. No harm would have come.' I laughed at myself and thought, 'What are these two voices within me?'"

ℴ * * * ℳ

Elizabeth had often wondered about those two voices within, which met many times over the next few years of her life, acting almost as two forces pulling her in opposite directions. She began to understand that it was the battle between the rational and intuitive mind, or the skeptical mind and the mind of faith, the finite and the infinite mind. It was the same battle that she knew was allegorically described in the great Sanskrit epic, the *Mahābhārata*, the longest poem ever written. The mind of the tangible has a difficult time when it comes into contact with the unknown and, being thoroughly bamboozled by it, often tries to think up excuses to prevent any further contact. But some part of Elizabeth knew that that unknown world was real. She knew it, and that short ashram stay had awakened an even greater curiosity and desire to understand it. At seventeen, she found a mystery before her which was tremendously transforming her life. She couldn't explain what that mystery was or where it would lead, but time and time again, it was to pull her back to that place and to that teacher.

℘ * * * ℭ

Elizabeth asked me, "Why do we strive after *that* which we cannot understand? On the physical level, a simple answer would be curiosity. But on a metaphysical level much more is at stake." She elaborated, "I cannot forget reading in a *New York Times* article about a doctor at the National Institute of Mental Health who, frustrated by the lack of a simple chemical solution to the puzzle of schizophrenia, liked to quote the satirist H. L. Mencken: 'For any complex question there is almost always a simple answer—that is almost always wrong.'[7]

"Many would say that if we did not ask ourselves questions for which there were no answers then there would be no technological advancement, no scientific investigations, no theoreticians, and no philosophers," she continued. But Elizabeth was not pursuing an ordinary question. The Oxford Dictionary defines metaphysics as "the theoretical philosophy of being and knowing, or the philosophy of the mind."

She had laughed at this definition. "How can the cognitive mind discuss the philosophy of the mind? A paradox is there somewhere, right? The mind is asking about the nature of itself. It is really this 'nature' to which the 'that' in my question referred: Why do we strive to know the nature of the mind, which we cannot understand with the mind? If a question cannot be resolved on the physical or mental planes, meaning by experimentation or calculation or through inductive or deductive reasoning, then where are we to find the answers? But this is the beauty of a teacher like Guruji. He teaches metaphysical experimentation. A truer 'science' cannot exist.

"Many have wondered why it cannot be simply told how to attain enlightenment. Several years after first meeting Guruji, I was perusing a university bookstore and overheard two young women complaining about the works of Carlos Castaneda, the anthropologist who tells of a world of mystical sensation and perception and of the teacher, Don Juan, who showed him how to see beyond the surface realities of life.

"They were saying, 'His books are really fascinating to read but they're only descriptions of the sublime state of mind. They don't really tell you how to get there.'

"But the true nature of enlightenment cannot be conveyed in books. Books are meant to inspire those who are on a path toward understanding the mysteries of life. The secrets cannot be told directly. Only conditions can be created to allow for the Knowledge to be revealed. Much preparation is needed beforehand, and this is what many fail to realize. The Knowledge comes as a blossoming. But the greatest obstacle to this blossoming is, ironically, the thinking mind. Thinking makes knowledge finite, and the Knowledge is of an infinite nature. Only with the infinite mind can it ever be tapped. It is this infinite mind which is tickled into operation by the metaphysical experiments of the Guru. And tickled it has to be, for the analytical mind shakes with trepidation at the thought of ceasing. And yet only in its silence can the Knowledge come shining through. So the Master has to trick the disciple's thinking mind.

"But the students of a Master also know that they are going to be tricked. And that is actually part of the fun of it. Just as when watching a magic show, we sit in total anticipation of being fooled. It would be a great disappointment if the magician did not succeed. So it is, in a way, sitting at the feet of a Master. We know he is going to trick us and we are hoping that he succeeds; because if he succeeds and we can have a glimpse of the infinite mind, its existence is proven in that split second of direct perception. We no longer have to merely believe.

"One technique Guruji teaches is how to magnetize the body. Science has just recently come to show the direct connection between body and mind, but the Masters of ancient times understood this synergism. It is easy to prove. Relax the body. Breathe deeply. Release the tension in the neck, the base of the spine, the bottoms of the feet, and the tension in the mind is also released. And what is creating the mental tension in the first place? The constantly moving thoughts. The Guru is of course going much deeper than just relaxing the body and mind. He needs the body to be magnetized so that the thinking mind will become magnetized. It is only in this state that the 'other dimension' can be experienced.

"Guruji would direct, 'Feel yourself without thinking. Self-knowledge does not come from without. It is within you. You will not obtain enlightenment. Enlightenment is your inner nature. You have to feel it. You have not to believe anything.'

"He would have his students lie down in a comfortable position or sit so that there was no pain or uneasiness," she explained.

And again, so that I would understand more clearly about going into this deeper state, she played another audio recording. Guruji's instructions were: "Feel pulsation of the life force in your chest—the soothing pulsation of your heart. Feel the pulsation of the life force in your entire chest, back, both shoulders, both lungs and heart.

"When you begin to feel pulsation in your entire chest and back, then feel pulsation in both arms, upper arms, lower arms, palms and fingers, in the form of blood circulation...

29

From the heart to the tips of all fingers and from the tips of fingers to lungs and heart through the circulation. You have to do *nothing*. You have only to realize, feel. Because the pulsation of blood is already going on, back and forth. Otherwise, without this circulation of blood, you would be dead.

"Feel the pulsation of the life force in the form of blood circulation from the heart to the neck, face, eyes, nose, ears, forehead, the head and brain, and from these to the heart. Feel the pulsation of the life force in the form of blood circulation to the abdomen, navel region, all abdominal organs and from the abdomen to the heart. Feel pulsation of the life force from the heart to the upper legs, lower legs, feet and toes and from these to the heart.

"Feel pulsation of blood from the heart to the entire body simultaneously: skeleton, muscles, skin, all organs. Now your television and radio are transistorized to enter the inner space journey which is far better than the outer space journey.

"Now feel the flow of electricity, *prāṇa*, from the heart to the entire body and atmosphere that surrounds you, and from these to the heart... For two minutes, feel the radio waves. How will you know the physical body? You will feel it no more. You will feel the body of electricity, the body of pulsation."[8]

Elizabeth told me she remembers when she first started practicing this type of meditation. "I thought to myself, 'Could it be possible to feel that pulsation over the entire body at once?' It seemed almost unimaginable. But then I did begin to feel some tingling in my hands. And with more practice my hands and back, then my hands, back and lower neck. I would practice while going to sleep; concentrating on one part of the body, envisioning that part, surrounding it with a white or blue light. Each time it was like a test to see if some feeling would come. And it did come. Concentrating one night on my leg with great intensity, feeling the pulsations, my leg suddenly disappeared. I lay there wondering where it had gone. I didn't even think

I could find it to move it. And what if I did that to the whole body?"

And there was only one way for Elizabeth to find out. She kept practicing. She found that as the body began to dissolve, an inner sound filled her head. Guruji described this sound as an electric dynamo, present in everyone. She read from her personal notes his explanation: "This is the inner *OM*. The Bible calls it 'the Word' and 'original light.' Mystics call it 'cosmic music.' *Kuṇḍalinī* yoga calls it 'eternal *Gāyatrī*.' It is the mathematical zero, or cosmic energy, playing with the mathematical point, or consciousness. The whole universe is the dance of the point and zero; soul and mind; Shiva and Shakti; Rādhā and Kṛiṣhṇa. As a man crosses mountains, rivers and oceans with a rocket during outer space travel, so the meditator crosses over all difficulties during his inner space journey with this sound, *nādam*."

℘ * * * ℭ

Elizabeth had come to know what was meant by altered states of consciousness. Meditation was not just sitting and putting oneself half to sleep by a form of self-hypnosis. It was instead a test, a test to see how much sensation the central nervous system could detect and then going beyond all sensation. It meant going deeply into each feeling, trying to expand it, to feel it all over the body, so intensely that the mind would begin to shout for fear of being overwhelmed, and then continuing even deeper. Expressing this phenomenon to those who had not experienced it seemed extraordinarily difficult for Elizabeth. Yet Guruji seemed to have no trouble guiding students to that point.

℘ * * * ℭ

"He would coax, 'Feel directly that your body has become a divine television, radio and computer. You will feel the whole universe is in your consciousness and that your consciousness is in the whole universe,'" she quoted from her notes, clearly moved by the power behind these words.

Elizabeth hesitated to talk about the Guru-disciple relationship. "It is difficult to discuss this relationship because as the disciple, many times it is impossible to understand what the Guru is doing. But as one starts to follow the guidance of a Master, to practice what the Master is teaching, the skeptical mind begins to dissolve. A natural trust arises between disciple and Master, a trust of unfathomable depth. This trust is needed for the real teachings to be conveyed. Because remember, it is not conveyed with words. It cannot be. Words belong to the universe of the senses. True awareness is beyond the senses, and therefore beyond words. Only indication can be given. Without deep trust, a deep communion, the disciple will miss grasping what the Guru indicates. Or the indication will be misunderstood. And disciples continually go on misunderstanding the Guru. When the thinking mind is present, then the disciple will miss. But with the trust, the devotee gains courage to drop the thinking mind, to let go of the ego."

℘ * * * ℭ

Elizabeth's relationship with Guruji was a close one. For her, every word he spoke contained the seeds of truth. So if he said, "Do not leave the ashram today," she would not question his instruction. But this trust was not unfounded. Many times in hindsight she saw the wisdom of his guidance.

℘ * * * ℭ

"It was during one of my earlier visits. I had gone to Guruji's cottage to say goodbye. I was to fly the next day to Georgia to see a friend and then return to Oklahoma to continue my university studies. Guruji looked into my eyes and said, 'No, no, no. Do not leave tomorrow. Leave the day after tomorrow.' Now this meant totally rescheduling my flight and calling my friend long-distance. But I did it. My friend was greatly dismayed. Our visit was to have been only a few short days anyway. We were in love and he could not understand why one more day at the ashram was needed. He tried to dissuade me. His arguments were persuasive. But I kept feeling the penetration of Guruji's gaze. After two hours on the phone, the job was complete. I would be leaving the day after tomorrow. So much trouble just to arrange for one additional day. I wondered why Guruji had said I should stay. What kind of test was this? I had read stories of how Masters tested their disciples. I felt this must be a test.

"Sitting in meditation that evening, a tightness came to my throat. Awaking the next morning, I could barely swallow, nor did my body feel like moving from my bed. I managed to get to the meditation room but sitting up was impossible. Every muscle ached. My head was clouded with fever. I retreated to the adjacent room to lay down. As Guruji passed by afterward, he asked if I was okay. I feebly responded that I was and that I would still do my karma yoga or work project after breakfast. He nodded and walked away. I did get up then, and foregoing breakfast, I went to the small print shop where I had been assisting with the publication of a brochure. The fever made everything move in slow motion. I don't know why I was trying to fight the dizziness. But it intensified suddenly and I could fight it no longer. I told Kathy, the woman running the press, that I had to lie down. She quickly guided me to a small back room where a futon lay on the floor. Even the memory runs in slow motion through my head. As I lowered myself down onto that mat, knowing I could not possibly stand one minute longer, starry lights appeared before my eyes. They were small, bright and shining, white and blue lights. I had never had such a vision. I'm not sure how long I slept. But it was toward evening when I awoke. The fever was gone. My throat was no longer sore. I had a feeling of lightness when I walked.

"That night during the meditation program with Guruji, it seemed as though something had lifted from me. I felt happy. I received Guruji's blessing to leave the next day. He never commented on my 'illness' and I said nothing to him about it. But an understanding was there. From experiences like this came the immeasurable trust."

TWO

~

It was an evening in mid-May when Elizabeth phoned the ashram to see how Guruji was feeling and to inquire about his summer plans. She had wanted to speak to one of his assistants. She hadn't expected to talk to Guruji. In fact, she had never asked to speak to Guruji on the phone. It seemed superfluous given the nature of her relationship with him. Theirs was a more silent understanding. She never felt the need to put any question to him directly. But when he spoke to her, she would listen very carefully. From his lips no unnecessary word would come, only the nectar of truth. To her amazement, on this evening in May, he was the one who picked up the receiver. When Elizabeth heard his voice on the phone, she felt everything within stop. Had he known she was the one calling? If so, then she wanted to be absolutely still in order to grasp his real message.

She heard his husky, accented voice calling out, "How are you? What are you doing?"

Elizabeth perceived that whatever answer she might give would be beside the point. He had not picked up the phone so he could inquire about her health. This was merely the lead-in question, in preparation for something more. So she made her reply short and nondescript. "I'm fine, Guruji. I'm here working."

He responded, "How about Denmark? Do you want to go?"

Immediately she got it. Without needing to know any of the particulars, she understood. He was not asking her to give pros or cons about whether she could go or not. His asking alone indicated that she should go. That was their unspoken understanding.

She replied, knowing he didn't really need any response from her, "Anything can be planned, Guruji."

He ended with, "Okay, okay. *Harih OM.*"

℘ * * * ℃

Those few words from him were enough. In that split second he had once again given her life a whole new direction. Something out of the unknown had just appeared before her. She felt dazed and admitted to me that her mind raced suddenly to George.

She had met George in England a year before. The moment she saw him, she said, it was as though a cannonball had landed in her stomach. It didn't sound like the most romantic way to describe love at first sight to me. But she explained that the unexpectedness and intensity of the moment far transcended romance.

"We know what it's like to have recollection of forgotten memories, but it's those times when we are reminded of something we can't believe we ever forgot that comes closest to describing the feeling of that first meeting. There was a sudden recognition, but of whom and what and why? He was a total stranger, and yet I knew that I knew him..."

In the middle of our talk, she stopped abruptly. Her eyes had a distant gaze to them. But in the next moment she returned to her animated self. She conceded that when we least expect it, the thing we're waiting for the most can suddenly drop into our laps. And so George had dropped into hers. She had traveled to England with Guruji. "Deciding to take that trip to England really was a divine test, for it came at a most inopportune time in my life.

"I had been working at a university as a technical writer for three years already. My boss had become well accustomed to my extended sojourns to the ashram in New York. Every minute of vacation time plus several leaves of absences he had known me to spend with some spiritual teacher. In an odd way, he seemed to respect that part of my life, although I doubted he really understood. He was a very pragmatic scientist, and talk about any state beyond the thinking mind probably left him shaking his head. But something in his scientific nature also prevented him from being totally closed-minded. The unknown is something with which scientists are quite familiar. Great scientific discoveries were manifested out of uncharted territories. I doubt he could deny that the human mind was one of the foremost unknowns confronting man."

Elizabeth was sitting back now, totally at ease. As she talked, her tone was soft yet with a certain precision. The memory of the trip was sharp in her mind but the recollection of it seemed to fill her with awe and wonder. Although I was very curious to know more about George and why the phone call with Guruji had brought him so suddenly to her mind, she wanted first to backtrack a bit and recount the circumstances and events just prior to their meeting. It struck me that their relationship, which had begun by a rather unusual encounter, had a mystery behind it that would be revealed in the story she was about to tell me.

She continued, "So my boss quietly let me come and go from my job without interfering or putting forth any strong objection.

"I had not been planning to go to the ashram that summer," the summer before the May phone conversation with Guruji. "But at the end of June I had completed a project at work and found myself with a few free weeks before I was to meet and work with a visiting research scientist from Japan. He was working in collaboration with my boss and I was assisting in the preparation of manuscripts for publication. My function was to take the rough drafts written in broken English by our foreign visitor and tie them into a coherent whole with proper presentation of data and deductive conclusion. A total of nine roughly formatted papers had already been written and were on my desk. But I had completed as much of the rewriting as was possible without further clarification from the author.

"Without a day's delay, I informed my boss that everything was ready for the meeting with our soon-to-be-arriving visitor and asked if it would be all right to slip off to the ashram for a few weeks. With a serious look in his eye, he consented as long as I was sure that I was prepared for the intensive meeting with Dr. Miura, the scientist traveling to our university on the invitation of my boss. Reassuring him, I departed for the ashram.

"Now the plans for England were already in the making. Guruji had been invited to give a ten-day intensive seminar on yoga at a retreat just north of London. He had been to England before and seemed pleased with the prospect of returning. I was thoroughly enjoying my ashram stay as usual, attending all the *satsangs* or gatherings with Guruji, feeling the nourishment that I had so been needing and craving after an absence of many months from him. Although I maintained a daily practice when I was home, the power of the meditations in the presence of the Guru is indescribable. Guruji always taught us to have attunement. If we were attuned to his being, his energy, then he would be working with us no matter the physical distance. Somehow, though, proximity with the Guru brought that attunement into flowering. Therefore, it was with great delight that we would ascend the staircase to his small apartment located on the upper story of a large house to read to him. We all knew that these reading sessions were for our benefit rather than for his, but he would never let on about this fact. He would sit cross-legged, his eyes closed in concentration, and listen to every word, asking us to repeat certain passages when the meaning was seemingly unclear.

"I was upstairs reading to Guruji when at the end of a chapter he waved his hand, indicating to put the book down. I laid the book on the maroon and blue tapestry rug covering the floor of his sitting room and waited. He looked at me with a slightly mischievous smile and said, 'Wouldn't you like to go to England?'"

"I sat and looked at him with eyes that had no answer. Of course I wanted to, but how could I possibly go? Guruji and the others traveling with him were planning to leave in three weeks. Feeling certain that the divine knew something I didn't, I did not give any answer. After a moment's silence, Guruji nodded and I continued reading.

"All odds seemed to be stacked against even considering going. But to tell Guruji that my job responsibilities were too great at this time to allow me to travel with him didn't seem right, either. I could feel the shift in my own energy with just the thought. So I opted to wait. I said nothing to anyone else about the inner conflict I was in. One thing I had learned from Guruji was the power of silence.

"He would say, 'Language in crude form uses words and speech and thinking, whereas language in subtle form works in silence.' I much preferred the subtle approach when in difficulty.

"Guruji liked to tell a story to illustrate the advantage of keeping quiet, about two swans and a turtle who had lived together happily for some time. One day food for the swans ran short and they were forced to search for another place to live. Not wanting to be left behind, the turtle asked if he could join them. The swans were happy to take the turtle with them. Seeing as he could not fly, they devised a clever plan. Finding a golden thread, the swans decided they would carry it in their beaks as they flew. They instructed their friend to hold onto the thread with his teeth. Just before take-off, they reminded the turtle to maintain absolute silence so as not to lose his hold. The swans took off in majestic flight, the turtle in tow. They flew over green valleys and snow-topped mountains and colorful canyons. But most breathtaking of all was the sight of the rosy pink sun setting over the ocean. The sky was a palate of orange, pinks and purples. Forgetting the thread, the turtle exclaimed in delight at the beauty. The moment he spoke, he began to fall away from his friends, landing in the ocean's depths."

The moral of the story needed little reiteration. There was a time for speaking and a time to remain silent. And wisdom had told Elizabeth to remain quiet while she figured out what to do.

She continued telling me how it happened that she ended up traveling with her Guru. "A few more days passed. While out shopping with Guruji and several others, he turned again to me and inquired, 'Have you decided about England?'

"Everyone turned and looked at me. I laughingly smiled at Guruji. He also smiled and continued with the shopping. After that, all deliberation came to an end. It was not a question of whether or not I should go, but how to explain the necessity of this trip to my boss at such a critical time in my work. I decided I had to write him a letter.

"The following day Guruji went into New York City. Except on rare occasions, I was almost always among those who accompanied him, not wanting to miss even a day in his presence during my short ashram stays. But on this day the car was full, and I was chosen to stay behind. I watched as they backed out of the drive, and suddenly Guruji's eyes looked straight at me with unbelievable intensity. The seriousness of his mood set off an alarm, a warning not to delay any further in making the necessary arrangements.

"The letter to my boss was already composed in my head. Immediately finding a quiet spot on the porch of Guruji's house, I began writing it down. Rereading it, I couldn't believe the boldness of its tone. But there seemed no delicate way to ask for four weeks' leave of absence at such a time as this in my professional career other than to state the circumstances directly, to state my loyalty to Guruji, and to give three possible solutions to the rather difficult position I was in, having to choose allegiance between the Guru and the boss.

"There had already been some discussion that I should be sent to Japan to complete the necessary work on the manuscripts, so my first two proposals suggested either flying directly from England to Japan or returning first to the university before my departure for the Orient. The third suggestion was my immediate resignation. I laughed at the last option, thinking he would probably fire me before I could ever resign officially. Acknowledging the difficulty of my position, I closed with a statement of respect for whatever decision he made.

"I typed it neatly, signed it, made two copies for myself and posted the letter. Surprisingly, from beginning to end it took almost the entire afternoon.

"Guruji never inquired again about my future plans. A phone call came a few days later from my boss's secretary. I was told to return as soon as possible to discuss the situation with him. It was evident where my priorities stood."

ℴ * * * ℳ

How to balance the secular with the spiritual life? This was the challenge confronting Elizabeth. Does one have priority over the other? Are there times in life when one should predominate? From where were the answers of such questions to come? Elizabeth knew that people unfamiliar with her spiritual quest would not be able to comprehend her decision. From their perspective it would appear that she was taking a foolish risk to strain her relationship with her boss, jeopardizing her career and professional reputation. Worldly responsibilities were not to be lightly shrugged off. "And yet," Elizabeth had often mused to herself, "who was it that said, '[…] let the dead bury their dead'?"*

---

* Matt. 8:22 (Authorized Version - abbreviated hereafter as AV, commonly known as the King James Version).

She recognized that her time for worldly living would come later. Guruji had invited her to go and that was enough. To be in personal contact with a living Master was too precious to sacrifice for anything. Her heart was telling her much inner work was needed, and she must do it while she had someone to show her how. It was her total trust in her teacher that gave her the determination to follow her heart. Since the age of seventeen, she had been questioning the purpose of life. Now ten years later she was surer than ever before that neither job nor money nor position nor prestige was going to bring her the inner happiness she craved. Trusting in divine guidance and pulled like a magnet toward her spiritual pursuit, she returned to see her boss.

She walked into his office with information in hand concerning the ten-day conference Guruji was conducting in England. She had strategy for how she was going to present her request. She had dressed appropriately in a blue tailor-fitted jumper worn over a white cotton blouse with dainty blue and white embroidery, topped off with a matching blue shoulder-padded jacket. Her blond hair was attractively styled and sprayed and she wore just enough warm beige make-up, rosy blush, soft eye shadow and lipstick to complement her businesslike appearance.

"Have a seat, Elizabeth." There was an oval table with four chairs in his office in front of his own desk. He gestured to a chair at the table while he sat down in another. She studied his face as she greeted him and took her place. The atmosphere was surprisingly calm. Elizabeth felt a strength emanating from her. She had not a trace of anxiety as she looked her boss directly in the eye. He must have seen that look of steady determination. He asked her in a quiet voice to explain her plans to him.

"As I mentioned in my letter, there is a foundation in England which has invited my teacher to lead a conference and I have been requested to go along as an assistant." The part about being an assistant was stretching the truth but it still seemed within the bounds of honesty. She handed the brochures to him, the front page stating in bold print: "World-renowned yogi/doctor invited as guest of honor to the Yoga Foundation of England." He made a sound which could only be described as interested surprise. He had not been aware of the reputable standing of this spiritual teacher. He read through each page quickly, noting that Guruji was slated to give two daily presentations throughout the entire conference.

"You know," Elizabeth continued, "I have a long association with my teacher which goes back over ten years now. This British conference on yoga is a very important one. The British are exploring even more readily than the Americans the therapeutic application of yoga exercise and philosophy, particularly for those who have physical disabilities such as multiple sclerosis. Yoga helps alleviate physical dis-ease, or the lack of ease within the body, and address the emotional stress which can accompany physical trauma."

Her boss was listening and nodding. So this was not a trip to camp out in the middle of Stonehenge or to sit on the Dover cliffs and watch the gulls fly by. There was credibility to it and evidence for need of assistance by her teacher did appear to be legitimate. He looked at this young woman whom he had employed for three years in a new light. If she had been requested to be an assistant to this yogi, then she had more training than he had originally imagined. At least it was Elizabeth's intention that he should think so.

She needed him to understand the dedication with which she approached this esoteric study. She did not presume to imply that she was one of Guruji's top disciples, but if appearances led him to that conclusion then she did not plan to contradict him.

"And how long would you need to be gone?" he asked. Guruji had said the trip would last one month.

Gazing quietly at her boss, Elizabeth replied, "My teacher plans to stay in England for four weeks. After the ten-day conference, he will go to London where he'll give several other workshops."

"Four weeks. That would put you back here in mid-September. If you'll look here on this globe," he got up and walked over to a globe sitting on his conference table, "I think you'll see that the distance is much greater flying from England to Japan compared to flying out of Los Angeles. I'll discuss with Dr. Miura how long he thinks you'll be needed to complete the manuscripts. It's my guess that two months in Osaka should be sufficient for you to pull everything together. Unfortunately, the winters can be very severe over there so you should leave as early in the fall as possible. Better be prepared to leave fairly soon after your return from Great Britain."

Everything seemed to have been decided quickly. Without wanting to show any surprise at the turn the discussion had taken, Elizabeth had sat calmly listening. She had not only been granted a month leave of absence but was actually going to be sent to Osaka. Her boss began explaining that a stipend of $1000 would be given to cover living expenses and another $1000 would be allotted for airfare. He hadn't even given her a chance to suggest resigning. When he smoothly turned the discussion to the status of his book on which Elizabeth had also been working intermittently over the past three years, it dawned on her that he was adding another point to their negotiation. In their discussion, he set a six-month time frame for its completion which was to be carefully overseen by Elizabeth.

He began jotting all this down on a legal pad: four weeks in London until mid-September; October through December in Osaka; January through June finish Chemical Structure book. Elizabeth felt honor-bound to agree to his terms and to commit to working another ten months for him after returning from England. He was a man to be respected. In his late sixties, it was rumored he'd been nominated for the Nobel Prize in chemistry several times by his colleagues. He was known for

44

the first systematic application of physical chemical principles to drug design, delivery and analysis. As a foremost leader in his field and author of highly acclaimed work, many younger research scientists stood in awe in his presence.

Elizabeth realized in retrospect that she had been too well trained in her position to be easily replaced. That had been her chief bargaining chip, quite unknown to her at the time. Trusting in the words of her Guru alone had given her the courage to broach the subject with her boss, and miraculously he had agreed to the leave of absence she so desperately wanted.

The sheet from the notepad was ripped out and taped on the wall behind her boss's desk, where it remained for the next ten months. Elizabeth courteously thanked her boss for allowing her this privilege to pursue a personal interest at the expense of her job, and she promised she would return ready to complete the projects that he had outlined for her. She worked for two weeks right up to the time of her departure for England, getting everything in order before her next absence.

THREE

~

The transatlantic flight from Newark International Airport to London's Gatwick Airport took seven hours. Elizabeth arrived at eight o'clock in the morning. She was traveling alone. Guruji and the others had arrived the day before. The conference was not in London, but an hour north of the city by train. After passing through customs with her baggage, Elizabeth followed the bright red sign with bold white letters: Gatwick Express Trains and Intercity Trains.

Just before passing through the gate to board the train which would take her into the city of London, Elizabeth entered a small concessions shop. She'd only eaten lightly on the flight and was now feeling a pang of hunger. Picking up a bag of potato chips, she knew they weren't terribly nutritious, but she was craving the salt. When she approached the counter, the cashier asked with the British accent still unfamiliar to Elizabeth's ears, "What would you like, miss?"

"Just the bag of chips, thanks." She placed the chips on the counter. "Chips, miss? We don't sell chips here." He said this in a surly tone, as though stating the obvious.

Surprised, Elizabeth looked down at the bag. "Ah, miss. These are crisps. You want this bag of crisps, is that what you want?"

"Yes, please." She looked at the package and saw clearly printed the word, "Crisps." It hit her suddenly that chips, as in "fish and chips" fame, meant French fries. She laughed at herself. No wonder the clerk had been taken aback. It was the second incident since she had stepped off the plane where she had found great amusement at the difference between British and American English.

"That'll be thirteen pence, miss." Having just exchanged $200 into British sterling, she handed him a ten pound note. With at least half a smile, he gave her back nine pounds and eighty-seven pence. She collected her luggage cart, which she'd left by the entrance of the shop. She was in good humor. Reflecting back over her trip, it had been easy, with few complications.

After disembarking from the plane just a few hours ago, she'd followed the throng of people onto the Gatwick Satellite tram which had carried them from the tarmac to the main airport terminal. The ride had been quick and smooth, and big white letters reading "Welcome to Gatwick" had greeted them as the tram pulled to a stop. The doors had glided open and everyone had stepped off and turned to the left to enter the terminal. Elizabeth had followed the signs for "All Other Passports," which meant non-British passport holders. Down a red, green, tan and blue striped carpeted hallway, around a few corners, she'd found herself at the top of a ramp which led into an enormous hall packed with people. Incoming Britons had also gathered in the immigration hall but were directed to a separate entrance. They were in the minority. This leg of their trip was not meant to be the same ordeal as it would be for the foreigners. Yes, even here in a country where the language was the same as her native tongue, and where she imagined the social customs were not that far removed from those she was familiar with, she was a foreigner. It had amused her. The conversation she'd had with the customs official also was in her mind.

"Please queue up on this side," had come the instructions from an airport attendant.

"There's one of those funny British words, 'queue', actually of French derivation," she had thought. This being the first incident where she'd noticed a difference in language usage, she'd unintentionally began making a mental list, and "queue" was first in line. Enjoying the humor of it, she'd wondered what would come next?

As she'd inched her way down the ramp leading into the hall, she'd surveyed all the queues. There must have been about twelve of them. She'd speculated, along with everyone else, as to which one would move the fastest. She'd chosen the one just at the bottom of the ramp and by chance nearest to the restrooms. Once establishing her place in line, she'd set down her carry-on bag and had asked the person behind her, "Would you mind holding my place?"

Those were different times, before terrorist threats instilled in everyone the fear of unattended luggage and airline agents asked, "Has anyone had access to your bags?" She'd left her carry-on bag holding her spot in line and had headed toward the small yellow illuminated square box with "WC" written in bold black letters. It marked the entrance to the restrooms. Ordinarily she wouldn't be so trusting of a total stranger. But she'd judged that the person must know that nothing of real value was in the bag or else she wouldn't just leave it behind. And that was in fact the case. It had been a relief to have those few moments unencumbered by the weight of luggage. She'd felt light and free, her mind calculating how many hours of travel still lay ahead before catching up with Guruji.

Upon returning to the queue, she'd tiredly noted that her bag was only a few feet from where she had left it, nudged along by the foot of the stranger. It soon became apparent that she had chosen one of the slower-moving lines. It had given her plenty of time to reflect on other occasions when she'd gone through customs and immigration. There was always some tedium involved: the wait, the questions, the luggage search. No one relished the procedure and yet its necessity was unquestioned. Finally at the head of her line, hoisting her carry-on bag into her arms, she had waited for the next available officer. It had been a woman. Elizabeth had cringed. Women officials more often than not gave her a harder time.

The questions had been innocuous enough. "What is your profession? Why have you come to Great Britain? Do you have adequate funds to support yourself here? How long do you intend to stay? How can you afford to be gone from your position so long?"

The last question had taken Elizabeth by surprise, making her feel momentarily uneasy. "Well, I work for a university and longer vacations are permitted." she had stated, trying not to waver or flinch. Could this official have any idea how great the stakes had been just to get to England? Fortunately no other explanation was needed on how she could take such a risk leaving her job. The official had stamped her passport with a six-month visa. Elizabeth had ascended the escalator to baggage reclaim. Her suitcases loaded onto a luggage cart, she'd been allowed to walk past custom officials unaccosted. Having strolled through the airport following the signs for the trains, she'd purchased the "crisps" and now was at the British Rail gate entrance. She decided the whole trip would have memories she didn't want to forget and vowed to write them down in a notebook.

"This way, love," the porter said with a self-assured smile. He carried her luggage down an escalator and placed it on the train that would take her into Central London. She gave him a generous tip and took a window seat. Still the official's question lingered in her mind, "How can you afford to be gone so long?"

Elizabeth felt the journey she was on was a test of her trust in her teacher's guidance. She was heading into the heart of London because she trusted in Guruji's wisdom. She wanted the knowledge that he could impart, the knowledge of the workings of the infinite mind. Transfer of such knowledge necessitated a close union, and this kind of union was possible only within the force field of absolute trust. Sitting on the train, Elizabeth was acutely aware of that protective force field radiating from her teacher and guiding her steps. As she watched out the window, the multi-tiered parking garages, tall apartment buildings towering above rows of chimneys, and the busy shop-lined streets all signaled the approaching city center. Just a few weeks ago she had thought she would be at her home in Kansas. But now she could feel a current pulling her gently along. Even though she was entering a strange city, alone, with still further train connections to make, she had no anxiety. She was watching her own life like a movie.

$\wp$ * * * $\varnothing$

This detachment had brought to her a calmness, she told me. She had read in Chapter One of the *Bhagavad Gītā*, "Good events or bad events should make no difference in one's bearing." She could feel the real meaning of it.

She recollected the number of times she had heard Guruji say, "There are two possibilities. For some people, they will run after God, and for others, God will run after them. If you do your work without attachment or desire for personal gain, God will come after you." She wondered if this inner calm was God coming after her. This was only allegorically speaking, of course, but that inner feeling had nevertheless been all-pervading.

This brought to her mind the prayer of Alyosha Karamazov, kneeling in the monastery hermitage before going to bed. She had copied this quote into her notebook. Dostoyevsky had written: "In [Alyosha's] fervent prayer he did not beseech God to lighten his darkness but only thirsted for the joyous emotion, which always visited his soul after the praise and adoration, of which his evening prayers usually consisted. That joy always brought him light untroubled sleep."[9] Elizabeth wondered how many people must have experienced that fullness in their heart when trusting totally in a divinity.

Elizabeth also had these words of Isak Dinesen written down: "To the Conscience of the world we may address ourselves in prayer, it will faithfully reward its faithful servants according to their desert [whatever is deserved], and its highest award is peace of mind. [...] They will [...] have experienced the supreme triumph of Unconditional Surrender."[10] That unconditional surrender, that was the trust: this Elizabeth knew. Elizabeth liked Dinesen very much. She might have felt some affinity with her, both being independent women, strong-willed, both acknowledging through experiences in their life the operation of a force more powerful than human intellect.

She read to me another quote from Dinesen, this one from the book *Out of Africa*: "I learned the strange learning that things can happen which we ourselves cannot possibly imagine, either beforehand, or at the time when they are taking place, or afterwards when we look back on them. Circumstances can have a motive force by which they bring about events without aid of human imagination or apprehension. On such occasions you yourself keep in touch with what is going on by attentively following it from moment to moment. [...] Things are happening to you, and you feel them happening, but except for this one fact, you have no connection with them, and no key to the cause or meaning of them. The performing wild animals in a circus go through their programme [sic] [...] in that same way. Those who have been through such events can, in a way, say that they have been through death,—a passage outside the range of imagination, but within the range of experience."[11]

Elizabeth laughed, saying that this was what was always happening in her life with Guruji. Even funnier was the fact that whenever Guruji had a chance, he would take everyone to see the circus. Elizabeth sensed it was not for mere entertainment. Maybe this was what he had been trying to tell everyone; that a death of the individual ego was needed before the higher order of things could be understood. "Otherwise, we are simply acting like circus animals," she said. She shook her head again, despairing that she was jumping ahead of her story.

"Now, back to London." She resumed her narrative. I wanted to know when George would appear in her story and she assured me he was coming soon.

ℰ * * * ℭ

Ickwell

The trip from Gatwick Airport into Central London took only forty minutes. The train pulled into Victoria Station. Elizabeth reached for the white slip of paper upon which she had written directions before departing the States. She had made a transatlantic call from her home in Kansas to the Foundation. A polite English lady had given the instructions: "Arrive at Victoria Station. Take the London Underground train, using the Victoria Line, to King's Cross. Purchase a British Rail ticket for Biggleswade. At Biggleswade, take a taxi to Ickwell." It sounded simple enough.

Pulling her luggage off the train, she quickly acquired a baggage cart and blessed the British for being so practical as to supply push carts free-of-charge for baggage-laden travelers. She walked down to the end of the platform and entered the central hub of Victoria Station. She was struck by its quaintness, not that it was meant to appear quaint. It was open and airy. Pigeons were flying freely. It had a high triple-peaked skylighted roof supported by an intricate network of steel trusses. In the middle were three Corinthian columns painted yellow and blue. There was a feeling of a bygone era, and oddly a familiarity about the place.

She maneuvered the cart across the spacious enclosure. Stopping at a newsstand in the middle of the terminal, she inquired about the train to King's Cross. The clerk pointed to an elevator and said, "Downstairs, miss. You'll see signs for the Victoria Line. That'll take you there."

After descending downward, the doors of the elevator opened. It was an entirely different place before her: white tiled floors, fluorescent lighting, rows of ticket machines. An agent in a blue uniform passed by and she asked again what her next step should be.

"Buy a fifty pence ticket. Victoria Line is right over there."

She bought her ticket. Leaving the cart behind, she shuffled her luggage past the ticket agent and stepped onto a long, steep escalator which carried her down to the Victoria platform. She had to decide between the northern or southern-bound trains. A sign clearly displayed all the stations on the line. King's Cross was to the north.

As she stepped onto the correct platform, a breeze came blowing down the tracks signaling the approaching subway, the "tube" as she learned the British called it. In England, a "subway" was an underground walkway. She boarded the tube with her bags. Fortunately, it wasn't crowded at mid-morning and plenty of seats were available. It was five stops to King's Cross. Posted above the windows was a map of the Victoria Line. The train would stop in Green Park, Oxford Circus, Warren Street and Euston before arriving at King's Cross.

The first object to catch Elizabeth's eye as she stepped off the train onto the platform at King's Cross was a bright yellow sign with black letters that said, "Way Out." It was meant to be taken literally but reminded Elizabeth of a "hip" American expression. She wondered why the British didn't use "Exit." It amused her greatly to follow the "Way Out" signs. She reckoned the Britons probably never gave them a second thought. This was the intrigue of overseas traveling. The most ordinary thing can seem extraordinary.

The "Way Out" sign led to another steep upwardly moving escalator. This station was much busier than Victoria. She stopped in the middle of all the people who were moving in every direction and many at great speed. This particular station, she later found out, was the junction for five tube lines as well as a British Rail interchange. Many of those hurrying were probably trying to make the quickest transfer possible from one line to another. Others were travelers like herself, carrying luggage or enormous knapsacks, moving slowly and awkwardly as they got their bearings.

Elizabeth found her way to the British Rail ticket office. She liked how easily the signs had pointed the way. She could not remember having had such an easy time in any American subway or terminal. The ticket to Biggleswade purchased, she found a seat on the train platform. It felt good to be back above ground again with sunlight and blue sky. It was a beautiful day. She'd had no chance to even notice the weather, arriving so early at the airport and shuttling from British Rail to the Underground and back to British Rail.

It was a welcome relief to just sit quietly. She was alone on the platform. The journey would soon be over. She closed her eyes for what must have been thirty minutes. It was pleasant to listen to the sounds around her, becoming absorbed in a thought only to be drawn again by some distant commotion.

More people gathered on the platform and the train pulled in. Elizabeth boarded, very glad not to have to carry her luggage far. The seats were long and covered in blue vinyl, fitting two people to a seat with pairs of seats facing one another. She took up one of these four-seated sections with all her luggage and sat down.

The train pulled out of the station. She settled back in her seat. She had not slept in almost twenty-four hours, but she couldn't sleep now. A lady across the aisle asked her where she was from.

"I'm from the States."

"So am I," replied the lady. "This is my first time in England. My son gave me this trip for my birthday. I'd been saying how much I wanted to see the English countryside. And I have family friends staying in Peterborough so I'm going now to see them."

Not feeling up to a long conversation, Elizabeth did not elaborate on her own trip. "I'm going to see friends, too."

The woman held a camera. She suddenly leaned forward and handed it to Elizabeth. "Would you mind taking my picture?" she asked. "This way I can show my son how happy I am to be here. And if you have a camera, I can take yours for you. It'll make a good memory." It was a fun idea. Why shouldn't she have a picture of her first day in England on the train to see Guruji. They swapped cameras and took the photos.

℘ * * * ℭ

Elizabeth showed me hers. She may have been tired, but she looked elegant, wearing a simple rose-colored dress and cream-colored raincoat. Her hair was brushed back and parted to one side. She had a distinct Grace Kelly look, even with her glasses, which she wore instead of her contacts since it was such a long trip. Overall, she appeared relaxed and happy.

℘ * * * ℭ

Looking out the train window, she kept trying to notice differences in the landscape which would reveal the fact that she was not in America. She always tried to do this when she traveled abroad. She had already been to Mexico, Russia and Japan (her first trip to the Orient had been when she was fifteen). On every trip, there were moments when she could deceive herself into believing that she wasn't far from home. It made her think that after all, people are people and land is land and it's all one world. Sitting on the train, the trees and flowers and houses in the distance did not look unfamiliar. But admittedly she was tired and any notable distinction could easily have been missed.

In this semi-dazed state, she arrived in Biggleswade. She had wondered many times at the strangeness of this name. It seemed no matter how it was said, it rolled off the tongue sounding British. She knew she was close to Guruji. Just a few more miles to go. She asked the ticket clerk, "How do I get to Ickwell?"

"The taxi will take you, miss. Just wait out there near the road and I'll call and let them know you're here. Should take about fifteen minutes. But don't worry. It'll come." She was very friendly. Elizabeth thanked her and moved all her bags to the roadside.

While she stood waiting, she watched the cars zipping past, taking the curves in the road at fairly high speed. It appeared the speed limit was not strictly enforced as in American small towns. She noted that the steering wheel of the cars was located on the right side. The license plates were longer than those in the States, with bold black letters and numbers on a cream or yellow background, and the cars were generally smaller than those in America. The service station on the corner advertised liters instead of gallons and the prices were in pounds not dollars. She was indeed in England.

From where she stood, she could watch traffic coming from three directions: right, left and straight ahead. She wondered from which direction the taxi would come. A coolness in the air began to penetrate her raincoat, and hunger and tiredness made her more sensitive to the chill. The taxi finally came. The driver loaded her bags into the trunk. "So it's Ickwell you want, is it, miss?" he said in a businesslike way.

"Yes, please," replied Elizabeth.

"Very well," he said, and off they went down the road. Elizabeth watched the car wind its way along, leaving the town behind. The few houses she saw were small and had beautiful flowers growing in front—authentic English country gardens. Their charm brought a smile to her face. The driver made a few turns and up ahead she saw a tall pole with red and white stripes around it and a decorative ball on top. He slowed the car and after crossing the main road continued straight ahead down a small gravel drive which passed not far from the pole.

He nodded his head toward it. "That's the Maypole."

Elizabeth looked again at it closely. How many times in her childhood had she read about Maypoles, with their streamers and children running around? And here was a real one, apparently a landmark in the area.

Passing a row of trees blocking the pole, Elizabeth saw horses grazing in the distance. The taxi was driving through a green meadow. Just ahead she saw a brick arch connecting two brick walls on either side of the gravel drive. The taxi slowed to a crawl as they drove over a grate of several metal pipes laid across a trench. She guessed it was to keep the horses from entering the main complex. There were no fences in sight.

The brick arch marked the entrance into a simple courtyard of substantial size. The first thing she noticed was that the roof of one of the buildings had caved in and the beams were sagging. The weather-worn gray of the wood showed that the dilapidation had occurred years ago. Other buildings looked well restored. In one glance, she took all this in. The driver turned to her and asked for three pound thirty. She handed him the money plus a little extra. He hopped out and unloaded her luggage. Elizabeth stood by her bags, her purse hanging from her shoulder. She thanked the driver and watched as he backed the car around and drove under the archway and down the drive.

FOUR

~

She had arrived at last. There was a row of cars parked in front of her. She knew other people must be around but she saw no one. She turned and walked toward a doorway. There was a short ramp leading up to its entrance. She carried her bags inside. The floors were wooden and worn smooth in the hallway where she stood. There were windows on her right looking out over the courtyard. A small table with a lamp was in the corner by the windows. Also on the right were three steps leading to a landing from which ascended a long staircase. The stairs were covered with a light green carpet. To the left was a display of books on a table against the wall. A doorway near the table opened into a room which she later learned was a sitting room. Glass doors were swung open at the end of the hallway. Elizabeth was just wondering if she should venture down that way to find someone when a woman came walking briskly toward her.

"Hello, hello," she greeted Elizabeth. "My name is Gretchen."

"Hello. I'm Elizabeth Dolman."

"So you're here for the yoga intensive?" she inquired as she sat down at the corner table and turned on the lamp. "Did you make a reservation?"

"Yes. I telephoned from the States last week. I'm a student of the Indian teacher who is here to conduct the intensive," Elizabeth explained.

"Oh, I see. Yes, he has already arrived with several other ladies. I'm looking here at the room arrangements. The three ladies are upstairs in a room together. There is a fourth bed there but I show a reservation for someone named Lee to occupy that bed. But let's see. You did bring a sleeping bag?" Gretchen turned to look at Elizabeth.

"Yes. I have one in this suitcase," Elizabeth said.

"Okay, I can put you in the Yoga Hall then, if that's all right with you. You'll be sleeping on the floor but we have mats." Gretchen held her pen poised over the reservation book.

"That sounds fine," Elizabeth agreed.

"Very good. That will be ninety pounds, then, for the ten-day stay."

Elizabeth counted out ninety pounds and was surprised to see she only had forty pounds left. However, she didn't expect that there would be many expenses during the intensive. Gretchen accepted the money and handed her a receipt. "You might like to keep your bags upstairs with the others. Let me show you their room," Gretchen offered, getting up from the chair. She was a squarely-built woman with short hair and a direct manner. Elizabeth learned later that she had a fourteen-month-old baby and her husband was a massage therapist.

Taking a couple of Elizabeth's bags, Gretchen led the way up the stairs. Elizabeth followed. At the top of the stairs, she turned to the left of the banister and walked down the hallway, turning left again through a doorway into a small walk-through sitting room, through another pair of doors and down a smaller hallway. Stopping in front of an arched window overlooking the courtyard, Gretchen knocked on a door on the right, directly across from it. Hearing a response she pressed down on the door handle and entered the room.

"Have a friend of yours here," Gretchen said, setting Elizabeth's luggage down. "Dinner will be in an hour." And just like that, she was gone.

Elizabeth walked in with a big smile. She had known these women for ten years, or more precisely, she had know two of them for ten years and one for six. They were like family to her. Being devotees of Guruji's, they all had Sanskrit names, as did Elizabeth. Guruji often gave new names to his students. It was to help them feel their own higher sense of self, and at the same time to direct their attention to the question "Who am I?"—an essential query on the spiritual path. Elizabeth's Sanskrit name was "Indu" and that was the name they knew her by.

"Ha, so you made it at last! We were wondering when you would arrive. How was your trip?" asked Uma, who was like a mother to Elizabeth.

"Fine, fine. Everything went just fine," Elizabeth reassured her. Hugs were exchanged between all four. They all sat down on the beds. The other two women were named Shakti and Mangala and they were like sisters to Elizabeth. It had only been three weeks since they had last seen each other at the ashram.

"So how did things go with your boss?" Uma asked.

"Did he get angry?" Shakti chimed in.

"I hope you didn't get fired," Mangala said with great concern.

"Well, it's a good story. But first tell me how Guruji is and how is everything here?" Elizabeth was eager to know.

"Guruji had a good trip," Shakti explained. "Mangala and I arrived a few hours ahead of his plane. We flew into Gatwick and made our way over to Heathrow Airport. Bookings were so tight that we had to come on separate flights. But it worked out okay. The Foundation sent a car to meet him. In fact, Harry Goodall came personally to welcome Guruji."

"Who's Harry Goodall?" Elizabeth wanted to know.

"He's the man who founded this place. You know it's called the Good Health Foundation. He is doing exceptional work in yoga. He has invited yogis to come from all over the world and he conducts classes and seminars himself throughout England, as well as sponsoring tours to India with people in his group," Shakti replied.

"But his approach with yoga is much more physical and mental than spiritual," Uma made the distinction. "He presents yoga as a tool to help relieve physical discomfort and remove anxiety from the mind. Of course, it certainly does do this."

"He seems particularly dedicated to helping those with physical impairments, like multiple sclerosis," Shakti said. "That's why you'll see ramps everywhere, for those in wheelchairs."

"Well, it seems to be quite a lovely place," Elizabeth responded.

"It definitely is," agreed Uma. "But I still suspect that Guruji will send a few shock waves through it before he leaves, if you know what I mean."

ஐ * * * ౭

They had all laughed. Guruji would certainly not contradict anything that Mr. Goodall had to say. Guruji's words would simply send everyone flying far, far beyond any personal identification with the body or mind.

Guruji would say, "You have to go beyond 'Genesis' to find liberation." Elizabeth described to me how he would then tell the story of the two different kinds of people. In prison there are the prisoners and the prison guards. Prisoners have no freedom. They are in bondage. The guards, although they spend much time in the prison, are free to walk out. In the hospitals there are patients. They always have to be in the hospital. But the doctors move both inside and outside. The gist of his story was that we should be like the guards and the doctors.

"Our body and mind are like the prison and hospital," Elizabeth reiterated Guruji's teaching, reading his words from her notebook. "We need to be involved with them to some extent because that is our incarnation. But we should have the freedom to transcend them, at least for a certain number of hours each day. We should not be in total bondage."

Guruji taught that this *dis*-identification with body and mind did not guarantee in anyone's life an absence of problems. There would still be ups and downs. But with disidentification, we would not feel suffering. Guruji had explained further, "Pain is necessary. We must face it in order to find its opposite. We must realize that living within the confines of body and mind means nothing but suffering. Only going beyond will bring great happiness. And that state of blissfulness is our real nature."

Elizabeth had also written down Guruji's comments when he was talking of the immutable—that essence within us which never changes: "Your real nature is immutable. That which existed before we ever entered the physical body is with us now." This idea had affected Elizabeth deeply. Although she could see the changes in her body and mind as they developed throughout her childhood and adulthood, she knew that there was an essence which had always been with her as far back as she could remember. It was something pure and innocent; carrying with it a feeling of love, trust, contentedness.

"Why do we lose touch with this part of ourselves as adults? It's because of the mind. The mind can be a blinding force which overshadows our real nature," Elizabeth said to me. She told how, with a pin and a stack of papers before him, Guruji had illustrated the mind's power during one evening program at the ashram. In one sudden motion he had jabbed the pin through the papers. By all appearances, the individual sheets were pierced simultaneously. But there actually was a time difference of milliseconds as each page was pierced. Looking earnestly at everyone present, Guruji had said, "The mind moves faster than those milliseconds of time."

It was for this reason that Guruji had devised so many tricks to short circuit the mind. In truth, his very being had the power to short circuit Elizabeth's mind. It was a subtle power discovered by devotees when around a true spiritual teacher.

One thing was for sure: the people coming for the intensive would at some point or other experience the real meaning of "yoga." In Sanskrit, yoga means "union." Many claim yoga gives union to the body, mind and spirit. They are not incorrect. But it's similar to reading the introduction of a novel and then being told that that's the whole story. The wise person will feel something is missing. Guruji gives the missing story. The real union to be experienced is the union of the individual soul with the Absolute Soul. With Guruji's help, Elizabeth had felt the possibility of that union.

She described one occasion during a group meditation when she had been sitting in silence in front of her teacher. Her eyes had been closed. She heard a voice in her head. She had never heard voices before but she heard this voice clearly. It said, "Be attentive." It was what she needed. Her mind felt momentarily paralyzed. A sensation came over her body, as though she was disappearing from her legs up. She felt on the edge of something, a nothingness. She wanted to see it, to be in it. But suddenly Guruji had given the signal: enough. Her concentration was broken. The feeling left but the memory of it remained. The seed of Knowledge had been planted.

In one of Guruji's essays, Elizabeth recollected these words: "Once you have tasted nothingness, you will desire nothing else." He had also spoken of the need to embrace one's own heart. If we could do that, he had said, then we would never long for the embrace of anyone else. Elizabeth had wondered what "embrace your own heart" meant. But she had felt that feeling when embracing that nothingness. It had been a feeling of fullness and completeness, a happiness beyond anything she'd known. Had not God advised Moses to tell others, "[…] I am That I AM […]"?* Elizabeth had never really been sure of

---

* Exod. 3:14 (AV).

64

its meaning. She thought she understood it better now. Was it "Be still and know I am no-thing"? Because in that nothing, Elizabeth had found everything.

"Guruji was right," Elizabeth said to me. "One glimpse of nothingness and one will desire only that. That desire wells up inside, to drop the mind and lose sensation of the body and move into that heavenly state; the state beyond the senses and the sensory-dependent mind." She continued, "Why people allow only their senses to define the universe is a point Guruji contests over and over again. The senses are not reliable in the first place. Guruji describes the unenlightened perception of reality as being similar to watching a 3D movie. You begin to feel like you're also moving with the images on the screen, even though you know you are separate. He illustrated this by remarking that if wild animals were projected, we would turn and run out of the theater, frightened. We had all laughed at such a ridiculous scenario. But the laughter was more self-ridicule than disbelief. Too many of us had seen a 3D movie."

Guruji hadn't missed the chance at Disney World to take them into the 3D theater. There had been no seats, only railings to lean against. They had stood and watched a plane fly over mountains and valleys and canyons. Elizabeth admitted she couldn't keep herself from swaying. It was as if the floor was moving. Not feeling dizzy was a challenge, but the railings were there for those who were unsuccessful, which most were. The senses tend to believe in the illusion. And humans declare to be true whatever the senses perceive.

℘ * * * ℂ

Elizabeth and the other ladies knew Guruji had brought his bag of tricks to Ickwell. After the laughter had subsided over the effect that Guruji would have at the Foundation, Shakti continued, "We all arrived yesterday and have been getting everything ready for the intensive which starts tomorrow evening. Guruji's room is just around the corner. He's been taking rest most of the day."

Mangala then asked, "Now tell us, Indu, what happened with you?"

ℬ * * * ℭ

Indu meant "moon." It was as familiar to Elizabeth as any nickname might be to anyone else, although it was much more than just a nickname. Guruji had given it to her during a yoga workshop in Fort Worth, Texas, many years before. She had been sitting in front of him amongst a group of people. He unexpectedly handed her a slip of paper with "Indu" written on it and said, "This is your name." There was no ritual or oath. She was under no obligation in any way. Guruji had perceived her true devotion to spiritual knowledge and the name was given to help her on the path of inner exploration. And she had quietly accepted it.

Since she went by "Indu" during this period of time, I will also use it for the sake of continuity in the narration of her story.

ℬ * * * ℭ

Indu began, "Well, I myself cannot believe how well things turned out." She gave them a brief description of the meeting with her boss and his proposal to send her to Japan in October, all expenses paid.

"My goodness, that's wonderful!" Uma was quick to congratulate her. "So how long can you stay over here?"

Indu smiled, "I've got a little over four weeks. My return ticket is for September 17."

"Guruji will be pleased. He was surprised when we told him you were coming," Shakti said.

Indu laughed. She wondered just how surprised Guruji could have been. She had parted from him three weeks ago without definitely saying she was coming. Before making such a claim, she'd known she had to talk to her boss. So she had bid Guruji farewell, giving him a few flowers and silently departing. But in her mind she had prayed, "May we meet again in England."

So now, at last in England, she was looking forward to seeing him. Not wanting to disturb his rest, though, she had already decided to go down for dinner and afterward visit his room to pay her respects. It was almost dinner time. As they were all getting up to go downstairs, she asked about the reservation for Carol Lee.

"Is Carol really coming?" Indu asked her friends, nodding to the empty bed.

"We have no idea. But if she doesn't, that bed is yours," Uma replied warmly.

"Where are you staying otherwise?" Mangala asked.

"Downstairs in the Yoga Hall—sleeping on the floor with my sleeping bag." Indu hoped she could stay upstairs with them.

The room was a nice size with four beds, two dressers, one closet and a sink. There were two full-size mirrors: one near the closet and one over the dresser. The room was situated on the south corner of the building with windows on two sides, allowing soft sunlight and a nice breeze to enter. But Indu had resigned herself to at least one night downstairs.

They all went down to dinner together. The aroma of tomato sauce permeated the hallway. They used the same staircase that Indu had so eagerly ascended just an hour before. They took a right after the banister, passed the table of books, and walked through the glass doors at the end of the hallway. Turning to the right, they walked down another long hallway with a polished wooden floor and a glass paneled wall on the left side that looked directly into the dining hall. On the right side was a bank of windows. The entrance into this table-filled room was at the end of the hallway.

The dining hall was not a large room. The back wall was again all windows looking out onto a flower garden. The glass panels allowed the light from the outer hallway windows to shine through. The atmosphere was charming. Six tables were set up in two rows of three. The food was served buffet style at a table by the door leading to the kitchen. A few people were already forming a line. The ladies joined the line, too, nodding hello to others in the room. Two people did enter in wheelchairs, one a man in his thirties and the other a child of about ten. Chatting with them at dinner, Indu learned that they were facing the challenge of multiple sclerosis.

The dinner was deliciously prepared. It was spaghetti with salad and fresh Italian bread. Nothing so extraordinary except for the sauce. Indu saw a young woman with a short bobbed haircut and a quick manner coming in and out the kitchen door to check things on the serving table. She was told that this person was the cook named Wendy. Indu silently blessed her for such a meal.

All the meals served at the Foundation were from a balanced vegetarian menu. Later in a discussion with staff members, she heard that the food was one highlight that attracted many people to come to the Foundation. Every meal was very carefully planned and prepared; vegetables were picked from the garden and breads and pastries were freshly baked. It was one of the Foundation's philosophies that if the body eats well, then other problems in life will be easier to address. It was a philosophy unanimously agreed upon by everyone there.

Only about ten people sat down for dinner that evening. But many more were expected the next day. Indu enjoyed the peaceful atmosphere and good food. But she was looking forward to greeting Guruji. He had also been eating at this time, for Mangala had prepared a tray and taken it upstairs to his room. So after clearing away their dishes, the four women climbed the stairs again and entered a small vestibule directly across the hall from the staircase. There were doors to the right and to the left. Guruji's was the one to the left. They knocked and entered.

Guruji was sitting on the floor at the foot of the bed with his dinner tray placed on a white towel before him. He had just finished eating and was wiping his hands and beard with a napkin.

"Look who's here, Guruji," Uma announced, pointing a finger at Indu. "Isn't she a happy sight?"

Indu smiled, bringing her palms together in salutation. Guruji looked at her brightly and also smiled.

"Very good that you came," he said in his distinct Indian accent. "How did you get here?"

"I took a train from London and then a taxi." It sounded simple when Indu said it even though it had taken a good day's travel to get there.

He nodded and said again, "Very good, very good."

ॐ * * * ૭૩

He had asked no other questions. Indu had also remained silent. She felt no need to tell him about her pending trip to Japan and her commitment to work for the next ten months after her return. On one level she felt he knew everybody's story and taking time to tell particular details seemed superfluous to her. He had already demonstrated his power of understanding beyond any spoken word.

Indu could not resist giving me one more example of this. She had been staying at the ashram for several weeks and was soon to be leaving. Feeling torn between her spiritual life and her secular duties, she had gone down to the lake on the ashram and walked to the old goat house. Someone had rebuilt it to be a small hut with a deck out over the water. There was a wooden lounge chair on the deck and Indu thought it the perfect spot to contemplate the circumstances of her life and the direction in which it was heading. She wanted to be with Guruji. Yet, she had completed one university degree in the sciences with honors, done some graduate work and had found good employment. She had, in other words, successfully completed her education and found a niche for herself in the outside world. But her heart was aching at the thought of leaving her Guru.

The story of Lord Buddha came to her mind. She sat watching the reflections in the water and thought about his life. He had been a prince in a wealthy kingdom, a loving father with a beautiful wife and baby. But something was missing. He could not see the meaning of life. He left everything to become an ascetic in the forest. After six difficult years, he collapsed under a bodhi tree in helpless despair of ever realizing the truth about human existence. That night he became enlightened. Indu found comfort in the story. Had not Buddha's heart ached in despair just as hers was?

After some time, she returned to Guruji's cottage only to hear that Guruji had been calling for her. She climbed the stairs to his small apartment. He was sitting on the floor in front of a low table and motioned for her to come near. She knelt down near him and immediately he placed his hand on her head. She bowed with her head to the floor and he gave her four heavy pats on the back. Tears suddenly flooded her eyes. As she sat up, they rolled down her cheeks. Her love for him was enormous. He got up and went into the next room. Returning with a book, he opened to a page in the middle. Indu did not recognize the book. She often read to him so it was not unusual that he should hand her a book, but this wasn't one they had been reading. She took the book and began reading aloud. It was on the life of Buddha. The same story that had just been passing through her head was on the page before her. Halfway down the page, Guruji reached over and closed the book. The emotion in Indu's heart was too great to be contained. Sobs came from the depth of her heart. *He knew, he knew* kept running through her mind. He knew what she had been thinking, he knew what was in her heart. He was a true Master, although she had never doubted it. But to see his powers so directly was always a profound occurrence for her. Her tears subsided. She wiped her eyes, blew her nose and sat waiting, looking down at the rug. Guruji handed her the book from which she'd read the day before and she began to read.

એ * * * ભ

In England, she now sat before Guruji once again. No, there was no need to tell him anything about her boss or her work. Uma asked, "Guruji, what shall we plan for this evening?"

"Evening time we can do a fire ceremony, chanting and have silent meditation out on the lawn," he said.

It sounded wonderful to Indu. They decided to start the fire at seven o'clock. The sun would set at 7:45 p.m. They would meditate through dusk. Mats would be needed so Indu agreed to bring them from the Yoga Hall. Shakti would prepare everything for the fire.

એ * * * ભ

The fire ceremony was beloved by all of Guruji's devotees. It was a Vedic tradition performed in an exact manner. The items needed were a copper pot in the shape of an inverted pyramid, dried cow dung, clarified butter called *ghee*, and rice. A piece of camphor placed in the bottom of the pot under a small pyramid of cow dung ignited beautifully into a tall glowing flame. After repetition of certain sacred words or mantras, *ghee* would be offered to the fire, or if it was sunrise or sunset then rice mixed with *ghee*. Indu was surprised how many hours the fire could burn with just a few drops of the clarified butter added every few minutes. A special combination of herbs was also used to give greater intensity to the flame and for the fragrant aroma they gave off.

The times of sunrise and sunset were particularly recommended in sacred texts for the fire ceremony. A subtle change occurs in the atmosphere, a shift in energy. Attunement with this shift seems to greatly facilitate the perception of energy movement in the body and bring about a heightened sensitivity. At any time of day, however, the fire charged the atmosphere surrounding it. Indu had read about this in a book by Paul Devereux entitled *Earth Lights*. She said that in it, Devereux explains that ions are the electrical charge distributed in the atmosphere. They are the electrons broken off from atmospheric atoms. On a clear day, ions tend to be more highly concentrated than when weather conditions are unsettled. She read his statement from her notebook: "The burning of fires also produces ions (of both charges) [negative and positive], which can augment the preponderant electrical conditions of a given environment. Thus the use of ritual fires in conditions suitable for ESP [...] could add their negative ions to enhance the suitable electrical conditions." [12]

For this very reason, negative ion machines have gained in popularity, even in offices and conference rooms. Corporations speculated that if people feel good inwardly, then productivity could only improve. The beneficial effect of negative ions had been proven scientifically. And yet, Indu reflected, the sages of Vedic times thousands of years ago understood the sense of well-being that the fire brought. She suspected that scientists would continue to find that there was a subtlety to existence of which modern man had become totally ignorant but which had been understood by the ancients.

Einstein once said, "If there ever comes a Third World War, after that we will be fighting with sticks." Reading the quote from her notebook, Indu felt he meant that civilization as we know it would disappear in the aftermath of another world war. Guruji had said that something similar to this had already happened in the past, and that some time in the future, people would not believe that television, radio or space travel had ever existed. It made Indu wonder about the people of prehistoric times. Possibly they had been living on a much higher level of cosmic attunement than modern man. But that attunement seemed to have deteriorated with the coming of the Bronze and Iron Age, the advent of industrialization. Material prosperity may have had a deadening effect on man's supra-psychic abilities.

Indu never thought of the fire as a religious ritual or a sacrifice to the gods. It was a scientific tool. It worked to enhance the meditative state. And that was the purpose for which Guruji used it.

℘ * * * ℭ

They left Guruji's room to freshen up, change clothes and prepare for evening program. Indu found the pile of mats in the Yoga Hall. She carried out ten to a site just beyond the flower garden that she had admired through the dining room windows. She placed the mats on the lawn at the corner of the building so that both the flower garden and the open pasture on the far side of the complex could be seen. An old, low stone wall made a large square barrier which separated the pasture from the beautifully maintained lawn of the complex. Indu had heard at dinner that by the next day tents would border the inside perimeter of the wall. But for now she saw a green expanse broken only by the picturesque stones beyond which grazed the horses.

It might have been the novelty of being in new surroundings, but Indu felt a magic in the air. She couldn't say what attracted her. It was just a sense that Guruji would not have come so far to just any ordinary place. There must be something more. That something she could sense but not identify.

At seven o'clock, Guruji came outside and sat in front of the fire pot. Their group sat on either side of him and several others came out and filled in the circle. Most seemed to have some understanding about meditation and held a healthy curiosity for this man in orange.

The fire was started. Mangala passed out papers which gave the Vedic Sanskrit mantras that were used, along with their English translation. They all chanted and Guruji added *ghee* to the fire at the end of each mantra. The sky was clear, the air calm. The time of sunset was approaching as the last rays of sunlight cast a tranquil glow. At the moment of sunset, Guruji added grains of rice to the *ghee*, chanting one last mantra specifically used for attunement with the setting sun. The fire was moved into the middle of the circle and all sat silently, watching the flame. These were Guruji's only instructions: "Watch the flame until it goes out." The trance-like state quieted the mind and brought a regular movement to the breath, both of which were extremely conducive to meditation. Indu could feel the people around her relaxing and breathing deeply. She also felt soothed and allowed herself to be mesmerized by the flame. Slowly it went out. She closed her eyes and felt the peace.

After ten minutes, Guruji again chanted a mantra which blessed the entire planet—its air, waters, vegetables and herbs, animals and people—, praying for all to coexist peacefully and to be free from pollution and disease. It was quite dark when the meditation ended and a coolness had crept into the air. All the things were picked up and moved indoors. Guruji returned to his room upstairs. Tomorrow at this time everyone would be finding seats in the downstairs sitting room to hear Guruji's first lecture. But his program had not officially started and he did not want to take any liberties to talk until formally given the floor to speak. So for now, he would remain silent.

At the top of the stairs, Indu bid goodnight to him. The other three women went with him to take care of last minute details before he retired for the night. Indu had never been involved in arranging Guruji's personal things so she naturally did not assume this role now.

Entering their room, she thought it looked like an obstacle course. Two beds were backed up against the wall in two corners. The other two beds projected out into the room at right angles to each other. And luggage was everywhere. She unpacked her towel and cosmetics bag and went next door to the bathroom. She had been looking forward to a warm bath all evening. When she returned to the room after her bath, the others were there. They sat around chatting about the plans for the next day and for the coming weekend.

Uma had heard of one event separate from Guruji's program which was to take place on Sunday afternoon. "I heard that there'll be a big welcoming celebration for two jugglers who have just juggled two hundred miles fundraising for the Foundation. Their jugglethon has apparently been quite successful."

Shakti shook her head, "Can you imagine *walking* for two hundred miles, let alone juggling? Good grief!"

It was a feat to be honored, they all agreed.

Soon it was ten o'clock and Indu knew exhaustion would soon overtake her. She gathered up her sleeping bag amidst the protests of the others that she should just sleep in the room. But on principle, she felt she should sleep at least one night in her assigned spot. She had only paid the camper's rate since she was not in a private room; that was what she had agreed to with Gretchen. She didn't want to go against her word. And if she did stay with them upstairs through the intensive, then she would offer to pay the full rate.

FIVE

~

The next morning, Indu had to admit she had not slept well. There hadn't been enough cushioning under her sleeping bag and it had gotten cold that night. Two of the walls in the Yoga Hall were lined with windows. She went upstairs at seven. Her friends were up, shuffling in and out of the bathroom. She got her cosmetics bag and waited her turn.

"How was your night?" Uma asked.

"Well, not too bad," Indu said. She didn't want to make a fuss.

Breakfast was served between seven-thirty and nine. Uma and Shakti went to check on Guruji and prepare his breakfast. Indu and Mangala met them downstairs. The dining room was already warmed by the morning sun streaming in through the windows. It seemed it would be a beautiful day.

Hot and cold cereals were served with fresh bread and butter. Through the door leading to the kitchen was a small room off to the left. It was the beverage room where they kept available any time of the day hot water for tea, coffee or instant hot chocolate. At mealtimes, juice and milk were also put out. Indu went in to get juice. At the other end of the beverage room was a large door leading to the outside. She peeked her head out the door. A narrow brick path led off to the right. To the left was a brick patio which extended along the side of the building and wrapped around at the corner to the other side. It was at that corner where they had had the meditation the night before. There was a low retaining wall running the length of the patio beyond which was the flower garden. A white wrought-iron bench, chair and table were there by the door, which looked inviting. But the air still had a chill to it so Indu ventured out no further.

As she turned to go back to the dining hall she saw a display of pictures above the tea table. Photographs of everyone on staff were hung on the wall with their name and position given below each picture. She looked closely at each face. They all looked nice. The face of one fellow caught her eye. She looked at his name. It was an unusual one, spelled "Nhoj." She guessed he must be from Scandinavia. The thought popped into her mind that maybe there was someone here whom she was supposed to meet. Had that been why Guruji had suggested she come?

℘ * * * ℭ

She had often wondered under what circumstances she might meet a future husband. She had seriously dated a few men. She was, after all, an attractive woman. But whenever she surmised that a fellow was not a potential mate, she would not delay in ending the romance, although the friendship was often continued.

A serious relationship took too much time and energy to cultivate and she was not about to make that investment unless the man had potential to be a good husband and was himself looking for a committed relationship. The problem had been uniting these two qualities. She had already had two friends suggest marriage with serious intent. But in close examination of her feelings for them, she knew something was missing. She could honestly claim she had loved them and they both had had admirable qualities, but both times her heart had said *not this one*. She had gone on looking for that one person she could love with all her heart and who would love her in the same way. Sometimes, she had even wondered if he really existed.

She strongly suspected, given her close association with Guruji, that her husband would have to be a man who was also in search of life's meaning. Otherwise, how could he tolerate her great devotion to Guruji and her love of meditation? Time for solitude and devotional practice was critical for her. Whenever she missed meditation for several days in a row, a feeling of depression would often creep in. Then everything she did would seem meaningless.

She explained this to me by reading a quote of Guruji's from her notebook. Guruji had talked about having "free-floating anxiety," anxiety without any cause. "Whenever we have the feeling that something is missing in our mental life, free-floating anxiety will set in," Guruji had said. "We'll try many things to remove it, a new relationship, a new lifestyle, a new career. But the real cause is the mental life. Only when we go beyond time and space can the anxiety be alleviated." Indu knew the truth of this. She told me that her anxiety had been so acute at times that even while meditating her heart had continued to beat rapidly even though she was sitting quietly. But her pounding heart had been the best biofeedback. The moment she had entered deeply enough into meditation, breaking through the mental grip of her mind, relief would come and her heart would suddenly slow down. She knew she needed to spend time everyday in the state "beyond," out of time and space. Where, she wondered, was she going to find a man who could understand this?

But as she stood in front of the staff photos thinking about her future, she knew it was in God's hands after all, or one could say, the hands of destiny.

℘ * * * ℃

Indu met the other ladies as they were getting ready to leave the dining hall. They stopped at the foot of the staircase in the entryway.

"So what's on the schedule for today?" Indu inquired.

"There is some shopping I need to do," Shakti said.

"I'll be sorting things in the room and helping Guruji with some correspondence," was Mangala's answer.

"Well, if no one needs me for anything, then I think I'll go for a walk." The idea had just occurred to Indu. But first she wanted to get a sweater.

They all walked upstairs to the room. She found her sweater in her suitcase and slipped back out. She stopped at the arched window just across from their bedroom door. It looked down onto the courtyard. She watched as a car pulled around and drove out of sight. A man appeared from the right, crossed the square, and headed into the doorway of the building to the left. The complex was in a quadrangle. Her building and the one on the left were at right angles to each other and were connected through the second-floor sitting room. From where she stood, she could go to the right and find a staircase leading down to the Yoga Hall, or she could go to the left, through the small sitting room which angled to the right, then down the hall past the main staircase and find a smaller spiral staircase at the end of that hall which went down to the laundry room and main kitchen. The upper hallway was in an L-shape. The door the man had entered was the service entrance that led past the same laundry room and into the kitchen/dining room area.

Indu was very curious about the entire place. She understood that it had originally been built in the 1600s. That would account for the dilapidated condition of the roof she had noticed when she'd first arrived in the taxi. She could see it from the window. It was a section of the far building, near the kitchen. From where she stood, she could clearly see that it was roped off to prevent people from entering. Beyond that ruin was a wall with a white door. The wall turned the corner of the courtyard and went up to a very tall, long stone structure which had once been the barn. Another brick wall extended perpendicularly from the barn and led up to the front gravel drive. Across the drive, the wall continued until it reached what had been the servants' quarters.

Indu went downstairs and headed out the front door through which she had first entered the day before. After exploring inside the courtyard or quadrangle, she walked back to the door.

A gravel path went underneath the archway above which was the second-floor passageway. Indu imagined it must have been the back entrance for carriages. The gravel path went along the inside of the low stone wall which enclosed the expanse of green lawn. Already that morning several tents had appeared, set up along its perimeter. Indu walked to the end of the path, which terminated at two stone posts securing a tall iron gate. Beyond that was the pasture and farmland.

Turning around, Indu got a majestic view of the complex. In one straight row she could see the old servants' quarters, now the residents' hall for staff, the Yoga Hall and above that the windows to their room where she hoped she'd be staying that night. The windows to Guruji's room were located on the other side of the second-floor archway. Below his room were quaint, white French doors that opened onto the downstairs sitting room. Extending beyond the French doors was a curved patio. The patio narrowed to a walkway which wrapped around the building. Indu knew it connected to the patio by the flower garden near the dining room. She started to walk that way, cutting across the green grass.

She passed the dining room windows and stopped at the door to the beverage room. She could either go straight down the small brick path or up over the retaining wall. She saw some stone steps on the far side of the garden beyond the retaining wall, so she let her feet carry her in that direction. When she arrived at the top of the steps, she was pleased by what she saw. A formal rose garden lay beyond. It was beautiful. The five long stone steps were bordered by tall pillars and led down to a grass runway which ran the entire length of the garden. The garden was laid out to the right and a tall ivy-covered brick wall to the left. Foot paths ran in and around the five separate rose beds which were bordered on the far side by another ivy-covered brick wall.

Indu walked to the end of the grass runway. It stopped at a low, iron gate which had been tied shut. A small sign on the gate read, "Private Property Beyond This Point." But Indu's curiosity could not be so easily thwarted. Swinging her legs over it, she saw on the other side another posted sign stating "Nature Trail," with an arrow pointing to the right. She could tell that the trail was not often frequented and feared that poison ivy or some other pernicious vine might be lying in wait. Another footpath, extending to the left of the gate, also seemed too overgrown to explore. But straight ahead she saw a pond. Its contour was almost entirely concealed by overhanging trees and a great abundance of water lilies. As she approached it she noticed something peculiar. Broad stone steps led right down into the water. Maybe at one time, she thought, people had enjoyed swimming and boating and had entered at this point. But there was now a foul smell of decaying plants and stagnant water. Who knows, she speculated, it may not have been used in over a hundred years. She stood for a few minutes, wondering about the history of the place. She was soon ready for the fragrance of the roses again and turned back toward that direction.

She gracefully lifted one leg and then the other back over the iron gate. The garden from that vantage point was exquisite. What a lovely estate this must have been she thought. She could just imagine ladies in long muslin dresses picnicking on the grass or strolling along the paths with gentlemen friends. She laughed at her own imagination. She was a romantic at heart. Checking her watch, she was surprised to see that it was time for lunch. She walked slowly back toward the dining hall enjoying the fragrance and colors of the flowers. It was a sensuous feast.

With a plate full of food, Indu found a seat on the ledge of the retaining wall outside the dining hall. The air was warm, the sky clear. Almost everyone was eating outside on the grass. Guruji also came out with a plate. Indu watched where he would choose to sit. He walked directly to the spot where the fire ceremony had been the evening before. Uma, Mangala and Shakti were with him, as well as another tall, well-built man in his mid-forties. Indu guessed that he was Harry Goodall. She thought she should go over and join them. But some part of her liked observing from a distance, although she did not want to appear unsocial. She decided to finish her meal, watching, and then get dessert and join them.

The number of people around seemed to have more than doubled since the evening before. Many were approaching Harry Goodall and Guruji, saying a few words before finding a grassy seat nearby. Indu heard through the beverage room door, "Custard is ready." That was the dessert. She hurriedly finished the last few bites on her plate and went in to get a bowl. She put several bowls on a tray and took them out to Guruji and the group.

She was well received.

"Come on, come on. What took you so long to come over?" Uma chided her.

"I was waiting for the custard. What did you think I was doing?" Her timing was perfect. They all were just ready for dessert.

Shakti made the introductions. "I don't believe Indu has met Mr. Goodall yet."

"No, I haven't," Indu said, "But I've certainly heard about you." She extended her hand to meet his. "It's very nice to be here."

"Well, I'm glad to have you all at Ickwell," he responded with polite reserve. "My staff and I are very pleased with the size of the group that's coming for the intensive. In fact, I was just telling your teacher about a phone call I had this morning from an old acquaintance of his, a man named Luke Michaels."

The name was not familiar to Indu but she gathered from the conversation that Luke had been a student of Guruji's over fifteen years ago when Guruji had been teaching in London. When Guruji had gone to the States, Luke had remained in England and become a fairly well-known teacher himself. He presently had a center in the south of France. But he was back in England and had heard through a yoga network that Guru-ji was visiting at the Good Health Foundation. He had called to tell Mr. Goodall that he would definitely be coming for the weekend. Other commitments prevented him from staying longer. The news had pleased Mr. Goodall because Luke was known to be a good yoga teacher and speaker. Luke had further volunteered to make the opening introduction of the guest of honor that evening.

Uma later told Indu of some of the other conversation between Guruji and Mr. Goodall. "He explained to Guruji that he would miss Saturday evening's program because of a special dinner being held in London for the two jugglers and their entire crew. They've just completed the three-week jugglethon. Their effort to raise funds for the disabled has been broadcast on radios and television across the south of England. Not only have they increased people's awareness of the challenges faced by the disabled but they've also brought in substantial pledges of support for the work at the Foundation."

"Sounds like they're a pair of heroes, all right," Indu said.

Walking through the front entryway after lunch, Indu saw a small poster about the jugglethon. It showed a picture of one fellow standing on the shoulders of another. The one on top was juggling, and upon closer inspection, she recognized him. He was on staff at the Foundation and she had seen his picture on the wall in the beverage room. It was Nhoj. She examined the face of the fellow below, but she did not recognize him from the staff pictures. "They certainly must be good jugglers," she thought.

Still tired from her trip and from the uncomfortable night's sleep, she lay down on the bed upstairs in their room for an afternoon nap. Jet lag had caught up with her. She slept straight through dinner. Even though the ladies had been coming in and out of the room all afternoon, she had not heard a sound. She awoke at six o'clock in the evening, just one hour before the evening program was to begin. She changed clothes, washed her face, brushed her hair, and dabbed on a little make-up. She always tried to be neat in her appearance. Shakti came into the room.

"You're alive again," she joked. "We thought you were gone for good. Uma fixed you a plate of food. She set it over there on the dresser."

Indu saw the plate covered in aluminum foil. "How sweet of her. Let me see what it is." She peeked under the foil and saw a baked potato, corn on the cob, baked beans, salad and a slice of homemade bread. "Gosh, this looks great. But I think I'll keep it covered right here until after program tonight. I'm not quite awake enough to enjoy it right now. Besides, it's almost program time."

"It sure is," Shakti agreed. "In fact, Guruji has already gone downstairs. I came in just to see if you were moving. Didn't think you wanted to miss the first program. It should be a good one. Luke arrived about an hour ago. He's downstairs with Guruji and Mr. Goodall now. A lot of people have come. You should see all the tents that are up outside. Must be at least twenty. Looks like a circus is in town."

Indu couldn't keep from smiling and said, "With Guruji in the show, it probably will be a circus." She then remembered a reference Guruji had made to circus life. He had said that people meeting together was like a cosmic circus, with everything performed in a very orderly and cooperative way, but still for fun, not to be taken too seriously. He strongly advised to stay detached and not identify with the circus as if it were real life. Contemplating the challenge of staying detached, Indu picked up her meditation shawl and went downstairs with Shakti.

Everyone was gathered in the sitting room. It looked like about fifty people were there. Indu saw Guruji sitting in front of the fireplace, cross-legged in a large chair. Luke sat to his right and Mr. Goodall to his left. Indu found a pillow and sat in the back of the room, directly in line with Guruji. In this way she could be attentive to Guruji and still observe everything around her.

Mr. Goodall finally stood up and drew everyone's attention. "Please find a comfortable seat. I think we can all squeeze in here." There were a few laughs as people adjusted their chairs and floor pillows to make room for others still coming in. Speaking slowly and distinctly, he began. "As many of you know, this is the first seminar of the eighth yoga conference held here at Ickwell, and we're very fortunate this time to have an eminent doctor, surgeon, author and yogi with us as our guest of honor. And that man is seated here next to me, Dr. Ramamurti S. Mishra. Now to give a more detailed introduction of our guest of honor is a man who has known Dr. Mishra for twenty years. He is himself a well-established teacher of yoga, and his name is Luke Michaels. Luke, I turn the floor over to you." Mr. Goodall gestured to Luke and sat back down.

Luke had pulled a straight back chair near to Guruji's lounge chair and also sat cross-legged. He looked to be in his mid-forties and had a small beard and long hair tied back in a ponytail. He was dressed in baggy orange pants and a light orange shirt. Several *mālās* or strings of sacred beads were around his neck. Indu liked his eyes. They were clear and focused. He made no motion to stand up. After clearing his voice, he began to speak.

"Harry has asked me to do something which is not the easiest thing for me to do. He wants me to introduce a man who in my esteem is beyond any introduction. His presence speaks for itself. Tonight, actually, I am meeting him again after not seeing him for many years. But although I have not been with him—in his physical presence, I mean—he has always been in my heart. It was my great fortune to spend several years with him way back when I was first entering on the Path. In no short order he transformed my life. And I'd only like to warn you all now that he's about to do the same to yours."

Laughter broke out in the room. Guruji gave one of his famous side smiles, where only the right corner of his mouth pulls up and the whites of a few teeth peek through. It was a smile that radiated mischievousness. Indu had seen it many times and it was a sure sign that the Guru was up to something. But Guruji then resumed his serious expression and waited for Luke to finish.

"All I can really tell you," Luke said by way of a closing statement, "is don't let appearances deceive you. You may think you see a small Indian man sitting before you. But you don't. You are looking at a giant, a universal giant, a cosmic giant. You only have to hear him speak and be with him to know this. He is no ordinary man. I bow humbly before him." With these words, Luke folded his palms together and bowed his head.

Giving him three solid pats on the back, Guruji then closed his eyes and waited for silence. The sound of his voice began to fill the room as he chanted three *OM* mantras, each one resonant and sustained. The entire room joined in. The room vibrated with the sound. He then pronounced, "*OM shāntih, shāntih, shāntih.*" The group chanted along, not necessarily knowing that they were chanting the Sanskrit word for peace.

Guruji began to speak. "Have you ever been in a planetarium? You can see the sun, the moon, the stars, whole galaxies. But where are you really? Sitting in a building. A planetarium is a great illusion. Our minds are like the planetarium. Our minds create such an illusion for us. But all we need to do is walk out. What is the illusion? Our problems, our illness. They show us that we are involved with the body and mind. But when we are not attached to the body and mind, then problems can become instruments of heaven. Then even our sickness can be the cause of our enlightenment. If we are attached to body and mind, then problems become instruments for our destruction.

"I want to tell you a little story to help explain this. There are four men standing out in the forest. Three of them claim to possess great knowledge and the fourth can only claim to have common sense. The four men happen upon a dead lion. The three men of knowledge decide to use what they know to bring the lion back to life. One uses his knowledge of taxidermy and dermatology to repair the skin. The other uses his knowledge of anatomy and physiology to put the bones together and situate the organs. The third man uses his knowledge of endocrinology and neurology to put the spark of life back into the lion. But the fourth man with common sense tries to warn them against doing such a dangerous thing. Let the animal remain dead, he says. But they ridicule him, saying it was more important to demonstrate the powers of their knowledge than to worry about the consequences. So the fourth man climbed a tree and waited. When the three men of knowledge succeeded in reviving the lion, the lion promptly ate them. We are all too busy with this lion and it is leading us to destruction. This lion is the body and mind.

"Mind cannot work without space and time. And space and time require cause and effect. All business of the mind involves matter in time and space. So we have two duties. We must work in time and space and we must go beyond time and space. If we do not ever take a rest from time and space, it will be just as debilitating to our lives as not taking physical rest.

"When you think, your mind transforms energy into matter. That is why we are tired at night. And matter cannot exist without time and space. Can you remember anything without time and space? Try. You will immediately be in some time and some space. Therefore, by means of the mind there is an exchange going on between matter and energy. Thinking transforms energy into matter. When you go beyond thought, then mind transforms the universe of matter into pure energy. It is just as Einstein stated in his law of relativity: $E = Mc^2$, which means energy equals matter multiplied by the speed of light squared, and conversely $M = E/c^2$. Matter and energy are connected through the mind.

"So why meditate? We meditate to go beyond the mind. Then only energy is left and we are that energy. That energy is our real nature.

"What is the difference between all religion and yoga? Religion deals with symbolism and yoga deals with reality. Religion is mental, caught in language and mind. Yoga deals directly with universal energy, with the ultimate reality. Without meditation, all of life is useless. Who created all war? Religion. Look in the history books and see how many wars have been fought in the name of religion. Thousands. It is because people have lost the power of meditation and they depend on the mind. Mind is the cause of wars. Heart is the center of unity.

"We keep trying to purify the mind. But can you really purify the mind? You have to go beyond the mind and body. Then your mind automatically becomes pure because you already are that purity.

"Emerson wrote, 'Everyone is God playing the fool.' It means we are fools because we identify with the physical and mental states. We need body and mind but do we feel it necessary to carry our houses on our backs everywhere we go? No. So we must come out of body and mind by means of wisdom. When you have wisdom, you can transform hell into heaven, sickness or difficulties into your enlightenment."

Guruji stopped at this point and again let silence fill the room. Everyone sat waiting, not sure what was to come next. If they had grasped even part of what Guruji had said, then they were well on their way to enlightenment. Indu suspected that Guruji's talk had penetrated more on a subconscious level than a conscious one. He often worked that way.

He broke the silence to say he would welcome any questions. "Please feel free to ask anything."

No one spoke for a moment. Then one man raised his hand. "Do you believe, then, that religions do not serve any good purpose in our present civilization?"

"Religions are useful," Guruji said affirmatively. "All religions—Christianity, Hinduism, Mohammedanism, Judaism, Buddhism—are like soap. We need to clean out the mind. Religions are good in the sense that they act like detergent. But after cleaning, then we must rinse away the soap. If the soap stays in, then the clothes cannot really get clean. Meditation beyond the thinking mind is the final rinse. We need to eat. But the following day we need to release what we took in or else we will become constipated. The purpose of the outer church is to lead one to the inner church."

Several nodded in agreement.

Guruji continued. "But don't misunderstand. I am all for Jesus, for Mohammed, for Buddha, for Moses. When Moses was on Mount Sinai and asked how to convince people that he had seen God, God said to tell them to 'Be still and know I am That I AM.' God did not say to read the Ten Commandments, the Bible, the Koran, philosophy, science, law. These things are all good. The Vedas, the Bible, the Koran clean our minds. When the mind is clean, then you can come home. As Jesus said, 'I and my Father are one.' There should be this complete identification because you and your God are one. But you are going out and out, and you must go in to meet God. And that is what Moses did. When he was climbing Mount Sinai a voice said to him, 'Please remove your shoes because this land is holy.' What does that mean? Moses wore no shoes. It means please drop your body, mind and ego. Only then can you visit God. Drop all personality and your real self will shine through. For where is God? God is within."

A woman raised her hand and asked, "So there is no such thing as the Devil?"

Guruji didn't hesitate before replying. "What is the difference between devotees of God and the Devil? They are both children of God. But demons have selfish motives and devotees have unselfish ones. God does not see the action; he sees the motive behind the action. If we kill to protect a nation it is different than if we kill to steal money. The motives are different.

"And if you are a real devotee of God then you will feel that both of these motives are within you. Some of our desires are selfish and some are unselfish. So this battle of good and evil is within us. But someone who is not a devotee of God will battle with others. If you don't believe me, then see the television."

Guruji nodded to a woman in the corner who had a raised hand. She asked, "What is a *mantra*?"

"The word *mantra* is Sanskrit. *Man* in Sanskrit means 'to think.' From this Sanskrit word comes the English word 'man' because he thinks. Although other animals think, man is the only creature who thinks, 'Who am I?' A cow does not wonder, 'Who am I?' 'Mind' in Sanskrit is *manah*. A mantra is a sacred word or phrase. So a mantra is that which protects the mind. When you repeat a mantra, you cannot think. The thinking mind contracts. You can then have a glimpse of the reality beyond time and space."

A woman in front of Guruji wanted to know about the "third eye." She had heard many references to it but she didn't know what it meant.

Guruji looked directly at her and asked, "Can you drive your car with your eyes closed?" The woman shook her head "no." Others in the room were smiling. It seemed that they had gotten the answer by that statement alone. But Guruji went on. "If you can drive your car with closed eyes, you must not have any doubt that you can drive even better with open eyes. At present we are blind. We are blind because we suffer due to the illusion of the body and mind. Only with wisdom can we break that illusion. Without wisdom you have no third eye. When you have a third eye, then you go beyond time and space. The third eye is not a physical entity. It is understanding your real nature."

Mr. Goodall glanced down at his watch and then spoke up before Guruji could take another question. "I'm sure over the next ten days you all will have a chance to ask as many questions as you like. But tonight, it is already quite late. So we'll end this session now with a few moments of silence."

People immediately adjusted their seats and many took deep breaths as they closed their eyes. They seemed ready to go beyond. Guruji had lit the fire. It wasn't so much his words but the inspiration that they had kindled. That was their power. And all seemed to have felt it. It was going to be an interesting ten days. Indu also closed her eyes to meditate.

Guruji's voice again resonated with three *OM*s. Everyone joined in. The third *OM* was followed by the three *shāntih*s representing peace for the body, mind and spirit. Guruji ended with a final "*Harih OM.*"

Before anyone had moved, Mr. Goodall stood up and addressed the gathering again. "I just want to add one thing. If anyone who has arrived this evening needs any assistance setting up their tents, or is wondering where to stay, Rhonda, Sarah and Marty are here to help you get settled. If you ever have any difficulties, please don't hesitate to ask anyone on the staff to help you. Now for those who might be hungry in the morning..." He paused to receive a flood of grins, "breakfast will be served from seven-thirty to nine. Dr. Mishra's program will be in the barn starting at a quarter past nine. Everyday we'll keep the schedule posted in the front entryway. Once again I would like to extend a big welcome to Dr. Mishra and his lovely staff. Why don't you ladies stand up so everyone knows who you are?"

The four of them complied with his request. Indu stood up from her position in the back, smiled, and quickly resumed her seat.

Mr. Goodall gave a final wave of his hand. "Everyone, get a good night's sleep." He turned then to shake hands with Guruji and make a few other comments. He did seem a little preoccupied but it was understandable. It was not easy being host to so many people. Indu thought he had been appropriately warm and gracious.

Guruji was heading toward the door with Uma and Mangala right behind him. Shakti was visiting with guests. Not really wanting to talk to anyone, and feeling pangs of hunger, Indu also followed Guruji up the stairs. She bowed with folded hands as he went to his room. With that lovely plate of food in mind, she quickly walked on to her room. It appeared Carol Lee would not be coming after all. Indu looked gratefully at the bed in the corner.

SIX

~

Before breakfast the next morning, Guruji called Indu into his room and handed her a slide carousel filled with slides. "This morning I want to show the slides of the universe. Can you locate a projector and set it up in the barn after breakfast?" Guruji asked.

It was natural that he should ask her since she was the one who had spent hours organizing the slides at the ashram.

"Yes, of course, I'll take care of it," Indu replied, eager to be of help. She took the carousel and went downstairs to look for Gretchen. She found her standing in the courtyard by the doorway which was the service entrance leading to the kitchen. Her baby sat on her feet playing with the gravel.

Indu approached her. "Hi, Gretchen. Is that your baby?"

"He certainly is," she stated matter-of-factly. "Do you need something?"

It was as if Gretchen had read Indu's mind. Although the question had been abruptly put, Indu appreciated the directness. "Yes, we need a slide projector for the morning program."

"Oh dear, let me think. We've got one somewhere but I'm not sure if it's working. Let me look in the office. You'll probably need an extension cord, too." She said this as she picked up her child. "Come on, Thomas. Let's go see what we can find." She walked toward the main entrance. Indu followed. Mr. Goodall had an office off the front hallway. The door was by the table with the books. Indu had missed noticing it earlier. Gretchen had the key and went in. Mr. Goodall was not there.

Indu asked, "Has Mr. Goodall already left for London?"

"Yes, yes. He'll be away the whole day." She was searching behind his desk in some boxes. "Ah, here's something, I think."

She dragged out a piece of equipment, but it did not look like a slide projector that would automatically rotate a carousel with the touch of a button. "How do you work this one?" Indu asked with skepticism.

"Oh, it's easy. But let's see if it works at all." She plugged it in and the motor hummed. "You're in luck," she said. "You flip this switch for the light and you slide this metal frame across with the slide in it. Then you put your next slide in the frame on this side and slide the carriage back to the far right again. You see. You just slide the two frames back and forth."

Indu accepted it, trying not to show any lack of gratitude although she couldn't believe they still used something so archaic. Carousel projectors had been around for a couple of decades. Nonetheless, she thought, "You take what you can get."

"Shall I bring it back here when we're finished?" Indu politely inquired.

"Yes, have someone unlock the door for you and just set it inside," she replied. "Now, there should be an extension cord in the kitchen utility closet. I'll have someone drop it off at the barn for you. The screen, I believe, is already in the barn up on the stage to one side."

Indu thanked her and carried the projector into the dining hall. After cereal and juice, she headed to the barn. Its two large, white wooden doors were swung back, held open with cinder blocks. Another entrance was at the other end of the barn with a smaller, standard-size door. Inside, Indu found the screen where Gretchen had said it would be, up on the stage to the left. The stage was a good size. It filled about one-fifth of the barn and had been built since the Foundation had owned the property. The barn was an ideal small auditorium, with its stone walls and a high pitched roof with massive wooden beams. It smelled of old timber. Over the grass floor a large piece of carpet had been laid, and smaller mats had been set to the side with stacks of chairs.

After setting up the screen, Indu positioned one chair a little distance from the stage to hold the projector. Someone had already plugged in the extension cord and left it lying conveniently within reach. She turned on the machine, set a slide into the metal frame and adjusted the focus. With the barn doors closed, she hoped it would be dark enough.

People began coming in and a few minutes later Guruji also entered. Shakti carried a tape recorder and set it up near an electrical outlet to the side of the stage. The series of slides Guruji was going to show about the universe and galaxies came as a set with an audio tape. At the special tone, the slides were to be advanced. Indu had already speculated on the adeptness with which she was going to have to maneuver the slides in and out of the metal frames. If she didn't keep things synchronized it would distract terribly from the presentation. She signaled to Guruji that she was ready.

The presentation went well although Indu had had to work to keep from laughing at the absurdity of the whole procedure. When the slides were finished, Guruji directed everyone to close their eyes. Mangala and Shakti moved quickly among everyone passing out small quartz crystals. Guruji sat cross-legged on a mat onstage. He began a guided meditation.

"Watch your mind." He paused for a moment. "What happens to your mind when you do not think? It becomes an ocean of radio waves. When you feel the radio waves, you cannot feel your physical body. With that sensation comes heavenly music, a ringing sound in your head, the vibration of electricity."

There was a power in the silences between Guruji's words. The atmosphere was charged by his magnetism, and by the effusion of his energy. Everything Guruji said to feel, Indu always tried to feel. It was as though he was acting as an amplifier, magnifying sensations which had gone unnoticed by her.

Guruji's voice, clear and deep, carried easily through the barn. "Now, feel the vibration and pulsation in your head and face, neck and shoulders, arms, palms and fingers. Feel electrical vibration from your palms to your heart and from your heart to your palms. Hold the crystal in the left palm. Close the fist of both palms to make it easier to feel pulsation. Feel pulsation in both hands, in your neck, face and brain. Feel like there is a burning flame in the center of the brain." Indu particularly liked this image. She could feel this light in her head and its presence affected her entire body. "Let the light of this flame pervade the lungs and heart, abdomen, stomach, liver, kidneys and intestines, pancreas, spleen." There was another short pause. "Lower abdomen, legs, feet and toes. Now you have the body of pulsation, of electrical vibration. Feel the whole room is vibrating with electrical waves. Go deeper and deeper. Have no fear. Sometimes you will feel you have no body. You are everywhere in the universe. The universe is you. The energy is the same. Feel this. You are the Absolute. Your body is burning like the burning bush which was seen by Lord Moses on Mount Sinai. This feeling is the burning bush. The more the fire is burning, the more the leaves and flowers and fruits are growing. It is no ordinary fire. It is not a physical fire, but a spiritual fire."[13]

A long period of silence followed. The more Indu tried to feel all the inner sensations, the more distinct the sound in her head became. When learning meditation, it often took time to detect the subtle inner changes. This was why discipline was required. But the crystal was a good aid. It acted to strengthen the pulsations, making it easier to stay attentive.

℘ * * * ℭ

Why the crystal worked was something Indu could not easily explain. But Guruji had often said regarding a question about a particular technique, "Scientists do not know why electricity works, why a filament in a vacuum will carry a current causing the vacuum to fill with light. Nobody knows, but everyone uses electricity."

Indu knew that crystals were absolutely pure substances whose three-dimensional structure was made up of identical, congruent unit cells repeated over and over again. "Somehow," she said to me, "they work to hold the attention inward and keep the mind focused. When the attention is uninterrupted, the mind and body become still. Only with that stillness can the metaphysical jump in awareness be made, that jump beyond time and space."

ﾝ * * * ﾈ

Guruji brought the meditation to a close by chanting *OM*. Everyone opened their eyes. Many began talking about their experiences and as Mangala and Shakti collected the crystals, several asked where the crystals could be purchased.

Shakti replied, "Any number of places sell them. But we'll make these available for purchase on the last day of the intensive."

"I'm so glad. I want to buy one. It's so peaceful holding it. I had such a nice meditation," an older woman said.

It was lunchtime. Many guests were still lingering in the barn as Guruji walked out. He went upstairs while Indu returned the projector. When she finally got her plate of food, she found he had come back down and was sitting on the grass near the same spot as the day before, eating intently. Indu had begun a conversation while standing in the lunch line with two ladies who were on staff at the Foundation. It seemed more gracious to take her seat with them than to go over toward Guruji. It gave a greater feeling of unity between the Foundation and Guruji's group. The ladies' names were Rhonda and Sara.

Rhonda was speaking exuberantly. "Can't wait for Nhoj to get back. He owes me ten quid."

"Better watch out, or he may ask you to donate it to the jugglethon," Sara cautioned with a smile.

"Well, I've already given. Besides that, I even bought one of their T-shirts. So you see, I've been advertising for them all over Bedfordshire. I've done my part." Rhonda turned to Indu and asked her, "Do you know what we're talking about? Have you heard about the jugglethon?"

Indu nodded her head. "I have heard about it. Seems it's been a big success. So, Nhoj is on staff here, is that right?"

"He is," Sara said. "He's been associated with the Foundation for two years now. Quite a good chap. He did something like this last year, but then he only juggled fifty miles. This year he wanted to do something bigger and better. So when his friend came along, they decided to make a real show of it. They made up an itinerary, contacted all the towns they were going to pass through and arranged to give small exhibitions as part of a fundraiser for the Foundation. They've been walking and juggling for three weeks. What a pair of clowns they are."

Sara and Rhonda then wanted to know more about how Indu had gotten involved with an Indian Guru, what she did for a living, how she liked England. She answered their questions. An American connected with an East Indian transplanted in England made for an interesting topic. But she did not elaborate too much. It was actually difficult to do so much talking and eat at the same time.

Lunch was soon finished and the ladies hurried back to their jobs. Indu had sat only a few minutes alone when Uma came up and asked, "What's up, ducksie?"

"Oh, not much. Where are you heading?" Indu inquired, figuring she had something in mind.

Uma gave a big grin. "Well, I was thinking about a little stroll down the road a bit. Would you be interested in joining me?"

"Sounds like a lovely idea," Indu said, happy for the invitation.

They both dropped their plates off in the kitchen and headed straight across the quadrangle and under the entrance arch, stepping carefully over the metal grate. They walked briskly down the gravel drive which was the main access to the Foundation. They had the utmost intention not to dawdle along the way since they needed to be back by two-thirty for the afternoon program with Guruji. But their walking pace soon slowed at the end of the drive where the Maypole and another monument stood, one Indu had not noticed previously. Indu stopped to look again at the Maypole. Uma went up to the other monument, which was in honor of some patron saint. They turned left at the main road and walked at an easy, relaxed pace. It was a sunny day. Uma pointed out the elaborate thatched roofs. Indu had to look hard to believe that they were really made of thatch. Not only were they thatched, but many had been ornately carved with curves and peaks at the apex of the roof. Thatched roofs, Maypoles and archaic slide projectors; this was a land of wonders, she thought.

As they walked, Uma told Indu about her two children, both of whom were grown and living in California. She began reminiscing. Seventeen years ago their whole family had spent a year living in England. Her husband had gotten some post at a university and the children attended an American academy. They hadn't missed the chance to travel all over Europe, although it had been a challenge with two young children. This was Uma's first visit back since that time.

They saw a small chapel and graveyard on the left of the road and decided to go and explore. Spanning the shallow roadside gully was a wooden footbridge, complete with decorative posts and roof. A winding gravel path led up to the front portico. They entered through the arched doorway. Inside was a vestibule where the schedule of services was posted. This charming house of prayer was affiliated with the Church of England. There was one central aisle with pews on either side. A large stained glass window was at the front. Statues of the Christian saints were set in recesses along the walls leading up to the altar. Two other women were also there discussing a special ceremony that would take place. A clergyman in black robes appeared and came up to Uma and Indu, inquiring if there was anything they needed. They both said no and thanked him, eying each other a little sheepishly since curiosity had been their only reason for entering. Not wanting to wantonly tread on anyone's sacred ground and clearly not there for worship, they slipped out discreetly and walked over to the graveyard where they oddly felt more relaxed. Uma sat down against a tree.

Indu stood next to her. Indu had never gone into an unknown graveyard for a moment's reflection. But looking at the grave markers, it was impossible not to reflect on the meaning of life.

℘ * * * ℭ

The spirit moves into a physical body and then moves out of the physical body. What is this movement? After much meditation, it had become clear in her heart. This movement or release from the body appeared to happen at death, but Guruji had said over and over that we are neither born nor will we die. She read to me his short clarification of this point, "As long as you are not enlightened, so long the world will be a dream because you are seeing through the body which is in time and space. But when you are enlightened, then the world is recognized as an illusion. This world is not real." The movement is not real, except when perceived in time and space. Beyond time and space there can be no distinction of "in" the body or "out" of it. Spirit is all the time eternal.

Indu laughed when she heard herself say this to me. "All the time eternal" was a grammatical *faux pas,* she quickly explained. She had read an article in a news magazine on tautology, the unnecessary repetition of an idea. It was certainly unflattering to have them pointed out and the author's example of one such tautology was from a recent broadcast of an address by a White House spokesman. It was: "The President is watching the current situation, which is ongoing at this moment." The triple overstatement was plain: current, ongoing, this moment. But I readily forgave her redundancy. Yes, "all the time" does imply "eternal" but I knew she'd meant it for emphasis. The Spirit is in us and in the universe simultaneously. They are not separate. Why we perceive them as separate is what Indu had been pondering on while standing under that tree. That was Guruji's whole teaching: we are not separate. She was happy that I understood and was just about to continue her story when I had to ask her again about George.

"Oh, surely you've guessed by now who he is?" she teased me.

"Is it the juggling friend?" I carefully proffered.

She nodded that it was. Meeting him was a moment she would never forget. And since it seemed she was finally at that point in the story, she picked up her narrative on the following day, the day the jugglers were to return to Ickwell. It was a Sunday, August 19.

ℬ * * * ℭ

They had all had lunch. Luke was playing the guitar out on the patio in front of the French doors. Again it was a beautiful day—the sky blue and almost cloudless, the air warm. Indu sat enjoying the music and watching the people. Everyone had a feeling of anticipation. They were all awaiting the return of the jugglethon crew. Guruji came downstairs just after two o'clock. Mr. Goodall began to give the signal that it was time. Word had come that the jugglers would soon be juggling down the gravel drive.

Whatever musical instruments were available were brought to the brick front entrance archway. The idea was to make as much noise as possible just as the jugglers came into sight.

Indu walked ahead with the others from the Foundation and found a place to stand just between the archway and the horse grate. She was glad to be part of the fun, there to cheer on two people with whom she had no connection whatsoever, to do it in honor of their great deed. She turned to see Guruji, who seemed to be enjoying the festiveness, walking slowly toward her with Mr. Goodall. Uma was also at his side. All three took a place just opposite her on the other side of the drive. Indu had brought her camera and it was a good chance to get a shot of them together, although only Uma looked her way. Minutes after that, someone called out, "Here they come."

All eyes were focused on the end of the drive. And there they appeared, too far in the distance even to see the juggled balls. There was a hushed silence as everyone watched them slowly advance. But when they were nearly halfway down the drive, the cheering and noise began. A minute before they were to cross the horse grate, Indu stepped from the sidelines and snapped a photograph. It was an unusual spectacle, two men walking with six balls flying through the air.

80 * * * 03

She showed me the picture. George was the one on the right, she told me. Even when I looked closely, the distance made it difficult to make out his features. After taking the picture she had stepped back onto the grassy edge of the gravel drive. The cheers had been loud and lively, with everyone making a great commotion. But she told me that once the two jugglers crossed the horse grate, the noise recorded in her memory faded into a blurred oblivion...

80 * * * 03

She saw only his face. Her eyes became transfixed by his face. Within seconds, he had walked past her. But it was enough time. If she had been impaled by an arrow or had a steel ball shot into her stomach, the physical sensation would have been

104

the same, she was sure. She stood momentarily stunned. She did not know what to make of this feeling.

There was nothing cerebral about this first encounter. There were no wandering thoughts, "Isn't he cute," "What a nice looking fellow," "Here's someone I'd like to meet." All she could think after the initial shock was, "If he's the one, he's shorter than I expected." Having stood so near him as he passed, she could judge that she was possibly even a little taller than he. But it was an inconsequential observation. She had no qualms about relinquishing the superficial image of "tall, dark and handsome." The man before her was "dark and handsome" and even that was irrelevant. Confronting her was something far beyond physical attraction. She did not care what his name was, where he was from or what age he was. The questions themselves never even entered her mind. Love was already pouring from her heart unreservedly. What she couldn't understand was how it could hit so hard and fast, and so totally consume her with such overwhelming intensity. This dazed state continued as she followed along behind the jugglers, her eyes riveted on his back as he juggled into the courtyard.

George and Nhoj proceeded juggling across the courtyard, under the second-story passageway and onto the semicircular patio in front of the French doors. Mr. Goodall soon joined them. Guruji sat on the grass to one side, with Uma, Shakti and Mangala seated near him. The two ball retrievers also sat toward the side where Guruji was. They were, as it turned out, the jugglers' respective girlfriends who had also walked the two hundred miles picking up the balls that the juggling duo missed. Indu, however, did not figure out this romantic involvement until much later.

Everyone gathered on the grass around the patio to hear as Mr. Goodall proclaimed the accomplishments of these two fellows, heaping laurels upon them. Four-foot long garlands of flowers and leaves were placed around their necks. To Indu, the two fellows actually appeared shy and embarrassed by all the special attention. They sat on the cement patio with their garlands comically falling around their legs and feet. Mr. Goodall stood formally beside them. Indu held her camera up, continually keeping her eye on George. Oddly, just as she was about to snap another picture, George looked her way. She gazed directly into his eyes through the viewfinder.

Mr. Goodall was saying, "...from Bournemouth to Plymouth, along the English channel coast, they juggled. In good weather or bad, among crowds of people or along isolated country paths. And it was not for personal glory. Every town they entered, or whenever they attracted a crowd, they stopped and spoke earnestly about the needs of the disabled, of those who find it difficult to walk a mere two feet, let alone two hundred miles. But they did not ask something for nothing. No, they gave to those people in exchange for their pledges of financial support. They gave of their talent, of their humor." At this comment both fellows broke into broad smiles. Mr. Goodall waited until the group's laughter had subsided before continuing. "They gave of their hearts, to thousands of people. And in response, although the figures are not all tallied, they raised an enormous sum in pledged support and contributions." This was met with great applause.

He went on to say that no words could really express his appreciation on behalf of the Foundation for their gallant efforts. He then made the request, though acknowledging their indisputable exhaustion, that they share with everyone their magnificent talent one last time. They had anticipated the invitation and seemed anxious to get on with the show. Immediately, they leaped up and hurried to their suitcases, strategically placed by one of their faithful crew, and pulled on over their shorts tattered baggy pants with suspenders. Nhoj topped off his costume with a white stuffed seagull, wings extended, mounted on a bright blue cap. George donned a navy blue beret.

Indu walked to the far side of the group where she could take in not only the two jugglers but also Guruji, Mr. Goodall and all those watching. Would anyone have the slightest idea that some unknown force was operating powerfully on her heart?

She walked closer to the front of the gathering, directly opposite Guruji. She raised her camera again to capture a shot of the three: Nhoj and George in action with Guruji watching. She suspected Guruji would know about her sudden turmoil. But what was she to do?

George and Nhoj put on a good show. They did three-, four- and five-ball juggling, baton tossing, and even something as silly as taking each other's hands and stepping over one another until they were precariously entangled, then ridiculously untangling themselves while still holding hands. Nhoj walked on glass and juggled with fire, as well as juggling three totally unrelated objects: a tea bag, a small bowling ball, and a knife. George juggled two balls with an apple, consuming the apple as it passed through his hands. Throughout their show, the banter between them or with the audience never stopped. One joke, undoubtedly used in every show, was timed to coincide with the inevitable dropped ball. With the proper gesture to convey the sexual innuendo, they gave the face-saving quip, "Well, dropped balls are a sign of maturity." The joke brought reels of laughter.

It was true. They were both talented. While watching the show, though, Indu had the feeling of being transported back to an earlier century—the country setting, the quaintness of the buildings, the people enjoying the rakish show of two boyish jugglers. There was a simplicity about it. She felt "time" and "space" playing a trick on her. She worked hard to shake off the feeling and return to what she knew was the twentieth century.

꽁 * * * ೞ

She laughed as she told me about all that had been racing through her mind at that moment, racing to understand the overwhelming emotions she was feeling. Had some memory from deep within been stirred, from a bygone lifetime, from a realm as yet untapped? Indu did believe in reincarnation and in the eternal nature of the soul, whether it be identified with a body or not. She intellectually accepted that evolving spiritually implied evolution through lifetimes until the eternal nature of the spirit is realized, and that this realization is enlightenment. Guruji had put it this way, and she read this quote to me: "As long as we are in the mind, then we will have birth and rebirth over and over again ad nauseam. We have seen a million parents, a million children. We will keep coming again and again until we get out of the mind. This takes wisdom."

It was during her meditations, when her mind became more still, that she truly felt the naturalness of disidentification with the physical body. Although it was not a frequent occurrence, she had at times felt an expansion of her being beyond physical confines when all sensations of the body were lost. Those describing near-death experiences also tell of a similar expansion, usually an upward movement, until they are gripped again by the pull of a physical bond. She had witnessed Guruji's ability to see and know without the senses, to work outside the limits of time and space. Clearly death of the body did not mean termination of existence since there could be awareness beyond the physical senses. Why couldn't this same awareness re-enter the matrix of time and space with a newly formed body? Could this not be one explanation for predilections and intrinsic tendencies? Why couldn't her unexplainable passion for George be a triggered recognition of a being she had encountered before, in another place, another lifetime? She said it was these types of thoughts that passed through her mind while she sat watching their show.

"What *was* I to do? Confronting me was the great mystery of my connection to George. I could only watch and wait for an explanation. I had eight days left at Ickwell with Guruji. In those eight days, I could only pray that an answer would come. And so my vigilant observation began. I may have appeared undisturbed—carrying out my duties, eating meals, talking with the guests—but my mind was continuously aware of George's presence or absence, my eyes always watching his movements, my heart searching for a sign that he, too, felt our mysterious connection."

Her description of those last days at Ickwell are totally focused on her observations and interactions with George. At the time, she had wondered if the poor boy had any idea that he was under such vehement surveillance. Of that she had remained uncertain for the entire week.

SEVEN

~

Her first exchange with George was to come that very same evening. Indu could not help but notice how quickly their paths had crossed with no intentional effort on her part. She hadn't seen him since the end of the afternoon juggling show. Dinner had come and gone, and he hadn't been there. It was six-thirty. She was on her way to round up mats for the fire circle. She remembered seeing them in the barn that afternoon. So instead of going directly to the Yoga Hall, where they had been on the previous day, she headed out the front door and across the quadrangle toward the barn. Just as she was about to pass the service entrance door, George suddenly walked through it.

To stand before him face to face... to speak to him directly... she had been hoping for this chance, but had not expected it to come so soon. If she did not speak up within the instant, she would be forced to express only a passing greeting of "hello." She had been walking with some momentum in one direction and he was moving in another. How to bring their paths together without betraying her real intentions? There was no time to think.

As though another voice was speaking, she heard herself say, "Would you mind helping me carry yoga mats out to the far side of the building? I think there are some in the barn."

"I'd be happy to," he said, turning to walk alongside her. He had a clear, distinct British accent. It was unlike any she had heard. It had a deepness, a quality, an unaffected refinement.

"Thanks," she said as casually as possible.

Without time for further words, they were at the barn entrance. The doors were still braced open. They both entered. They were alone together, standing within feet of each other. She was working hard to feel what the vibration was between them, all the while maintaining a relaxed countenance. She quickly realized as she looked around the barn that the stack of mats had been moved. They were nowhere in sight. She guessed they were back in the Yoga Hall. But George seemed truly eager to be of help; seeing the large carpet lying on the ground, he was quite ready to roll it up and carry it off. He did not understand that individual mats were needed for the meditation circle. As he held one corner of the carpet asking, "How about we take this one?", her love for him welled up inside of her.

She could only hide it by saying quickly, "No, no. This won't do. Thanks anyway. I'll run and get some from the Yoga Hall." With rapid steps, she walked out the doors, keeping her eyes set on the Hall which, once inside, would hide her blushing cheeks.

She laid the mats out on the lawn. Many guests came, but she did not see George. She hadn't explained to him what the mats were for or that the meditation was about to take place. She'd not even commented on his juggling show. Had he thought it strange that she'd left so quickly? Possibly he had not even given it a second thought. This was the mental turmoil she often found herself in: trying to conceal her love and at the same time trying to ascertain what his feelings were. Although it was a ridiculous situation, nonetheless, that first night after their meeting she went to bed with a strange happiness. She knew he was somewhere nearby and that tomorrow she would see him again.

She did not see him at breakfast or at Guruji's morning session. Having had a good night's sleep, she wondered what had really happened to her the day before. But when she finally did see him sitting in the dining hall eating lunch, she knew it had not been just a strange dream. Her heart was still in trouble. She tried not to even look at him. He was sitting with Nhoj and the two women who had been the ball retrievers along with several other friends. Indu got her plate and went out the beverage room door. Uma was sitting on the white wrought-iron bench and Indu joined her.

ℰ❀ * * * ℭ❦

Although these women traveling with Guruji were all good friends of hers, Indu told me that she never had any intention of confiding in them about her love for George. She didn't want anyone to know. She felt that any discussion of it might disturb some natural force. She felt herself enveloped in a cone of silence, an inner isolation. But the power of silence she had already come to understand.

Silence helped to protect and conserve the energy surrounding any event or mystical teaching. This was something every true seeker learned. Guruji had given the counsel: "Know everything but behave like an ignorant person. Don't tell anyone when you have reached some deeper understanding. They will not be happy. They may kill you." It always brought to Indu's mind the lives of Jesus, of Joan of Arc, of Mahatma Gandhi. It was their destiny to speak of what they knew. But certain people had not been able to tolerate what they spoke and those who did understand could not save them. So unless one was ready to meet that end, Guruji advised, "Keep quiet." Although this was a different situation, his advice still seemed appropriate.

ℰ❀ * * * ℭ❦

Indu ate lunch in as normal a fashion as she could. Uma was in a good mood. She loved being back in England. The afternoon program was going to be a group rebirthing. Indu had gone through several of Guruji's rebirthing sessions. They were pure psychotherapy. She also suspected that they had a strong activating effect on the *kuṇḍalinī*.

ℰ❀ * * * ℭ❦

Indu explained to me that *kuṇḍalinī* was a mystical force that was present in every human being at the base of the spine, but usually in a dormant state. Few people knew about it even though they may have had sensations caused by its movement. I asked what could make it move and she told me, "Any number of things, which is what makes it dangerous. Guruji has said that many people in mental hospitals are really victims of the *kuṇḍalinī* energy. But without consciously understanding what is happening inside the body, the mind manifests extraordinary explanations which give all appearances of psychosis, neurosis and paranoia. Not able to cure the problem, doctors simply fill their mental wards. It's lucky for the person to meet a spiritual teacher who can give reassurance that the surge of sensations, the tremendous inner sounds, or even the unexpected vocalizations are actually omens of heaven and not to be feared. With proper spiritual guidance, their anxiety can be allayed and they can live relatively normal lives."

She went on to say that being in the presence of an enlightened being could also awaken the *kuṇḍalinī* and that this was the ideal circumstance. *Kuṇḍalinī* aside, Guruji's rebirthings were dynamic and intense. Using special breathing techniques, the mind would be lulled into a state of relaxed receptivity, much like that of a baby's mind. Babies enter the world totally receptive to every stimulus encountered. How else could they learn as quickly as they do? But as adults, we build selective defenses for protection that block reception from the subconscious and superconscious levels. The breathing techniques Guruji used were designed to open the defense barriers and allow these other levels of consciousness to break through. But for many, the process brought up deeply repressed emotions. This release was the healing. By becoming more receptive and open, it was easier to perceive the unity of all souls, finally shattering the illusion of individual separateness. Guruji said time and time again, "We must go beyond dualism and feel absolute oneness. There is no 'me.' The real beauty of life lies beyond dualism."

℘ * * * ℭ

The rebirthing was scheduled to begin at half past two in the barn. Indu entered the barn with Guruji. Uma was already there instructing people to lie down comfortably and just relax. Not sure what else she should do, Indu laid down, too. Shakti and Mangala began giving the directions on how to breathe. Guruji did not speak much throughout these sessions but only kept watch for those who were ready for his direct assistance. Regardless, the space was charged with his energy.

Indu felt a tap on her foot. She opened her eyes. It was Guruji. He motioned for her to come to a man lying on the stage and directed her to place one hand on his abdomen and one hand on his forehead. He then silently showed her how to demonstrate the breathing. She began doing the slow rhythmic breathing, making the sound of an air stream in the back of her throat. The man naturally began to follow her rhythm. It took great concentration for those participating to stay with the breathing for the duration of the session. If one persevered, however, then the psychic breakthrough could come.

Indu saw that Uma, Shakti and Mangala were also walking from person to person giving individual instruction. This was the first time Indu had instructed during any rebirthing. But Guruji was giving her on-the-spot training. He signaled for her to move to another person and do the same thing: one hand on the abdomen, one on the forehead, and breathe. What was magical to Indu was that as her breathing became synchronized with each person's, a flow of energy could also be felt moving from her body to theirs and from theirs to hers. It brought her briefly into a union with them. She would then move away and they would continue breathing on their own.

Indu had seen George the moment she had entered with Guruji. Alison, who had been George's ball retriever and was his current girlfriend, although Indu was still not sure about their association, was also lying several feet from George. Indu realized as she was walking from person to person that she would eventually come to George. He was lying about ten feet back from the stage over toward the barn doors. The other three ladies were working more toward the back of the barn.

She quietly approached him. He had on olive green pants and a maroon shirt opened at the neck. His eyes were closed. She knelt beside him, marveling at the beauty of his head: dark hair, dark eyebrows, tanned complexion. She placed one hand on top of his shirt over his abdomen and the other she rested gently on his forehead. He did not move or open his eyes. She began to breathe the deep rhythmic breath. He began to follow. She could feel his abdomen slowly rising and falling. She did not take her eyes from his face. For those few moments their energy merged. In the split second before she was to withdraw her hands, Indu felt the tingle of tears about to fill her eyes. She pulled back and turned to another person. She had touched his head and he had not even known it was her. If she was not allowed by the cosmic Mother to have any further contact with him, at least they had had those moments together. A virtual stranger he was, but his soul was not unknown to her. And those few moments of rhythmic breathing had allowed some essence of their beings to reunite, or so it felt.

She had been aware that as she was breathing with George, her deep personal attraction to him had made it difficult to concentrate on her role as guide, and then the tears had made it impossible to continue. Still she had managed to stay with him for three minutes. Looking back, she realized that the breathing had triggered an emotional release in her, which she'd had to interrupt for fear of disturbing George.

Throughout that rebirthing session she passed by several times and just looked at him. She knew she dared not approach him again since he would surely pick up on a self-conscious vibration from her, which she didn't want to happen. She wanted him to have a good experience with Guruji's rebirthing. Any awareness of her presence would have been too great a distraction from his own inner process. Besides, she was also sure Guruji would notice her broken concentration if she went near George. To assist in rebirthing, it was critical for her to remain clearly focused at all times. Rebirthing was such an intense experience, it required everyone's full attention, participants and instructors alike. She did not want to disappoint Guruji by losing her focus.

At the end of the sessions, Guruji put on a cassette of flowing music and suggested that everyone begin moving naturally and freely to the sound. Indu loved these dance periods. They were a catharsis in themselves. For many there had already been a lot of release: crying, shaking, laughing, moaning, giggling. Part of being the instructor was to be by the side of anyone going through such manifestations—to hold them if they needed it, to laugh with them, to feel compassion for whatever they were feeling. The idea of the free movement was to encourage everyone to further drop their inhibitions and feel the aliveness of their being. It was really a relief to move so freely after such a long period of concentration. For anyone who had not experienced an outer manifestation, they could still feel an inner release by this process of free expression.

Indu stood at the front near the stage to demonstrate. Her movements were graceful and smooth. She felt a natural flow of energy moving her arms and legs to the rhythm of the music. Everyone seemed to feel a sense of relief. Out of the corner of her eye, she noticed that George was just sitting on his knees, meditating. She wondered why he didn't try some slow movements. But he sat absolutely still the entire time. Afterward Indu was greatly rejuvenated. She realized she had needed the rebirthing more than she'd ever imagined. Her heart, though, was still preoccupied with George. After the session, he and Alison had disappeared across the quadrangle.

That evening there was a special guest speaker, a Scottish priest. Guruji and his group walked together into the Yoga Hall. Mr. Goodall invited them to take a front-row seat on the floor. Indu noticed George and Alison sitting together against the wall. The nature of their relationship was becoming clearer and clearer to Indu. It hardly gave consolation to her heart. If they were a couple, then she would simply have to try to smother her feelings and hope that the next week would go by quickly. Throughout the lecture, she caught sight of them sitting shoulder to shoulder holding hands. She resolved at that moment to make every effort to avoid having any interaction with George. Nonetheless, as she was walking out of the Hall after the talk, as much as she wanted to resist the temptation, she could not help glancing back over her shoulder toward him. He was still sitting with Alison and seemed totally oblivious to whether she herself came or went. She suddenly felt silly about the whole situation and was even more determined to keep her distance from him.

How much of a coincidence it was, she would never know. But the following afternoon Guruji had a strong hand in bringing her directly into contact with George again. She had succeeded the entire morning and lunchtime to avoid even looking in his direction. That afternoon in the barn, Guruji was to teach a group of about fifty people a special yogic technique called "oil *neti.*" He described it as feeding the brain. The process involved placing two small test tubes half-filled with sesame or almond oil into the nostrils and tipping the head back, allowing the oil to drain up into the sinuses. The oil reached a permeable membrane at the back of the sinuses allowing nutrients to easily pass through the blood-brain barrier and directly supply the brain itself. No one was obligated to do the technique but almost all were willing to try.

Indu had been a faithful practitioner of oil *neti.* She had done it daily for a year and then had slowly tapered off, doing it now only on certain occasions. Guruji had divided the group into four sections. Uma, Mangala and Shakti each took charge of one. A visiting student of Guruji's named Sally, who had come up from London for the day, took charge of the fourth group. Sally had studied with Guruji for over fifteen years herself. Indu had been sitting on the side, watching. She had taught oil *neti* before, but not to so many people at one time. She was admiring how Guruji could pull off such a thing. It was a messy affair, oil and tubes and tissues everywhere. She had nonchalantly noticed that George was in the line instructed by Sally, who was working up on the stage. The stage was a good spot because people could lie back and tilt their heads over the edge allowing good support for the neck and a good angle for the oil to drain into the nose. George's turn was coming up. Just as he was lying down for the treatment, Guruji suddenly signaled for Indu to come and relieve Sally. Whether Indu wanted to or not, she would be the one to teach George oil *neti*. She wondered if it was providence that was encouraging her association with this enigma of a soul. She knelt down beside him and he looked up at her.

Immediately she was moved again by how beautiful his eyes were. Intrepidly he greeted her, "Hello there."

She nodded, trying to appear unconcerned. "Are you ready for this?" she asked as she began pouring the oil into the tubes.

Watching her, he inquired, "Have you done this yourself?"

"Oh, sure," she reassured him, "many times. It's wonderful once you get used to the feeling of the oil flowing past the throat and into the sinuses. The most important thing, though, is to keep the back of the throat closed off with the tongue, like this. . ." Unabashed, she demonstrated by opening her mouth to show the position of her tongue. It was an important point. Otherwise, the oil would be swallowed or could enter the windpipe. Sealing the esophageal and bronchial pathways was the whole trick to the process. If coughing started, the chin would have to be tilted back down, thus preventing any flow into the sinuses.

He mimicked her example to get the feel of it. She told him, "Don't worry about anything after the oil drains in. I'll take the tubes away and hand you a tissue. Just relax and breathe deeply twenty times, in through the nose and out the mouth. Then give a few quick breaths like this..." Again she demonstrated, showing how to do a sniffing breath, and again he mimicked her.

"Okay, let's do it. I'm ready," he said, showing little apprehension.

Indu gave him the tubes and he placed them in his nostrils. She brought her right hand to the back of his head for support as he laid down. To be leaning so near him, his head in her hand, it was almost more than she could bear to keep her feelings concealed.

Within seconds, the oil left the tubes. He had properly sealed the back of his throat. Taking the tubes away, she saw a few drops of oil gliding down his cheek. Instead of handing him the tissue, she took it herself and wiped them away. She did it automatically. But as she was tenderly wiping his cheek she became fearfully self-conscious. Had he noticed? She immediately began to speak to distract his attention from her gesture.

"Very good. Now just relax and breathe. Give the oil time to go as far into the sinuses as possible. You really did very well for the first time." She was pleased. He had done beautifully. He continued seriously performing the breathing. Indu sat quietly by his side, watching his chest move up and down, admiring the black curls of hair that peeked out at the top of his shirt and the prominence of his Adam's apple.

After taking several sniffing breaths, he sat up, looking flushed in the face. He gave a rosy smile, reaching for more tissue and said, "That's a very unusual feeling."

Indu replied, "Once you get used to it, it seems like nothing."

"It will take a few more times before I'm that used to it," he said, flashing a big grin back at her. "Are there any other instructions after this?"

Looking into his eyes, she could have drowned in their depths. She made herself turn her eyes away, using the pretense of collecting tissues and wiping up spilt oil. "Just take it easy for awhile," she said. Looking back up at his face, she added with strained seriousness, "Some oil may drain back down in the next hour or so. You might want to keep tissues with you."

"Nope, got a good handkerchief for that, right here," and he said, patting his side trouser pocket.

For a split second she thought she saw a flirtatious glint in his eyes, but decided it was just his joking nature and nothing to be taken personally. Inwardly, she had relished every moment with him. But outwardly, she turned and motioned for the next person to come up on the stage, silently indicating that she would say nothing more. She must have shown fifteen people oil *neti* that afternoon. She had gotten so involved in it that she hadn't stopped to look around until just toward the end of the session. She had then become aware that George was still in the barn. When she glanced his way, their eyes met and for seconds, they held each other's gaze. Then once again she looked away. It seemed funny to her. She had assumed that he had gone away. She wondered if he'd been there the entire time. It didn't matter anyway, she told herself. She proceeded to clean up the stage. Dinner would be ready soon.

EIGHT

~

It was Wednesday, August 22. Indu was downstairs having breakfast with Uma and Shakti. Both were in high spirits. The intensive was going well. The guests seemed to be enjoying Guruji's programs. As qualified therapists, Uma and Shakti had also become friendly with several of the therapists on staff. A registered nurse, Uma was trained in acupuncture and Shakti in Swedish massage. They'd had several involved sessions with the Ickwell staff, comparing notes and exchanging treatments. But that was not the only reason Uma wore such a big smile. This was the day that she would give her workshop on acu-yoga.

Acu-yoga was a combined discipline showing how certain hatha yoga postures were closely related to particular acupuncture meridians and points. Meridians referred to the energy pathways in the body and acupuncture points were located along these lines of energy. A needle inserted or pressure applied at a given point would either stimulate or depress the subtle energy flow along that pathway. Uma would demonstrate how the yoga postures could do the same thing, to help the energy move along the meridians. She had gotten much of her training from Guruji, who was a master acupuncturist. In the class, a general background of this ancient Chinese healing art would be given, describing the five elements—fire, earth, metal, water and wood—and how bodies differ depending on which element predominates. Pressure on specific points, either by hand or posture, would be shown as a method to alleviate specific discomforts and help re-establish balance in the flow of energy.

Shakti teasingly interrupted Uma's avid description of the class. "And what is the afternoon program?"

Not noticing the interruption, Uma continued with just as much enthusiasm. "As for the afternoon, we'll be showing videos on underwater birthing."

℘ * * * ℃

This was also Uma's specialty, Indu explained to me. As a nurse, Uma had been the midwife at many deliveries. Underwater births were deliveries in which the mother was resting in a tank of water. This method of birthing was pioneered by a researcher and swimming instructor in Moscow named Igor Tjarkovsky, who had used it as a birthing method for many years. He claimed that the shock of birth was much less if the infant was born directly into a tub of warm water, a familiar environment to the baby since it is surrounded by fluid for nine months in the womb. He had found that the water was soothing for the mother, too, and made labor less painful. Although many physicians practicing Western medicine were still skeptical about the procedure, it was gaining popularity, particularly with the pioneering efforts of the French physician Dr. Michel Odent. Uma had met with Dr. Odent and had already delivered four "water babies." One of the videos to be shown that afternoon had been filmed during her most recent water delivery. Indu then told me the funny turn their conversation took.

℘ * * * ℃

"Well, seeing as everything's been going so well, I do hate to bring up some disquieting news, particularly at the breakfast table," Shakti said, but the smile on her face eased any immediate anxiety.

"Pray tell us, what's happened?" Uma asked, remaining as blasé as she could.

"Our supply of dried cow dung is running extremely short." She gave a long pause while looking back and forth between the two. "We have enough for perhaps one more week of fire ceremonies. I doubt greatly that London has a large demand for this agricultural commodity, which means that once in the city, we may have trouble replenishing our supply." Shakti emphasized her last statement, making it clear there could be no postponement in the search for dung. The fact that several days were needed to dry the carefully-shaped patties meant that this was the day for a friendly stroll through a nearby cow pasture.

Indu didn't doubt whom they had in mind for this excursion. "I'm definitely getting the feeling I'm going to miss this morning's program," she said with quiet acquiescence. Turning to Uma she joked, "But please don't take it personally. I would certainly prefer your lecture to demonstrating my expertise at shaping flat, circular cow patties. However, I sense a higher duty calling." The fact was that she welcomed the chance to be separate from the group for a while, as it would keep her from having to see George for the morning.

"The only question is," she thought out loud, "where to find some cows?"

Uma suggested, "You might ask Gretchen. She seems to have answers for most questions." They couldn't keep from laughing. How do you ask a very straight-laced, English lady where to find dung? But Gretchen would be the first one Indu would ask.

By chance, while stacking her breakfast dishes in the racks, Gretchen walked by. "Gretchen," Indu called.

Gretchen stopped on hearing her name. "Yes," she said, waiting for further communication. She was without doubt not a Gemini. For her, the fewer the words the better.

Indu got straight to the point. "Is there a dairy farm nearby?"

"Do you want fresh milk?" she inquired, probably thinking the Foundation might be able to supply the need and save an unnecessary trip.

"No, it's not fresh milk that I want. It's a bit delicate to explain. But a dairy farm should have what I need." Indu tried to finesse the question.

"Oh, I can guess what you're wanting," Gretchen said, breaking into a big smile. "I've heard what it is you burn for the fire circles." She didn't appear taken aback by the topic. "The best person to help you is Kevin. He knows someone who owns a farm just down the road."

"Where can I find him?" Indu asked, relieved that without any sign of dismay Gretchen did have the answer.

"Well, he's probably back at the residents' quarters," she replied. "I'm going that direction. Why don't you come with me and we can see what he says?"

They walked together down the little hallway, past the laundry room, out the service entrance, and across the quadrangle. Indu was hoping she wouldn't run into George. Kevin was in the small residents' kitchen making tea. Indu recognized him. He was one who came regularly for the fire circles as well as to most of Guruji's programs. He was a burly fellow standing about five feet nine, with curly hair and good-natured eyes. He was happy to be of service.

"We can go anytime. Right now if you want." He stood solicitously, ready to move at her request.

"Well, actually, right now is a pretty good time." Indu couldn't believe how easily things were falling into place. "I just need to run and change clothes."

Seeing her white pants, he agreed, "Nope, I wouldn't go out in the pasture wearing those."

Indu was impressed by the alacrity with which he volunteered for the dung search. Talking to him in the car, however, she realized he had a genuine affection for Guruji and felt honored to do any small task for him. Indu was touched to hear him speak. Given his usually quiet demeanor, she would never have guessed how strongly he felt.

The farm was only a five minute drive away. He turned into the brown-graveled driveway of a small farmhouse. It looked cheery in the morning sun. Flower boxes filled with red and white petunias were at the windows. Blue periwinkle bordered the sidewalk along the front of the house. A barbed-wire fence separated the pasture from the yard and stretched from the roadside straight back alongside the driveway and out of sight. Watering troughs and a barn stood a distance from the house. Although there were no cows in sight, there was no getting around the smell in the air, indicating their proximity.

Kevin ran up to the side door. Indu saw a woman pass in front of the window and seconds later the door opened. Kevin was totally unabashed. "Morning, Marilyn. Do you mind if my friend and I visit your cows? We want to pick up some droppings for a study she's doing."

"My goodness, what a request. But certainly, you're welcome to go in the pasture. Right now the cows are on the other side of the barn. Just help yourself to whatever you need." No details were asked and none were given.

"That's grand of you, Marilyn. We won't be long." Kevin went quickly back to the car to get a box and shovel, which he had brought from the Foundation. Indu got a "thank you" in, too, before the woman disappeared back inside the house. There was something Indu liked about the direct manner of the British.

She and Kevin carefully opened and closed the long wooden gate to the pasture and headed around to the far side of the barn. The cows were there. Cow patties, old and new, were everywhere. Indu needed the freshest possible. Though timid at first due to the intrusion, the cows soon surrounded them and approached closely. They were large animals, standing as tall as Indu. She had a moment's hesitation when several grunts came and tails flicked nervously. She looked at her bovine friends. Their eyes were big and blinking, with moisture covering their flared nostrils and saliva drooling from their chins. She found her position pleasingly humorous.

Kevin also stood in the middle of the herd waiting for her to give instructions. Indu had just begun looking for the freshest pile when a splattering sound was heard. She turned to locate the cow. "That was very accommodating of you," she said to the cow as she approached it. The cow skittishly moved away. "I think this is the freshest one, Kevin." He laughed as he swung the shovel into it. It was a bountiful deposit. The box was soon full.

Looking down at the green mass, Indu said, "Now the fun part is about to begin, assuming we can get this back to the Foundation."

Kevin lifted it up in his arms, saying, "That we can do." They both headed back to the car. The dung had an earthy odor. The obtrusive smell from a bovine herd was not from fresh dung. In fact, cow dung had been reported to be "not a bad remedy" for burns.

By the time they arrive back at the Foundation, Indu still had an hour before lunch to hand-shape the dung into saucer-sized patties, half an inch thick. These she would lay out to dry. Kevin carried the box to a cement platform behind the barn.

"The one last thing I need are screens, or something like that, on which to dry the patties," Indu replied to Kevin's query of further aid. She did not want him to feel obliged to do any of the "creative" work. He disappeared to find some. She began scouring around in a small covered stall which opened to the back of the barn. Lying under sawdust on the floor she found two wide-mesh screens. Kevin soon returned carrying a metal grid which he had found in the garage.

"I didn't have much luck. Only this." He handed her the grid.

"That's okay. I found these wire screens in there," she said, pointing to the stall. "Now, you've done enough. I know you must have other work you need to do. I greatly thank you for your help." Looking brightly into his face, she pretended to shoo him away. She had enjoyed his company.

He gave a grin and said she should just call him whenever she needed anything. He really meant it, too. He disappeared again around the barn. From that time on, they had a warm friendship.

Indu finished the job shortly after lunch had started. She placed the screens in the sun and hoped no one would be too shocked if they walked back there. It did make a funny sight.

She went in through the service entrance door and washed her hands in a bathroom just across from the beverage room. Piling a plate full of food, she went outside through the beverage room door. Right away, she saw Kevin sitting on the grass by the flower garden and surprisingly Uma was sitting with him. One other lady, named Leslie, was there, too. Seeing Indu, Uma waved to her to come join them.

"Do you know Kevin?" Uma asked, attempting to make the introduction. When Indu and Kevin both laughed, Uma responded, "So it appears you two have already met."

Kevin spoke up, "Indu and I spent all morning together."

Leslie's eyebrows shot up. "What were you two up to?"

Indu quickly interrupted Kevin's first few words. "Kevin helped me with a little project this morning." She smiled at

Kevin and looked at Uma, "You know, the topic we were discussing at breakfast."

"Oh, did that already get taken care of?" she exclaimed.

"With Kevin's help, it did." Trying to change the subject, Indu introduced herself to Leslie, whom she had seen before but never spoken to. Indu pondered silently, "Here we are, people brought together by happenstance under an azure sky by a flower garden for lunch. There is again a quaintness about it. Why do I keep feeling as though memories from a distant time are being stirred up?" The whole scene reminded her of some painting by Monet, Manet, or Cassatt.

Then George came up with a plate of food and a smile for everyone. "Is there enough room for us out here?" he asked with a jocose wit. Alison followed not far behind.

Kevin gestured with grand formality, "By all means, pull up a seat."

Sitting in a semicircle, everyone talked at once. It was the first time Indu had seen George wearing a *kikoi*, an ankle-length cloth wrapped around the waist. A loose cotton shirt covered his chest. Although she had seen men in *lungis* before, which looked similar, they had usually been worn by East Indians. The *kikoi* appeared out of place in the English country setting, but she liked him in it. He looked masculine and at ease. While contemplating all this, she tried to keep up her conversation with Kevin. She did like him.

She and Uma finished at the same time and excused themselves from the group. Indu completely avoided George's eyes as she left. They went up to their room to rest before the afternoon program began. Shakti and Mangala were also there. It was pleasant in the room with the afternoon sun filtering in and a warm breeze passing between the two windows.

Out of the blue, Uma remarked, "You know, my heart could be melted by one of those jugglers."

Shakti questioned, "Which one?"

"The one named George. What eyes he has. He just sat across from me at lunch," she replied.

"I like the other one, Nhoj. Reminds me of someone I used to know," Shakti readily confided.

"Okay, how about you, Indu? Which one has taken your fancy? Or haven't you noticed either?" Uma asked.

Indu was not about to reveal the torment in her heart. "Oh, if I had to have a preference, I suppose it would be George, though Nhoj is sweet, too." She hoped the truth would become one of the best kept secrets of her life. If only the next five days would hurry and pass quickly. The others continued talking and she fell into a light sleep. She awoke to their movements as they prepared to depart for the program.

They went past Guruji's room. Since Uma could give the introduction to the videos, Mr. Goodall had arranged to visit privately with Guruji that afternoon. Videos in hand, the four ladies walked across the quadrangle to the barn. A television and video player had been rented by the Foundation for the occasion. It was set up in front of the stage. About half the usual group was already gathered. After saying a few words, Uma started the documentary on the work done by the Russian doctor on underwater birthing. Soon after it had started, George and Alison came in and sat down toward the front of the barn. Indu doubted they had even seen her standing against the wall directly across from the large barn doors.

It was hard for Indu to keep her eyes focused on the video. Without turning her head, she could see them peripherally. They were sitting next to each other and every now and then exchanged comments. It did seem to Indu that Alison was the one reaching out toward him. Who knows, though, she thought, maybe they think they will have children together one day.

The second birthing video, which had been made at the ashram, was intense to watch, waiting and waiting through the labor for the delivery to come. At some point, George and Alison changed positions and Indu couldn't see them without turning around and of course, she didn't want to be that obvious. After the videos were over, the barn quickly emptied except for George, Alison and Nhoj. About to leave herself, Indu did not want to appear to be obviously ignoring them and went up to say hello.

Nhoj asked, "So where were you in that video? We saw the other three ladies assisting at the birth, but not you?"

Indu explained, "I had to leave the ashram just two weeks before the baby was born. This was the first time I saw the video, too."

Alison was sitting cross-legged on a chair. "Frankly, I wouldn't want that many people around while I deliver. I mean, after all, the father and the doctor is enough. Forget any video camera."

"Well, it was done for educational purposes," Indu said somewhat defensively, "to help promote underwater birthing. But we're all like a family there."

Nhoj asked if the water really did help with the labor pains.

"I can't speak from experience, but many say that it does. Some women choose to go through the labor in the water and then deliver conventionally."

George then asked, "Do you have children?"

Indu looked at him and shook her head "no."

She immediately felt awkward. It might have been because George's eyes had caught hers. Was it her mistaken perception or was something being silently communicated? Then again, even Uma had said his eyes had a magnetic pull. She motioned to her stomach, saying she was hungry and left the barn. She did not see them later at dinner. Maybe they had all gone out together, she thought.

NINE

~

The barn appeared to be filled to capacity as Indu approached the white barn doors. She was a few minutes late to the morning program. When she saw the crystals laid out in front of Guruji, who was sitting on the stage, she soon understood why everyone was crowded toward the front. She was about to sit on the ground just inside the doorway when someone passed her a blanket. She knelt down on it and soon felt the morning sun warm on her back. There was a reassuring calmness—the smell of the barn, the crystals, Guruji, the sun. "How nice," she thought, "to enjoy living, to take nothing for granted. I wish I could always feel this way."

ℵ * * * ℶ

She paused for a moment in her story to tell me about Guruji's talk on resurrection. She read his words from her notebook. He had said, "The body is a moving grave burning with anxiety. But we are not the body. Resurrection means to come out of body identification while your body is living. To reach that state in meditation, it helps to remember we are not this food body, product of a seed and sperm from parents. We are not that. Silent mind will bring the secret of existence. Without knowing this secret, we will always feel that something is missing." It now made even more sense why Guruji had wanted to show the underwater birthing videos.

Indu had experienced that feeling of something missing when depressed. Was it that missing sensation which blinds one to the full enjoyment of life, creating instead anxiety and depression? Guruji had said that when one meditates and goes beyond thinking, then the unconscious mind can operate through the conscious mind. Otherwise, there can never be original thinking, only rumination. "When you meditate," he had said, "you will feel some force operating through you. You will feel it and you will have to express that feeling because you will be so deeply inspired."

℘ * * * ℂ

Indu felt inspired sitting that morning for meditation. At least for those moments she could feel her anxiety dropping and a deep gratitude taking its place, a gratitude that was amplified by the translucence of the crystals arrayed before her. Were they not beautiful creations of nature? Had they not taken millions of years to form? How could the mind not be transported by them? How could we not sense the energy emanating from their crystal depths? How could we not feel that same energy vibrating in ourselves? These questions arose from her heart. Were we not all one energy, one spirit? She felt herself being pulled deeper and deeper into meditation. The entire barn was quiet. Guruji had only instructed that everyone should sit and gaze steadily at the crystals. Indu opened her eyes and focused on one large crystal in the center of the display. She let its purity and beauty expand inside herself. At the end of the meditation, she felt a light sweat all over her face.

Looking to her right, she saw George sitting just behind her. He had also come in late. She nodded to him in such a way as to convey it had been a powerful meditation. Seeing that he was sitting on the ground, she inconspicuously unfolded her blanket. It seemed so automatic to do it. George readily accepted. Minutes later Uma came by handing out crystals. Giving Indu one, she handed the remaining two to George. Another brief meditation was to follow, this time squeezing the crystals tightly in the palms of the hands. Out of the corner of her eye, she saw George making fists around each crystal. She could not deny the happiness in her heart to have him so near.

Guruji began the guided meditation: "This is for *kuṇḍalinī* awakening and natural healing for psychosomatic manifestations. Close your eyes. Relax the body. Do you know that behind your physical and physiological body there is a body of electricity? Feel this current pulsating through the entire body. Relax deeper and deeper. Hold the crystal in your left hand and make fists with both hands. Feel a vibration and pulsation in your palms. Follow the flow of electricity from your heart to your palms and back to your heart. Feel it through the shoulders, upper arms, lower arms, palms and fingers and from them back to the heart.

"Back and forth, to and from the heart. Follow the flow of electricity from the heart to the neck, face, to the entire head, up to the brain and from them back to the heart. Feel the flow of electricity from the heart to the entire back, upper abdomen, lower abdomen, all abdominal organs, and from them back to the heart. Follow the flow of electricity from the heart to the upper legs, lower legs, feet and toes and from them back to the heart. Feel the flow of electricity from the heart to the skeleton, muscles, every joint of the body and from them back to the heart. Feel the flow of electricity to the entire surface of the skin and from the skin back to the heart, from the heart to your entire body and from your entire body to the heart, simultaneously. Feel the flow of electricity from your body to the atmosphere surrounding your body and from the atmosphere back to the body, back and forth. This electrical current is all-pervading, like radio waves. Your body is like the remote control. Feel the movement of electricity from your body to the sun, to the moon, to all planets, all stars and all galaxies, and from all of these back to your body of electricity. Feel the flow of radio waves and radar waves from your inner space to the outer space and back to your inner space.

"When you have awakening of *kuṇḍalinī*, it will be the sensation of a powerful flow of energy. You will have the following signs: a vibration all over the body, tingling, heat or chilling sensations, sensations of well-being, sensations of happiness and bliss. You may lose the sensation of body consciousness altogether. You may hear sound currents: a humming or buzzing sound in your head, the sounds of church bells, evening crickets, ocean waves, rainfall like Niagara Falls. You will experience inner light. You may have the sensations of flying and of various electrical jerks in the body. You will feel that you are the blue sky, pure awareness, pure consciousness. You will be beyond any identification with the physical body. When you regain body awareness, you will find the body is in a divine healing process. You will find happiness and bliss beyond human language. And then you will know your true form." [14]

After the meditation, no one wanted to move. The first thought that came to Indu's mind was that she would soon lose the nearness of George. She had intentionally tuned into his presence during the meditation, feeling the electricity moving from her heart to his and back. Would something in the purity of the crystals and the power of the meditation make it clearer what her connection was to him? But no sudden insights came. She only felt her heart overflowing with love for him. Maybe that was the answer, she told herself. Maybe she should not try to suppress the love she felt in her heart, not that she should exhibit any outward affection. Why not simply let the love shine through silently? Nature would respond if anything was meant to happen. In this, Indu believed. If it was meant to happen, then she would not need to do anything to manifest their meeting. She turned and looked at him. His eyes were still closed, his fists clenched around the crystals. His face had a peaceful expression. Simply let the love flow, she told herself as she watched him. When he finally opened his eyes, she turned her head away. She stood up to stretch. Others too were getting up, as did George. Indu turned toward him again, smiled and then leaned down to pick up the blanket.

"Thanks for that," he said.

Indu replied, "Someone loaned it to me. The least I could do is share it. In fact, I'm not sure who it belongs to. Let me see..." She looked about the barn trying to recognize the person who had handed it to her as George began mingling with the others. Deciding to leave it on the stage, she approached near where Guruji was seated. As she did, he motioned for her to come over.

He leaned toward her and spoke. "I need you to prepare something. Come and see me upstairs before lunch." Indu agreed that she would. She was happy to think that there was something more she could do to help him.

Everyone had been impressed by the crystal meditation. Many crowded around the crystal display, experimenting by holding different crystals in their hands.

"I've never felt anything like that," one elderly woman was saying. "You know, it felt like God was hugging me. I just kept wanting to hug him back."

When Indu turned back to the spot where she had left George, she saw Alison with her arms around his waist. But she felt no pang in her heart and no feeling of "loss." She trusted in Nature. She had to trust in it, for it was the only way she could tolerate the deep feeling he stirred in her. Guruji was just walking past. She fell in step alongside him, walking silently. Uma was not far behind. They went upstairs to Guruji's room. He sat down quickly in a corner chair. He had put out a lot of spiritual energy that morning. Through every crystal, he had also been vibrating. Of course, he would never say what exactly he had been doing. He was a mystical Guru. But clearly his physical body was ready for a rest.

Uma offered to get him food right away but he declined, saying he would take only something to drink and eat later. She went to prepare fresh juice.

Indu stood before him. He looked up at her and smiled. There was a long pause. Then he spoke: "What I would like is for you to find some colored paper: blue, red, green, orange and black. The colors, though, should be pure colors, not hues or shades or mixtures—pure and bright. Then, if you could cut large, round circles out and mount them on large sheets of white paper. The white paper I think we have. Shakti will know. She arranged those things. Do you think you can find this paper at the store?"

Indu had watched his face and his hands as he spoke. She never took for granted being in his presence and always tried to pay close attention. She assured him, "There must be some stationery or art store in town. I'll get a ride from somebody. When do you need them ready?"

"Not until Sunday. So you have a couple of days," he said.

When she asked if there was anything else she could do, he simply motioned that she should go eat lunch. As she pulled the door shut, she could see that his eyelids were already closed.

She went downstairs. Lunch was just being served. Already a line had formed before the buffet table. Indu took her place in the line and began filing down the length of the dining room, looking out the windows onto the garden. She had been so caught up in gazing outside that it wasn't until she was almost at the buffet that she saw George sitting in a chair up against the opposite wall. Alison was right next to him, leaning into his shoulder. She was talking and laughing. He was smiling and saying something, although he did not turn to look at Alison.

Still Indu had a strange peace in her heart. Let be what will be and that would be enough for her. She filled her plate and went into the sitting room next door, happy to find an old padded armchair vacant across from the fireplace. It was too damp to sit on the grass outside. A summer rain had drizzled down just thirty minutes earlier. Many people were milling around, moving in and out of the room carrying plates. After finishing, Indu sat wondering if maybe a nap wouldn't be nice before the afternoon program. But her eyes kept falling on a piano in the far corner of the room.

It had been awhile since she had played. She decided she could probably remember one ragtime tune which she'd memorized long ago during her more studious piano training. She had never memorized any classical music. She set her empty plate on the chair next to the piano and eased down onto the bench in front of the keys. It was slow coming back. But after missing several notes and starting over, she finally made it through a Scott Joplin rag. She knew a couple tunes from a Broadway show, so she began to make the same effort over them, with just about as much success. She'd never had any ambition to be a great pianist and had studied solely for her own amusement. She was soon ready for a nap. Depositing her plate in the dish rack in the kitchen, she went to her room.

That afternoon there was another rebirthing session. Again Indu laid down, this time up on the stage and off to the side. She wanted to get the feel of it, of lying in the barn and breathing the slow rhythmic breaths. But after only a couple of minutes, she heard Guruji call her name. She got up quickly. He signaled that she should begin the breathing instruction. She did it as he had shown her before, moving slowly from one person to the next. She saw where George was lying and chose to work on the other side of the barn. People were familiar and more relaxed with the process and consequently a greater number of emotional releases were experienced than before.

Well into the session, Indu came to Alison, who was lying with her eyes closed, observantly doing the breathing. Indu knelt down beside her. As she placed her hand over Alison's abdomen, she noticed that the belt around Alison's waist was too tight. She spoke softly to her. "I'm going to loosen your belt a little for you."

Alison nodded her chin without opening her eyes. After loosening it, Indu saw her take a long, deep inhalation. "Yes," Indu said, "that's much better." Loving George as she did, it saddened Indu to think that if George ever returned those feelings it would inevitably hurt Alison. Indu didn't want any hand in causing anyone suffering. All the more reason, she told herself, to leave everything in the hands of divine Nature.

Over an hour had past. Guruji turned on the music. Uma said, "Now let your bodies flow with the music. Stretch and move and begin to breathe naturally. Feel the breath flowing down your arms and into your legs. Feel the body's energy come alive with this breathing. Feel as though you are floating."

The barn became alive with dancing bodies. They had gotten the idea. Toward the end of the music session, Indu saw Alison and George side by side on their knees, Alison's arms hugging him in close. He was also hugging her. Indu watched without envy. It was a touching scene. Maybe something in the rebirthing had been released for both of them.

As she turned away, she felt a touch of regret that she might never be able to hug him that way. Alas, Nature was a strange teacher, she told herself. Still, she couldn't help but notice there was a reserve in the way George held Alison. Indu had not noticed him making any obvious amorous advances. Always it seemed the energy was flowing from Alison to him. Something in their relationship appeared strained, but Indu could not count on her perception being accurate. What was clear was how much Alison cared for him. Indu wondered if George felt smothered by all the attention.

Indu made a promise to herself. "I will not do the same. Unless it is equally returned, I shall not express my affection."

After dinner was over, she went out to check on the cow patties behind the barn. Several men on staff were carrying wood into the middle of the quadrangle. She remembered there was to be a campfire that night, a good old-fashioned night out under the stars with music and singing and a roaring fire. When she got back to her room, she asked the others if they were planning to go, but no one showed much interest. They all claimed to have personal things to do. Indu wasn't sure she felt like any jubilant camaraderie since she hadn't gotten very close to any of the visitors or staff, except maybe Kevin.

Nonetheless, after the evening fire circle, when the other ladies had gone back upstairs, Indu lingered in the quadrangle to see what was happening. Chairs had been set up and mats laid out. They were already kindling the fire. Soon the logs and twigs would be aflame. Near the fire pit was a reserve of wood which would easily last three or four hours. She laughed, thinking that it was, after all, just a different sort of fire circle from the one she had just attended. The vibration and intent were different, but the fire held her. The flames were already alive inside the wood pile, flying out between the logs. People were beginning to gather round, filling chairs, some with blankets, others with instruments. A table had been set up by the barn doors and ice cream was being served. "What fun," Indu thought as she went over to join the line.

Turning back toward the fire, she saw Alison, George and Nhoj standing together. She didn't think there was any harm in going to say hello. She walked up and greeted them, standing near Nhoj. Nhoj smiled and leaned toward her. "You know," he said, "there's some apricot brandy in one of the kitchen cupboards which really does taste delicious over this." He indicated his own.

"Is there really?" Indu smiled. "Which cupboard exactly?"

He broke into an even bigger smile and explained the location of the concealed bottle. Indu thanked him for the information and headed for the kitchen. She later found out that the three had been surprised at her eager acceptance of the idea, apparently thinking she was a strict purist. One thing was sure: none of them had a clear idea about any of the women serving Guruji, except that they were obviously devoted to this very intriguing man called a yogi.

Indu found the bottle in the cupboard just as Nhoj had described. The kitchen was deserted. Pouring a splash over her ice cream, she hurriedly put the bottle back not wanting anyone to notice she was helping herself, albeit at the invitation of one of the staff. She returned to the fire to find them still standing there.

"Did you get some?" Nhoj asked.

She affirmed that she had. He again broke into laughter.

She looked at him and said, "Well, it is good." She liked its warmth and the relaxed sensation it brought.

Just eight feet from where she stood, George and Alison sat down on one of the mats. No suggestion was made for her to join them. Nhoj, too, disappeared. Finding herself standing all alone, she turned around and saw Kevin sitting in a chair behind her. Seeing an empty chair next to him she sighed that maybe she wouldn't have to be alone after all.

He greeted her warmly as she walked up to him. "Is this seat taken?" she asked him.

"Not at all," he said, patting the chair. The dusk was rapidly giving way to night. The glow from the fire cast beautiful light and shadows on everyone's face. Indu spied Nhoj again on the other side of the circle. He was propped up on his elbow with his girlfriend at his head. Her name was Oola. Indu chatted with Kevin, looking now and then at George and Alison who were directly between her and the fire. The singing began with English tunes that everyone knew. Having gotten up to discard her plastic dish, Indu returned to find Kevin gone. She saw he had joined the musicians. George was also holding a drum between his knees trying to keep rhythm. Alison held finger cymbals.

Indu found herself alone once more. Still, she was amused by the whole scene. And with the position of her seat, she could gaze directly into the fire and see George's silhouette and no one could tell that she was watching him. She saw how often Alison kept putting her hand on George's leg or arm and observed that he did not extend the same gesture to her. There was definitely something strange about that relationship.

Indu enjoyed the music and sang along when she could, but she soon grew tired of listening to unfamiliar songs and of watching George and Alison side by side. Although it was only ten o'clock and the singing was in full swing, she picked up her meditation shawl and walked quietly across the quadrangle to the front doorway, assuming she'd gone unnoticed by anyone, but specifically George.

Her intention had been to go directly to the room but one book on the table in the hallway caught her eye. It was a large book on Mahatma Gandhi with pictures. She stood for awhile flipping through it and reading the captions. Getting interested in the story, she sat down in a chair by the small corner desk. There was good light to read by and through the window she could hear strains of music. But her mind was quickly absorbed in the life of Gandhi.

ℰ * * * ℭ

Indu told me that at his ashram in San Francisco, Guruji kept a large picture of Gandhi on one of the walls in the meditation room and often spoke of the noble ideals that Gandhi had held. This small man wearing a simple *dhoti* and round wire-framed eyeglasses had overpowered the entire British Empire with one mantra. It was famous all over India and no one can chant it now without thinking of Gandhi. Indu obligingly chanted it for me:

> *Raghu-pati rāghava rājā Rāma*
> *Patita pāvana Sītā Rāma*
> *Rāma, Rāma, Rāma, Rāma*
> *Sītā Rāma jaya Sītā Rāma*

According to Guruji, Gandhi's life was living proof of the power of mantra. Guruji described this mantra as a prayer to the Lord of Movement, our whole life being filled with movement—movement of the body, of the mind, of the senses, of our consciousness. *Raghu-pati rāghava rājā Rāma*: it is the Absolute Inner Being who is Master of all movement, pervading all motion. Wherever the mind goes, already consciousness is there. Therefore, Guruji would ask, who is king of the body? Not the senses, or mind, or ego. Eternal consciousness, *Rāma*, is the king. *Patita pāvana* asks, "When you are lost or fallen, who purifies you?" The answer is *Sītā Rāma*. It means Lord of Life, Lord of Supreme Nature.

Indu had heard Guruji tell the story of the time he'd met Gandhi. It was an unusual meeting and they exchanged no words. It had been in the early morning. Guruji's habit then was to jog before going to work at the hospital where he was a doctor. It was the day Gandhi was to give a speech in Bombay to commemorate a special occasion. Security was extremely tight around the pavilion where Gandhi was staying. At that afternoon's public speech, a crowd of over a million was expected. Guruji wanted to meet Gandhi but did not think it possible under the circumstances. Guruji and Gandhi had one common bond. Gandhi had at one time gone to see Guruji's Guru to ask for counsel on some matter. Indu knew of the bond that exists between those under the guidance of the same spiritual teacher. It's nothing that is spoken. It simply exists.

Taking his usual path that morning, Guruji had seen another man jogging toward him from the road to the right. It was at a corner where he usually turned left, which would have put him on the same path as the approaching man. As he looked again, he recognized Gandhi. Unsure what he should do, he hesitated at the intersection. As Gandhi passed, he waved his hand that Guruji should join him. For a stretch of several miles, they jogged silently side by side. They parted as Gandhi headed back toward the pavilion.

ℰ * * * ℭ

Totally absorbed in her reading, Indu was startled when someone came walking through the doorway. It was George.

"Hello," he said with his usual charm.

She had been reading for over an hour. She sat wrapped in her meditation shawl, the book in her lap. She still heard the music in the background and had been aware of it only subliminally.

She had been in another world, and felt a moment's hesitation being pulled so suddenly back to the present. Markedly subdued, she looked at George and responded, "Hi. Is it winding down out there?"

He had walked in and gone up to where the schedule was posted for the following day. As he looked over it intently, he replied, "It should be over by midnight. It's already getting pretty mellow. What have you been reading here?" he asked, trying to see the book.

Indu held it up to show the cover. "It's a lovely book on Mahatma Gandhi."

"Really. Mmmm. Well, I noticed when you left. I hope you weren't terribly bored." His eyes were beautiful, looking directly into hers.

Indu thought, "So he did notice." But to George she simply said, "No, I enjoyed it very much. I thought I was tired until I saw this book and I haven't been able to put it down. It's been nice listening to the music from in here."

"Yes, you do look quite peaceful. Well, I won't disturb you any longer. Do get some rest, though." He left again through the same door.

Indu stared down blankly at the page before her. She reflected on every word they had spoken. With George fresh in her mind again, she wondered if she could possibly get back into the history of Gandhi. She told herself, "I shouldn't let my mind be that possessed by this mysterious one." She perused the page and found her place. Soon again she was immersed. She sat for another hour and went upstairs only after finishing the book.

೧ * * * ೞ

Gandhi's story had been inspiring, she thoughtfully commented to me. "If we could all have such lofty aims and walk so reverently toward them, life would certainly be richer for it." This she remembered had been her thought at the time. To find anything in life whose pursuit brings fullness and meaning to existence was a real secret to happiness. We both agreed.

She knew that her spiritual quest was the one driving force in her life. But while in England, she could still feel a restlessness in her heart stemming from uncertainty about the future, which she prayed was under the control of divine planning.

She read to me something else that Guruji had said: "Be sure, without planning no one can live. But find out *who* is planning. Sometimes in your life, the time comes when nothing works. It is at that time that the real planner is working. Usually only in retrospect do we understand this." He gave several examples of how when something unexpected happened which unsettled our personal planning, our first reaction often tended to be a disgruntled one. He told the story of the man who fell and hit his head on a rock. His head was cut and he was in great discomfort until he looked at the rock and saw that it was made of gold. The cut on his head became a blessing. Indu had two more examples. There had been a more recent story in the news about a man who had forgotten his passport and was denied passage on an airplane. He was upset until he heard that the airplane had crashed shortly after takeoff. Then his misfortune became a gift. Also in the news was the story of an actress who had been nominated for an Academy Award. The report related how she might never have become an actress if she had not been thrown from a truck at the age of eighteen and been forced to spend several months in a hospital. It was during the hospital stay that she decided to become an actress. Previous to that, she had gone to Israel and was thinking of joining the Israeli Army. Only after the accident did she find the real direction for her life.

Guruji had said, "Sometimes the mind and senses are just like monkeys, putting us into extreme confusion so that we cannot make any decision. Then what should we do? Only by meeting with your inner Guru, your *Sadguru*, can you know. The more you meet with your *Sadguru* through meditation, the more you will realize he has a plan for you. And yet you always think you are planning."

Guruji's most beloved example of this was a story from his own life. He had been in Kashmir taking a few days of rest from his medical studies. In the meantime, his family had received an important letter regarding possible employment at a hospital. On the front it said, "Immediate Response Required," but they had no idea where he was or how to reach him. His father had gone to Guruji's Guru with the problem. The Guru told them that he hadn't been given any forwarding address either.

Back in Kashmir on that day, Guruji ran into an agent from Air India. The moment this man saw Guruji, he came up to him with a profusion of greeting that left Guruji extremely embarrassed because he did not recognize the man at all. The man graciously invited Guruji for breakfast and Guruji did not know how to refuse. The man even paid the bill. Guruji was in a quandary. Who was this man? It had become too late to ask. The man then pulled out a ticket which he happened to have in his pocket. "This is a special ticket," he said, "for flights running between Kashmir and Bombay. The ticket is good on all Air India flights for the next month and can be used without limitation, as many times as you wish. And the best part, the ticket is free." It was a special promotional deal advertising their new route between the two cities for the summer. There was only one catch: the ticket had to be activated that day to be valid for any time during the rest of the month. "By chance," the man asked Guruji, "would you like to go to Bombay today?" Since that was where his family and Guru were, Guruji decided to accept the ticket, wondering the entire time how strange it was that he did not even know who this man was. When he arrived at the airport in Bombay, he was shocked to see his family there to meet him. How was it possible, he asked them? He had not notified them. But his father told him of the Guru's advice to be at the airport to meet that particular flight.

Guruji had thought it had been his own decision to go back to Bombay. But he came to realize that some other force had decided ahead of the time. It was divine planning. Guruji explained, "When divine planning and your planning are the same, then you can never know whether it is your planning or divine's. It is only if your planning is opposed to divine planning that you will have difficulty. But then recognize that your difficulties compel you to see God. God has to work through you. He has no choice. It will be either knowingly or unknowingly; either you will know it or not. For devotees, they know. Just find out the uniqueness in you and you will see in what way God can work through you."

On that trip to England with Guruji, at that time in her life, that was all Indu wanted to know. What was her uniqueness? What was it she could do to serve a divine purpose? One man had won independence for an entire nation. She had heard these words from Guruji: "Meditate and you will feel some force operating through you. You will feel it and you will have to express it because you will be so deeply inspired." All she could do at that time was to meditate and see what inspiration came to her heart. That would be God's signal.

ℰ ✻ ✻ ✻ ℭ

It was quite late at night when she entered her room. A soft glowing light emanated from the top of the dresser. The others had left a candle burning to help her see her way.

TEN

~

It was Friday morning. There were only four days left of Guru-ji's program at Ickwell. Just after the morning program in the Yoga Hall, Guruji tapped Indu's arm and said, "She will help you find the colored paper," and pointed a finger at Alison, who was busily talking to others.

It was a puzzle that Indu mulled over. "How is she going to help me? She doesn't even have a car." Kevin was the one Indu had intended to ask for help. She and Alison had exchanged only a few words which had hardly put them on friendly terms. She walked out of the Hall passing Alison, wondering what was to come.

After Guruji retired to his room to rest before lunch, Indu decided to look for Kevin anyway. She went out the front door and headed toward the residents' quarters. She felt shy about walking in and calling for Kevin. She peered into the garage next door, above which was the main office. She hoped to find someone whom she could ask. But the garage was empty. Hearing footsteps coming from the residents' quarters, she hurried back out, thinking it might even be Kevin. Instead, she saw George and Alison. As she approached them, George gazed steadily at her. He asked, raising one eyebrow, "Did you finish your book last night?"

Alison's head turned first toward Indu, then to George. Indu thought to herself, "This woman can't be so naive as to not notice some attraction here. What to do?"

But to George she replied, "Well, as a matter of fact, I did finish it." She looked at Alison and said, "I made the mistake of picking up one of the books on the front table last night just before going upstairs and I couldn't stop reading. It was on Gandhi's life." Alison nodded but did not appear impressed.

Having seen her coming from the garage, George asked, "Were you looking for something in there?"

"Well, I was actually looking for somebody who could tell me where I might find Kevin," Indu replied without thinking it necessary to say more.

George arched his eyebrows and puckered his lips. "I can tell you," he said, "where he probably is, but that won't be of much help to you. You see, on Fridays he goes to visit relatives in Luton. Don't know when he'll be back. Should be tomorrow sometime."

Indu's ponderous expression must have made Alison curious. "What did you need?" she asked.

"It's something for Guruji," Indu started explaining. "I need to find some colored paper, but of specific colors. Guruji wants to teach another meditation technique called *trāṭakam*. It's when you look steadily at an external object, in this case colored circles. This helps build concentration. The next step then is to close your eyes and see the impression left in the mind's eye by that object." She wondered if Alison and George had any idea what she was talking about.

Alison remarked, "I've heard that certain colors of light can have different healing powers. Does gazing at the different colors have different effects on the body's energy, or something like that?"

Indu was surprised that Alison had this much understanding about the influence of colors on healing. Clearly she was more astute than Indu had given her credit for being. "I can't really say how the different colors affect the nervous system. But what does happen is that the afterimage of each color is its complement. So after gazing at a blue circle, upon closing the eyes one should see a reddish-pink disc in the mind's eye. Gazing at black will produce a white disc." Guruji had used colored circles at the ashram, so Indu had experienced the phenomenon many times. *Trāṭakam* with a candle flame was also popularly used but often beginners found it more difficult to recognize and maintain the afterimage. The image from colored paper was more conspicuous because of the sudden change in color after closing the eyes.

Alison seemed interested but said half apologetically, "Too bad. We're just going out, otherwise I'm sure George and I could have taken you into town. But we're not even going that direction."

George was more candid. "We're going to Cambridge. And it's true, we were just preparing to leave in a few minutes. Otherwise I would have been glad to take you to town. Alison has never been to Cambridge and I wanted to show her the university there."

"Oh sure, everyone knows about Cambridge University. I'd like to see it myself sometime." Indu said this as she was backing away, trying to show she didn't want to interfere with their planning. "But thanks for telling me where Kevin is. It saved me a long search." She meant this as a joke, but neither one was laughing. It crossed Indu's mind that perhaps American humor was different from British.

She had just turned her back when she heard George call out, "Hey, do you want to go with us?" Indu turned around and saw he was glancing at Alison, trying to get her to confirm the invitation. Alison remained silent, fidgeting for something in her tiny handbag. Seeing Indu's hesitation, he insisted more strongly, "Come on, you'll have fun. We'll probably be back before the afternoon program begins. Cambridge is only thirty minutes away. And who knows, maybe you can find your colored paper there. In fact, I know there's a Heffers there." He again turned to Alison, trying to convey that they could help her after all.

"What's 'Heffers'?" Indu asked. She was quickly thinking. The idea of going anywhere with George had enormous appeal but she would not have thought it proper to accept if it was just for pleasure. It would have been too obvious an intrusion. By the look on Alison's face, it was going to be an intrusion anyway, but at least with a purpose. Heffers, as it turned out, was a group of specialty shops for children's books, university books, stationery and artists' supplies. They were all located within the vicinity of the university.

"But I need to change clothes and tell someone I'll be gone." Still dressed in yoga clothes from the morning program, she did not feel properly attired to go out on the street.

Was there a tone of eagerness as George said "Go ahead—we'll wait for you," she wondered?

"Really? Well, that's wonderful. I'll be right back down." At least from George it did seem the invitation was sincere. Uma was in the room when she walked in, which was just what she had been hoping. While she changed clothes, Indu told her about the invitation to Cambridge and why she was going.

With a playful pout Uma said, "I'm jealous. I'd love to go see Cambridge again."

Sure that neither George nor Alison would mind if another person came along, Indu suggested, "Why don't you come, too? There's plenty of room in the car."

Uma shook her head, "No, I can't, but thanks. I've already scheduled an appointment for right after lunch. You go and have a good time. But I'm still jealous, and with George of all people." She rolled her eyes upward and swooned.

Indu played innocent. "Oh, come on. His girlfriend is going, too." She hoped her inner excitement wasn't obvious. She dashed out the door with a wave of her hand.

George and Alison were waiting in the quadrangle by a for-est-green car. It was an older model. Indu didn't recognize the make. "Is this one yours?" she asked and George proudly acknowledged that it was. "What model is it? I've never seen one quite like it."

"It's a 1957 Morris, in pretty good condition." At this comment Alison let out a laugh. "Well, there may be one or two things that need adjusting," he said.

Indu smiled at Alison and climbed into the back seat on the driver's side. George had reached in and literally lifted the whole seat up and forward to make room for her to pass through. She still wasn't used to the steering being on the opposite side to American cars. "To think," she mused to herself, "this car is as old as I am."

Indu would have been content just to sit in the back and watch the scenery for the entire drive. Except from the train and her walk with Uma, she hadn't seen much of the countryside. But George wasn't going to miss his chance to find out more about at least one of these rather unusual Americans. He had one question after another. So that he could hear her, she moved to the middle of the back seat. From that position, he could also see her through the rearview mirror. She, however, could see only his eyes, his beautiful dark brown eyes which were magnets to her own. They met time and time again in the mirror for what were much longer than glances. "How can he drive and take his eyes off the road so often?" she wondered.

Feeling she had talked enough about herself and also eager to find out more about him, she asked a few questions of her own. "So what will you do after the summer? Remain at Ickwell?"

He shook his head "no." "There's a juggling convention in Germany in September which I'll be going to and then after that I'll be heading to Greece." He sounded definite about his plans.

Alison spoke up. "We'll be in Frankfurt, isn't that right?" She was looking at George.

"Frankfurt it is," George confirmed.

Indu caught the word "we" and understood its implication. But she decided to ask anyway. "You'll be going to Germany, too?"

Still looking at George who was watching the road, Alison answered, "Oh, yes. I do a little juggling myself."

"And you'll also go on to Greece?" It was a question just short of prying, but it was one Indu felt she had to ask.

"Yes, that's right. Greece should be very nice this time of year, eh George?" Alison replied, tapping George's elbow. He glanced over at her and nodded. The subject suddenly changed to plans for the afternoon. Cambridge was just ahead.

"After we park the car, our first stop should be King's College. This part of the university was founded in 1441. There's a nice chapel there. Then we'll just cavort a bit. You know, we might even run into Nhoj." Looking again in the rearview mirror at Indu, he continued, "Nhoj came in earlier this morning with all this paraphernalia. Probably right now he's standing in Market Square trying to attract the lunch crowd with his flying fire balls. He likes playing with fire." He raised his eyebrows up and down like Groucho Marx, making Indu laugh. She saw that his eyes watched for her reaction in the mirror.

She responded, "Yes, Nhoj is quite impressive juggling fire."

Serious again, he remarked, "Nhoj has a fantastic one man show. He really has talent. It far surpasses mine, but then he taught me what I know in the first place." He seemed proud to claim Nhoj's friendship.

Touched by his modesty, Indu responded, "It takes a little talent to juggle two hundred miles."

"No," he denied, "that just took patience—and stamina, enormous stamina."

They had driven into Cambridge and were passing alongside a canal. Small gondola-like boats could be seen hugging a dock. George cocked his head in their direction. "That would be fun sometime, a little boat ride through Cambridge."

Alison almost purred, "It would be romantic."

From that, Indu surmised it wouldn't be something they'd do as a threesome. But she did have to agree, it would be romantic, especially with George.

George found a spot for the car near the college. "Let's take a little look-see round about and just before coming back to the car, we'll pick up your paper."

They were soon walking on the campus of Cambridge University. Although many of the buildings were surrounded by scaffolding, the grandeur of the site was not lost. The scaffolding was part of a major cleaning effort to remove decades of soot and corroding pollutants from the granite and sandstone. George showed Indu how badly eaten away the delicate carvings were around the portal of the chapel, a structure completed in 1536. In hopes of preventing further damage, the cleanup was being undertaken. The chapel, already cleaned, glowed in comparison to those buildings still streaked black from long exposure to elements unkindly laced with modern pollution.

Inside the chapel were signs that great expense had been taken to preserve the original structure: the uniquely designed fan-vaulted ceiling, the marble floor, the beautiful pipe organ, the high arched stained glass windows telling the story of the Old and New Testaments, a gift from King Henry VIII. It was a splendor to behold. Indu watched George and Alison walk down the center aisle. "I should give them time together," she reflected, suddenly feeling a little bit of a tag-along. She amused herself by reading a display in the center of the nave about the reconstruction effort being made. As she was about to walk to the other side of the display panel, she ran right into George. While she had been reading one side, he had been reading the other.

"I thought you were at that end," Indu said, lifting her thumb up over her shoulder toward the altar. "How did you get back down here?"

"An angel whisked me up and dropped me here," his witty tongue quipped.

She shook her head in playful exasperation. She liked his humor and its naturalness. However, the thought flashed through her mind, "Why did he part from Alison?"

When leaving the chapel, George exclaimed, "Look here! There's going to be a chamber choir concert tonight and on the weekend. I'd love to come back to hear it. Imagine the acoustics in this place." There was no pretentiousness in his manner. His desire was genuine.

Indu admiringly took note. "So, he likes classical music. Quite a nice thing for a fellow to enjoy." She wondered if he would make it back, perhaps with Alison, to hear it.

Just before leaving the campus, Indu asked if they would take her picture in front of the central green. Alison volunteered but snapped the picture while Indu was still smoothing her hair mussed by the wind. Indu knew the moment the shutter clicked that the picture would not be a good one. But it didn't matter enough to bother with another since she had limited film. They then headed toward Market Square.

Standing on the northeast corner of the Square, they looked for Nhoj but saw no signs of a gathering crowd. "He must be working another corner," George made the obvious guess.

As Indu's head turned, also trying to spy any signs of a street show, she heard the distinct sound of kissing lips. There was nothing subtle about it but Indu did not turn her head. It was supposed to be a sly kiss, she assumed, but it seemed more an intentional statement of the romantic involvement between Alison and George. "Was that meant as a message for me to keep my distance from George?" she suspected. She intended to do her best, particularly on that trip. But oddly, many times his eyes met hers while walking in and around the shops.

Reaching the corner of Petty Cury and Sidney Street, George pointed down the street saying, "I knew we'd see Nhoj." Nhoj was one block ahead walking toward them. His seagull cap was prodigiously set on his head. With a unicycle in one hand and a motley carpetbag in the other, he was a risible sight. They met on the opposite corner. Indu did not delay in pulling out her camera. Nhoj solemnly posed with George and Alison on either side of him, George with a mellifluous smile. Looking through the viewfinder, she could again feel George's eyes holding her own. Their inimitable power distracted her for several seconds from pressing the shutter button. No one seemed to notice.

Giving a sound slap on Nhoj's back, George said, "We were just at the Square looking for you."

"That's where I'm heading now. Why don't you come watch? You can stand in the crowd and make a big fuss. It will draw even more attention." Nhoj began to shake his head up and down, making the wings of the seagull flap.

George feigned innocence, "Would I do such a thing? Besides," he said, "we're on our way to Heffers Art Shop over on Kings Street. Indu needs to get colored paper, on orders from Guruji." He said this lifting one finger to the sky.

"So be it. So be it. Go ye merry way and be well, as I must go mine to regale the crowds and catch the shillings." Indu laughed. Could Shakespeare have said it better?

The art store was the perfect place. There was a wide selection of colored art board. The only question was in the selection of the most vibrant colors as specified by Guruji. Indu and Alison began holding each color up, laying the best on a work table and stepping back several feet. Peering through cupped hands braced against their cheeks to block out extraneous light and movement, they began to check the afterimages of each color.

"This is fantastic," Alison declared with closed eyes after staring several minutes at an orange board. "The afterimage is an amazing violet light. It's wonderful." Back and forth they compared their visions. Until then, Alison's demeanor had been stolid toward Indu. But any uneasiness between them melted for the time being. Indu was pleased to hear her impressions. Alison was adept at catching the afterimages quickly. George appeared bemused by the whole selection process, not attempting to give any opinion of his own unless asked, and even then his exuberance in preferring one color over another was only mildly expressed.

"You pick whichever you think is best," he said finally as he sidled up to another part of the store. The sudden congeniality between the two women must have been bewildering.

The colors were at last selected and the cardboard sheets rolled up and paid for. George glanced at his watch and suggested, "Shall we take a quick look at Nhoj's show before we head back to the Foundation?" He confessed to having professional curiosity as to what kind of crowd could be attracted at the Square. He had a street show of his own which he was thinking of performing, assuming the audience was large enough to make it profitable.

Nhoj was in the middle of his show and was just pulling on the protective mitts for the fire part when they walked up. Indu didn't know why, but she felt more anxious watching him this time with the fire than she had the Sunday before. "Isn't he being more daring?" she wondered as she watched him throwing the balls higher and higher and reaching out wider and wider to catch them. Suddenly catching two in one hand and the third in the other, he made a deep bow which sent the crowd into applause. Coins went flying into his upturned hat. His finale was a five-ball juggle while riding the unicycle.

Indu understood from George that Nhoj was a self-taught showman. "There has to be something floating loose in your blood to make you do that," he said, pointing to where Nhoj was happily accepting the coins of accolade from the people. "To really make it profitable, you have to be good."

Nhoj joined them minutes later. His face was bright red. "Fire get a bit close, ol' chum?" George bantered as he patted one of Nhoj's cheeks.

"Nonetheless," Nhoj retorted, "me pockets are heavy, whatever the travail." He was not to be outdone by George.

In earnest, George asked, "Is it pretty good?"

Nhoj nodded, "I've done three shows and made about twenty-three quid."

"Good God, that's marvelous. That's outrageous. And that's for only two hours of work, including transportation. You're not going to stop now, are you?"

"I think I've got one more show in me. That'll be enough. I'm not feeling that covetous today." He tossed a smile toward Indu.

An idea suddenly came to Alison: "You know, Indu, you might like to see a little more of Cambridge and ride back with Nhoj." She glanced over to Nhoj with a big smile.

"Oh sure, I'd be glad to give you a lift back. No problem," he answered unswervingly.

Although not unkindly spoken, Indu sensed an ulterior motive behind Alison's idea. Feeling caught in an awkward spot, Indu did not want to offend Nhoj by choosing not to stay with him or exasperate Alison by remaining in their company. So, she simply spoke honestly about her concern to get back as soon as possible in order not to miss too much of the afternoon program. It was a legitimate excuse that was amiably accepted by all. It was a relief to be back on the road to Ickwell.

The time passed quickly with George and Alison humorously telling stories of the jugglethon expedition, like the time it rained so hard George and Nhoj could barely see the balls in front of them and yet they'd kept juggling. Or the day, as Alison remembered, when George was so tired he'd dropped every other ball, which kept her running all day long. She nudged his shoulder, "Or were you doing that on purpose?"

He exaggerated a look of shock. "Are you kidding? That day nearly destroyed all my confidence as a juggler. And it certainly didn't help my self-esteem."

Just as they were nearing the Foundation, he pulled a small news clipping from the glove compartment. "Was thinking of sending this to my mom." He handed it to Indu.

Indu read it carefully. It warmly extolled the jugglethon fundraising effort. After finishing it, her eyes went back to the names in the first sentence. She read, "George Acroilus."

"Is 'Acroilus' your last name?" she asked, intrigued by its unusual sound.

"Yes. Rather a mouthful, isn't it? What's yours?" He again sought out her eyes in the mirror.

"It's Dolman. Not nearly as exciting," she said. "What nationality is your name?"

"It's Greek," he replied.

Indu handed back the article. "It's very nicely written. You should keep a copy for yourself."

"You think so? What... to show the grandkids that their eccentric old grandfather was an eccentric young man?" Smiling, he folded it up and returned it to the glove compartment.

It was two-thirty when they finally arrived back at the Foundation. A glance toward the barn showed that the afternoon program had already started. Lifting the colored paper out of the car, Indu said a warm thank you to both. It had been a successful trip.

"We were glad to have you along, truly," George said with equal graciousness. "But we never did stop for anything to eat. Aren't you hungry?"

"Maybe I am a little, now that you mention it," Indu replied, realizing she'd had nothing since breakfast.

"Well, I'm starved," Alison remarked with one hand on her stomach.

"Come on, then," George said, motioning toward the service entrance, "Let's go raid the pantry."

Hesitating a second, Indu said, "I'll meet you in a few minutes. First I need to run these things up to the room." She had the rolls of paper tucked under one arm.

"All right. We'll be sitting on the back patio," George replied as they parted company for the moment.

Putting the paper on her bed and freshening up, Indu was pleased with the jaunt to Cambridge, to have had a chance to really talk to George, to have laughed with him, to have looked so many times into his eyes. It had been a magical three hours. And Guruji had been right. Alison had been the one to help her select the colors. Staring down at the shadows on the carpet, she sat for a moment, a half-smile illuminating her face as she wondered at Guruji's incomprehensible wisdom. It had baffled her many times before. Pulling herself out of the reverie, she suddenly felt in a hurry to get to the program. She could wait until dinner to eat. She took the back stairs down to the kitchen area and walked through the beverage room. She wanted to let Alison and George know that she was going ahead. Peeking around the door, she saw them sitting on the white bench.

"I'm going to run to Guruji's program. It's not that long until dinner." She glanced down at her watch as she said this.

"It's just as well," she thought to herself, feeling she had interrupted a conversation they'd been having, "we've been a threesome long enough for today."

Leaning with his elbows on his knees, George looked up at her and said, "We'll be coming soon."

Nodding at him, she slipped back inside the house and quickly walked to the barn. Guruji was standing at the head of a massage table set up in front of the stage. A volunteer was lying with copper coils on his abdomen. Indu knew what was going on. This was Guruji's technique to graphically demonstrate the sensation of electromagnetism.

℘ * * * ℂ

If anyone had had trouble understanding what he had been describing during the meditations or had been unable to feel the pulsations and vibrations while holding the crystals, they could not miss it with this technique, she explained to me. Even if one had felt the pulsations during meditation, this technique confirmed that the pulsing sensations were from the electromagnetism of the body. After feeling it with the coils, one could not doubt that the body was an "electric dynamo" just as Guruji described.

By running a small electric current through the coils and holding magnets against them, pulsations would begin to vibrate through the palms and up the arms. Intently focusing on the magnetic pulsations, a deep relaxation would be induced. So powerful were the pulsations that many described a melting sensation, as though the body were disappearing into the electromagnetic waves. Others described a peaceful state or a feeling of lightness and inner calmness. Anyone who ever believed that meditation was merely self-hypnosis was the most surprised by this technique. Without repeating calming mental suggestions or following anyone else's guidance, it was possible to enter a truly altered state simply by feeling the current and watching it with unbroken concentration.

Again from her notebook, she read Guruji's explanation, "What is the difference between deep sleep, meditation and death? Death is permanent, but deep sleep and meditation are like temporary death. The difference is that in meditation, we are aware of our death, and that is what brings liberation. In deep sleep, unconsciously we enter the Absolute. But with meditation, we enter the Absolute with awareness. The body may be male or female, but the soul has no gender. In deep meditation, when attuned with that inner pulsation, gender also disappears.

"Our problem is not in the external world. Our problem is disconnection from the radio waves, from our higher self, which we can feel through the electromagnetic energy. When connected with that energy, any calamity can transform us into enlightenment. To live all the time in the mind is just another form of suicide. Earthly man is like a disconnected telephone. Who are we? Without getting out of the body, out of the senses, totally disidentifying with the body, we cannot know anything. Meditation is light. Without light we cannot see. Meditation on the electrical current and on the inner sound current, which is one in the same energy, we will feel we are the blue sky. We will feel a power like the ocean vibrating. We have many bodies: the body of food and matter, body of electricity and breathing, body of the mind, body of higher understanding, body of bliss. When the baby is in the womb, it does not breathe but there is electricity. When we die, we do not breathe but there is electricity. The last four bodies do not die. They are eternal."[15]

∮ * * * ∯

Shortly after Indu arrived at the barn, Guruji signaled for her to come and stand at one end of the table. He wanted her to cup the feet of each volunteer, showing her how to fold her hands around the outside of the feet. Shakti was standing at the other end with her hands bracing the head. Indu guessed that the touching hands helped reassure or "psychically ground" the person and thus allay inner anxiety and self-consciousness about the coils and the crowd of observing eyes.

When the first treatment was over and she was no longer needed to hold the feet, Indu turned to sit down and immediately saw George and Alison sitting just inside the barn doors. She herself sat several feet back from the table, and when Guruji encouraged all to come in closer, the reshuffling of seats brought George forward, putting him shoulder to shoulder with her. In fact, they were almost in the exact same place as they had been the day before. When the next volunteer was ready, Indu got up and again cupped the feet. It gave her a nice feeling, meditating on the pulsations occurring naturally in her own body and attuning inwardly to the person experiencing the coils. Guruji had everyone in the barn doing that very same thing, closing their eyes and attuning to that current within themselves. In this way, empathetically everyone was getting a treatment simultaneously.

When the fourth volunteer was lying on the table and weighted down by the coils, Guruji called George to come stand alongside. He gave George a magnet for each hand and had him hold them against the coils. The person lying down was also holding magnets in the same way. He then had Shakti put one hand on the person's head and one on George's. Just touching the coils with a magnet would send an electrical current through it, enough to run the rhythmic pulsations down the hands and arms. With his eyes closed, George nodded that he could feel the current up his arms. Before closing her own eyes, Indu looked across at Shakti. She wished for just that moment that she could have traded places, to have her own hand touching George's head.

When George sat down, Alison volunteered. Guruji had her lie down, directing Shakti to place the coils under Alison's shirt to touch the skin. As this was done, Indu became acutely aware that George was closely watching.

"How deep is his connection to her?" Indu wondered as she cupped Alison's feet. "How is it that I've ended up coming between these two? What is the *karma*?"

෴ * * * ෴

Karma was not an easy thing to understand, Indu commented to me, let alone explain to anyone else. It could be most simply equated to Newton's Law: "for every action, there is an equal and opposite reaction." Essentially, that was the Law of Karma: as we have done in the past, so we shall reap. For every one of our actions, we must expect a reaction, even though it may take several lifetimes to catch up with us. It will, nonetheless, definitely come. It was for the same reason that Jesus taught, "[…] whatsoever ye would that men should do to you, do ye even so to them: for this is the law […]."*

෴ * * * ෴

Indu knew there was something karmic in her connection to George, for upon merely seeing him without doing anything, a deep reaction had stirred in her heart. Sitting with her shoulder pressed against his, she was eager for the outcome to manifest. Would they remain just passing acquaintances in this lifetime or would there be more? Only three more days were left.

---

* Matt. 7:12 (AV).

ELEVEN

~

The next morning after Indu had eaten breakfast, something happened which made her even more convinced that there was a bond between her and George. She had gone back upstairs and was about to enter her room when she glanced out the arched window opposite the door and saw Alison and George walking across the quadrangle toward the kitchen service entrance. They were talking intently about something given the gesticulations George was making. Indu's eyes followed their movements. They stopped outside the service entrance to talk with a man named David who had just walked out. Her eyes were fixed on George, whose back was to her, although she caught his profile now and then. He stood with his feet solidly planted and his hands now in his pockets. It was like watching a silent movie, and Indu could not pull her eyes from the scene. Not aware of thinking anything, she gazed unwaveringly, focused solely on George. Then it happened. Just before passing David and following Alison through the doorway, he slowly turned around and looked in Indu's direction. She stepped back from the window, not wanting to be seen but still watching him steadily. She wondered what he was responding to by turning but his eyes only seemed to vaguely search the space before he turned back around and went inside.

Her eyes still riveted to the place where he had stood, she felt mesmerized. "Did he feel it?" she thought. Had he sensed something from the intensity of her gaze? Otherwise, why had he turned around? Had he actually felt her presence? These thoughts stayed with her through the morning.

She worked that morning in her room drawing and cutting out colored circles. She had brought a small plate from the kitchen to trace around. She found she could get five nine-inch circles from each cardboard sheet, as well as six small ones. Not wanting to waste any of the paper, she decided to make as many sets of circles as possible, if for no other reason than to give away to people who were interested in the technique. Without sharp scissors, the project turned out to be more time consuming than expected. By lunchtime, she was still not finished. She would simply have to work through the afternoon, but there was going to be a guest speaker, so she knew Guruji would not require her services. At noon, she unhooked the scissors from her sorely bent fingers and went downstairs to eat. She noticed how funny her balance was and that if she closed her eyes, afterimages of all shapes and sizes kept floating across the black inner space. She laughed to herself. What she had done was almost three hours of *trāṭakam,* first cutting out squares and then reshaping them into perfect circles. Her visual nervous circuitry had been put on overload. She felt intoxicated.

Just as she entered the dining hall, Alison and George came in behind her. "So where have you been hiding all morning?" he calculatedly asked her, his eyes narrowing with the inquisition.

"I did play hooky this morning," Indu admitted. "But for a good cause. I've been cutting out circles."

"Ah, the fruits of yesterday's labor," George retorted.

"The funny thing is, I'm dizzy from it," she said, explaining the sensation whenever she closed her eyes, to the amusement of both George and Alison.

But after getting a plate of food, she did not feel drawn to sit with them. Either from shyness or insecurity in her relationship with both, she chose instead to join Uma and Shakti at the spot where Guruji usually ate. She saw that Alison and George had gone to eat with Nhoj and several others from the staff who were sitting by the flower garden.

After dropping off her plate in the dish rack, Indu felt pulled to sit down again at the piano in the lounge. This time her memory was refreshed and her fingers moved easily over the keys. She played straight through five songs, ending with the Maple Leaf Rag. During that last song she became aware that George was sitting by himself in a chair at the other end of the room. She finished playing but sensed a surging heat of self-consciousness moving over her. "How long has he been sitting there listening?" she wondered. "It would be quite natural," she reasoned, "to stop and chat with him a bit before heading back upstairs, and a good opportunity given that Alison isn't present." But a sudden nervousness welled up inside of her.

As she walked toward him, he looked up at her with a welcoming smile and said, "Very nice."

As much as she wanted to, she could not bring herself to stop and talk, too afraid that the trepidation she was feeling would show. Instead, she returned the smile and replied, "It's fun." She paused not even a second before walking out of the room.

"Did he think it odd," she wondered again, "that I didn't stop?" Still, it had been another moment of strong eye contact.

"Can I possibly contain all these feelings and not let him know?" she asked some unknown presence as she went upstairs. In their few encounters, she had had no choice but to delicately conceal her longing to be with him. The circumstances had so far made it impossible to do otherwise.

At the top of the landing, she met two little girls of about ten, one of whom she knew was named Wendy, just like the cook. "Where are you going?" Wendy exclaimed upon seeing Indu, reaching for her hand.

"I'm going to my room," Indu calmly responded, taking the little girl's hand and giving it a teasing shake as she moved down the hallway.

"Can we come, too? Oh, please," Wendy pleaded.

"But I'm going to be working," Indu tried to explain. "Don't you two want to play outdoors?"

"We've already played outdoors. Can't we come watch you work? We won't bother you."

Hard-pressed to say no and imagining that they might be entertained by cutting out some colored circles of their own, she invited them to join her. As luck would have it, no one else was in the room who might have objected to the girls' jabber, for they did not stop talking for one second. But Indu found it an amusing diversion. They left for only a few minutes to run and find scissors once they saw what the project was. Indu even hoped that they might come back with something sharper than what she had been using. The ones they brought back, however, were not, although they willingly let her try each pair. Spreading everything out on the floor, Indu cut out small colored squares for them to play with. It warmed her heart to see them happy with scissors and paper. She remembered enjoying the same pastime, cutting out paper dolls as a young girl.

A light knock at the door had barely just caught her attention when she saw the door slowly open. To her surprise, George's head and shoulders peered around. There was a shyness in his manner as he looked at her, sitting on the floor in the middle of the room with the little girls on either side. His usual light air and quick tongue were replaced instead with a somber and serious tone. He looked steadily into her eyes, not venturing further into the room.

"I'm searching for Uma. Do you know where she is?" His eyes did not leave her face nor did hers leave his.

She answered, "I haven't seen her since lunch. She may be down in the clinic giving a treatment."

"I wouldn't want to bother her in that case." Still his eyes did not leave hers. Not the appearance of the room, nor the two little girls, nor the mess of colored paper all around seemed to interest him. He gave a brief explanation. "Nhoj and I are heading back into Cambridge today and when I spoke with her yesterday, she expressed a wish to go, too. So I came to make her the offer. I'm sorry I missed her. See you." He ducked out before Indu could make any pledge to bear the message to Uma.

The entire encounter could not have been more than a couple of minutes, but the intensity of it left Indu motionless for many seconds afterward. This time he was the one to shy away when the moment for a private exchange had presented itself. What had happened to his usual jovial nature? Why the lack of any other friendly comments? Had he really been in such a hurry? Had he perhaps felt the same sudden anxiety which she had felt just hours before in the lounge? Were strange feelings stirring in him also and were they perplexing his heart as much as they had been perplexing hers? These were questions for which she knew there might never be answers. For the time being, the only thing she could do was immerse herself in the girls' chatter and the project in front of her.

Still, it was hard to quench the spark of excitement in her heart which was further ignited by any thought of the event which would take place that evening in the barn. Scheduled to start at nine o'clock was another old-fashioned pastime, a barn dance. If he came at all, she knew Alison would be on his arm. But the thought of simply seeing him dance and possibly catching a dance herself passionately filled her heart with eager anticipation.

George was nowhere to be seen at dinner. It was therefore again a surprise to see him appear an hour later at the fire circle. This was perhaps his third time attending. He sat several feet away from Indu and very seriously concentrated on the meditation. The air was warm with a slight breeze. A soft citrine twilight engulfed the sky. The arrhythmic song of the crickets filled the shadows of the encroaching dusk. There was a stillness in the movement of the yellow flame, which glowed an incandescent blue at its center as it slowly began to die out. The smoke billowed illustriously skyward, tingeing the air with an evanescent redolence. While everyone sat silently before the slow prelusive march of night, Guruji's deep, rich voice rose with ineffable vibrancy. All joined together with him to repeat the prayer of peace for the planet.

Strains of music could be heard floating from the barn as the musicians began to warm up their instruments for the dance. George silently departed and Indu followed Guruji upstairs and then went to her room. From that distance, the sound was soft and gentle and enticing. But she saw that the other ladies were making no preparation for appearing anywhere outside that night.

She finally asked, "Isn't anyone planning to go to the barn dance?" She felt a little inhibited to be the only one making a fuss about getting dressed up for it.

"Don't think I'm feeling like a barn dance tonight," Shakti replied.

Mangala was also shaking her head, "Barn dance or ballroom dance, it doesn't matter. I don't go out much for those sorts of things."

Indu turned to Uma. "Aren't you just a little tempted, just a little curious to go down and see what's going on?" she asked, hoping she could wheedle Uma into it.

Her attempt did not totally fail. "Yes, yes. I'll probably come down after awhile to beguile a few minutes," Uma said. She clearly was not planning to move anywhere immediately.

They lacked, she knew, her strong motivation. She probably wouldn't have cared to go herself if it weren't for George. She was going solely on the hopes of seeing him. Undaunted by their disinterest, she pulled on blue jeans, an orange shirt and tied a scarf around her neck to give a country touch to her outfit. She dabbed on make-up, brushed her hair, slipped on her shoes and asked Uma for her opinion. "Do I look ready for a barn dance? Does this look all right?"

Shakti interrupted, "All right? You look darling. Everyone's going to wonder, 'What happened to that quiet young woman who always wears white?'" Everyone laughed. She thanked them for their approval and waved as she disappeared out the door.

She stopped at the arched window and looked across at the barn. It was lit up and full of people. The band was about to begin playing in earnest. She went downstairs and walked across the quadrangle. She stopped at the big white doors of the barn and peered in at the musicians. There were two fiddles, a harmonica, guitar and bass. The harmonica player stomped his foot three times and the music began. It was a polka. Indu didn't know the polka and she had a feeling she wasn't going to know many of the dances that night. She stood watching the couples. "If worst comes to worst," she consoled herself, "I'll just watch for thirty minutes and go back up to the room." She stepped back outside and walked down to the other end of the barn where the smaller door was. She went inside. Many others were crowded toward that end, watching and sipping wine.

"Where did you get that?" she asked the man next to her.

He pointed a finger. "Down at that table. There's plenty of it."

"It does look tempting. Think I'll try some." At the table she asked for a glass of red wine.

"That will be seventy-five pence, miss," the tall gentleman said.

"Oops," she gasped, "I didn't bring any change with me."

He handed the glass to her anyway, saying, "You can pay me later when you get change." He had a broad smile. Indu accepted it.

As she turned from the table, she saw George walk in with Alison. He was again wearing his olive green pants with a soft pink shirt opened at the collar. He looked handsome. They were standing against the back wall. She walked over. George looked surprised to see her. "Gracious, look at you. You're in jeans. I almost didn't recognize you."

"Come on. I don't always wear white. Only around Guruji."

"It's just a shock to see you in colors. But you look very nice." He seemed to want to apologize for his outspoken remarks.

Indu caught his eyes for a split second before she turned to greet Alison. She commented on how nice Alison looked, dressed in a wrap-around skirt and a loose blouse. George left the ladies while he went to get two glasses of wine. Alison wore an unusual beaded necklace, so Indu inquired about it. "Your necklace is striking. Is there a story behind it?"

"Not really," she replied, rolling the beads between her fingers. "This is just one that I made months ago. I do a lot of bead work and try to sell things at bazaars or fairs. It brings in a little income. You should come and see. I have beads all over George's room."

George returned with the wine. Alison asked him as she took her glass from his hand, "George, aren't there beads in your room?" She smiled coquettishly up at him.

George confirmed, "Good God, there are beads everywhere. I mean, it has gotten out of hand." He somewhat seriously reproached her.

Nudging his arm, she retorted, "Oh, George, it will only be for a few more days. After the Bank Holiday on Monday, I'll pick them all up." Alison turned to Indu. "Monday is a holiday all over England. There will be a small bazaar here at the Foundation and I'm going to have a booth to display my work. So right now I'm busy making as many pieces as possible."

To Indu, all this information simply conveyed that Alison was sharing a room with George, indicating that their relationship was serious enough. She tried to keep any feelings of disappointment from spoiling her happy mood. A voice began calling out the instructions for the next dance. No couples were required, just three large groups with equal numbers of men and women. Indu joined one group and George and Alison another. Step by step, instructions were given before the music began. It was fun trying to keep up with the instructor's calls during the dance, but toward the end, Indu's group was nothing but a mass of confusion. Indu doubled over in laughter as the song ended.

But she'd also made another discovery. She'd forgotten her belt and she knew her pants weren't going to stay up much longer unless she got one. She ducked out of the barn and walked quickly back to the room. They were surprised to see her return so early.

"I just came back for a belt," she explained, breathless and rushing.

"Is it any fun?" Uma cautiously asked.

"Fun? It's hysterical. You should have seen the dance we just did. A total disaster. It's definitely good for a few laughs." Her rosy cheeks and exuberance finally infected Uma with a desire to see for herself.

"If you can give me a couple of minutes, I'll walk back down with you," she said as she got up from the bed where she'd been reading.

Together they walked across the courtyard, which was ringing with the sound of music, shuffling feet, laughter and the booming voice of the instructor trying to prevent total chaos on the dance floor.

They passed George, Alison and Kevin standing outside the back barn door and gave them friendly nods as they went by. Indu had remembered to bring money with her so she went up and bought herself another glass of wine and one for Uma, and also offered to pay for her earlier one. The man seemed impressed that she'd remembered. "No," he said, "that one was on the house."

Uma was already engaged in a conversation with a pleasant looking gentleman. Indu slipped the glass into her hand and stepped back out to say hello to Kevin and of course see George. The three of them were still standing near the door. "We were just commenting on how you and your mother have a lot of mannerisms in common," Kevin told her as she walked up.

"My mother?" Indu questioned. "You mean Uma? She's not my mother, at least not biologically speaking, anyway. But she and I are very close. Probably mother and daughter from a past incarnation, who knows."

"Well, it's true," George agreed. "You two do a lot of things alike. For instance, see how she's holding her glass of wine right now." They all looked through the door where Uma could clearly be seen holding her glass in her right hand, her left arm folded across her chest. "You see," George said vehemently, "you were standing just like that a second ago. I was watching." Indu had to laugh at the similarity herself, and at the fact that George should have noticed.

They all went in to join the next dance, which was just about to start. This time they were in the same group. Indu was pleased. "Now, I'll really get a chance to see him dance. He does seem to be having a good time." No partners were needed for this dance either. Having equal numbers of men and women, each man would end up dancing with every woman by the time the dance was over. Indu watched as the dance progressed and her turn to dance with George approached. They wouldn't really dance, but simply swing arm in arm in circles a couple of times.

He looked at her just as they were about to meet in the center. They skipped toward each other and linked elbows for the twirl. She felt the pull of his body against hers and the pressure of his arm on hers. Within ten seconds they were both back in their respective lines at opposite ends, clapping and smiling and watching the next couple swing. Outwardly, she appeared gaily caught up in the spirit of the dance but inwardly she was pensively thinking, "Let me just make it through these next two days." She tried not to look at him for the rest of the dance, and shortly afterward he left with Alison.

She sat along the wall watching Uma gliding through a waltz with the same gentleman to whom she'd been talking earlier. More and more people were gradually leaving, with several mingling outside the barn. Seeing that Uma had been asked for one more dance, Indu got up and, lingering only a few minutes by the large white doors, she slowly headed back across the quadrangle.

TWELVE

~

The Yoga Hall was filled for the Sunday morning meditation with Guruji. A chair was at the front of the room on a small platform. Guruji had asked Indu to prop the white sheet with the black circle against the back of the chair. This would be the first color for the *trāṭakam* meditation.

Uma stood before the group to give a brief explanation. "*Trāṭakam* means concentration with open eyes." She spoke slowly and smoothly in a gentle voice. "It is a powerful technique which will help you in stilling the restless mind. You need to sit comfortably and in a position so that you can see the colored circles without obstruction. During this meditation, try to gaze at the color without blinking. After several minutes, close your eyes and focus inwardly on the point between the eyebrows.

"Now I'm sure you've all had the experience of gazing at Christmas tree lights and then closing your eyes afterward and seeing little starry lights in front of you. Or you may have been mesmerized by the flame of a candle and then found that when you closed your eyes you could see an image of light in your mind's eye. You didn't know that you were naturally practicing *trāṭakam*, did you?" There was a wave of head shakes and smiles throughout the room.

Uma went on. "When you close your eyes after *trāṭakam* on the circle," she motioned to the black circle behind her, "try to hold onto the inner image, which you'll see as though it's in the middle of your forehead. Hold it for as long as possible. Then let your eyes rest. We'll change the circles five times, using five different colors. What you'll notice is that the image after each color is different. At the end of the session, I'll ask what different inner colors everyone saw. Just remember to gaze steadily without blinking. It's important, however, not to gaze so long that you tire the eyes. If you begin to feel eyestrain, then stop the practice of *trāṭakam*, close the eyes and completely relax the eye muscles. Before we start a new color, we'll have everyone rub their hands together like this." She demonstrated a rapid rubbing motion of her two palms. "You should rub until you feel some heat. Then cup your hands over the eyes and let that heat penetrate back behind the eye to the optic nerve. Now, I don't want to say too much more. You can only know the real benefit of this technique by practicing it. But some of you may wonder where to look on the circle. I would suggest that you try two different places, looking directly in the center or just along the periphery. In either case, you may notice an aura-like effect. This means that you may see a complementary colored shadow illuminating the border of the circle itself. This complementary color should be the same color that you'll see in your mind's eye. Are there any questions?"

She looked around the room. One hand went up. She nodded in that direction. "Should we keep our glasses on or off?"

"I should have said something about this. It is best to practice all *trāṭakam* with eye correction off. For that reason it might be a good idea to shift all near-sighted people to the front of the room. So please, do change your seat so that you can comfortably remove your glasses." Uma waited while a few people moved forward. Seeing that there were no other questions, Guruji gave three resonating *OMs*. And the meditation began.

After the black circle, Indu put up the red one, then the orange one, followed by the green and ending with the blue. There were many "ahs" as the afterimages of each color were seen. Everyone was excited at the end to describe their inner visions. Indu went up to Alison after the program and thanked her again for helping select the colors. She then told her that she had made a set of circles for her. Alison seemed truly pleased to hear it.

At lunchtime, Indu carried her plate outside to the patio, which she found almost deserted. Although George and Alison and others were eating off to the side by the garden, Indu decided she would perch on the small ledge of the retaining wall and eat alone. Shortly after, however, Uma came out and sat down on the wrought-iron chair directly across from her. Without turning around to look, Indu was aware of George's voice rising and falling in conversation behind her. He brushed past her left shoulder as he carried his dishes inside but said nothing, as though he hadn't even seen her. The others dispersed a few minutes later and even Uma excused herself. Left alone, Indu felt in no hurry to leave her perch on the wall. She was thinking. She would simply have to resign herself to sublimating the feelings she had for George. She was mulling this over when out of the blue George reappeared with an orange in hand.

Their eyes met as he came toward her, and before Indu could say a word, he seated himself on the ledge as well. There were a few moments of silence as he began to peel his orange.

"So, did you enjoy the dance last night?" he asked in such a casual manner that one would have thought it just coincidental that he should be sitting next to her.

"Very much so," Indu replied. "It was my first barn dance."

"Really? Surely they have barn dances in the States, don't they? I mean, there's so much farm land there. I would have thought it an American tradition," he responded, seeming to want to hear more about where she was from.

"Well, it may have been at one time, but it's since been replaced by baseball and football," she joked. "There's dancing, of course, but not so much in barns. You know, the barn here really is a unique one." She meant it tongue-in-cheek, but he again didn't catch her humor.

"So what do you do for fun?" he asked, glancing at her. Their eyes met for a second before Indu looked away.

She chuckled, "What do *I* do? I travel with my Guru to England."

"Oh, you know what I mean. Besides this part of your life, what else do you do?" He was intent on getting an answer.

"When I'm not with Guruji, I work at a university as a research assistant," Indu began. "And when I'm not working and want same entertainment, then I go see a movie or I go dancing."

"You dance very well. I watched you last night," he said. She thought she saw a twinkle in his eye.

"What? Last night? I clapped my hands more than I moved my feet," she replied, trying to make light of his comment but happily taken aback that he had been watching.

"Well, you did that very well, too," he responded, tossing an orange slice into his mouth.

"Okay, so tell me what you do when you're not juggling or traveling off to Greece?" Indu returned the question.

"Me? I'm... I'm in between jobs right now. Just before coming here I was working in Scotland at a small hotel. It was more for experience than for pay. I have a degree in hotel administration and catering."

"That sounds like a good profession," Indu nodded with approval.

"Well, it's a good vocation for now. Actually, I'm pretty good with the catering end of it. If you ask for a bourguignon or bouillabaisse, you will get bourguignon or bouillabaisse, or something close to it." They both laughed. He continued, "But then Nhoj sent word about this jugglethon idea and I have to admit I was feeling a little restless up there. So to the Foundation I came."

Indu asked, "You've known Nhoj a long time, haven't you?"

"Let's see. It must be at least five years. We met in a park in London. I was just passing through and I saw this guy tossing five balls in the air in a wide circle. Quite a few people were watching him so I stopped and watched, too, and was amazed to see what he could do. Afterward, being the congenial fellow that I am," he looked affably askance at Indu, who sat smiling and nodding, "I went up to him and introduced myself by asking, 'How long does it take to learn to do that?' He started teaching me right then and there. That's what impressed me about Nhoj. He's so giving. He wasn't standing there showing off. He was there to share with people something he truly loved. For that alone, I admired him."

"Will he be going to the juggling convention in Germany, too?"

"Yes, we'll drive down separately but leave here at the same time." Indu finished the last bite of food on her plate and George consumed the last succulent slice of orange. Indu wondered if that would be the end of their talk.

But George turned to her with a serious inquisitiveness in his eyes. "So what do you know about opening the third eye?"

"Oh, I'm hardly the one to ask. I don't know that much about the higher knowledge. And whatever I do faintly grasp, I can't put well into words."

"Well, I don't know what it was, but after this morning's program with the colored circles, I've had the strangest feeling in my head." His hand went up to the back of his head and neck and then moved to his forehead.

"Is it something painful or like a pressure?"

"No, it's not painful. Feels more like a weight, a heavy fullness."

"All I know is that it's a powerful meditation technique. It hits the entire nervous system and no doubt the *kuṇḍalinī*, too. Have you heard about *kuṇḍalinī*?" she asked. He nodded that he had. "Well, when that spiritual energy starts moving, it can produce any number of manifestations. When some of that energy hits the brain, I can only imagine that the third eye is thrown open. Of course, nothing physically changes, but wherever intuition comes from, wherever the inner light comes from which can be seen with closed eyes, wherever the quantum leap in logic comes from, that's where the third eye is. It allows us to see beyond the five senses."

In all earnestness, he asked, "So what are we supposed to do when we feel something like this?"

"I've heard Guruji say that if any physical sensation is painful or uncomfortable, we should first seek medical advice. But if everything is physically fine, then have no anxiety and just keep meditating. It's really a good sign to have something like that happen. But if it gives you a lot of trouble, some massage can help."

"It's kind of a mysterious thing, this *kuṇḍalinī*," George said. He looked down at his hands, stretching his fingers out with only the fingertips touching.

Indu thought to herself, "There are a lot of mysteries, my love, a lot of mysteries."

To him she softly said, "Many things are hard to understand."

"Yes, many things are." He seemed to reemerge from some distant place. "Have you heard anything about 'ley lines'?"

"'Ley lines'? No, what are they?" She looked for a moment into his eyes. The inner self-consciousness and shyness she'd had the day before were gone. She felt comfortable talking to him now, wondering what he would say next, wondering what she would say next.

"Leys are geographical alignments thought to have been deliberately structured by prehistoric surveyors." His voice was subdued as though he was speaking venerably of something. Right away Indu sensed that another mystery was unfolding. She sat perfectly still and listened to the rest of his description. "The leys are really invisible lines that connect a series of sacred sites. Many believe that along the leys powerful energies are moving and that prehistoric man had been aware of these energies and marked high energy spots by erecting stones and constructing stone circles. The leys can range from two to twenty-two miles in length and there's a very unusual correlation of paranormal sightings along them, like UFOs and ghosts. Oddly, too, a lot of the great cathedrals were built on the leys, like St. Paul's in London, also St. Martin-in-the-Fields and Canterbury Cathedral as well as Salisbury Cathedral. In fact, Salisbury Cathedral is on the same ley as Stonehenge."

Indu was fascinated. "So our prehistoric ancestors weren't so naive after all." She slightly quivered with a wave of horripilation as she said this.

"Have you seen any of the prehistoric sites here in England yet?" he asked.

"No. I've only been in England ten days and it's all been spent here. I do hope that I can, though, before leaving."

"Well, there's one standing stone not far from here. You can get to it by cutting through the rose garden and going over the iron gate."

Indu knew exactly the direction. So he too had jumped that iron gate and gone exploring. She laughed, thinking, "Had some energy pulled me that way?"

"I'd love to see it sometime," she said.

"I can show you anytime, whenever you're free," he offered.

There was a moment's silence between them. Realizing that she had lost track of time, she glanced at her watch. Time had almost stood still in her inner world but the outer clocks had not stopped and there were only a few minutes before the afternoon program was to begin.

"My goodness, how did it get so late?" she exclaimed. "I must dash to get ready. It's almost time for program."

"Is it that late?" He too was surprised. "What is it this afternoon?"

"By popular demand, another rebirthing session. Guruji only planned to do two but so many requests were made, he changed his planning."

"They are pretty intense. I've had some interesting experiences during the last two," he said.

As she stood up with her plate, she looked into his eyes. Why were they so familiar? "Will you come for this last session?" she asked.

"Yes, I'll be there. He's a very unusual man, your teacher."

"He is," Indu agreed, gazing over his head at the flower garden, smiling unconsciously. She looked back at his face. His eyes were on her.

"I hope we can talk again," he said.

"I hope so, too."

Again there were seconds of silence as their eyes held each other. He continued sitting on the retaining wall. "So, I'll see you in a bit then for a little breathing practice." He began the slow deep breathing with his eyes crossed. She loved his comical nature but she was glad to have seen his more serious side. As much as she wanted to remain near him, she felt the intense pull of her duty. Guruji would want her present at the afternoon's rebirthing. She hurried to get to the barn on time.

The third session was again powerful. Everyone seemed to be feeling the surge of energy. It was as if with every intake of breath, they were soaking in this energy and with every exhalation they were experiencing a greater and greater release. Just at the peak of the session, when hearts were wide open, the walls of the barn began to vibrate as a low-flying jet soared over the barn. It had never happened before and it was surprising that it flew so close. Then another went by and again the barn shook with the low, droning rumble of the engines. Indu could feel the sound penetrate right through her. She stood motionless. Within seconds a third roaring vibration filled the barn. Then silence, a silence so profound that no one moved or even wanted to breathe. Guruji stood, eyes closed, meditating.

The silence sank deep. Then suddenly it was broken by Guruji's voice, which with just two words sent a virtual shock wave through the barn, bringing everyone back to life with fresh tears and emotion. All he said was, *"Harih OM."* Because of the way it sounded, he had often jested that it was Sanskrit for "Hurry home"—hurry home to your real nature, your real self, your real home. But nobody needed to be told its meaning. Guruji had spoken in a language that no one knew but everyone understood. That was the magic of stillness, of true silence. An understanding beyond words can come through. The tears turned into laughter and relief and everyone began hugging the person nearest to them. It came as an automatic response after feeling such an outpouring of emotion.

Indu hugged an older woman near her named Hazel, who was on staff at the Foundation. She was a gentle and quiet woman wearing powdered blush and coral lipstick. Indu had said only a handful of words to her during the entire week, but there was no hesitation in their embrace, cheek to cheek. She looked up at Indu with eyes twinkling with tears. "I just feel so happy. A heaviness is gone that I didn't even know I was carrying." She sighed deeply with her hand over her heart and closed her eyes. Indu looked over at Guruji who was walking toward them to turn on the music. As he passed, Indu's eyes caught George's and they exchanged almost imperceptible smiles. During the music he stood gently swaying to the rhythm with closed eyes and Indu let her body move as it pleased, stretching in all directions with graceful movements.

Afterward, Guruji disappeared quickly back up to his room. Indu followed soon behind him along with the other three women. The courtyard became alive as people slowly dispersed.

ᖇ * * * ᘓ

How Guruji worked his magic during the rebirthing sessions, Indu couldn't say. She emphasized that Guruji rarely spoke about what he was doing. Instead, he said that personal experience alone was the best teacher, that no words would be more powerful than one's own inner realization. My conversation with Indu was about just this, the wonder of the spiritual path. Without embarking on such a journey, rarely do we permit real silence into our lives; rarely do we move beyond language. The Master's challenge was to entice us to listen deeply, to feel the pulsation of energy, to move into the dimensionless form of being, and to recognize the amazing realm beyond the boundary of the mind.

ᖇ * * * ᘓ

The next time Indu saw George was that evening back in the barn. Rows of chairs had been set up facing the stage for a concert by a group named Kaj Bid. Their music was made from the most unusual collection of instruments that Indu had ever seen on one stage. They had a double bass and xylophone set up in back. Up front they played different pitched penny whistles and strangely shaped ocarinas while the leader of the group sat in a chair cranking a hurdy-gurdy. Their music was exquisite. It was lightly ethereal and teasingly playful. It was impossible not to smile while listening. Guruji sat in a front-row seat and seemed to thoroughly enjoy it. Indu sat on the ground in front of him, leaning against the cool stone of the barn wall.

Intermission came. She looked over at the second row on the other side and saw George sitting alone. Alison had been beside him earlier. "Do I dare?" she thought to herself. Before she had much time to deliberate, she felt a force moving through her. It stood her up and walked her past Guruji toward the second row. "Do I know what I'm doing?" The question needed no answer, for George was looking directly at her.

With a slight surprise in his voice, he said, "Hello again." He had been left the only one sitting in the row. It seemed all the others had stepped outside. Why had he stayed, sitting alone like that? Something in their talk that afternoon had broken any protective shield which might have given her the will power to stay leaning against the barn wall. Sitting alone, he was like a magnet to her heart. Could a similar force have pulled him out to sit on the retaining wall this afternoon? Why was there this attraction, beyond any conscious incentive? "Would you like to sit down?" She barely caught his words, feeling in a trance-like state.

"Is it free?" she redundantly asked. Obviously, no one was sitting there.

"Looks pretty free to me, except for the ghost. 'Go on, shoo, shoo,'" he waved his hand over the chair. "Now it's quite available."

"What I meant is," Indu tried to explain as she sat down, "will someone return for this seat?" Of course, she was thinking of Alison but George didn't seem concerned.

"Do you like the music?" he asked.

"It's very different from anything I've heard, but yes, I do like it. I think Guruji is enjoying it, too. It looks like he's going to stay through the intermission."

"This music is what I think you could call eclectic folk. But they're a fairly popular group. They played at last year's Yoga Festival and were so well received that Mr. Goodall invited them back."

Indu suddenly saw that Mangala was standing right in front of them. She held out a glass of wine to Indu. Quite puzzled, Indu accepted it. "What's this for?" she asked with a furrowed brow.

"I just wanted to do something to return the favor you did for me after dinner. When this man came in," she pointed to a wheel barrel that had been brought in filled with ice and wine bottles, "I thought you might like a glass. I hope you want it." She stood with folded hands and a hesitant expression.

Indu reassured her. "You silly. You didn't need to treat me. But since it's here," she looked up at Mangala with wide eyes and a smile, "I certainly will enjoy it." Mangala returned the smile, obviously pleased, and walked away.

"You must have done her quite a favor," George quizzically commented, looking at the full glass of red wine in her hand.

"It was nothing. I simply gave her a foot massage up in the room. She didn't ask me to. I just wanted to. She really didn't need to do this, though," she said.

"She must have just wanted to." He smiled.

Before she'd taken one sip, Alison returned. Indu felt a moment's awkwardness but Alison quickly sat down in the row of chairs in front of them, turning to catch George's attention as she pushed her chair back to be closer to him. Indu had hoped that Alison wouldn't come back. "I should have known better," she thought sheepishly.

To Alison, she said, "Someone just delivered this glass of wine, would you like a sip?"

"No thanks," was Alison's response, spoken as indifferently as possible, although not in an unfriendly way.

Looking at George, she made the same offer, "Would you like some?"

"You go ahead," he spoke reservedly. Was it because Alison was there?

Indu took a sip. The warmth of it felt wonderful.

Turning toward George, she again asked, "Are you sure?" She lifted the glass to him.

He accepted it this time without hesitation, took a long sip and handed the glass back to her. Alison, sitting facing the stage, missed the exchange. The musicians were back and within seconds the barn was filled again with music. Indu put her lips to the rim of the glass where his lips had touched. Without saying a word, she passed the glass back to him. When he took it, his fingers touched hers gently. She diverted her eyes toward the stage. They had only passed a glass but her heart knew that there had been more.

As he passed it back to her, he leaned toward her. Still without looking in his direction, she cocked her head to hear what he would whisper. "What does 'Guruji' mean?"

As she whispered back she had to press against his shoulder so he could hear, "*Guru* means 'remover of darkness' or in other words, a spiritual teacher. The *jī* is added for respect. It can be a suffix for any name. So you could be 'George-*jī*.'"

He pulled back a little and before her eyes could evade his, they met, parted by a hand's breadth. It was no fleeting glance. Indu had to turn her head for fear of revealing too much of what was in her heart. She took another sip of wine and then was intrigued to see Nhoj standing in front of the audience, on the floor just to the left of center stage. From a bag he materialized three softball-sized bright silver balls. A gentle flowing sound with steady rhythm welled forth from the stage and Nhoj began to juggle, the balls rising and peaking over an invisible bar in exact rhythm to the music. The barn was dark, but the light from the stage reflected off the balls, making them glow. Indu watched the silver globes, entranced.

"How amazingly beautiful," was all she could think. Nhoj kept the balls in motion, as steady as a metronome. It must have been ten minutes before he finally missed. His concentration had been phenomenal. An energy had been established between him and the balls and the audience. When the ball fell, a spell was broken. Even though the music continued playing, the audience applauded as he took his seat. The musicians, smiling joyfully, soon brought the song to an exuberant end.

Indu again handed the wine glass to George who accepted it, again touching her fingers with his as he took it. There was not much left. He took a short sip and gestured to give the glass back, but she waved her hand refusing, offering him the last swallow. They had passed the glass three times. There seemed something sacred in the number.

Throughout the last half of the program, Alison had remained tolerantly with her back toward George, watching the stage and Nhoj. Indu hoped the significance of what had passed between herself and George had gone unnoticed. It was the furthest desire from Indu's heart to cause any jealousy or disturbance. But some force of nature seemed to be operating powerfully. Before the music ended, Guruji stood up and unobtrusively walked to the back of the barn, followed by the three other ladies. He had not even looked in Indu's direction, but she felt it was her place to be with him. She could not simply ignore the passing of the Guru.

She whispered softly in the direction of both Alison and George, "See you," and exited with the others. The music magically filled the quadrangle and grew faint only after they entered the house.

As the others went on upstairs, something on the book table caught Indu's eye again. It was a book on yoga for the handicapped written by Mr. Goodall. She had been perusing it for several minutes when she heard George's voice by the door. He was talking to two elderly ladies. He had stepped in just far enough to see Indu, who was still looking at the book, although having a hard time concentrating. Indu turned toward the stairs as the ladies walked away. With one hand on the banister, she faced George. If there was such a thing as a "poignant pause," then she knew this was one of them. The pause seemed momentarily endless, as his eyes watched hers and her eyes watched his. Then a smile broke across his face and he said, "Well, goodnight."

Indu replied the same and turned and walked up the stairs. Why had he stood just inside the door anyway, she wondered? Maybe he had only escorted the ladies gallantly across the quadrangle to the house. For a split second she had thought they might resume their talk of the afternoon under the cloak of the night sky. But neither had made any indication of remembering that they had agreed to talk again. She laughed at herself. "Why do humans hesitate to say what is in their hearts?" She knew she was guilty of it many times over and there was nothing she could do about it. "The timing has to be correct," was all she could intuit from her heart's shyness to reveal its love. "Yes, timing is important," she mentally agreed with her heart.

But sitting on her bed with so many thoughts, she was much too restless to sleep. "Maybe hot chocolate would help," she thought. All was quiet downstairs except for a couple of people in the kitchen whom Indu only heard but did not see. She mixed the instant cocoa powder with hot water in the beverage room and went out the kitchen service entrance. The music had ended and the barn was dark. Only a few people were still around. She sat down on top of the ledge by the door and looked out over the quadrangle. Her thoughts were on George. One week ago, they had met. And now she would be leaving the day after next.

Where was he now, at that moment? Could he feel that she was thinking of him? Could he know that she was there, watching for him? It was true. As each person approached, she peered through the darkness to see if it was him. "No again... No again."

"How can I be so silly as to imagine he will come because I'm sitting here thinking of him?" But she could not remove the image of his face from her mind. Sipping from her cup, she saw a figure walking along the side of the Yoga Hall. Even though she knew it to be highly unlikely, nonetheless she felt a moment's expectation as she watched the figure approach. Then she froze. He was again wearing a *kikoi* with a blue and white pullover sweater. It was George. She followed his every step as he got nearer and nearer, feeling inside herself a slow beating pulse running from her chest to her head. Their eyes met through the darkness and smiles crept across their faces.

"What are you doing sitting out here?" he asked, stopping a few feet in front of her. "I thought you'd gone off to sleep."

"I decided I wanted a cup of cocoa so I came back down." He stretched his neck to peer down her cup, which was now half empty. "So how about you, are you just out for a stroll or are you up to something?" she asked.

"I'm absolutely up to something," he said. "A whole group of us are chatting over in the residents' cottage. But, quite honestly, I got a little bored and restless. So I decided, why not trot off for ten cups of tea for everybody."

Indu couldn't help but laugh at his expedition. "Ten cups of tea! Don't they have a kitchen over there?" She remembered seeing one when looking for Kevin.

"Well, it's true, there is one. But I also felt like a walk. And I like challenges. 'Can I carry ten cups without spilling a drop?'" He rubbed his hands together anticipating his clever skill at doing it. Indu guessed he must have learned the trick in his catering experience.

He went inside but Indu didn't follow, surprising even herself.

Something held her glued to the spot. He had come. She had been thinking of him and he had come. Even he did not know why he had come, that she had been calling and calling. Had his psyche somehow registered it as a restless feeling? Could it be possible? She wondered.

Her cup was empty. She went in knowing she'd find him in the beverage room. He had a tray with ten cups in front of him and had just finished pouring the water over the tea bags.

"Tea for ten," she said, announcing her presence. "That sounds like a Broadway tune."

"'Broadway', that's in New York, isn't it?" He was adding honey and milk to each cup.

"Mmmm. Have you ever been to the States?" It was something she had wanted to ask earlier.

"No. No, I haven't. Never felt any strong urge to go for some reason. But I'll probably get there some day. Where in the States are you from originally?"

"I was born in Oklahoma. Do you know where that is?"

"It's in the middle somewhere, isn't it?"

"Somewhere around there," she mocked teasingly. His eyes twinkled when he looked up at her.

"Boy, does he look dashing," she thought, watching him lift the tray onto the palm of his right hand. She stepped back to let him pass. He stopped before heading down the hallway to the kitchen service entrance. He turned and looked at her again.

She was leaning against the doorjamb to the beverage room, wearing a white cotton skirt and a white Indian-woven cotton shirt. Her eyes were green-blue, her hair light brown with natural streaks of blond. Her cheekbones only hinted that her grandfather was one-quarter American Indian. Her skin was a light golden brown. Was she as much an enigma to him as he was to her? For just a second, she thought she saw a perplexity shadow his eyes.

"Well," he said, "nighty night." And he disappeared down the hall to the door.

She repeated it in her head, "Nighty night." It had been a long time since someone had said it to her, since her childhood. Hearing it from his lips brought back the same warm, secure feeling as it had when she was a child.

THIRTEEN

~

It was the last day of their stay at the Foundation. It was Monday, August 27, the Summer Bank Holiday in England. Guruji's program had ended the day before with the final rebirthing session. This day, there would be a special noon meal and then a small festival/bazaar held outside on the open lawn. Everyone who had come with a tent had been asked to dismantle it by eleven o'clock that morning to make way for the individual booths that would be set up. Guruji's group would also put up a table displaying his Sanskrit chanting cassette tapes, pamphlets and books, as well as incense and incense holders which someone had donated. The day had been designated as the "Garden of Music Day." Several musical groups had been invited to play during the afternoon and of course George and Nhoj had been asked to give one last juggling show.

After eating breakfast, Indu went back up to the room for an hour to start packing for their departure the next day. At ten o'clock, she decided she should make an offer of assistance to the staff to help prepare for the afternoon festivities. Upon leaving the room, she ran into Hazel, who was standing by their door looking out the arched window.

Indu greeted her: "Good morning."

Hazel didn't respond immediately but turned slowly toward Indu. "I just don't understand it," she said. She looked back out the window, raising her hand to cover first one eye, and then the other.

Indu was concerned by her solemnity. "Is something the matter, Hazel? Do you have a problem with your eyes?"

"I just don't know how to explain it. I haven't been able to see well in years. Even with my glasses, everything has still been fuzzy. But it's gone." She was looking out toward the barn. "Without my glasses, I can see each brick over there. For so many years I've had difficulty with my eyes. And now, since that last rebirthing session yesterday, something has happened." She turned again toward Indu, raising her hand to her own throat. "All I can remember is that something happened here," she said, rubbing her neck. "I heard a popping sound in my throat. I lay very still because I didn't know what it was. And then afterward, my eyes began to change. I thought I was imagining things, but this morning I can see. It's a miracle. That's all, dear. It's a miracle. And I just don't understand it."

Indu was at a total loss for words. Healings like this were known to happen spontaneously around real Masters but she didn't want to say this. It seemed inappropriate to make any statement regarding the mystical powers of her Guru. She stood next to Hazel looking out toward the barn. "It's God's grace," she said to the sweet gray-haired woman. "It's very hard to understand God's gifts." Hazel took hold of her hand and squeezed it. Indu gently squeezed back. No other words were needed. She stood for a moment in silence with Hazel and then started to excuse herself.

Suddenly coming out of her daze, Hazel responded, "Yes, yes, yes. Lots of work to do today. We should have lots of people coming. Still much to do before the afternoon. My, yes." She patted Indu's arm and walked down the hall. Indu turned to go the other direction, down the main front staircase.

Venturing out into the quadrangle, she wondered where she could be of most use. She went over to the barn. A couple of men were inside doing electrical wiring. Already chairs and mats had been moved out.

"Anything I can help with?" she asked quietly.

"No, dear. We've got it all under control here," one of the gentlemen replied.

Heading back outside, she saw Kevin carrying some heavy equipment. She waved her arm to catch his attention. "Hi, Kevin. What have you got there?"

"It's going to be a ride for the children once we get it set up. It will be like riding an electric buggy. See, these are the tracks." He patted the metal railings he had balanced on his shoulder. "Could you step back a minute? Don't want to catch your toes." She quickly complied, watching him hoist them down in front of the barn.

Once relieved of his burden, he looked up at her, smiling. "So what are you up to?"

"Well, that's what I wanted to ask you. How can I be of some help around here?" She felt sure he'd have some idea.

He thought for a moment and replied, "I'm hard put to say. Picking up garbage you see on the grounds might be the most helpful thing, if you feel up to it."

She thanked him for his suggestion. Looking around the quadrangle, she did notice one glass bottle and a few paper scraps but otherwise it was fairly well picked up. She went in the house to deposit them in a waste bin. It dawned on her that maybe extra hands could be used in the kitchen making lunch. She went through the dining room, past the beverage room, through a small kitchen annex where the pantry was, and pushed gently on the swinging door that went into the kitchen.

Quite surprised, she saw George sitting on a stool at a table in the center of the kitchen cutting vegetables. She had totally forgotten that he had mentioned the day before about preparing the lunch that day. "How could I have forgotten?" she thought. He turned and saw her standing with the door braced against her shoulder.

"Do you need any help in here?" She put the question directly without giving any greeting or making reference to the night before.

He shook his head. "No. Don't think so. Everything's pretty much taken care of here." Indu glanced around. Already there were three ladies helping.

"Okay. Just thought I'd check," she said, affably smiling and quickly retreating from the doorway.

"Does he think I intentionally came in to see what he was do-ing?" she wondered. "Truly, I had no idea he'd be there. Some-thing just pulled me to the kitchen. Oh, well," she sighed, amused at her own inner defenses. Feeling fatigued from her search for work or possibly from her anticipation of their de-parture the next morning, she went back up to the room for a nap.

At one o'clock, she awoke, startled to see the time. She had slept through lunch. But it didn't matter because for the last three days, her appetite had been continually dwindling. On that day, it was virtually gone. She went downstairs, think-ing she should at least help in setting up the table for Guruji's things. She met Shakti out on the lawn.

"Where do you think is the best spot, Indu?" Bare tables were lined up along all three sides of the stone wall. "My choice," she continued, "would have been that spot," and she pointed to the first table on their left, just at the head of the gravel walk by the second-story arch. Alison had already picked that table. Indu had seen her there just seconds earlier.

"Well, how about the first table down by the iron gate?" It looked like a pleasant enough spot to Indu, being at the end of the gravel path.

"We'll probably have to settle for it now. It just seems so far back. Guruji's things should be prominently displayed. He's been their guest of honor after all. They should have allocated the best spot to him." Clearly, Shakti was miffed.

"They probably wanted to leave it up to us. We should have been down here sooner." It wasn't much consolation at that point.

"Okay. Let's take that one." She agreed with Indu's selection. "Can you round up a sheet or decorative cover for the table and I'll collect the box of things to be put out." It sounded like a fair division of labor to Indu. She went back into the house and upstairs to the linen closet. Fortunately, one of the housemaids was there.

"Could you help me?" Indu asked politely.

"Yes, dearie. What do you need?"

"Would there be a cloth somewhere that I could use to cover one of the tables outside?"

"Well, I don't know. Let me see here." The housemaid glanced in the linen cupboard in front of her. "Let's look down here." Indu followed her down the hall to another closet. The maid pulled a large white sheet from it. "Would this do for you?" She held it out.

Indu accepted it distractedly because her eye was on a light orange plastic drape lying on the third shelf of the closet.

"How about this orange plastic?" She put her finger on it. "Could we use this to help protect the sheet from any stains?"

"Oh, why not. That's a good idea." She presented both to Indu. "You can just return them to the laundry room downstairs when you're done, sweetie."

"I certainly will," Indu reassured her. She hadn't really wanted the orange plastic out of concern for the sheet. She thought it would add a nice touch of color to the table and be more exciting than just the plain white. As she walked out of the house, she saw someone eating a bowl of gooey granola. It was the dessert from the lunch. She still wasn't hungry, but it did look good.

She secured the cloth and plastic to the table with tacks generously provided by a man at the next table. From a distance the white and orange colors looked nice. Since Shakti had not yet returned, Indu decided to go back to the dining hall for a bowl of the granola dessert. As she walked across the lawn toward the back patio, she saw George standing by Alison's table helping arrange the jewelry. After getting her bowl, she went outside and sat at the far end of the retaining wall where she could look out over all the activities on the green and where she could see George. The band, standing on the patio in front of the French doors, was warming up and adjusting speakers for the best acoustics, about ready to start playing. There was a festive feeling in the air. Indu sat eating slowly, feeling totally out of synch with the high energy vibrating from everybody.

What was she feeling? She wasn't sure. It wasn't melancholy. But she did feel withdrawn. At one point, as she was watching George, he stopped and looked in her direction. For a moment, they looked at each other across the lawn. She could feel his gaze was as intent as her own. Or was it? The distance was too great to see the expression on his face. He then turned back to his task. Kevin came by and sat for a while next to her. As she talked to him, she was aware that it would probably be the last time that they would have to visit.

"Would you mind if I wrote to you now and then?" he asked with a shy smile. "You see, I'll be returning to Australia in a few more weeks. Sometimes I get to feeling out of touch there and it helps to keep in contact with friends."

"Kevin, I'd love to hear from you. Here, let me give you my address. Do you have a paper and pen?"

"Well, as a matter of fact, I have my address book right here." He pulled from his pocket a small green book.

She wrote down her address in the States and told him, "You'll definitely hear from me, too. You've been a real friend, always right there whenever I needed help. I'll never forget that."

"No, no, it was nothing. Really, I enjoyed it. I mean, I know I'm shy and awkward at times but you accepted me plain and simple. Well, I liked that." He was speaking with a humbleness that moved her heart.

"You know what my feeling is?" Indu asked him.

"No, what?"

"If more people were like you, we'd have a happier world. Truly, I mean it." She turned and gave him a hug and a tiny kiss on the cheek.

He was sweetly embarrassed and stood up immediately saying, "Gracious, I never heard such flattery. Don't believe a word of it either." But his grinning face showed he was pleased by her words.

"Well, I best get back to my work. This shindig is going to start soon." He strolled off across the patio toward the quadrangle.

It was two o'clock. Indu saw Shakti and Mangala out at the table. It was a beautiful sky-blue afternoon. Most of the booths had been attractively decorated. Indu was amazed at the transformation brought by the morning's work. Where twenty tents had once stood were now at least twenty booths, equally as colorful. And people were everywhere, coming and going with last minute details. Yet the light, airy music of the band brought a calmness to all the bustle. Amid the commotion, order was being made. Indu knew she should be helping at the table. Slowly getting up, she moved as though in slow motion toward the far corner, carrying her bowl with her. She would return it to the kitchen when she dropped the table coverings in the laundry room. She casually glanced around but did not see George. "It doesn't really matter now," she thought.

Shakti and Mangala had done a good job. The table was nicely arranged with flowers and incense burning, and they were pinning a Sanskrit poster showing the *Gāyatrī* Mantra to the front of the drape. The *Gāyatrī* Mantra was a well-known mantra which, simply translated, meant: "Oh Lord, please let me see Your Shining Light so it can guide my way." Indu knew that the "Shining Light" was ever-present. It was only up to each person to see it and follow it. She began to inwardly repeat the mantra. No matter what personal heartbreak she might have, her only goal in life was to do just that, to see the Light and follow it. But how easily it could be obscured by personal desires and ambitions. She knew the ego had to be dead to the world before the world of light and love could be experienced. After several minutes of repeating it, she actually did feel heartened, and she was determined to enjoy the afternoon.

Shortly after the official start of the festivities, Indu again saw George. He was walking slowly down the line from booth to booth. She tried not to pay much heed as he approached their table.

"So what have you ladies got here?" he said with a cocked smile and squinting eyes, as a rogue of Dickens might have peered over something he was about to snatch. He certainly did look the role, for he'd already changed into his tattered juggling clothes, the blue beret tilted on his head. Indu let Shakti do the talking, although she couldn't keep from watching every bit of the transaction. He had already acquired several of the cassette tapes, so he purchased a box of incense and one of Guruji's small booklets.

"Much obliged to you ladies, truly much obliged," he said, and he slipped back into his vagabond character, tucking the things under his arm and moving stealthily to the next table. Indu had to laugh at his antics. She could only console her heart that it was a love affair, a romance, never meant to come to pass. "One cannot argue with the hand destiny plays," she murmured to herself. She would be glad, though, when they were gone the next day and it was all behind her.

The juggling act was soon to begin and it was something Indu wanted to see. One thing that had seemed odd to her, though, was the cringe or grimace George had made when Shakti had mentioned it to him. It was as if he wasn't looking forward to performing; or was it just overriding modesty? Nonetheless, while watching the show, Indu thought she did detect a certain stiltedness in his motions. "It can't be from self-consciousness. He's done this too many times. It surely couldn't be because I'm watching. No, how silly of me to even think so. Some days are simply better than others." As she carried on this inner dialogue, she began to move slowly toward Alison's table. She felt it would be a kind gesture to buy some small token from her.

She put on a big smile as she approached the table. "Looks like George and Nhoj are at it again."

"Yes. I think they really love the attention. I'll probably always remain a closet juggler, but George has been saying I should start doing some performances, maybe even joining their act sometime."

Had she wanted to intentionally emphasize her position in George's life? Was Alison his partner-to-be? "Maybe she is," Indu thought. It was a battering to her heart to think so.

Seeing a pretty copper, brass and silver bracelet, Indu asked the price.

"It's four pounds."

It seemed reasonable, so she bought it and sincere thanks were exchanged on both sides. The juggling show had ended by that time. Indu had begun to walk slowly back toward the table when her eyes fell on a yellow T-shirt displayed behind one table. It showed two hands juggling three balls and said "Jug-glethon" in big black letters. It had to be one of the promotion-al shirts for the fundraising. On the back it gave a little map of the coast of the English Channel, showing Plymouth and Bournemouth. The caption read: "Juggling 200 Miles for the Disabled."

"Do you have one in medium?" Indu asked.

"The only ones we have left are in that basket." The lady point-ed to a basket near Indu's feet. Folded neatly in a plastic bag, Indu found a medium size. The price was three pounds.

It would be a nice memento but she wondered if the memory would be more painful than enjoyable. Regardless, it would be a memory of him to go along with her few pictures, so she decided to buy it.

Sitting down at the table to help sell the books and tapes, she saw George from a distance back at Alison's booth. As people came and went, the afternoon passed quickly. Many who came by had attended the ten-day intensive and were eager to share their experiences. They all marveled at how much Guruji had taught and how much there was to learn.

"It will keep this lifetime busy, anyway," Indu said, agreeing with them.

Then at five-thirty, as though a magic bell had rung, the ten-day retreat officially came to an end. Already many of the families and couples had come by to say goodbye and gone on their way. The crowd had been slowly thinning for the past hour and the time had finally come to dismantle the booths. Surprisingly, Nhoj walked up to offer a helping hand. Indu thought it exceptionally kind of him. He lifted the box in which Shakti had packed the books, tapes and other things not sold. He hoisted it onto his shoulder and carried it up to the house. Indu followed behind with the table coverings and her bowl.

"Where would you like me to set this?" he asked just before going through the front doorway.

"In the hallway underneath the table with the books should be okay for now. Thanks, Nhoj." She liked him very much, although they hadn't gotten to know each other well.

"And don't worry about those chairs at your table," he added. "I'll bring those in next."

"You're wonderful," Indu said with a big smile.

"Yes, I know." He gave a quick smile back as he disappeared into the house.

Indu continued across the quadrangle to drop the sheets and plastic cover in the laundry room and the bowl in the kitchen. She also needed to find two plastic bags. It was time to collect the cow patties. "Don't think Mr. Goodall would appreciate it if I left them behind the barn." The very thought amused her greatly as she saw them lined up on their racks on the ground. Most of them were dry, although one corner of a rack had been covered by shade and the patties had already picked up some evening dampness. She'd have to remember to set them out again when they got to London. She placed the wide-meshed screens back on top of the sawdust in the stall, and with the two bags of dried dung in one hand, she lifted the wire grid in the other. This she wanted to return to the garage where Kevin had found it.

Leaning it against one wall, assuming Kevin would see it, she emerged from the garage carrying a plastic bag in each hand. She didn't worry about concealing them as she doubted the average passerby would be able to even come close at guessing what they really were. She had just stepped from the garage when George and Nhoj appeared from the residents' quarters. George went toward his car, but Nhoj came up to her.

He pulled a candy bar from his pocket and split it in two. It was chocolate caramel, Indu's favorite. She switched both bags to one hand and accepted it.

"How did you know I was wanting something sweet?" she asked him.

"It was easy. Most people carrying cow turds are desirous of something." Nhoj was not the average passerby. No doubt he had heard some tale from Kevin.

Indu went along with his teasing. "How did you know that's what it was? It was supposed to be a secret."

"Must have been a cow in a past life. I can spot those turds anywhere." He opened his eyes wide and mooed. Indu threatened to hit him with one of the bags if he didn't stop, which he did quickly, backing away.

"Didn't realize women in your occupation could be so dangerous." He covered his head and pranced across the quadrangle, making Indu laugh.

George was standing with his head under the hood of his car. She wondered if he had heard any of the silliness with Nhoj. He seemed so engrossed in adjusting some wire that she even hesitated to say anything as she passed by him. She was fully resigned to the fact that nothing would happen between them. Just as she was deliberating, he twisted his head and smiled at her. Giving her most noncommittal smile in return, she decided to stop.

"What can a few last words hurt?" Her mind was trying to be as detached as possible but in her heart she recognized it to be one last glimmering chance to connect with him.

Not really knowing what to say, she held up the two bags of dung. "I almost forgot my booty."

"Yes, I heard about that. Did they dry?" She was surprised by his serious tone. She thought he'd enjoy making a few jokes about it, like Nhoj had.

She answered with equal seriousness. "Yes, they did, for the most part."

"So you're off tomorrow, is that right?" he asked.

"Tomorrow morning. A minibus will take us all into London where we'll be staying for a few more weeks." She felt a sadness as she said it.

"So, will Guruji give programs there, too?"

"Oh, sure. He gives programs wherever he goes. Doesn't matter how many come. He'll give a program to one person if they're sitting in front of him ready to meditate," she said.

"Mmmm," he nodded. "That's the sign of a real teacher."

Again at a loss for words, their conversation about the standing stone came back to her mind. "Well, too bad we never did get a chance to visit that stone you told me about." She said it only as a casual remark, a way of acknowledging the memory of their nice talk together. It was already past six o'clock and dinner would be served soon, a little later than usual because of the festivities of the day. She still had many things to do to finish preparing for the departure.

She anticipated some remark about how time had gotten away, that so much had been happening, or that hopefully she'd get to see some of the more impressive stone markers or circles before she left England. It was for this reason that her breath came to a total stop. Her anticipation had been wrong.

He was saying to her, ". . .it's not too far away. If we hurry, we can make it before the sun sets." He was suggesting that they go that very minute, that they drop everything they were doing, or planning to do, and go immediately.

She quickly regained her composure. "Do you have time right now?" she asked, having difficulty concealing her amazement.

"Sure. I want to show you." He stood facing her, looking into her eyes. He was dead serious about the proposition.

It was agreed upon. She would run and drop the bags off in her room and he would meet her downstairs in the hall by the books in five minutes.

FOURTEEN

~

She dropped the bags of dried dung on her bed, brushed her hair and quickly headed back downstairs. George was not there yet. She waited a minute in the hallway. Ordinarily, she might have browsed the books on the table, but she was feeling much too excited. She walked into the sitting room. It had a soft, warm glow to it from the evening sun. Walking over to the French doors, she immediately caught sight of George standing near Alison's booth. They were talking as Alison packed away the rest of her jewelry. Then, sending a dull ache through her heart, she saw George lean over and sweetly kiss Alison on the cheek. It had not been meant for anybody else's eyes and yet hers had seen it. Her heart sank.

"How absolutely silly I am to have even thought about pulling those two lovebirds apart. Where has my mind been?" She didn't think it possible to chastise herself with enough severity.

She stepped away from the doors, not wanting to be seen, and walked back into the front hall. She thought the best thing to do was to go out the front door and meet George at the booth where she could then say to Alison something like, "George is only going to show me where the stone is. He'll be right back." That way they'd both know that her intentions were admirable and that her real interest was in seeing the stone.

She was just about to walk through the front doorway when suddenly Guruji appeared with Shakti behind him. He stopped a moment to look at her. Without saying a word, she folded her palms together in salutation and stepped back a few feet in order to allow him to pass. He turned to Shakti, who was holding two small objects. One was wrapped in red tissue paper and the other in blue. He took the two objects from Shakti's hands and gave them to Indu. It was his way of indicating that she should follow him upstairs. She knew this without him saying a word. She let the two of them pass and then she, too, fell in step behind.

"Will George wait if I'm a little bit late?" The thought passed through her mind as she started up the stairs. That moment George came through the doorway of the sitting room. She leaned over the banister and whispered she would be right back down in a couple of minutes. He did not seem disturbed by the delay and made a silent gesture that he understood. Guruji had already reached the top landing so Indu hastened up the stairs with the two parcels.

The door to Guruji's room was just about to close as she slipped inside. She entered his room, still holding the door open with her foot, and handed the two paper bundles to Shakti. She hoped by keeping the door ajar that it would show her desire to depart as quickly as possible. But Guruji did not give any indication that she should leave, so she entered the room, letting the door click shut. She realized that her meeting with George might never come to pass.

Shakti began to unwrap the two objects. "Wait until you see what Guruji bought this afternoon at the fair," she said. That quickly she produced a blue, hand-decorated goose egg. "Isn't it exquisite? And look! It has little windows." She pulled on a tiny glued pearl knob and a hinged piece of shell swung open. The inside was just as delicately decorated as the outside, with colored mesh and tiny wildflowers all glued in place. She pulled one little knob after another until all four little windows were open, each supported by tiny gold hinges. It was darling, she had to admit. But why had Guruji bought such a thing?

"And look at this one." Shakti then produced from the blue paper another goose egg, only this one painted shiny black with gold trim. "And this lifts completely off here." She demonstrated by pulling up on a tiny gold bead glued to the top. The secret compartment inside was delicately lined with a sparkling gold and black fabric. It had to be one of the most unusual looking objects that Indu had ever seen. "You see, it comes with this little stand, too." The stand was a small gold ring with three dainty legs that curved outward.

With a twinkle in his eye, Guruji took the black one from Shakti's hand and held it out to Indu. Indu took it from him, puzzled.

"It's for you," Guruji said simply. "Keep it carefully. It is mystical."

Indu was stunned. To receive such a gift from one's Guru, so unexpectedly, was not without a deeper meaning. In that moment, Indu felt her heart surrender completely to him. Shakti also seemed surprised by the sudden presentation of the gift, but Guruji immediately asked her to run and find a member of the staff with whom he wanted to meet. As she went out the door, he sat down on the edge of the bed. Holding the gift gently in her hands, Indu knelt down on the floor at his feet. She knew of no words that she could speak. If one has ever beheld the glorious painted depths of the Grand Canyon, or spotted a whale from the bow of a small fishing boat, or stood in Red Square in front of the multifarious onion domes of St. Basil's Cathedral, the exultation experienced during each of those times, each an experience in Indu's past, did not come close, even when combined, to the joyous overflow of emotion which was now pouring from her heart.

"How ignorant I've been to even think of leaving him for one minute to see anybody else. How can I have been so blind..."

Her thinking was interrupted by Guruji's voice. "Can you manage to pack that safely? Otherwise, it will break." How the practical and mystical could be so beautifully blended in one man was beyond Indu's comprehension.

She replied, "Yes, I'll find a box and pack it carefully." Again she sat in silence, this time watching to keep any thought from intruding into her mind. Trying to consciously attune herself to absorb the energy vibrating from this one small man left her motionless. Suddenly the door opened and Shakti entered again.

"Guruji, that lady is nowhere to be found. I looked everywhere."

"Okay. No harm." He then raised his feet off the floor and lay back on the bed. It was only his physical body that needed rest. His other "bodies"—body of electricity, of cosmic mind, of cosmic understanding and of cosmic consciousness—were still radiantly vibrating, and would be eternally. Shakti unfolded his wool shawl and covered him from chest to feet.

Indu waited, expecting him to indicate a book she should read. It would have been the most natural thing. Many times she had read to him while he rested. But he made no motion for her to read. Instead, closing his eyes, he slowly raised one hand, indicating that nothing else was needed. Shakti turned off the light. Indu stood up and moved toward the door, keeping an eye on her Guru who lay with his hands folded across his chest. Was he silently giving his blessing for her to meet George? She had been willing to renounce it completely just to sit at his feet. Now he was ushering her back out into the world of *sansāra*, the endless wheel of pain and happiness, out of which she must find her own way. But she went with his blessing and that made all the difference. He could not "give" her enlightenment. He could only indicate. And when she was ready, she would find it waiting. In the meantime, she would have to balance her spiritual *sādhanā*, or devotional practice, with her secular, worldly life.

As she quietly saluted him and slowly backed out the door, she remembered Guruji's answer to the question, "How to be meditative and at the same time work in the world on the physical plane?" He had said, "We must go up and divinize everything, make everything divine: friends, enemies, love and anger. Let all be holy."

Twenty minutes had elapsed since she'd come upstairs. She went back to the bedroom and hid the egg under her bed. She had already asked Shakti not to mention anything about it to the others.

ℰᴑ * * * ℭℬ

Indu explained to me why she thought Guruji had given such a gift to her: he had forced her to confront the choices in her life and decide in which direction lay true happiness. The gift had been his way of opening her heart to see the choices in front of her. It wasn't a lesson which could ever have been taught with words. Her heart had clearly chosen to be in divine company, totally surrendering worldly attractions. She could feel that that decision alone had suddenly released her from a bondage inside. It was a feeling she had never experienced before, an openness, a flowing, a freedom. Her decision made, she felt totally protected to enter back into worldly life, into the life in which George was waiting.

ℰᴑ * * * ℭℬ

Before leaving the bedroom, she picked up her meditation shawl. She would be happy now to just sit and meditate by the stone without detaining George unnecessarily. As she was walking through the small upstairs sitting room connecting one wing of the house to the other, she happened to glance out a window overlooking the green lawn just as George looked up. She couldn't remember ever noticing the window before, but now her eyes met George's through it. He had again been standing at Alison's table. He quietly nodded up to her and said a few quick words to Alison. Downstairs, they met at the front door, exactly where she had met Guruji only thirty minutes before. Could George have any idea of the change in her heart? Did he know he was free to come or go, that her expectations would not hold him?

It wasn't that her feelings for him had changed. If anything, they were only continuing to grow stronger each time she looked into his eyes. She suspected she would love him for the rest of her life no matter what he did that evening. Yet it was a love that she knew would never interfere with her spiritual path, and that knowledge made the love flow even stronger. But to the extent that it was within her power, she would conceal her feelings. That was unless of course by some force of nature something came from him.

"Come on. We'd better hurry. I thought for a minute you weren't going to make it." There was a brightness in his eyes. He seemed happy to see her. He led her past the kitchen service entrance, past the dilapidated building to the white wooden door in the far corner of the quadrangle. He pulled the door open. Indu had often wondered what was concealed on the other side but had never taken time after her first day of exploring to find out. It opened onto a shady path which led to the vegetable garden. After stepping carefully over several rows of squash and carrots, George took her down a brick-laid path which curved to the left. Although Indu had never been down it, she suspected that it would take them to the patio behind the house and her suspicions were correct. It was indeed the path she had seen leading off to the right of the beverage room door. Before reaching the patio, however, George hopped up onto the retaining wall and proceeded behind a row of trees which skirted along the front wall of the rose garden, ending just at its entrance by the stairs. He hooked a right down the stairs and then side by side they walked the length of the green runway leading to the small iron gate.

"It's beautiful, don't you think?" he asked, looking over the rose beds.

"Yes, it is," she agreed, remembering how she'd admired them the first time she had traversed the same path.

They came to the gate bearing the sign, "Private Property Beyond This Point." George made no mention of it and neither did Indu. He gingerly lifted his legs over the iron posts and offered his hand when it was her turn. But she refused, saying, "No, I can manage. I've done it once before."

"You've come back here before?" he said with no uncertain surprise.

"Yes, but I didn't go much beyond, only up to that pond."

"Well, we're going to turn left and go down here." He nodded with his head. "But be careful. There are nettle plants all along the way which can be obnoxious and painful. Used to always get into them when I was a kid."

She had no trouble envisioning him as a young boy in the nettles. She smiled to herself. But how wise he had grown, expertly guiding her along a virtually concealed path which grew narrower and narrower, twisting under a tree or around a clump of brush. She did not try to follow close behind, but instead allowed plenty of room—friendly distance, but distance nonetheless. She did not want him to suspect that he was anything more to her than a guide to the stone. He shouldn't know what a darling figure he made to her, still dressed in his juggling outfit, winding down this tiny path, glancing back to make sure he hadn't lost her. No, he mustn't know yet how endearing he was to her heart.

He stopped at one point for her to catch up. Indu was glad for the moment's rest. They had been walking quite a distance at a fast pace. She took a few deep breaths and then something in the air tickled her nostrils. She stood still, aware that all of her senses were alert. Unbeknownst to her, she had turned her body to stand directly in line with the stone as yet concealed. George was watching curiously.

"Is it nearby?" she asked, not really wanting a confirmation of anything she'd detected sensorially, or extra-sensorially, as the case may be. But her standing position and her question coinciding with the proximity of the stone led him to conclude that she knew it was.

"Can you tell?" he asked with a tone tinged with respect.

She was surprised by his question. Consciously, she didn't know what she had perceived. She replied, "Oh, I don't know if I can tell. But is it?"

His wide-eyed smile showed that it was. Staying now closer behind, Indu saw that the path circled around to the right. It suddenly widened, with dark earth appearing between the trampled straw. It was a more frequented path, but one that emerged from nowhere. Ducking under several low-hanging branches, Indu saw the stone in a small clearing ahead. It stood three feet tall, was wider at the base than the top, and had four clearly defined sides and a flat top.

For just a moment, Indu forgot George's presence. She approached the stone slowly. Without any forethought, without any preconceived idea, she began to move her hands very near its surface but not touching it. Her instinct was to feel it, but to feel what? What was it that she expected to feel? She didn't know. She couldn't say she had seen some aura or a flashing vision. But she saw it standing there with the glow of the evening sun around it, speckled with light as the leaves of the overhanging tree swayed above. She had no doubt this was a mystical place.

Quickly her innate suspicions were confirmed. Moving her hands within an inch of the stone's surface, she felt a pocket of heat on the side of the stone opposite the setting sun. She shifted her hand up and down, testing the area around the hot spot and the warmth in her palm disappeared. Moving it back toward the spot, it returned. Now unable to restrain her curiosity, she gently rested her hand on the surface just below where she'd felt the heat. The surface was cool. It was not radiating heat. She realized George was watching her rather aberrant behavior. She was glad he was there. She wanted him to feel it.

"George, come and see what you think?" She turned and saw he had been standing five feet away, watching her.

"What are you doing?" he asked, not knowing what she wanted from him.

"Just move your hand near the surface and see if you can feel any heat."

He squatted down on the other side and put his hand close to where hers had been. He had beautiful, strong, well-shaped hands. He moved one slowly up and down the side of the stone until it came to hover over one spot.

He spoke with amazement. "You're right. There is something here. What is it?" While he asked, he also touched the stone, trying to find the origin of the heat.

Indu began "feeling" other areas. The side toward the sun was the "coolest." She located another hotspot on her side and then her hand glided up to the top.

"George, up here. It's really coming out the top." She was so captivated by it that it was almost a minute before she could pull her hand away to make room for his.

"So tell me what this is. Where's the heat coming from?"

He assumed she knew something more than she was admitting. But she didn't. She was equally as bewildered as he was.

"I don't know anything. You're the one who knows about standing stones. You tell me." It was a playful challenge.

"But if you didn't know about it, why did you try to feel it in the first place?" he asked with an intensity in his eyes.

"I just felt like doing it. I don't know why," she replied. It was a mystery that seemed to root them to the spot. Their hands at times passed very near to each other but never touched. Indu noticed he wasn't in any hurry to depart. She pulled her hands away from the stone and looked candidly at him. She felt her guard slowly dropping. Had the stone melted her resistance about revealing her feelings? Had something changed in him, too? Had some door finally been unlocked between them?

Seeing her withdraw from the stone, George looked up to meet her eyes. Their eyes held each other for much longer this time than ever before and neither tried to hide the intensity of feeling building between them. She knew what she wanted to ask him. Had she finally found the courage to say it?

Unable to contain it any longer, she spoke. "You know, I've had a funny feeling since meeting you, like there's some connection, a karmic connection between us."

"A karmic connection?" He continued to gaze into her eyes. "I don't really know what that means. But I have felt a need to talk to you, and I'm not even sure what about. Maybe I was thinking that you could teach me something."

"Now what can you possibly learn from a strange American, wearing white most of the time and traveling with a Guru?"

"That's what I've been asking myself," he said, rubbing his chin pensively. "But I have a feeling there's a lot."

Indu had a strong desire to move around to his side of the stone. As she stood up, he made a warning gesture behind him.

"Watch out for the water."

"There's water there? Let me see." She walked a few feet to the other side of the stone.

"It's a natural spring. I've read they're fairly common around standing stones."

The spring was four feet from the stone and was itself not more that four feet across. It was quite alive with movement as the water bubbled up from some unknown source. Indu stepped back from it and sat down on the ground next to the stone. It put her very near to George and she sensed him leaning away.

"Poor fellow," she thought, "he seems almost frightened of this crazy American girl."

They were almost shoulder to shoulder, which was really too close for any serious talking. She saw a stump just to her right and as smoothly as possible, she scooted herself around so that she could perch on top of it. George also shifted his seat around to face her, squatting about two feet away.

"So tell me, what does that ring on your finger mean?" he asked, looking at her left hand. "You're not married, are you?"

"No, I'm not." The question surprised her.

"I didn't really think that you were. Is there some significance to it, though?"

The ring was a silver one, with an unusually delicate basketweave design. There was a reason for her wearing it. "When I'm traveling, it's convenient to have a ring on the left finger, particularly one that can pass as a wedding band. It's to discourage advances from strange men."

"I see. I thought you might have taken special vows to be with a Guru, so in that sense you were married to that life," he said.

"I'm a devotee, not a nun. No, there are no restrictions to speak of. We're free to do whatever we want. But of course real devotees are highly protective of their spiritual energy. When *kuṇḍalinī* starts stirring around, you really don't want to do anything that will pull it back down. As the energy moves, it brings a natural high all its own. So you begin to watch everything in your life: who your friends are, who your relationships are with, what kind of work you do, what you eat, what you think. Because everything affects that energy. I believe that's why the Ten Commandments were written. It wasn't to show man what is morally good and morally bad. They're meant as guidelines for protecting spiritual energy."

George asked, "What is this energy? Where does it come from? I think that's what I don't understand. It's something that everybody has, right?" Indu could think of only one analogy, but she didn't know if she could properly explain the relationship between the two.

"Doesn't everybody have a sex drive? Where does that energy come from?" Asked rhetorically, she continued without pausing. "There's no simple answer. But believe it or not, sexual energy and *kuṇḍalinī*, or spiritual energy, are related. That's why many following spiritual paths try to be celibate.

"Again, it has nothing to do with virtue or chastity. But you can see, if the *kuṇḍalinī* is moving upward and the sexual energy is moving downward, it can be counterproductive," she said, still looking intently at him. "You know, I was reading that book on Gandhi's life the other evening. In it they described how Gandhi struggled to control his sex drive because he recognized the power behind that energy. It's really too precious to just release heedlessly. He was determined to be master over it and at some point in his life, he did."

"Yes, I'd like to have that kind of control. I can see it would be a very practical thing." He spoke with the utmost earnestness.

She was touched by it. "There is one yogic discipline which is very helpful for gaining that mastery. Have you ever heard of *tantra*?" she asked, this time waiting for his reply.

"No, I don't think I have."

"Tantra is feeling the oneness of ourselves with the rest of creation. It's a word often sorely misused to mean free-love or sex. That's because people don't know what they're talking about. Tantra alone has nothing to do with sex per se. If you are sitting and meditating and feeling the oneness with the air, or with the universe, that's tantra. And if you're intimately embracing someone dearly beloved and that feeling of oneness comes, that's also tantra. But in that kind of embrace, you try to ride the wave, so to speak. You try to stay just on the edge of sexual release for as long as possible. Very interesting things can happen when you do this. Of course, I've not had much experience with this myself, believe me. But I do know something does happen. Because the energy is not being released, it can start to activate the more subtle energies in the body, like the *kuṇḍalinī*. You can feel a tingling along the spine, or a profound ringing in the head, or just an overall dizziness. And suddenly you're not even thinking about the sex drive. You've lost all awareness even of the body and all you feel is the oneness. It's the most blessed feeling. To me, that is what lovemaking is all about. Just sex is terribly boring and often draining."

"Yes, that I've experienced, feeling totally drained. But I wasn't sure what to do about it."

"Oh, well, there's a lot you can do. But it must be with the right person, and you also have to take a close look at everything else in your life, at your desires, your goals, at the general direction in which your life is moving."

"So, it's a whole way of life," he said.

"Yes, it is."

Just after she'd spoken, they both heard the sound of approaching footsteps. Indu looked past the stone. A man appeared. He was advanced in age and gruff in appearance, with a cap pulled down over his forehead and a long shotgun cradled in one arm. He stopped just feet away from them, obviously displeased to see them.

"You're trespassing. Do you know that?" he said in a harsh voice.

Completely surprised at herself, Indu felt not one bit intimidated. She looked calmly into the man's face and said, "We certainly didn't mean any harm. We only wanted to sit by this stone for a few minutes. We'll be leaving soon."

"Well, you'd better. You shouldn't be here. If the owner were to come by, you'd be in big trouble, big trouble."

"Yes, we understand. Thank you." Her composure was unwavering.

He made a grumbling sound, ducked under the tree branches and was gone. Indu listened as his footsteps grew fainter and fainter. George had not said a word. Indu looked down and smiled at him.

"I got this feeling when I was talking to that man that we were protected by this stone, like there was an invisible force field. Really, I don't think we need to worry about anything. We're protected."

To herself she wondered, "Why do I sound so emphatically sure?" She noticed George looking at her with no such quizzical thought. Then it hit her that she was taking on too much of an authoritarian role: she the "perched-on-stump" teacher, he the "sitting-on-ground" student. She didn't want that. She slowly lowered herself to the ground and leaned against the stump. Looking at the stone, she couldn't deny that she did feel protected. She heard George's voice drawing back her attention.

"How old are you?" he asked, apparently feeling no need to apologize for his directness. At some point during the last hour they had transcended formality.

Indu was curious. "How old do you think I am?"

He studied her for a moment. "You must be around twenty-five."

"Well, I'm not twenty-five."

"Older or younger?"

"Older."

"You're older?" He asked innocently, perplexed. "Are you twenty-six?"

"I'm twenty-seven." Now it was her turn. "How old are you?" She tried to guess before he spoke. Would they be the same? He certainly wasn't older, but how much younger?

He ended her quandary. "I'm twenty-four."

They looked silently at each other. So she was three years older than he. The statistic mattered little to her heart, but she couldn't resist commenting, "Didn't you say your birthday was in July?"

He nodded.

"So you actually just turned twenty-four."

"That's true," he said with an almost sheepish grin.

That meant that they were exactly three years and two months apart. Her mind was like that. It liked to make numerical calculations. Even as a child, she was always counting something: the eggs in the refrigerator door, the polka dots on her dress. The number wasn't important; it just gave her comfort knowing.

George's countenance showed it mattered little to him that he was younger. In fact, it seemed to make sense now that she should be the one explaining the deeper facets of life.

The creeping twilight made Indu remember that dinner would soon be over. Her watch showed it to be seven-thirty. "You

227

might want to go eat," she said. "It's gotten quite late. You must be hungry."

But he shook his head "no," saying he wasn't particularly hungry at the moment. They talked on.

Indu spoke more about the movement of the spiritual energy: how she had first recognized it, how it had drastically altered her life, why a Guru's guidance was invaluable, and which meditation techniques she enjoyed the most. An hour flew by. There were still so many things she wanted to tell him. Neither one showed any signs of growing restless. He reminded her, "Isn't it almost sunset? Don't you want to get back for the fire?" There was a twinkle in his eyes.

"You stinker," she thought. "You know full well I'm not about to leave."

She gave him an acquiescent smile which said for her what she still dared not put into words: "How can I possibly leave you?"

Verbally, she said, "Seems to me we're having our own meditation here. Won't hurt to miss the fire this once." Their eyes danced together in the dusky rays of light. And they talked on.

FIFTEEN

~

At one point, sitting near enough to behold each other through the darkness, Indu saw that George was rubbing his arms. "Are you cold?" she asked, only then conscious that the temperature had dropped since the sun had set.

"No, it's the bugs. Aren't they getting you?"

"I don't feel a thing," she said. "But here." She handed him her meditation shawl which had been in her lap the entire time. "Why don't you wrap up in this?"

He accepted it gratefully. She liked seeing it draped over his shoulders.

He had asked one question after another, trying to figure out who she was. She had talked relentlessly, telling about her present life, about her vocation to write, about what she thought her past lives had been, about her romantic entanglements with two men whom she believed had been her father and her son, respectively, from previous incarnations and what it was that made her think so.

Then she stopped, astonished at herself. "What have I done, telling so much?" she thought, as she looked over at him. She had never talked to anyone like this before.

The silence hung momentarily between them. Then he reached out and gently patted her shoulder. It was the first time there had been any intentional physical contact between them, not counting the swinging twirls at the dance.

"In a way, I wish I could know what my former lives have been or in what direction this life will go." He spoke pensively.

"I don't know anything, really. They're just strong feelings I get."

"But I can't recall ever even having those kinds of feelings." There was a shadow of disappointment in his voice, as though he had missed something by neglect on his part.

She wanted to reassure him. "The main advantage I can see about knowing anything from another lifetime is simply to see that the present life needn't be taken so seriously, as though it's the final moment. It's just a continuation of one's spiritual evolution, only in another physical body. Guruji says our spirits are neither born nor do they die. It's only the body that goes through that. He also says that if we did know our past lives, if they suddenly came flooding back into our memory, we'd commit suicide right away."

"Why is that?" he asked.

"Guruji says we're overwhelmed enough as it is with the problems of this lifetime. If we fill our minds with all the problems of previous lifetimes, we'd short-circuit our nervous systems."

"But wouldn't we gain the wisdom from our mistakes?"

"But that's just it. All the wisdom we've ever acquired from our former lives is with us right now. Our psychic bodies are eternal. That's the whole point. Guruji says whenever we have a vision, whether we're dreaming or awake, what we are seeing is the psychic body."

Indu suddenly felt goose bumps run down her exposed arms. It might have been from their discussion but she also felt a dampness and chill from the air. Her shawl could easily wrap around them both and they were already sitting close enough to share it. It seemed natural to ask if she could use a corner of it. He readily unfolded it and draped half of it over her shoulders. It felt warm from his body and it brought them closer in the enveloping darkness.

There was a moment's silence before he asked his next question, which he delivered carefully. "Even though we don't need to remember, what do you think was our past relationship?"

It was a loaded question. How many times had she asked herself the very same thing? She ingenuously responded, "I have the suspicion that we've actually had not only one previous incarnation but more than one, which would mean that more than one relationship has existed. One might have been as a teacher, another as a sister or brother." She was trying to remain gender neutral since the spirit itself has no gender. That was the point she wanted to make.

"Do you think we were ever lovers?"

"How could we not have been?" she thought. "Have I not held you tenderly many times in my arms? Have I not lovingly kissed those cheeks?"

But she thought it wiser to temper her answer. "It's very possible. I have noticed that whenever I see you and Alison together, there is some reaction inside of me."

"You're kidding?" He sounded astounded to hear it.

"It isn't anything like jealousy. I don't even think I can describe it. I simply suspect there is something karmic behind it."

She knew he was looking at her. She could feel his eyes penetrating the obscurity of the night. She turned her head to meet that pair of eyes which now she could barely discern but which she knew so well. Their talk had been long and intense. Their hearts had been moving closer and closer. Words could no longer speak what was moving between them. Only the hug that followed could. The moment she felt his arms around her, the last barriers protecting her great secret fell. Her arms wrapped around him with all her love pouring from her heart. His movements were slow and relaxed. He held her tightly. It was more than an embrace. The intensity increased until they were almost clinging, as if daring not to let go for fear of losing one another.

His hand moved up to stroke her head, pressing her cheek to his. She returned the caress, feeling their heads braced together, and then relaxing apart only to press against each other once more. It was beyond any dance imaginable, a dance of two meeting again. With each sway her lips brushed closely to his only to move away. Would they meet? Neither seemed to know. There wasn't a need that they should. The energy surging between them was so comfortable, so natural, so alluringly familiar. What more could make it sweeter?

She then deliberately leaned back. He loosened the grip of his arm around her and brought his left hand down to her lap. It was that hand which had just hours before glided near the surface of the stone, searching enigmatically for the energy radiating from it. They had both felt it then and they were both feeling something now, an energy which had almost been left untapped. The thought sent a shudder through Indu's heart. She reached blindly for that hand, holding it tightly in her own, bringing it slowly to her lips. Yes, she would kiss the palm that had felt the stone's heat. With all its sensitivity, it would feel her love, too.

Her lips only lightly touched his hand, and when she looked toward him again it was as though a wave moved through them both. She felt his body lean into hers. So gently, so warmly, their lips finally met. Their passion was tender and real. Separated by galaxies, by universes, by lifetimes, they had somehow returned to the one they knew, to the one they loved.

Their lips parted reluctantly.

George was the first to speak. "Have you ever felt anything like this before?"

"Have I met anyone like you before?" she thought, her hand still holding the back of his head. Still thinking to herself, she marveled, "Have I felt anything like this before in this life-time? If I had, could I possibly ever have forgotten? Never."

To him she replied, "No, I've never known anything like this. Have you?"

"No," he replied.

She searched to find the words that could express what they were feeling, something so new, yet so familiar, so intense. But George was the one that uttered them. "So love is eternal after all."

It was so simple. Whatever their relationship had been before, they had adored the other with the deepest of love and that love, like a magnetic force, had pulled them back together. "Yes," she repeated to herself, "Love is eternal."

But the harsh reality of time stood boldly before them. They had avoided its tainting fingers beyond the possible limits. He had brought her to see the stone and six hours had passed like six minutes. They stood up, the shawl still wrapped around them.

Holding her closely, he whispered, "Do you know how rare it is for two people to feel this? God, we are so lucky."

She still couldn't believe that the man whom she had guarded-ly watched for all those days, who had moved her heart from the moment he had appeared before her, that he too had felt the depth of their connection. He had been pulled to her just as she had been to him. Breaking through this ethereal moment, her mind obstinately intruded, leaving her to chuckle coyly.

"What is it?" he asked softly.

"When I was twenty-one, a psychic told me that I would marry at twenty-eight. I wonder if it will be true."

"That's in one year. Maybe I'm..." He stopped before finishing. Indu understood. They were in love. But to proclaim one's love and with the same breath to speak of the future, to try to shape that love into a structured mold of something called "marriage," it would have been like moving from the wilds of Africa to a zoo. Neither one of them was ready for that. They both let the subject drop.

But it did make her think of the more immediate future. She was still scheduled to leave the Foundation in less than twelve hours. He was supposed to leave for Germany in ten days. She would leave England in three weeks. From Germany, he would move on to Greece. After three weeks in the States, she would fly off to Japan. They were going in every direction except the same one.

Would life be so cruel as to pull them apart? She remembered a line from Richard Bach: "Is it possible for soulmates to meet and then to separate forever?"[16] Was that what was to happen to them? She couldn't imagine that it would be true. How could their bond of love let it happen?

They stood for a long time holding each other near the stone. It was a magical spot and neither wanted to leave.

"I wish time were standing still, but I know it's not." He spoke softly.

"Yes, I know," she said. "'Be active in the world but be not of the world.'" Indu couldn't help but quote this lesson from the *Bhagavad Gītā*, even though it was about being unattached to the doer-ship of actions. "What we feel is not of this world, but vanished the world has not. As much as I hate to say it, I still have laundry and packing to do. We'd better head back."

Lifting the shawl from his shoulders and draping it around hers, he took her hand and led the way. But he did not turn down the same small path from which they had come. Instead, after ducking under the tree branches he went straight for a short distance and then cut across an open field. A half moon cast a cool radiance bright enough to see the dark shadows of trees along one side of the field. How different now, returning with him, walking in step by his side, his hand squeezing hers. The distance between them was gone.

They had circumambulated the rose garden and approached the house from directly behind. At the edge of the field was the carefully maintained lawn of the Foundation. Indu could see light glowing through the dining room windows.

They walked around the flower garden and stepped down onto the brick patio. As they drew nearer to the light, Indu watched as George's face became more and more distinct. For hours he had been but a warm shadow near her. Now, she could clearly make out his aristocratic nose, his dark eyebrows, his deep, alluring eyes. He stopped by the windows and turned toward her. Their eyes joined again, as they had so many times over the past eight days since he juggled past her, but now there was a difference. If it's true that eyes are the windows to the soul, then it was no wonder that theirs had been drawn together time and time again. Nature was very wise.

Cautious about being seen together, they vigilantly entered through the beverage room door. A bowl of grapes had been left on the counter. They both reached for a handful. Indu had eaten little but the granola all day long. Although she was far from feeling famished, the grapes were a welcome sight. She watched George watching her eating grapes while he himself popped several in his mouth. The light from the hallway shone brightly into the small room, contrasting starkly with the dark veil of night to which their eyes had grown accustomed. It also brought a sharp realness to what had passed between them. At the same time, it prohibited any contact. For the time being, their love had to remain clandestine. He was in a much more compromised position than she, since his relationship with Alison was far from over. Propriety necessitated discretion. But the light revealed that the magic they had felt was not a dream, not a fleeting affair. In darkness, emotional exchange can be inflated to the level of romance only to have the fantasy shattered when confronted face to face with the same person under more illumined circumstances. But that light only showed the glow on their faces and the adoration beaming from their eyes.

"Do you want to see how I really eat grapes?" he asked, smacking his lips and arching his eyebrows at the keen prospect of demonstrating yet another talent.

"Don't tell me you juggle them into your mouth," she said, feigning ennui. She had come very close to guessing. He tilted his head back, tossed a grape high into the air and executed a perfect catch, showily devouring the reward. She could not repress a gleeful grin at the perfection of his performance. It was comic relief that they both needed after having spent such a profound period by the stone.

She fixed hot chocolate and he a cup of tea. "Would you like tea biscuits to dunk?" he asked.

"Mmmm. I would like some."

"Good. Me, too. I'll bring the whole package." He hunched over, rubbed his hands together and disappeared into the hallway to the left. He quickly returned carrying a red roll of McVities Digestive wheatmeal biscuits, something new to Indu. They sat down side by side, arranging the grapes, round biscuits and drinks on the small table below the pictures of the staff. Every minute alone with him was precious. She knew they would soon have to part.

"Ah, me bag," he said using the Cockney colloquialism as he jumped up again. "Let me run get it. I left it in the kitchen earlier." He was back again in less than a minute, carrying a well-worn canvas shoulder pack. He pulled from it his date book.

"So, Miss Indu Dolman, what's the best address to reach you these days?" He held a pen poised in his hand. Before Indu could respond, there was a sudden bang of the service entrance door. She and George waited to see who would appear in the hallway. It was a young woman named Lucy and her friend.

Seeing George and Indu sitting by the table, she pulled her friend into the tiny room and plopped onto the counter across from them. "Fancy meeting you here at this hour, George," she merrily quipped.

"Oh, come on. Can't a bloke have a cup of tea in peace?" he asked, showing his usual acerbic humor. Sipping their tea and cocoa, they both tried to exude a nonchalance in the hope of convincing Lucy that all was innocent between them. For Indu, though, it lent the moment an awkwardness which she didn't enjoy. Fortunately, Lucy found it necessary to leave after exchanging only a few casual remarks. Indu and George then resumed their talk, seriously discussing their respective future plans.

"You're going to Japan?" It was said more as an exclamation than a question. Indu had just briefly outlined her obligations for the next year. "That's wonderful. For how long?"

"It's only for two months, from October 9th to December 15th."

"You must be quite good at what you do," he said with admiration.

"I like what I do, at least I like the writing."

"Well. So much for the jet-setting part of our lives. What about this next week? Do you have the address in London where you'll be?"

"I think Shakti posted it in the front hallway for anyone who wanted to come see Guruji. I don't know it offhand. But next Friday we've been invited to Liverpool."

"Really? Liverpool?" he replied, obviously intrigued by the information.

"Yes. Did you get to know Margaret and Paul?" she asked. He nodded that he had made their acquaintance during the intensive. "Well, they have a yoga center of their own in New Brighton, just outside Liverpool. They want Guruji to do a workshop at their place this coming weekend."

"It's uncanny." He had a whimsical expression.

"What is?" she inquired.

"My aunt lives about an hour from there and as a matter of fact, my mother is with her right now. Last time I talked with them, they were wanting me to pay a visit and even suggested this coming weekend. I half promised that I would."

"George, you're not thinking what I'm thinking, are you?" she said with unbridled expectation.

"Don't know that they'd totally appreciate me disappearing off to Liverpool in the middle of my visit with them. But with the right amount of sweet cajoling, I could probably manage it."

It was an odd coincidence. The prospect of meeting again in five days brought gratified smiles to their tired faces. Indu looked again at her watch. It was two o'clock in the morning. They had been together for over seven hours. Clearing the table of the dishes and crumbs, they knew it was time to part from one another.

Only the consolation of knowing that they would try to rendezvous again at the stone in the morning eased the reluctance of having to say goodnight. They hugged and kissed lightly before heading in opposite directions, he out the service entrance that opened onto the quadrangle and she up the front stairway.

She heard the service entrance door click shut. He was gone. How had it ever come to pass that their hearts should finally connect just hours before she was to leave? It was a mystery she would forever hold in high reverence. After stopping at the bathroom, she pulled on a nightgown and silently crept into bed. Sleep came quickly. She was glad to catch a few hours rest before trying to do all that had been left undone that evening, forsaken so she could explore an avenue of life which had brought her unimaginable, resounding happiness.

She awoke at six o'clock. The others were still asleep. Hurriedly pulling on clothes, she ran down to the laundry room where she had left a bag of laundry ready to go into the already occupied machine. Blessed by small favors, she saw that someone had kindly run it through the washer for her. All she had to do was get it dried and folded and into her suitcase. Clothes safely humming in the dryer, she dashed back up to bathe, don her contact lenses, shave her legs, dabble on her usual touch of make-up, and slip on the same rose-colored dress in which she had arrived. When she checked the mirror just before running down to the laundry room again, she thought she saw someone radiantly glowing back. She didn't want to concede the truth of it, fearing that such a concession would make her joyous secret more evident to those who saw her that morning.

Just as she was folding the last few things into a laundry basket, Alison appeared at the doorway, leaning around the door to hang a wet towel on a hook. Indu had no way of knowing what Alison knew about her time with George. Her demeanor seemed complacently composed, so Indu spoke as kindly as possible, hoping there wouldn't be anger lurking just under Alison's facade.

"I really am sorry about monopolizing George last night," she said. But before she could make any excuses for the exceptional length of their evening visit, Alison interrupted her train of thought.

"Oh, no. It's quite all right. It gave me a chance to visit with Nhoj and Diana and we listened to some unbelievably beautiful Tibetan bell music." There seemed to be no strain in her words, which eased Indu's conscience greatly, although she knew the relief was only for the moment. Alison would eventually find out how deeply in love she and George were. It would cast the only glum shadow over their reunited spirits, that Alison would suffer from their reunion. She prayed Alison would not despise them both.

With her suitcase packed, she went downstairs to have breakfast, expecting to finally see George. She tried to think of what to say or how to act toward him in front of the others, but he wasn't there. Instead, Nhoj came by and greeted her.

"It really is sad to see you all leaving."

"I can't believe the ten days are over either," she responded, gracefully accepting his kind words. "It is lovely here. I've enjoyed it very much."

"Listen. Do you think you could do me a favor before you go?" he asked with a slight hesitancy.

"Of course," she said. "What is it?"

"I need some help learning the *Gāyatrī* Mantra. If you have time this morning, could you go over it with me?"

"That's the best thing you could have asked." She was pleased by his request. "Here, I've just finished eating. Why don't we do it right now? We can go out and sit on the steps by the rose garden."

"Grand. Let me run and get the paper with the words written on it. I'll meet you back there in just a minute."

Before going out to the garden, Indu went upstairs to her room and found a box with Guruji's cassette tapes. There was one she thought Nhoj would particularly like. It was recorded during a special fire ceremony and had all the mantras chanted at the fire circles. Nhoj had come frequently to the sunset meditations. Locating the mantra sheet that went with it, she went down the stairs, out the beverage room door and across to the rose garden steps. Nhoj was there waiting for her. They sat down on the top step. The sky was overcast and the air felt heavy, but the roses made everything colorful and fragrant. It was an idyllic spot to learn a mantra.

"My Sanskrit pronunciation is not nearly as good as the others'," Indu warned before they started.

"That's all right. It's mainly the melody that I can't keep in my head."

They chanted it once through together, then they took it line by line.

OM BHŪR BHUVAH SVAH
TAT SAVITUR VARENYAM
BHARGO DEVASYA DHĪMAHI
DHIYO YO NAH PRACHODAYĀT OM

"What can you give me as a close literal translation?"

"Hmmm. It would be something like, 'The in-going, the out-going, the balancing forces, may we meditate on that, that sacred Light of the radiant source of creation. May it inspire our minds.' That's pretty close, anyway. Do you want to chant it again?"

He agreed. They chanted it at least ten times together. Nearly thirty minutes passed sitting before the majestic display of roses chanting Sanskrit. Indu felt a closeness to Nhoj just knowing what a good friend he was to George. She was glad she could be his friend, too. She gave him the cassette tape, the mantra paper and a big hug. He was happy to return the hug and was very grateful for the tape. It seemed right that her goodbye to him should be special.

Having only paid the camping rate to sleep in the Yoga Hall with her sleeping bag, Indu felt obliged to drop by the office and offer to pay any balance she might owe. Heading across the quadrangle with her purse, she saw George for the first time that morning walking from the residents' quarters toward her. She caught sight of Alison coming down the steps shortly behind him. She knew she could do no more than smile. He smiled in return but his eyes betrayed the strain he was under. She did not have to think hard to guess what it was. The shadow of gloom was slowly descending. As Alison passed, Indu tried to smile just as pleasantly to her but perceived that it wasn't so equally returned. "Alas, what to do?" she thought as she entered the office.

"My goodness, don't think of paying another penny," Gretchen said. "You worked very hard during the intensive. I saw you during the programs. You've more than contributed for your stay here."

Indu was greatly relieved. She had come with enough to get by but she was far from being amply endowed financially. "I would like to at least become a member of the Foundation so I can be on your mailing list. How much would that be?" she asked. It was a precalculated gesture and she already knew it would be around ten pounds.

"You certainly may. For overseas, it will be twelve pounds. Here is the form you need to fill out."

Indu wrote down the necessary information, paid the money and made the proper affable remarks about enjoying her stay at the Foundation before leaving the office. Back downstairs she saw George by his car. She approached as nonchalantly as possible and they quickly agreed to meet in ten minutes by the white door leading to the vegetable garden. They would then run to the stone where they could hold each other one last time. Just looking at each other was painful, for they dared not exhibit any sign of their inner passion, and yet she so wanted to raise her hand to touch his head and hold it against her own.

She flew upstairs to grab her camera and set her suitcases outside the bedroom door. The bus driver would be coming to help carry the bags downstairs. Indu hoped she could disappear without attracting notice. But seeing her readied state, Mangala had no compunction in beseeching her assistance. "It would be such a great help if you could get these checks cashed at the office. They were collected in the sale of the tapes and books while we've been here. I'm sure the office can do it for us here and save us the trouble in London."

Indu could not say no. She felt honor- and duty-bound to do it first before meeting George. Carrying her purse and camera, she went as fast as she could. They congenially greeted her again in the office and made the necessary exchange. She profusely thanked them again and dashed out into the courtyard, walking as casually as possible toward the white door. George was waiting for her on the other side.

He took her in his arms and whispered in her ear, "You look smashing in that dress. I wanted to tell you before."

She suspected it was more the radiance in her eyes than the dress that bedazzled him, but the only response she made was to plant a kiss soundly on his cheek.

"Come on," he said. "Let's not get started here. It's onward to the stone."

They took the route through the rose garden, virtually running the entire way. Only at the last turn under the tree branches did they slow to a walk. The stone stood conspicuously alone, leaning ever so slightly toward the bubbling spring. It was a spot she hoped to return to someday, hopefully with George. Slipping her heels off so as not to tower over him, they embraced at the same spot where they had stood the night before, his arms tightly around her and hers around him. Holding him, she was excruciatingly aware that time was short.

"George," she said with a tenderness she had never heard in her own voice, "I brought my camera. It only has one picture left on it. Shall we take one together?"

"How can we do it?"

Indu reached into her purse and produced the camera. "We can place it on top of the stone and set the timer."

He went over and knelt down near the spring while she balanced the camera. Setting the timer, she hurried to George's side. Both of them facing the stone, they waited. "It will be a magical picture," she thought, her first with George and taken in the presence of the mystical stone.

"Beep, beep, beep..." came the timer's warning just before the click, and then the film began its automatic rewind since it had arrived at the end of the roll.

℘ * * * ℃

The moment was captured forever: two souls, deeply in love, having spent only hours together, and most of them shared at that very site by the stone. Indu showed me the picture. It was touching to see their two heads leaning toward each other, their apprehensive smiles that spoke a million words. What were they doing? How had it happened? What would come next? Would they be able to ride the obtrusive waves that they had already seen coming between them in the ocean of the world? Those sentiments were oddly enhanced by the angular tilt of the picture, probably from the unleveled surface of the stone or its leaning position. What did strike me was the strange resemblance which Indu and George bore to one another.

℘ * * * ℃

The time was pressing hard on Indu's heart. She hated to break the spell of their last moment by the stone but her anxiety over possibly keeping Guruji waiting was too great. They had been gone over twenty minutes and it was all the time she dared allow. Their departure was set for eleven o'clock and it was only five minutes away. They hugged one last time and brought their lips warmly together.

Hurrying back through the rose garden and out the white door into the quadrangle, they were stupefied to hear that everyone, including Guruji, had converged on Nhoj's room to listen to the Tibetan bell record. George and Indu joined the group, crowding into Nhoj's tiny upstairs space. Guruji was sitting on the bed. Unintentionally, Indu found herself positioned between George and Alison. It was uncomfortably too symbolic of her real position in their relationship. But there was no other place to move. Closing her eyes, she tried to meditate. They sat for thirty minutes listening. The name of the album was *The Singing Bowls of Tibet* and the sound was absolutely ethereal.

"So this is how Nhoj practices his meditation," she thought, impressed to realize how sensitive he was.

After the music was over, everyone went down and gathered around the minibus. The time for goodbyes had arrived. Indu gave several farewell hugs and then found herself standing in front of Alison. Alison accepted a hug, but Indu could feel it was weakly returned.

"How much does she know?" Indu wondered. She had meant to ask George at the stone but it simply hadn't entered her mind. George was standing calmly next to Alison. "So I get to hug you one last time," she thought as she leaned toward him. She hoped it wasn't overtly apparent how much feeling was between them. She even tried to time the hug so as not to be too short or too long. But she could not prevent it from being a tight one. Their eyes met again for just a moment afterward.

ဆ * * * ҩ

Indu commented to me that this was but the first in a series of goodbyes that they would have to say to one another over the next few weeks, in person and by phone.

ℰ) * * * (ℬ

Being the first to climb onto the bus after Guruji, Indu took a seat at the back and waited for the others to finish their good-byes. The five of them and their luggage filled the bus. Its door glided shut as the driver put it in reverse and turned the wheel. Everyone from the Foundation gathered near the service entrance to wave final farewells. Shifting into forward, the bus moved slowly across the quadrangle. Indu looked back over the seat, as did the others. Mangala and Uma popped their hands out the windows to return the hardy waves. Indu waved through the rear window. She tried to look at all the people gathered but found it hard to break eye contact with George. She did so for a fleeting moment and then their eyes held each other once again until the distance was too great. The bus had passed under the brick entrance archway and was well down the driveway leading out of Ickwell before Indu sat forward again.

ℰ) * * * (ℬ

The ten-day retreat which had brought them all from the States to England was now behind them. She could not believe how much Guruji had loaded into those ten days. Even for her, a devotee of over ten years, the exposure to so many techniques in one period of time had been intense. Assisting as she had done had also given her invaluable training in working consciously with people to feel the movement of energy. Indu told me that it was only in retrospect that she could fully esteem the value of this training, and he had done it without her even knowing.

ℰ) * * * (ℬ

As they moved speedily along the highway to London, Uma, who happened to be sitting just in front of Indu, turned around with a coy smile. Indu suspected right away what was coming.

"So, where were you last night, if you don't mind me asking?"

Indu didn't feel that there would be any harm in telling anyone now, particularly since everyone would know in five days— that is, if George did make it to New Brighton.

"I spent the entire time sitting by a prehistoric standing stone just near the Foundation. I tell you, I could really feel it had some power," she replied honestly.

Uma hesitated not a second with her next question, presented with her usual, undeniable candor. "And were you alone?" A big smile spread across her face.

Indu's impish grin gave away the answer.

"Okay. So who was it?"

Playfully, Indu replied, "Can you guess?"

"Was it Nhoj?"

"No," she said, surprised that Nhoj had been the first one suspected.

"Was it Kevin?" That was a more likely guess since her friendship with him had been uninhibitedly expressed.

"No." Indu wondered if she would guess the right one at all.

Uma thought a moment and then asked, "Was it George?" Indu nodded. With another big smile Uma ardently replied, "I approve!"

Indu felt a warm rush in her cheeks and simply grinned back. Nothing more was said during the ride to London.

SIXTEEN

~

They arrived at a large, old house in Hampstead, a village in north London. The owner was an elderly Indian gentleman who had known Guruji for over twenty years. Guruji had stayed with him once before during the late 1960s. He was affectionately called "Muniji." A short, rotund man, he often wore sweaters in need of mending. But he wore them with dignity. That's what Indu remembered most clearly about him—he had a regal dignity.

The house had been divided into ten apartments, each with a kitchen, but bathroom facilities were shared on each floor. Knowing Guruji was coming to London, Muniji had arranged for his largest apartment to be available. It was on the third floor of the house and had four rooms: two small bedrooms, a well-proportioned sitting room and a kitchen. His other apartments were either under lease or under repair. It should have seemed cramped for five people, but oddly it wasn't. They ensconced Guruji in one bedroom. In deference to age Uma was assigned the second bedroom, leaving Shakti, Mangala and Indu to share the sitting room.

The furnishings in the sitting room were practical. There were two large oversized chairs, a day couch which Shakti used as a bed, a coffee table, a small desk, a chest of drawers, and the refrigerator, which was too large for the kitchen. Two other mattresses lay on the floor, pushed up against the walls. Suitcases lined any extra space on the sides. During the day, drapes were tossed over the bags and personal items tucked away. The room was kept neat since visitors came daily, taking seats on the beds, forming a circle around one of the oversized chairs where Guruji sat.

The kitchen, too, was a wonder to Indu. It could not have been much larger than a walk-in closet with a large porcelain sink, a miniature four-burner gas stove, a minimal countertop with cupboards above and below and one row of open narrow shelving. Yet for all its compactness, food for ten to fifteen people would come parading out of it to be graciously served buffet-style on the coffee table. Guruji was a wonderful cook. It was a pleasure for him to feed those who were with him and those who came to see him. The first question asked of anybody entering the flat was, "Have you eaten?" and almost regardless of their answer, a plate of Guruji's cooking would be dished up and served. Indu described how one time when they were walking from a tube station through a subway (an underground walkway), he stopped at a souvenir shop and purchased an apron emblazoned with the color-coded map of the London Underground. It was thereafter pulled on whenever he was in the kitchen.

There were two things which struck Indu as unusual. One was the coin box in the sitting room which had to be fed prior to any use of the gas stove or gas-heated radiator. It was a pay-as-you-go system. Fifty pence coins, the only sterling agreeable to the rectangular box near the baseboard of the door, became a valuable resource to keep on hand. The second unusual characteristic was the fact that there was only one phone in the house, a pay phone located in a phone closet on the second floor. Muniji's room was right next door and Indu came to know that many times in a day he would answer its ringing bell and go running up or down a flight of stairs to find the desired party.

ℰↃ * * * Ↄℰ

"That apparatus took ten, twenty or fifty pence coins or a one pound coin," Indu told me. "At each insertion there would be a break in the connection for a few seconds while it ingested the coin. God forbid you should make a long distance call and have only ten pence coins. The constant interruption for coin deposit could add an incredibly high incoherency factor to the conversation." Indu found this out the hard way just two days after her arrival.

But to jump to that point would leave out one enigmatic anecdote pertaining to the mystical hand of the Guru which involved a phone call from George on Wednesday, the day after they had arrived in London.

ଛ * * * ଓ

It was at their morning visit to the stone that George had promised to call the following evening between seven and nine to further discuss the possibility of meeting in New Brighton. To Indu's dismay, it was decided on Wednesday afternoon that the group would leave at six-thirty that evening to attend a religious Indian *pūjā*, or ceremony, at the home of Muniji's sister. All afternoon Indu prayed that George would call early. At 6:20 p.m., Muniji came into the apartment saying that there was some delay and that he'd be ready to leave shortly after the agreed-upon time.

Indu could not remember ever waiting so anxiously for any call. All she could do was keep glancing at her watch and straining her ears to catch the first possible ring of the phone. When she finally did hear a ring, she went bounding down the stairs only to find that it was for another party. Guruji was patiently sitting in his chair waiting for Muniji as she walked back into the sitting room. She tried to act as though she had just stepped out for some inconsequential reason although she was out of breath from running down the stairs and then climbing back up. She had not told anyone of George's pending call. Despite her pretense, she couldn't help suspecting that Guruji knew exactly what she was up to, but it wasn't something she would ever bring up for discussion with him. All she could do was sit down again and wait, praying that George should call very soon.

But no call came and Muniji announced that he was ready to leave. The apartment door was locked and they all filed down the stairs, Guruji leading. Indu could not believe that there could be any coincidence as powerful as what happened next. The phone rang as Guruji passed by the phone closet. It was seven o'clock. Without hesitation he reached inside and lifted the receiver. It immediately struck Indu as strangely unusual. It made no sense for him to be concerned with a completely unknown caller.

"Why is he picking up the phone now?" she wondered, knowing it could be for any of the twenty people in the house. But then she heard her name and saw him thrusting the phone toward her. Surprise was on everyone's face as they shuffled past her, following Guruji downstairs. It was not an unknown caller after all.

Indu took the receiver and spoke anxiously into it. "Hello?"

"Hello, Indu. It's George. Who was that who answered?"

"It was Guruji. We were just leaving the house and he passed by the phone when it rang." She knew he could not grasp the real significance behind the news. "In fact," she continued, "they're all downstairs waiting."

"Listen, Indu, I'm actually very near to where you're staying."

"You're in London?"

"Yes, Alison and I came in today. I drove down to Farnham to visit relatives of mine and on our way back to the Foundation we came to see some old school friends. Do you think I can see you this evening?"

"It would have to be quite late. We won't be returning until ten o'clock or so."

"Do you have to go?" he asked, sounding disheartened.

"It's for a religious ceremony, George. I can't just back out at the last minute. Is there any way we can meet at around ten-thirty? Will you still be in London?"

"Yes, we'll still be here. Okay, I'll call you back tonight around ten."

"I'll be waiting. I really do want to see you."

"Me, too. Well, bye for now."

"Goodbye."

They had both talked quickly, Indu aware the entire time that Guruji and the others were waiting. She hurried down the stairs and out the side door of the house. She knew they had gone out that door but they were nowhere in sight. She was standing in the driveway to Muniji's house, which was surrounded by a seven-foot-tall stuccoed wall. She ran out to the street's edge and saw them waiting at the bus stop on the corner diagonally opposite Muniji's house. Indu walked up to the group, trying not to look distressed, and stood silently. The others continued their conversations, although Indu suspected that curiosity was high as to who the caller had been. Minutes later the bus was spotted coming toward them. It was then that Guruji turned and asked her, "Who was it?" There was a glistening sparkle in his eyes.

Indu replied, "It was George." She was not certain if Guruji even knew who she meant. But he nodded as though he understood and got on the bus. With that one utterance, everyone knew.

Shakti whispered as she seated herself across from Indu, "I knew it was someone from the Foundation."

Indu gave a casual smile, not yet ready for them to infer too much from the call. Nothing more was said about it until she was walking down the sidewalk toward Muniji's sister's house.

Seeing her near him, Guruji asked another question. "Where is he?"

She answered simply and directly. "George and Alison are in London tonight."

He raised one hand to signal it was enough. Indu said no more.

The ceremony lasted until ten o'clock. Indu had painstakingly watched each minute pass from nine-thirty on. When they finally arrived back at eleven o'clock, she knew she'd missed George's call but she prayed he'd try one more time. She even stood for twenty minutes by the phone. Muniji came downstairs after bidding Guruji good night and asked if she was having difficulty. She shook her head and explained about expecting a call. But by 11:40 p.m., it seemed hopeless. She returned upstairs with a sadness in her heart and went to bed.

The following evening she felt compelled to call George to see if he was still thinking about a rendezvous during the weekend. She also wanted to tell him that they had not returned until much later than expected and that she was sorry she'd missed his call. Shakti had also called the Foundation that day to relay a message from Guruji to Mr. Goodall. Indu had heard her say that with a single twenty pence coin she had been able to put the call through. It seemed surprising that the phone rates should be so low. The Foundation was over forty miles outside London. Not realizing that twenty pence would only give one minute, she carried only sixty pence down to the phone. It was still early in the evening but meditation with Guruji would begin within thirty minutes in a room on the first floor. Muniji had made that room into an Indian temple with a beautifully decorated altar and other devotional pictures and objects displayed. It was also a room far removed from the telephone. Indu knew that any call coming from George would go totally undetected. She hadn't been able to explain to him yet that the phone was a community one, and that if no one answered, it didn't necessarily mean that she wasn't there. Having been unsuccessful at contacting her the night before, if he didn't reach her again that evening, she worried he might become discouraged. Doubt can raise a shadow over a passionate heart, cloaking even the most endearing feelings, or so she feared. She did not want him distraught, thinking she was out of reach.

Gretchen answered the phone. Without identifying herself, Indu asked for George, wondering if Gretchen recognized her American accent. Asking Indu to hold one minute, the line went quiet. Indu imagined, "Poor Gretchen, what if she has to go running around the Foundation to find George?" But she had no sooner finished the thought when George's voice greeted her ears.

"Hello?"

"Hello, George. It's Indu. What happened last night?" A mechanical sound came over the receiver. More money was needed. Indu quickly deposited her other twenty-pence coins, fretfully realizing her mistake.

"Hello? Are you there?"

"Yes, yes, I'm here."

"It got very complicated last night. I couldn't call you back after all."

"You didn't. Well, it doesn't matter anyway. We didn't get back until very late. George, listen, I didn't bring enough money with me. I'm calling from a pay phone."

"Okay, I'll call you back. When's a good time?"

"Tonight. How about around nine-thirty?"

"It might..." The line was cut off.

It had been a very odd exchange, so short and interrupted by the coins, but at least he would call back.

And he did, at exactly nine-thirty. Fortunately, evening program with Guruji had ended at a quarter past nine.

"Too bad we got cut off," she said. She'd felt badly about not having enough change before. "There's only one phone in this house and it's a pay phone. This house is like an apartment building. So if you ever call and a stranger answers, we're staying in apartment number five."

"Apartment five. Right. I'll try to remember."

"So, is everything all right there?" she asked. She noticed a tenseness in his voice. The deep mellowness she loved was missing.

"Indu, it's been an awful mess. Alison is quite upset."

"I was afraid of that. I wondered how you were going to get away last night to come see me with Alison with you."

"Oh, it's worse than that. The friend we stopped to see also happens to be a former girlfriend of mine. She and Alison have become good friends. So there I am, one former girlfriend, one current girlfriend, and I'm trying to get away to see another woman."

"Oh, George . . ."

"They made me feel like an ogre. What's worse is that there was a lot of truth in what they said."

"So what did they say?"

"It seems I've ended up hurting the people who have been closest to me. You see, things didn't end smoothly with Julie either. So suddenly a lot of those hurt feelings came back up and Alison jumped in to vent hers, too."

Indu understood now why his voice was strained. He had been thoroughly pummeled. But was he so wiped out by it that he no longer wanted anything more to do with her? It was a distressing thought but she braced herself for the worst. It was still all in the hands of God, she reminded herself.

"I'm sorry about that. I feel responsible too for Alison's anger. I like her a lot. The timing just isn't very good for us. So, do you still want to try and meet this weekend?"

"Well, I really haven't spent much time with my mother since she's been in the country. I may have been a little overzealous about making those plans."

"Where do your parents live anyway, George?"

"They live in Kenya, just outside Mombasa."

"In Kenya! Your mother is British and your father is Greek and they live in Kenya? But you have such a refined British accent, George."

"Ah, the product of many years in boarding school at Sherbourne."

"Your parents sent you to boarding school in England?"

"It was the only way to get a decent education. From the age of eight I was shipped off."

"Since eight! So young."

"Yes, barely out of nappies."

"Then George, it seems that you should be with your mother. I'm sure she'd be very hurt if you just disappeared during your visit to drive off to Liverpool." It was Indu's attempt to be stoic.

"That's what I was thinking, too. To walk in and say 'hi' and then 'bye' would definitely not be the loving-son thing to do. But maybe after giving my mother and aunt two days, I could break away on Sunday and see you for a bit."

"Well, except, George, we're supposed to leave on Sunday to come back to London. I don't know yet what the schedule will be."

"Can you give me the phone number and address of where you'll be?"

She had thought ahead of time to bring it with her and she recited it over the phone.

"I'll give you a ring then," he said, "and we'll just have to take it from there."

"Look, George, don't put yourself in another difficult position. If it doesn't work out, then that's okay. At least we tried."

"Let's wait and see. Right now, I don't know what's going to happen."

When she hung up the phone, she could only hope she'd see him again. By the end of the three hour train ride to Liverpool the next afternoon, she had reconciled herself to the fact that uncertainty would continue to shadow her love for George. Obviously the conflicts in his life would have to be resolved before their relationship would have a chance. What that would mean, she wasn't sure. One thing that sorely came to light was that he probably had more reservations about the ideal nature of their match than she ever would. She trusted her gut feelings and they were telling her that he was the one she should be with, that there was a reason for their coming together, although as of yet it was intangible to her. But she could easily perceive that he, on the other hand, would have many doubts. Not that it would mean he loved her less, but he simply wouldn't know what to do about it.

"He must resolve things with Alison, and that alone could take several months," she thought during the train ride. "For me to cause any sudden break between them would bring bad karma down on my head. That's not what I want. He must also give proper consideration to his mother. One cannot go through life hurting those loved the most."

$\wp$ * * * $\wp$

The hum of the train, the jostling motion, the towns and countryside gliding past had all given her a neutral framework in which to watch her objective and rational mind. She told me that she knew what she was doing. She was letting her mind build a shield around her heart, a shield that would be needed to confront the reservations which he would inevitably put before her, the decision he would make regarding his relationship with her, and the disappointment her heart would feel being separated from him.

She said her extraordinary sensibility had further influenced her thinking on the train: "Why should I interfere with his life anyway? Besides, the relationship can happen only if he truly wants it. The hard fact is that the proverbial ball will be in his court." These thoughts had given her a strange solace, putting her at ease with herself and with the world flying past the window.

$\wp$ * * * $\wp$

Margaret and Paul's house in New Brighton was beautiful. They called it "Reliance House." It was painted light green with white shutters and stood four stories tall. From her bedroom on the fourth floor, she could stand at the window and look out upon the Irish Sea. Evening meditation had included just their small group. The workshop wouldn't start until the next morning. Those who came to study yoga with Margaret and Paul had been contacted about the upcoming intensive with a "true yogi."

Guruji had retired for the night. Indu stood in the living room talking to Paul and another couple, Bill and Claire, who had also attended the program at Ickwell, when Margaret stuck her head in the doorway saying there was a phone call for Indu. Indu hadn't even heard the phone ring.

"Hello again." It was George.

"George! I certainly didn't expect any call tonight. Where are you?"

"I'm in Chester at my aunt's house. How are you?"

His voice was warm and lovely, a notable difference from their last conversation. Foremost in her mind were the thoughts she'd had on the train. "I'm okay. We just finished a lovely meditation with Guruji."

"So do you have some idea about the schedule for tomorrow?"

"Tomorrow?" She wondered why he was asking about plans for Saturday. "Well, there are two sessions: one from ten to noon and another from two o'clock to five," she said. "I think I heard Uma say that there would be a crystal meditation in the morning and rebirthing and massage in the afternoon."

"Indu, if I came up tomorrow, would you have some time to see me? I really need to know because if you won't, then it would make more sense for me to stay here."

"George, you're thinking of coming tomorrow?"

"Only if you can guarantee that you'll have time."

"George, if you get here, there will definitely be time."

Having heard her name mentioned and knowing full well who it was, Uma walked by and signaled that Indu should give George her regards.

"George, you've just been greeted silently by another member of our group. Can you guess who?"

There was a moment's pause before he answered, "Was it from Uma?"

"You're absolutely right. So you are a little psychic, huh?" She was happy he had gotten it right.

"No, I just felt a nice connection with her at the Foundation so I could only imagine it might be from her," he replied with modest discretion.

She mentally noted his comment, thinking, "So, he felt something toward her and she frankly admitted having an admiring eye for him. Good grief, maybe we're all three connected in some way."

She snapped back to attention. George was saying, "So how would it be if I arrived around eleven o'clock tomorrow morning?"

"George, I've been thinking a lot about our situation since your last call."

He quickly responded, "What have you thought?"

"Look, George, you've got to work through things with Alison first before we can ever figure out what's going on between us. It simply wouldn't be good karma for me to interfere with that," she said, repeating almost verbatim her thoughts on the train. "So please don't you and Alison give me bad karma."

He laughed and replied, "As far as it is within my power, I definitely won't do that."

That wasn't telling her what she wanted to hear. "Now, what does that mean?" she brooded momentarily. "Does it mean he's planning to end things with Alison or does he simply want to see me one more time before they both go driving off to Germany?" The ambiguity piqued her heart.

She decided to continue by voicing her concerns about his mother. "It's important to spend time with her, George. I'm sure she misses seeing you. So really you should probably be with her."

"Indu, there's no problem there. I checked it out with her. If I'd gotten a funny feeling about it I wouldn't have planned it."

"All right, then. If you want to come tomorrow, I'll be most happy to see you."

"Goody, goody!" was his happy reply.

It was such a silly thing for him to say and yet it struck her as sweet. Often as a child, she had said those very words at the prospect of anything that was to bring her happiness.

"But Indu, can you give me the address again?"

For some reason she hesitated to ask anyone in the other room for the address. She decided instead to run up the three flights of stairs and get it from her own address book. She returned to the phone, breathless. It was set that he would arrive around eleven o'clock the following morning. She hung up the phone on the edge of elation. He was going to come see her after all. She had tried to be rationally objective, voicing all her concerns. Her heart had acquiesced and nobly tolerated the assault of her logical deliberation. Could it not help rejoicing in its ultimate triumph? Before everyone went off to bed, the entire house knew that George would be coming. Her composure and casual air could not hide the glow on her cheeks and to her bemusement, everyone seemed quite pleased to see it.

SEVENTEEN

~

You can plan and plan and the unexpected will change everything. This Indu profoundly pondered while standing at the bow of a Merseyside ferry. She waved farewell to a group of actors standing on the pier. As they waited for the movie camera to get into position, they waved back at the young woman in white who was slowly pulling out into the Mersey Strait which separated New Brighton from Liverpool. She watched the pier and the actors grow smaller and smaller with distance.

It was eight-thirty. Early that morning Claire and Bill had suggested that a quick visit to Liverpool might enjoyably fill the time before Guruji's program began. The only one who had been interested was Indu. She stood on the bow feeling in a time warp. Even upon driving up to the pier, the three of them had been amused to see so many vintage model cars parked at the dock entrance. When they began seeing people wearing beautifully stylish apparel from the 1940s, they knew something was amiss. At the ticket desk they learned that the pier was being used as a film location for a TV movie, the title of which amused Indu even more: "American Dreamer."

೮೦ * * * ೮೪

"That's exactly what I felt like, an American dreamer, as I waved to the people in mid-calf straight skirts, heels and fur wraps, top hats, overcoats and canes. I had to blink hard to shake the feeling that somewhere I'd lost forty years," she told me.

"How easy it is to get caught up in the images before us," she continued. "When we die, all images disappear. They no longer exist. We so heartily believe in sense-perceived images during the entirety of our waking, conscious lives. And except for death, the only other reprieve we have from them is in deep sleep or meditation. And because of our belief in these images, we endure lives bound by the senses."

"It can only be in dropping this belief—in letting go of the images—that we can realize our true form, as Guruji tried so hard to make us understand. In that absolute inner silence, there can be no images." Indu knew this to be true. On several fleeting occasions she had felt the immense freedom of bouncing beyond the mental barrier. There had been nothing there and everything had felt complete. She knew she was not on any blind path to salvation. She had felt that release. It was just as Guruji had described.

"The proof is in the pudding," she said to me, laughing as the expression popped into her head.

℘ * * * ℭ

She got a wet view of Liverpool. It began drizzling as soon as they disembarked from the boat. But she was glad to have gone, just to get a feel of the famed city from whence the idolized Beatles had emerged. As she understood it, the city was under great economic strain and unemployment was higher than in most cities in southern England. Yet not for a minute did it leave her mind that within hours she would be seeing George again, although she made no mention of it to Claire and Bill.

At ten o'clock, back at Reliance House, they gathered with about twenty other people down in the meditation room. This room was a renovated basement, accessed separately from the house. It had been designed with a separate entrance so that classes taught would not impinge on the private family life of Margaret and Paul, who had two teenage children.

Indu had been absorbed in Guruji's talk when she caught a nod from Mangala indicating the back of the room. When she looked, she could see only his head, for he had already sat down. But when their eyes met, she felt the same rush. Those glorious eyes! He grinned when he saw her and she flashed a smile back. It would have been impossible for them not to show the happiness they felt. Although he couldn't see it, there was a vacant seat next to her. She motioned for him to come and he did. As he silently slipped in beside her, she tried not to show any emotion, not even extending her hand. Sitting straight in front of them was Guruji, who gave George a welcoming nod while he continued talking.

At the start of the program, Uma had handed out crystals to all the guests. Just before the guided meditation, Guruji stood with a crystal in his hand and came forward to give it to George. Indu was surprised by the gesture. She had been just about to give George her own.

After the program ended, everyone filed out and walked back to the house for lunch. Indu and George stood placidly together on the driveway outside the kitchen door showing no signs of amorous intent. Just the fact that he was there was enough to show the serious interest between them. Possibly suspecting that they were feeling shyly uneasy, Uma stopped in front of George and expressed a strong desire for a "hello hug." Indu stood watching as George happily obliged. She patiently waited until their embrace ended before she pointed out that she herself had not yet been so honored. That was all it took. Feeling no longer awkward about what others would think, they were finally able to hold each other once again.

"Lunch is served," Margaret called from the kitchen.

"Are you hungry?" Indu asked him.

"No," he said slowly, and then sniffing the air, he moved toward the kitchen door. "But I might just take a quick gander." Indu followed him in. He turned to her and asked, "How about you, could you eat a little?"

Indu shook her head in resignation. "Afraid I haven't had an appetite in several days. But you go ahead."

"Let's eat later, then. Can we go somewhere to talk?"

It was twelve-thirty. The rebirthing would start at two o'clock. They had an hour and a half before they would both want to be back. Indu knew Guruji would want her assistance and George was looking forward to another session.

They slipped out the front door, hand in hand, and started walking down to the beach. "You know, George, I didn't expect to see you at all this weekend, particularly not after that last phone call in London."

"Indu, I'm so sorry about that," he said, squeezing her hand. "I know I was terribly abrupt. There was just so much confusion at the time, with Alison, with trying to make plans. And you were there in the middle of it. I mean, I wanted to see you and suddenly everything got so complicated. I knew I was making you feel miserable and I didn't know what to do. I was feeling miserable myself."

With those words she could forgive him anything. "Where is Alison now?"

"She's in London. She went in to see Julie again. I'm supposed to meet her at the train on Tuesday. She's really being very strong about this. In fact, this is probably a good experience for her."

"George, that's an awful thing to say. It sounds terribly cruel." It really had struck her as a condescending remark. She sensed right away that the topic was a sensitive one.

"Look, Indu. I don't want to hurt anyone. What I meant about Alison was this: In her past relationships, she's always had the upper hand. Men did what she wanted. They adored her. Right now, she has another boyfriend in Israel who cares about her very much and yet she chose to come and be with me."

"How did you two meet in the first place?"

"She's also from Kenya. There was a party with some friends and she was there. And I have to admit, the attraction was initially a physical one. But then she decided to come to England, too, and things between us got more intense."

"So, George, tell me, exactly how have you left things with her?"

"I've told her that nothing has changed in the plans as far as I'm concerned. I'm still going to Germany and she is still quite welcome to join me. She said probably after that she might go visit that boyfriend in Israel. I'll still go on to Greece and then I don't know what next. I honestly don't know what the best thing is to do in a situation like this except be as honest as I can. I'm trying, I'm really trying."

"I know you are, George. I know it can't be easy. I certainly didn't plan for anything to happen between us. It simply did. It's far beyond me to understand it."

"That's just it, Indu. I can't understand it either. There's just so much about me you don't know. I'm not who you think I am. There are all sorts of shadows lurking in my past. I'm not the sort someone like you should be getting involved with."

"What do you mean, 'someone like me'? Who do you think I am?"

"You're a serious, disciplined, devout woman. You're dedicated to a spiritual path, and it's beautiful to see. And I simply don't fit anywhere into that picture. I'm not on any spiraling spiritual quest. I don't even know if I have the yearning to be. It's all too new to me. And here you've been doing it how many years?"

"I've been with Guruji for ten."

"You see. Ten years ago, I was a crazy young kid, in trouble a lot of the time. Not for anything horrifically bad, just mischievous. Don't know that I've gotten much better in my twenties. Sure, basic values I've got. I don't steal, I don't intentionally hurt anyone, I abide by the law usually, I try to be a good son and a good brother to my sister. I want to be happy, and pretty much I am happy, but it's in a carefree sort of way."

By this time they had reached the beach. The Irish Sea was splashing over their feet, causing them to sink deeper and deeper into the sand. Indu stood facing him, her fingers linked behind his neck. "George, I don't know how to put this without sounding like a crazy mystic. But whether you realize it or not, you have a pure heart. I felt it right away. Don't you know that God is infinitely more concerned with the motivation behind what someone does than with the action itself? Tell me that your motives are impure, that you callously ignore others' feelings, that you intentionally engage in flagrant behavior, that everything you do is for selfish reasons."

"Indu, you know that's not the case. But that's not the point."

"But it is the point, George. Many apparently pious people are doing just that. One great teacher used to say, 'Beware of pious egoists wearing dayglow orange.' The religious movement is filled with people with whom I wouldn't spend five minutes. They profess to believe in God and then viciously condemn the person next to them and God save the person who lives across the street. It's like the fortune cookie I once got. It said, 'In God we trust. All others must pay cash.' The hypocrisy is unbelievable. So you've had some adventures, run around, pulled some pranks, but there are clear signs, George, which show you are on God's path."

He seemed abashed to hear her describe him so resolutely. With a furtive glance her way, he asked, "What sort of signs do you mean?"

"The most obvious are your radiant eyes, although it is difficult for me to be totally unbiased here." He leaned toward her and placed a warm kiss on her lips. After the interruption she continued. "I mean it, George. The eyes definitely reflect the heart. Another is your voice. There's a quality to it that reflects even more about your past lives than the present. It is written in scripture that those who have been true followers of God will have a genuine vibrancy to their voice. You, my sweet, have got it."

"No, no, Indu. You're painting too rosy a picture."

"You see, you're also charmingly modest."

"Now that's enough," he retorted, finding it hard to hide a grin.

"One more thing, then I'll stop."

He took an intolerant deep breath, but he was listening.

"Your juggling, George. You may say you're not following a spiritual path, but I see your juggling as being your meditation. It takes an enormous amount of concentration to juggle for a long time. It takes discipline to practice. Doesn't it have a soothing effect on your mind?"

"If I'm alone it does. If I'm giving a show, though, I'm very self-conscious, always trying to think what to do or say next."

"Nonetheless, you've been doing it for four years. To get as good as you are has taken a lot of work, a lot of practice and a lot of concentration. I think you may even be pursuing it because it does put you in an altered state, whether you consciously recognize it or not. I think you've been searching for that just as I've been."

"You make it sound so natural, Indu, so natural that we should be together." There was acquiescence in the way he spoke. She wondered if he had really thought he could convince her otherwise.

As a deliberate tease, she asked, "You know what Guruji says, don't you?"

"You know much more than I," he replied, assuming another serious statement was coming.

"He says, 'You know you are enlightened when you know you are a first-class fool.' I'd say it looks like you're very near enlightenment."

He grabbed her behind the neck and shook her gently. "Is that what you think, you crazy mystic?"

She broke from his grip and ran down the beach. He pursued closely behind. When he caught her by the hand, she wrapped her arms around him. They stood for a moment and tightly embraced. "I don't know who you are," she thought. "All I know is that I love you."

They walked up a ramp to the top of the sea wall where there were cement benches. As she sat, she felt the relief of being shielded from the wind. The sun's warmth penetrated her skin. After sitting a moment in silence, he again began to speak disparagingly of his character.

"The only thing I may have going for me is I can usually recognize good criticism."

"So who's been giving this 'good criticism'?" she asked skeptically.

"Nhoj and Alison."

"And what is it that they find necessary to criticize you about?"

"They say I should be more outgoing and less reserved."

Her outburst was immediate. "Hogwash! They should mind their own business."

George was taken aback by her stern words and came rushing to their defense. "But Indu, I agree with them. It was constructive criticism. I really do find it a great challenge to do the street theater. I don't have the natural flair that Nhoj has."

"George, Nhoj is a natural extrovert. That doesn't give him any right to criticize you for being more of an introvert. You can't say one is better than the other. You can't."

"Well, you can when it comes to performing. I really think it's something I can work on."

"Okay. If you're dead set on doing street theater, and if Nhoj was making that observation to try and help your performance, then fine. But just to blatantly say that someone should be more outgoing is like trying to push everyone into the same mold. You simply can't do it."

"And Alison says that I'm inhibited in public, that I don't exhibit any emotion, that I stay very controlled."

"But George, for the past hour you've been expressing your feelings and affection beautifully to me, and we're in public. And when we were back at the house in front of everyone you gave both Uma and me exceptionally expressive hugs. If you ask me, I see nothing inhibited in you." She didn't mention that she had noticed at the Foundation that he had rarely reached out toward Alison. She had viewed his stolidity then as a reflection on the relationship, not on him personally.

George had to acknowledge that what she said was true. With her, he had felt no inhibition, except perhaps only when they were both feeling shyly awkward.

Indu boldly continued. "George, don't get me wrong. I like both Nhoj and Alison very much. But there is something I learned as I began to grow with meditation—my close friends could no longer understand me. I simply was not conforming to their ideas of socially acceptable behavior. And that was because my lifestyle and thinking had changed. As a consequence, I realized I had to let go of a lot of friendships, friendships that I had striven to maintain for years under unusually tenuous circumstances. Scriptures state that one must be careful with whom one chooses to associate because there can be negative influences. It's better to be alone, and even better to be with those who pull you up spiritually."

"Indu, they're my friends. I know they meant well."

She realized she may have gotten carried away delivering her sermon. She had not meant to be judgmental of his friends. She stayed silent for a moment and then took his arm and said, "That's fine. Whatever you want. But I have to say I like you just the way you are." Their eyes met and he seemed to bask in her unfathomable love.

In that innocent abandon, he asked, "Do you think I need a Guru?"

Indu leaned back against the cement wall trying to think how best to answer. "One does not need a Guru, but having one can help, especially if *kuṇḍalinī* starts to manifest and other strange experiences happen, such as out-of-the-body experiences or visions or sounds. You can feel you're going crazy unless someone is there to reassure you. None of those things really apply to me and yet my whole life has been turned around by knowing Guruji. But the Guru-disciple relationship is hard to understand even for me. It's unlike anything else. I would never say that you should have a Guru. But I would only hope that you would never feel jealous of my devotion to Guruji. I don't relate to him as a man. It's so far beyond the physical realm."

"Yes, I can understand that. It's just that I don't know if I should search for a Guru. I just don't know. I haven't been. I haven't felt any need for one. But I've never really thought about it. I feel so ignorant."

"Well, my feeling is that Guruji has some connection with you whether you want a Guru or not. But it's nothing to worry about. In fact, you've probably met many hidden Gurus and not even known it."

"Mmmm," he murmured, "so are you a hidden Guru in my life?" He raised her hand to kiss it.

"Yes, as you are for me," she replied.

"And to think, we really don't even know each other. Just count: seven hours by the stone, four brief phone calls and the past hour. And yet, I feel something...something..." he said as he again looked deeply into her eyes.

"If either one of us ever figures out what that 'something' is, we'll have solved one of life's greatest mysteries! And my love," she said, looking down at her watch. "It hasn't been the past hour but the past hour and a half."

"It's already two o'clock? How can time go by so fast? We're going to have to jaunt all the way back in order to make it in time."

"Let's 'jaunt' on then," she said, reiterating his word but not sure if he caught her tease.

They made it back in time. Indu walked to the front of the room and George lay down in the back. She had no intention of approaching him during this session either, although how different the circumstances now were. Quite a few present were older women. Indu began walking from one person to another, placing one hand over the abdomen and the other on the forehead. After the third or fourth round of breathing, she stood up feeling dizzy, knowing it was probably largely due to not having eaten. She stayed light-headed throughout the entire session.

ℬ * * * ℭ

One time, as she was moving to the next person, she saw Guruji sitting by George's side. He was pinching the bridge of George's nose. Instinctively, although she wasn't sure why, she'd turned away. "I felt it best to let the Guru do his work without my eyes intruding. I wouldn't have understood anyway," she said to me.

Interestingly enough, George had told her at a later time that something very peculiar did happen after Guruji left his side. George had continued the breathing and then had suddenly become overwhelmed with a tremendous sexual feeling. He had prayed that no one would look his way and notice that he was aroused. He felt dumbfounded as to why it had come. "I did not try to give him any explanation at that time when he told me about it," Indu said to me, "but I knew it was a significant indication. Guruji had simply hit his *kuṇḍalinī* powerfully. One very great spiritual teacher wrote in his autobiography that during some of his deepest meditations he would discover he had a throbbing erection after being in the most sublime state. It was the *kuṇḍalinī* energy and he knew it. It was simply hitting the lower energy center in the body before moving up the spinal column to the brain. But can you imagine, poor George, not understanding anything and being in such a state through most of the session?" But it had been another signal to her that his energy channels were open and receptive to the Guru's touch, that he must have done great spiritual work in a past life.

ℬ * * * ℭ

At the end of the session, Indu felt her hands vibrating with tingles. She stood at the front of the room with her arms down at her sides. She suspected a lot of energy had been moving through her. She knew it was the work of Guruji. He looked toward her, seeing her standing thus, and gently smiled. As everyone was getting up, three women approached her all at once and asked her name. Two of them had opened their eyes during the breathing and she had given them beaming smiles.

"It was such a wonderful experience. Peace. I've never felt such peace. You have a marvelous touch, dear. Here," one of them said, putting a pen in Indu's hand and holding out a pad of paper. "Could you write your name here? I don't ever want to forget it."

Indu was truly bewildered about what they thought she had done. She could only imagine that she had somehow channeled energy from Guruji to them. She obliged by writing her name. She'd never received such attention before and she was very eager to thank them for their kind remarks and slip past to find George.

He was also engaged in a conversation in the back of the room so she gestured as she walked past that she'd be waiting for him outside. She ascended the stairs and found the back driveway much quieter. After the session, there had been such a rush of energy that everyone had started talking at once. Several others came up the stairs from the meditation room and then one of the three ladies appeared. She came and took hold of Indu's hands.

"There's a healing in your hands. You know that, don't you?" She reached up and stroked Indu's cheek.

Indu could only try to deny it. "Oh, I don't really know anything."

"Then I do," the woman ardently replied. "You are a saintly soul. God bless you."

The last thing Indu wanted was for George to hear or see any of this unusual attention. "This is something better left unspoken. I don't know that he's ready to hear about mystical channeling of the Guru's energy. The fellow isn't even sure what a Guru is, let alone what a Guru does," she thought.

She earnestly returned the same blessing to the woman. "And may God bless you."

It seemed the right thing to say, for the woman smiled angelically up at her and went on her way. Thirty seconds later, George appeared.

"I was wondering when you'd come out," she said as casually as possible, not letting on that anything unusual had happened. But she felt dizzy. Inwardly she was spinning from relating on so many levels: with George, with the woman, and with Guruji.

"Sorry to keep you waiting. I stepped into the loo while I was down there." Indu already had loo, the informal term for bathroom, on her British words list. "But I've got to tell you," he continued in the same breath, "that I'm absolutely famished. Shall we go partake of the feast we missed earlier? Gosh, I hope there's something left."

"Come on," she said, thinking food might help her, too. "I'm sure we can find something."

There was indeed plenty of food. It was quiet in the house, for the others were enjoying tea and fruit in the basement. There would be only a short break before the next class started. It would be Swedish massage and Indu doubted that Guruji would object to her absence.

They opened the refrigerator and found four containers covered with plastic wrap. "Oh, boy, we're in luck," he boyishly exclaimed. She liked seeing him so delighted. She fixed a small plate for herself although she still wasn't really hungry.

Margaret came in and Indu quickly apologized. "Hope you don't mind we're raiding your kitchen."

"My goodness, you kids go right ahead. That's what the food is here for." She picked up a book from the counter and disappeared out the door.

"They've been so kind to us. They're a lovely couple," she said, referring to Margaret and Paul.

"Yes, they are. I enjoyed getting to know them at the Foundation."

Indu set her plate on the table and then suddenly remembered that she'd left her sweater in the meditation room. She wanted to get it before the next class started. She told George to go ahead and start eating.

Downstairs, people were milling around carrying teacups. Guruji was sitting at the front of the room. She respectfully nodded to him as she retrieved her sweater. But before she could turn away he motioned for her to come toward him. "So, I won't be able to sneak out after all," she thought. She would never consider opposing any request from him. She only hoped there would be some way to tell George about the change in plans.

"Yes, Guruji. Is there something you need?" From the look in his eyes she expected a question about her obvious desire to disappear.

Instead, he reached into his pocket and produced a small brass statue. It was a figure of a seated Buddha. As he handed it to her he said, "Give this to your friend." That was all. He held up an open palm indicating that she was free to go. An ocean of gratitude flooded her heart. He was again giving his blessing for her to spend time with George.

"Thank you, Guruji. I'll give it to him right away." Words to express anything more failed her. He seemed to know her heart anyway. He simply smiled and looked down at something on the table in front of him.

George was sitting alone in the kitchen, well on his way to finishing his entire plate of food. Indu sat down next to him at the end of the table and looked at him silently.

"Is everything all right?" he asked, keenly aware of the silence.

"Yes. More than all right. Something just happened."

"You know, you do look different, even more radiantly beautiful. What happened?" He had a bright twinkle in his eyes.

"Guruji asked that I give this to you." She placed the small Buddha in his hand.

"He did?" he said, examining it closely. "How extraordinarily kind. Well, I shall keep it always. So maybe he doesn't mind that I'm here after all. I was a little afraid that he might."

"No, I would say he definitely doesn't mind," Indu replied.

She could see he was both pleased and relieved. Setting the little figure on the table, he got up to fill his plate again. He then covered the food platters and placed them back in the refrigerator. She watched his every move as she tried to eat the few bites on her plate. After eating, they washed the dishes, he pocketed the Buddha and they went into the living room.

The family dog came in behind them and positioned himself at George's feet. George was glad to rub its ears and stroke its back. Indu wondered how she was going to explain to him about the sensitivity of her skin and the need for him to wash his hands before he even so much as touched her cheek.

හ * * * ෆ

She told me that later in a letter, George would recount the incident, describing that before she had spoken a word, he had known there was something wrong. He had "felt" something from her. He'd gone on to marvel at how much of their communication was unspoken. Indu had recognized this at Ickwell but she never told him of the time he had turned "unconsciously" when her eyes had been riveted on the back of his head or the time he had appeared out of the night to see her sitting on the ledge by the kitchen door. Again, it was the mystery of their connection.

හ * * * ෙ

He readily agreed to wash his hands. "Indu, I do want to hold you and of course I'll wash my hands, but I can't hold you here. Anyone might come walking in. Could we go up to your room? Would it be inappropriate?"

"No, it would be much better than here. The only problem is that I share it with Shakti. But at least for an hour or so she'll be busy in the basement." He washed his hands and they reached the third floor unnoticed by anyone.

"My God, you didn't climb up and down all three flights to get the address when I called last night, did you?" She nodded affirmatively. "But you weren't gone even thirty seconds. No wonder you could barely talk when you got back to the phone. I didn't think you could move that fast. I'd actually like to see you do it."

"I doubt I could do it again. I took the steps three at a time all the way up." She was pleased her feat had not gone unnoticed by him. She opened the door to her room and they went in.

EIGHTEEN

~

It felt wonderful to be alone and without the likelihood of any intrusion. She led him over to the window. "Come and see the view," she said. They stood arm in arm looking out over the sloping rooftops to the distant waters of the Irish Sea. The silence between them was peaceful. That peace pulled them closer and closer until they were in a tight embrace, his lips soon finding hers. And then another hug and another kiss and somewhere time passed.

Finally feeling a weariness in his legs, George sat down on her bed. Indu settled on his lap, her arm around his neck. After another span of warm silence, a question came to Indu's mind.

"George, does Alison know you're here with me now?"

"No. I didn't tell her that I was going to see you," he said.

Indu was greatly relieved. The idea of Alison feeling hurt and abandoned on that weekend when she and George were feeling so much love and affection for each other made her heart cringe.

"I didn't lie to her, though. I wouldn't want to do that. And she'll probably find out anyway, knowing Alison. But you really don't need to worry about her." He could see the pained look in her eyes. "Alison is a very tenacious woman. She usually knows what she wants, when, how and why. For a long time she's been clinging to her relationship with me, but not for the reasons you'd think. It's as though she's latched onto me out of an insecurity, not because of a deep connection she feels to me. And if I'm not there, she'll probably latch onto someone else. The best thing would be if somehow through this whole thing she could come to terms with what it is she inwardly needs."

"Be careful, George, not to rationalize away all her hurt feelings. This must be very difficult for her."

"Don't get me wrong. Indu. I love Alison. I don't want to see her sad. I don't want to be the cause of any unhappiness for her. Above all, I want to stay her friend." Indu felt a pang of apprehension when she heard him say that he loved Alison.

"How silly of me," she thought. "He should love her, being intimate friends and all. It would be even more hypocritical if he had spent all that time with her and not loved her in some way. I suppose he's trying to say that there are different kinds of love. There's the compassionate love and then there's the tender and ecstatic love, and God knows how many others. Love is not an uncomplicated thing. And you throw in a little karma..."

"Indu, did I lose you?"

"No, I'm right here. I just want things to work out for everyone."

"I think they are. That's what I wanted to say."

Indu heard footsteps coming up the stairs while they were talking. She sat perfectly poised, not intending to move even if it was Shakti. Just after George finished speaking the door opened.

Surprised, Shakti apologized for intruding. "Sorry, didn't mean to barge in. I didn't know you were up here."

Indu and George sat shyly a minute longer, hoping it was obvious that nothing too intimate had been interrupted. Realizing that Shakti wanted to change clothes, Indu removed herself from George's lap and he made a gentlemanly retreat. Indu stayed behind to talk to Shakti and find out what was happening next.

"We've all been invited to a new Hindu temple in Liverpool to see the performance of a well-known Indian dancer," Shakti explained as she slipped off her yoga pants and shirt and freshened up at the sink in the corner of their room.

Indu began thinking quickly. "How can I possibly get out of this one without upsetting anyone, particularly Guruji?" But she began brushing her hair and applying lipstick in case she had to go. She already had on a soft white cotton skirt and a flouncy long-sleeved white blouse. It wasn't dressy but it looked attractive. She decided not to change.

Shakti came up next to her at the mirror and said, "I hope you won't take this the wrong way, but I think Guruji brought you to England just so you'd meet George." Indu could tell that in her own tactful way, Shakti was trying to say that she saw Indu's alliance with George as one of unquestionable destiny.

Indu laughed at the delivery of her statement and said, "You know, I've been wondering that same thing, too."

Ready to head back downstairs, Shakti's last words were, "If you're going to come, we're leaving in the next five minutes," followed by a wink.

"Well, it doesn't look like Shakti will raise too many objections if I stay behind," she thought. She picked up her purse and went next door to find Uma still hurriedly getting dressed.

"Don't want to disturb you, but could I ask one question?"

"Sure, darling," Uma said, continuing her preparations. "What is it?"

"Do you think it would cause any problem if I didn't go this evening?"

A knowing smile planted on her face, she replied, "It probably won't make that much difference to anyone." She paused a second and added, "Is that what you wanted to hear?"

Indu was taken aback by her bluntness and quickly responded, "Not at all. I really want your honest opinion before I approach Guruji with the idea. I don't know how important this thing is tonight, or who invited us, or what's been said about it."

"Well, my honest opinion is that it certainly feels right that you and George should be together."

Indu gave Uma a one-armed hug across the shoulders and hurried downstairs. Margaret was sitting in the living room visiting with her husband and George. Indu walked in and knelt down next to her. Seeing the inquisitive look in Indu's eyes, she leaned forward to confer privately. The men carried on the conversation between themselves.

In a half whisper, Indu asked, "Margaret, would you have any objection if George and I stayed behind in the house? We haven't really had much time together."

"Why, not at all," Margaret graciously replied. She made a motion to stand up. "Let me just get the spare keys for you. They're out in the kitchen cupboard." Once in the kitchen, she gave one instruction. "If you do go out, please just lock the dog in the kitchen. When he gets lonely, he tends to make little puddles, if you know what I mean."

"Of course. I don't think we'll be going out. But if we do, we'll lock the dog and the house," Indu said.

Margaret smiled, then remembered one other thing. "Just so you won't be startled by any strange sounds, at around nine-thirty my father will be coming in. But he has his own key and will probably go straight back to his room and go to sleep." Indu had heard earlier that Margaret's father was living with them but she hadn't yet met him.

"Thanks, Margaret. I appreciate this."

"You two have a nice evening. You deserve it." Indu could easily glean from her comments that Margaret also seemed to approve of George.

During their discussion in the kitchen, however, Guruji had already slipped down the hallway and out the door. Uma informed her, "Guruji is sitting out in the car, darling."

"Oh, dear," was all Indu could think to say, standing in the hallway with a look of perplexity across her face.

Uma held up two sweaters in front of her. "Which one do you think will look better with this outfit?"

Looking them over quickly, Indu replied, "The bright orange one looks more dressy, if that's any help."

Turning back to inspect the colors in the hall mirror, Uma choose the bright orange one. As she went out the front door, she again looked at Indu's face and gave a hearty smile, seeming amused by Indu's love-torn heart.

Indu stood frozen in place, not knowing what to do. She wanted to say something to Guruji but the timing just didn't feel right. But not to have his blessing to remain behind also didn't feel right.

In the middle of her quandary, Uma poked her head around the front door. "Just mentioned to Guruji that you wanted to stay behind," she said, "And his reply was 'Okay, okay, okay!' Don't think you need to worry anymore." She blew a kiss and disappeared back out the door.

"I have his blessing, thank God," she thought, feeling in that instant a heavy anxiety vanish from her heart. Margaret came down the stairs, patted Indu's arm and called her husband to follow her to the car. Paul emerged from the living room and waved a farewell as he closed the front door behind him. Totally oblivious to any of the ordeal she'd just gone through, George appeared cool and calm in the living room doorway. Indu backed around into the kitchen and sat down at the table. George was right behind her.

With joy in his eyes, he said, "We're actually all alone with the whole house to ourselves, and no one else around."

She looked up at him, knowing that their time together was a gift from heaven. With total and complete privacy, they went back up to her bedroom. They closed the door and stood at the foot of the bed looking into each other's eyes, her arms on his shoulders, his around her waist.

"George, do you know I was engaged once?"

"Was this recently?" he asked, obvious surprise in his voice.

"No, when I was twenty-three." It may not have been recent for her but his twenty-third year had just passed and he had been nowhere near ready to consider marriage.

"Who was he and why didn't you?" he asked. It must have intrigued him that she hadn't mentioned anything about this at the stone.

"He was a graduate student, like I was, working on a Ph.D. in organic chemistry. Somehow, after we were engaged, I got pregnant. Needless to say it wasn't what either one of us had planned. Then before I knew what was happening, I miscarried."

"How awful for you, Indu." His empathy was genuine.

"Really, it was a blessing in disguise because after that, something changed in our relationship. Two months later we broke off the engagement. I realized then that I carried the family trait to miscarry. My mother miscarried once and had to work hard to keep my sister and me. Modern science may have a lot to do with me being here." She meant it as a joke but he wasn't laughing. She went on, "My grandmother miscarried six times. It's probably not the best genetic trait to have but it did save me from what no doubt would have been an unpropitious marriage. Fortunately, though, we did stay friends."

"Are you still in contact with him?"

"No. He finished his doctorate and just before he left town, he came to say goodbye. He was heading off somewhere to do post-graduate work."

"You know, I can feel your life hasn't been an easy one. I don't think you've enjoyed yourself much."

Indu thought a moment. "My life has been kept on a level keel, for the most part. I certainly haven't suffered terribly. My childhood was happy and normal, adolescence a bit rocky trying to do well in school and fit in with the right group. But my nature has always been serious. And after I met Guruji, I began analyzing everything."

"Ugh, I'd go crazy if I analyzed everything in my life. I like to just live in the moment and take what comes," he said.

"Well," she observed, "our natures are contrasting but not necessarily opposing." She had already noticed that he was much more easygoing than she.

He concurred. "As a pair, we might not be too bad. I probably do need to be more serious about certain things in life and I could help you see more of the fun-loving side." He seemed amazed by his own words. "I mean I'm just saying that it can be very healthy to match up with someone of opposite character."

"It would keep things interesting," she said, aware that he had suddenly hesitated to state too boldly what their personal future prospects might be.

She pulled back from his arms and plopped down on the bed with her head on the pillow, feeling relaxed and at ease. George, on the other hand, came and sat with apparent uncertainty on the edge of the bed. He hesitated only a moment before leaning over with a gentle, loving kiss. He then curled up next to her and they held each other. With his head on her shoulder, she felt sublimely happy. He was dearer to her than she could ever describe to him. She herself still did not understand why. The sun's warm glow through the window soon turned cool as the gloaming approached.

"Indu, the sun is setting. Do you want to meditate?" he asked.

She thought it was a lovely idea. She stepped into Uma's room to look for a candle and returned to find him sitting cross-legged on the floor with his back to the window and the Buddha sitting to his left on the carpet. She placed the candle between them, repeating the sunset mantras as she lit the flame. "How nice for the three of us to meditate together," she thought, looking down at the little bronze statue. She closed her eyes and watched a tranquil wave flow over her mind. But she was inwardly aware that he was sitting nearby. Alone, she would sit in meditation for at least thirty minutes, gazing with closed eyes at the point between her eyebrows, or submerging in the electrical pulsations running through her body. But this time she would not become too inwardly engrossed, not when her precious moments with George were so limited.

After fifteen minutes, she opened her eyes. George's were still shut. She watched him silently. It was a rare occasion for her to share any moment of meditation alone with a man whom she loved. In the first place, she'd been in love with few men and in the second place, those whom she had loved had had little propensity toward meditation. But here he sat, a man who claimed yoga as a newfound interest, a man she had loved the moment she set eyes upon him, a man sitting now so earnestly before her in meditation. But with her penetrating gaze on him, he soon opened his eyes. Together their eyes danced across the flickering flame, grown bright by the darkness of the room.

"Whatever our destinies may be," she thought, "I will never forget those eyes." She stared into them deeply and he into hers. A smile slowly crept across his face and a soft, self-conscious laugh bubbled out. "Not sure why, but I suddenly feel a little nervous," he said.

She demurely shifted her eyes away from his and relaxed her posture, turning to lean against the bed. Finding his eyes again, she reached out and caressed the side of his head. He set the candle next to the Buddha and slid over to her. A long, tender embrace followed. In her heart, there was not the slightest anticipation. Time stood still. Her mind could think of nothing except her love for him.

Withdrawing slowly from her arms, he smoothly lifted his shirt up over his head exposing his tanned chest, masculinely adorned with black, swirling ringlets of hair. With an equally smooth motion, she removed her own shirt, baring her shoulders, leaving only her white cotton T-shirt to conceal her small, round breasts. She looked again into his warm, gentle eyes. It was enough just to be close with him, to finally be able to let the love pour from her heart and receive his love into hers. Only one week ago had been the barn dance at the Foundation. How hard she had tried that night to hide her feelings from him. Could she have ever guessed that one week later they would be sitting in the shining glow of a candle on the fourth floor of a stately home overlooking the Irish Sea? No, it would have been a fantasy too impossible to come true. And yet...

Breaking the spell which had captured them both, he unexpectedly announced, "I'm thinking of moving onto the bed." He looked searchingly into her eyes. When she didn't respond or make any movements, he hesitantly faltered, asking quickly, "Is it all right?"

She was weighing the implication of his words, but she knew in her heart she wanted nothing more than to once again feel his body close to hers. With a subdued smile she replied, "Yes," as she slowly got up and stood refinedly before him. He stood also.

ॐ * * * ॐ

I looked across at her and saw a pensively distance gaze in her eyes and a flicker of a smile passing across her face. I wondered if she wanted to skip over discussing the intimacy they had shared, the memory of which was clearly playing through her mind. But she did continue, explaining how she had slipped the waistband of her skirt over her hips and laid it neatly on the bedpost at the foot of the bed. Modestly keeping her panties and T-shirt on, she had pulled back the sheets and climbed under the covers. Unbuckling his belt, he quickly had laid his trousers over the same bedpost, similarly leaving on "the cutest pair of navy blue underwear I've ever seen," she drolly described them to me. The warmth of his body against hers had felt so natural, so familiar. The barrier of her skimpy T-shirt was soon gone and they had lain wrapped in one another's arms.

This was the extraordinary thing that she said to me. Here they were two bodies, enraptured and entwined, his pressing down on top of hers, her legs cradling him, their lips softly caressing, and yet physically, she had not been aroused. Already overwhelmed by her love for him, there was no other desire. She wanted only to merge all that was her into him. She wanted him, body and soul, to be within her. To label such a meeting with a three-letter word seemed sacrilegious to her. If it had to be named, and any name of this union she nonetheless believed was fated to be misconstrued, why not call it "submersion," submersion of one being into another? But language poorly caters to the heart. As the word "sex" inadequately describes a profoundly intimate union, so the four-letter word "love" falls short of any differentiation in love for one's dog or one's country or one's beloved. Only in the heart can the difference be told.

ഇ * * * ൦ഴ

The energy running between them built up such a heat within their bodies that a warm, dewy sweat covered their skin. Yet their movements together were slow and unbidden. She knew she wanted to give him what was precious to herself, her most intimate embrace.

She turned his head to bring his ear to her mouth and softly whispered, "Will you come inside?"

Intensely passionate, he gazed into her face. Blinking as though coming out of a deep reverie, struggling to relate to the issue at hand, he asked, his voice breaking, "But Indu, what about birth control?"

Being only the fifth day of her cycle, the risk had not even entered her mind. But she liked that he had asked. She only wondered if he really understood that she only wanted to hold him within, just as she had been holding him and nothing more—just to feel the fullness of him within and to become submerged in that fullness.

All she could think to say was, "George, I hadn't exactly meant we'd…" She broke off her sentence.

ഇ * * * ൦ഴ

Somehow from her half sentence he had understood what she couldn't find words to say. He had sprung from the bed, and at the same time they both had disposed of their last modest coverings. She laughed when she told me about it, remembering how he had leaped back under the covers before she could see anything but two round, firm buns. What followed, she prefaced her story, was one of the most comical intimate moments she'd ever experienced.

291

In tantra, in a spiritual sexual union, no climax is needed and in fact is avoided. But Indu suddenly had realized that maybe it was asking too much. How could she possibly explain that it was not passionate sex she wanted but a union without physical barriers?

George had gently rolled back on top and they tenderly had embraced again. But she still had no feeling of arousal and had been counting on the love pouring from her heart and the natural movement of hormones to arouse him. What she hadn't allowed for was his ever-so-slight anxiety of what was really expected from him. He must have suspected that theirs was not meant to be an ordinary union. The outcome had been a humorously reluctant erection; it was there, but then it wasn't. Upon quickly perceiving the difficulty she had thought, "Poor George, I say I'd love for him to come inside and then leave everything up to him."

But to do anything for the sake of arousal would have felt unnatural to her. In tantra, preconceptions and expectations are dropped and the natural movement of energy between two people, flowing unrestricted, undirected, is what carries both to unbelievable heights of loving ecstasy. But that wasn't exactly where they were heading that night. She confided to me with candid good nature that simply getting into the right position, with her finally moist enough and him with a solid enough erection was a hit-and-miss proposition which finally succeeded.

She knew that heat in the stillness of love was described in ancient scripture as the stirring of the *kuṇḍalinī*. When again warm dewy sweat had quickly covered their motionless bodies, she had been immensely happy to feel it. She had held him closely and felt so full and at peace. The erection had not lasted long, but once inside it did not matter. Those few precious moments had been enough.

ℰ ✻ ✻ ✻ ℭ

George lifted his head with a recondite look in his eyes. He implored, "Has this ever happened to you before?"

It was the same question he had asked at the stone after their first kiss. Had she ever felt such a magic, the heat of passion in the stillness of intimate love, the fullness, the peace? "No," she thought, "Only with you, only with you." There were no words to express her joy. She reached up and caressed his damp forehead.

But he continued. "I've never had this problem, really. I don't know what happened." She realized suddenly that he was referring to his inability to stay aroused.

"But George, it's been beautiful for me. I'm not sexually aroused either. I just wanted you as close as possible."

"That's what's funny. I can't get aroused." By this time he had slipped out and they lay close to each other. "This is embarrassing," he said, speaking in a whisper.

"But George, why should it be? It's been lovely."

With his best farcical delivery, he replied, "But I'm Greek. You know Greek men have their reputations to uphold." His cocky smile moved her with its unbelievable sweetness.

"But that's the whole point, George. The attraction between us, our connection, it's not a physical one. It's something far beyond, beyond anything I've ever felt."

"Yes," he grinned, "There's no doubt it's beyond."

Laughing, she said, "Well, birth control may never be a problem but we might have trouble having children."

"Children!" he exclaimed. "Are we planning children now?" he teasingly taunted her.

"I only said *if,*" she retorted, smiling abstrusely.

The sweat was cooling, the energy subsiding. There was a winsome comfort and security feeling his arms around her. As much as she regretted the thought of the moment ending, she knew the hour was late. She pulled back from his tight hold to look at her watch.

"It's ten-thirty. We have maybe ten minutes more at the most."

But then, an abrupt noise came from downstairs. They both froze. There were voices, too. It was not just Margaret's father. In the same second, they bounded out of bed.

NINETEEN

~

As she walked with George down the stairs, she wondered if they could keep their faces from revealing how intimate they had been. Rounding the second-floor banister, they ran into Paul. He looked at them casually without reacting.

Trying to be perfectly natural, Indu asked, "How was the dance?"

Paul replied, "Oh, it was fine. But right now I'm trying to get back into our room."

"Did the door get locked?" George inquired.

"Yes, somehow in the rush to leave it did and the key is inside," Paul explained.

"If you think it would work, I could climb out a window and go around outside," George offered.

"Oh, no. That's all right. I just told Margaret and she gave me this other key to try. Thanks anyway, though."

Indu felt an awkwardness for just a moment. But chatting with Paul had helped to make her feel more grounded. Just as they were about to walk into the living room, Guruji came out. When he saw them, Indu discerned a twinkle in his eyes and a grin through his beard. He raised one hand in greeting and said, "Ah, hello, hello." He walked slowly past without stopping. Indu bowed her head in salutation.

Amidst all the commotion as they entered the room, she heard Shakti exclaim, "Oh, my, they look just ... Oh well, never mind." Glancing quickly toward her, Indu saw another twinkle and grin.

"Good grief," she thought, "it must be evident to everyone. But no one seems too unpleased."

℘ * * * ℰ

Indu interjected here to explain what had surprised Shakti. In a conversation the following day, Shakti apologized for making any remark, but had simply been amazed at the striking resemblance between her and George. "At that moment, you looked exactly alike and you were both glowing. It was really touching to see," she had told Indu.

℘ * * * ℰ

If the others noticed anything, they remained discreetly silent about it. Margaret was relaxing on one sofa and Claire and Bill on another. Indu went over and sat next to Margaret, and George sat across the room in the chair where Guruji had been sitting earlier. They were discussing the evening's outing. Several Indian dignitaries had been at the temple and Guruji had been quite a focus of attention. Indu was tickled by Margaret's obvious diplomatic appraisal of the performance they'd seen.

"Well, it was very nice—good dancing," which translated in Indu's mind to mean she'd found it challenging to appreciate.

When there was a break in conversation, Indu took the chance to inquire if there were any late-night restaurants nearby where she could get a milkshake. It was already past eleven o'clock. Although she really would have enjoyed one, Indu had actually contrived the question so that she and George could make a graceful departure from the house. She knew that for them to just disappear would have been inappropriate. She also didn't want anyone to be startled if they heard her coming back to the house late at night.

No doubt surmising the motive behind the question, a five-minute discussion nonetheless ensued as to the most likely location of such an establishment. Paul was concerned that most restaurants would be closed at that hour.

"But Paul," Margaret chimed in, "how about that place down the road? It's a fast-food chain, on the left-hand side of the road."

"Well, that place might be open, but I don't know that they serve milkshakes. They might, though. You could head in that direction. There are some other restaurants down that way. You do have a car, right?"

"Yes," George affirmed, going along with whatever Indu was planning.

"Okay, just remember this is Victoria Road," Paul said, pointing to the road in front of their house, "and the crossroad there," he pointed to the right, "that's Brittany Street. Wouldn't want you kids to get lost."

"We'll lock the door behind you," Margaret said, "and you keep the keys with you and just let yourselves back in." Turning to George, she asked, "George, can we fix you up with a bed for the night? Don't have a room open but these sofas are comfortable." She patted the olive green floral satin cushion next to her.

"That's awfully kind, Margaret, but I am expected back tonight."

"How far do you have to drive?" Paul asked.

"My aunt lives only an hour away in Chester."

"Oh, I hate to think of you driving so late at night. You be careful now," Margaret cautioned, sounding like any loving mother would.

"I certainly will. You've both been very kind. I want to thank you for having me here." It was the polite thing to say, and Indu was impressed by his poise.

"George, you're welcome anytime. I mean it," Margaret said. "We'd love to see you come back again."

"Now," Paul broke in with a grin, "we'd better let these young kids get on their way." He reached out to shake George's hand. As Margaret got up to give George a hug, Indu excused herself to get her purse. Farewells had been completed by the time she came back downstairs. Indu felt grateful that everyone was being so good-natured about bidding them out the door at such a late hour. But she knew she had to have more time alone with George. She simply wasn't ready to say goodbye to him. As casually and naturally as possible, they finally made a graceful departure.

They walked arm in arm to his car. Indu was surprised not to see the Morris. "Where's your other buggy?" she asked.

"Well, I sold it to my mother."

"Your mother bought it?"

"It was an extremely kind gesture on her part. She was afraid to see me drive all the way to Greece with it and she also knew I needed the money. My grandfather kindly gave me this one, claiming it a grandfather's prerogative to do so. It's seven years old and runs well." It was a white 1977 Polo with black interior.

"Sounds like you have a few people watching out for you."

"I'm very blessed in that respect. We all try to watch out for each other. But I'm probably the one who needs the most watching," he said with his classic smile. "Actually, what I wanted to do was sell this Polo to get enough money to really fix the Morris, make it a vintage car. I hated to part with it. But my mother said she doubted her father would give me this car if he knew that's what I was going to do with it. And he would have been absolutely right. That wouldn't have been the wisest thing to do. Hope I'll be that wise when I'm his age. If it runs in the family, then there may be hope." He glanced over at Indu and exhibited another beaming smile.

"So what will your mother do with the old Morris when she leaves the country?"

"Oh, she's going to try to sell it but in the meantime she'll use it to get around in. I greatly suspect she won't get as much as she paid. She made me a very generous offer."

"What mother wouldn't to a son she loved?" Indu said, glad to think that he had such a mother.

"Yes. I'm afraid I'm spoiled rotten. And I love it."

Indu did feel a sadness about him giving up the Morris. She had fond memories of that car, riding in its back seat, looking into its rearview mirror. And it was all just over a week ago. It seemed like years.

She walked around the car to what to her was the driver's side. She still wasn't used to the position of the steering wheel in British cars. In the passenger seat, she had the weird sensation that she was driving with no hands.

They drove two blocks and found the fast-food place Margaret had mentioned. It was still open. They parked the car and went inside. No milkshake was on the menu. The ambiance was not a pleasant one so they didn't stay. As they walked out, George noticed another restaurant up the street.

"Look. There's an Indian restaurant and it looks open. You know, we didn't eat any dinner, only that plate of food at three-thirty."

"Now that you mention it, I am hungry." It was the first time in days she had really felt hunger. And except for the few spoonfuls of food that afternoon, she hadn't eaten in almost thirty hours.

They went inside. The restaurant was deserted. A waiter came forward right away. "Are you still open for business?" George asked in his most distinguished voice.

"Yes, sir. We are. May I suggest this table here," the waiter replied, motioning to a booth comfortably set against the wall.

The restaurant was decorated in muted greens with plants hanging in the corners. The muffled sound of a television could be heard coming from behind the bar.

The waiter promptly inquired if they would order drinks. Indu shook her head "no," and George declined, accepting the menu instead.

"I have an idea," he said. "Why don't we order several dishes and split them. That way we can taste more things." Indu thought it was a fine idea. "So what would you like?"

She looked at the menu but didn't recognize any of the names. "You go ahead and select what you want," she said. "If we can check with the waiter to make sure it's vegetarian, then I'll be happy."

When the waiter returned, George was ready with the order. "We'd like a serving of *baigan sabji* and *aloo gobi*, one dish of *bhat* and *pudina* chutney. Also, two *puris* and two lime waters please. Now tell me, is anything there not vegetarian?"

"No, everything is vegetarian. Are you both vegetarian?" They nodded their heads "yes." "Ah," the waiter said, "very fine, very fine. This won't take long." As late as it was, he was in a very congenial mood.

"Now tell me, what did you order?'" Indu asked after the waiter left.

"Well, hopefully just eggplant, potato and cauliflower with cooked rice and a mint chutney and a little bread."

"We're going to eat all that?"

"Aren't we hungry?" he asked, smiling.

She wondered how, at twenty-four, he'd gotten so knowledgeable on Indian cuisine and here she was the one with the Indian Guru who loved to cook. She had a feeling this endearing fellow would surprise her many times over. They sat looking at each other, their hands stretching across the table to squeeze the other tightly. When the waiter came with the lime waters and napkins, they relaxed back in their seats, pulling their hands apart, not wanting to show too much ardent affection. He returned a few minutes later with the food, an enormous amount.

"George! What are we going to do with all this?"

"They are generous here, aren't they," he said with eyes wide. "This may be a bigger challenge than I thought." They laughed at having so many dishes before them, and going so quickly from famished to full.

With plenty left to go, George leaned back slowly and said, "My goodness, if we'd split just one dish it would have been enough. I can't eat another bite."

"Nor can I. But it was good."

Relaxing in her seat, Indu's ear suddenly picked up on a familiar voice from the television. It was an actor she knew well, but his name escaped her. Her curiosity piqued, she finally could tolerate it no longer.

"George, I have to see who's on the television. I'll be right back." She slipped out of the booth and went up to the bar. The waiter and bartender were engaged in a casual conversation.

"Do you need anything, miss?" the waiter said, standing up to greet her.

"No, I just came to see what show you have on," she said.

"On the telly? It's an American film. Are you American?"

She acknowledged that he had guessed correctly as she peered up at the television to see what face was behind the voice. "Of course," she thumped herself mentally as the name popped into her head. Watching for a few seconds, she contemplated how odd it was being so far from home, in an unfamiliar place, with someone who knows so little about her life and hearing a voice she'd known since childhood. It gave her a pleasantly incongruous feeling. She returned to the table.

"Did you know who it was?" George asked.

"Yes, it was a famous actor starring in an American war movie, World War II, I think."

"Do you go to the cinema a lot when you're at home?"

"I like to go. If there's a good movie in town, sometimes I'll go for a little escape."

The waiter came up to take away the dishes. "So where are you from?" the waiter asked, looking at George.

Indu was surprised to hear George claim Kenya as his point of origin since he had spent just as much time in England. She wondered if he'd been born there.

The waiter looked back at her and continued, "I wanted to go to America. I even have relatives who live in New York. But it takes a lot of time to get things arranged."

She gave a sympathetic nod. "Sweet fellow," she thought. "Can he have any idea how intense a time this is for George and me and how much we want to be alone?" He gave a little more of his background and told of some of his ambitions and then withdrew carrying the tray of dishes.

Indu was relieved that they were alone again. It had been a strain during the day trying to interact with others when all she wanted was to be with George. By this time she'd forgotten the question about his birthplace.

Her mind was nearing emotional overload, and all the time she was aware that soon they would need to part.

George pulled out two small photos of himself. They were black-and-white shots taken in a photo booth for sixty pence at a tube station. One did not look much like him. But the other was adorable. He was wearing a white shirt and a slightly crooked tie and gazing directly into the camera. His eyes stared straight up at her from the picture.

"You can have one if you like," he said.

"I can? In that case..." She chose the crooked-tie one. She loved his serious expression, his gently curving chin, his angular nose, his dark eyebrows, his slightly mussed hair, his mesmeric eyes, and even his crooked tie. It was a tiny little picture, but one that would be carried and treasured.

She also had three small color shots of herself. They were left over from a strip of four also taken in a photo machine in the London tube station. The fourth one had been used as identification on her Underground train pass.

"Anything there you'd like?" she asked. Two were solemn, the other silly. He studied each one but shook his head.

"None are really you as I know you," he said. It was true. She'd used the best one for her ID card. She took them back.

They both leaned away from the table and regarded one another for a long, silent moment. George then earnestly leaned forward, placing his forearms on the edge of the table. He bent his head down, looking vaguely at something which was not before him. Lifting his head again, he asked, "Indu, would you consider marrying me?"

℘ * * * ℭ

It was a question she had not expected so soon. Two weeks ago he had innocently juggled past her, oblivious that anything was about to happen to his life. Yet the obstacles that they had surmounted just to be at the Foundation at the same time were phenomenal. If they had never met, would either have known that something was missing from their lives? Could either have met anyone else and fallen just as deeply in love? Or was their meeting destiny playing its hand? When she imagined her husband-to-be, had he been running along the beach in Mombasa, or flying off to boarding school with tear-drenched cheeks at the sorrow of leaving his parents? Had he been the fellow that had almost gotten thrown out of school except for the kind intervention of a school rector who had seen a promising light hidden behind the devilish boyish pranks? If he had never learned to juggle, if she had never met her Guru, would destiny have found another way for them to meet? Or no... did everything in their lives up to that time which had brought their paths to cross suddenly have new meaning, new purpose? Had not everything in her life and his been essential to bring them together?

"Would I consider marrying you?" she had thought. "What else could I possibly be considering?" But that was not the answer she would give him. Her love for him was certain. Still, she needed to know exactly how deeply intertwined their destinies really were. She would have to test the karma.

When I asked her what this meant, she explained. "Destiny is karma realized. Karma manifested will shape one's destiny in the present as well as in the next life. One's destiny is therefore a careful balance of actions and reactions, thoughts and words, kindnesses and negligences, many of which have been carried over from previous incarnations. And once a karmic play is written into one's destiny, it's very difficult to avoid. According to Guruji, destiny is very powerful. It cannot leave you alone."

That's what Indu wanted to know. How powerful was her destiny with George? Would it bring them together for this lifetime or would their meeting alone be enough to satisfy the karmic debt, like in the story of the pie and the coins. She then related this story to me.

A beggar was walking along a street and caught a whiff of freshly baked apple pies. Stopping at the gate of a house, he saw the pies cooling in the window. He stood, feeling intoxicated by the aroma. The master of the house spying the beggar angrily approached him, demanding, "Give me five rupees."

The beggar cried out, "What for? I have done nothing. I did not touch the pies."

But the reproving man replied, "The enjoyment you have had from smelling these pies is worth five rupees. A taste would be worth twenty. So pay now or I'll take you to court."

The poor beggar, lacking funds, was dragged into court. The judge listened while the man explained the charge. After hearing the case, the judge paused a moment in deep contemplation, and then said to the prosecutor, "Okay, give the beggar five rupees."

The arrogant man immediately objected, "No, no, no. It is the beggar who owes me."

But the judge persisted. "Please, go ahead and give the beggar the five rupees." Reluctantly, the man did so.

"Now," the judge said to the beggar, "drop the five coins on the floor." The beggar followed his orders and let the coins fall, creating a pinging clatter as each hit the floor.

"There," said the judge to the man, "you may pick up your coins now."

"But I don't understand," he replied.

"It is justice," the judge answered. "The sound of the fallen money is the just compensation for the smelling of your pies."

That simply, the debt was paid. Were things to be that simple between her and George? Was their mere meeting enough to fulfill the karmic requirement? These were the questions that confronted her. Why, one may wonder, would she not just follow her heart? I asked the same question, to which she answered with another story. It was one she had heard soon after meeting Guruji.

A man devoted to his Guru went out one day to reverently pick flowers from a nearby garden, planning to lay them at the feet of his beloved teacher. But while walking among the fragrant petals, he suddenly beheld a maiden lovelier than any flower he'd ever seen. His heart smitten with love, he presented his bouquet to her. He lived happily with her for the rest of his life, never returning to see his Guru.

In his next life, he was born as a she. She was sitting at a roadside stand selling flowers one day when the same Guru came along. Spying the girl, the Guru immediately recognized his long lost devotee. He approached her but she did not recognize him.

"May I help you, kind sir?" she asked.

The Guru replied, "I only want to ask you one question."

"My ears are eager to be blessed by your words, O holy one. Pray speak," she reverently beseeched him.

"Why did you leave me so? I have missed you all these years."

With those words, tears flooded her eyes as she recognized her beloved teacher from her lifetime past. From that day forward, she who had been "he" again followed with devoted heart the path of the Guru.

Indu wanted her heart to always be with her Guru. She had vowed as a young woman in her late teens that if ever she did fall in love, she would keep the spiritual teachings of her Guru foremost before her. And now her beloved was sitting before her. She had watched how destiny had brought her to her Guru, and she had watched how it had brought her to George. Now she would challenge Nature until it was shown that their karma could not be cleared in any other way except through marriage. She knew if she married him for any other reason it would only create more karma than it would resolve, ultimately hindering any spiritual growth. No, she would challenge this love until she had no strength left inside to challenge it. She would examine it, dissect it, analyze it, question it, and pray that someday she would understand what she was supposed to do with it. And she began at that moment by not giving a direct answer.

℘ * * * ℭ

With a smile and a teasing voice, she replied, "Are you asking me seriously right now to marry you?"

His serious visage broke into a grin. He looked across at her intently. She had answered his question with a question which had left him holding the bag. Feeling the pressure of her question and her gaze on him, he blurted out, as if by force, "No, I'm not."

He suddenly relaxed and pretended to wipe his brow as though narrowly escaping danger.

Indu watched him go through his antics and then said, "When you are seriously asking, I will give you a serious answer. It's not a question to be considered lightly."

"You're absolutely right," he said. "Now that we've made it through that one, I have some pictures of my family to show you. Would you like to see them?"

She replied with the first words that came to her mind.

"Ah!" he exclaimed, "that's my answer."

"What, what?" she thought, startled by his outburst. "What did I say?" But she quickly realized what she had said.

She had said yes to seeing "pictures of her possible future in-laws." He had his answer. She felt wholly embarrassed that she'd given her position away. But in her heart she loved him more than any man she had ever known, and the possibility of their marriage had entered her mind long before it had ever entered his.

Ⅎ * * * ℳ

He had been more than pleased with himself for seeing through her evasive front. She told me that in a letter she would later receive from him, he quite forthrightly remonstrated that she made it difficult for him to discern what she was thinking and feeling. She knew the complaint was justly put. Possibly unfairly to him, she had never told him of the karmic challenge she was placing on their relationship. She explained to me that she simply could not. She could only hope that if their lives were destined to join, then whatever was spoken or unspoken between them was also part of the "plan" to bring them together. If it was really meant to be, then destiny would reign supreme.

She had known her slip of the tongue was also part of this metaphysical experiment. Even when trying to consciously watch what she was saying, her heart had come through. There had been nothing to do except meet his eyes with a broadly acquiescent smile.

℁ * * * ℛ

He laid the pictures before her on the table. One was taken a year ago after he'd fallen into a hot spring. It showed him pointing to his healing leg three weeks after the fall, still raw and red and looking incredibly painful. Another was of his father standing on the porch of their house in Kenya. She noticed he, too, wore a *kikoi* like George had, and she liked that. His mother, a gentle-looking woman, stood in one picture next to her husband, both looking content.

"They make a nice couple," she said in genuine admiration.

"It's been a good marriage. They've set a very high standard for their children." It sounded as though he had equal expectations for his own marriage.

"Who is this?" she asked, looking at a picture of an attractive woman, tan and well-proportioned.

"That's my sister, Melinda."

"She's lovely." Indu looked more closely at the face. There was a slight resemblance. "How old is she?"

"She's eighteen months older than I am. She's studying marine ecology in Australia. We're quite close." Indu's mind quickly calculated that that would make Melinda eighteen months younger than herself.

The last two pictures were views of his parent's home. It was a beachfront property, beautifully maintained. The family was obviously of adequate means. But he could have told her that he was a pauper and it still would not have changed the feelings in her heart. In fact, nothing he could have told her would have dimmed her love for him.

"These are very nice," she said, handing the pictures back.

"Indu, I've never told you my full given name."

"There's something more than George Acroilus?" she asked, curious as to what had been left out.

"My full name is Spyridon Rex George Acroilus."

"Spyridon?"

"He's the patron saint of Corfu."

She remarked with a mischievous glint, "Sounds terribly noble." But thinking about names, she wondered what spiritual name Guruji would give him if the opportunity arose.

The waiter brought the check. Indu automatically reached into her purse for money but George absolutely insisted that he would take care of the bill. She was charmed by his insistence and by the mature and manly way in which he did it. It was not her custom to let a man pay her way, but offered in such a chivalrous manner, she couldn't refuse.

Back in the car, they decided to head to the beach. She had thought a midnight stroll along the water's edge might be romantic, but a cold, whipping wind changed her mind. Instead, they parked the car down near the water. After a warm hug and kiss, he asked, "Do you know what I found out from my mother just before I came here?"

"I haven't the faintest idea."

"My father used to be stationed in New Brighton when he was in the service. In fact, my mother came here to see him. It was before they were married. Who knows," he looked across the beach, "my dad may have even brought some other woman to this very beach before he decided on marrying my mom."

"Ha—or before she decided on him," Indu playfully replied, but she suddenly became serious. "You know, that does make it doubly ironic that we should end up meeting again here, of all places."

To herself she mused, "Could that be why his mother did not object to him coming to see me?"

They silently held hands. She knew that soon goodbyes would need to be said. Tiredness was slowly overpowering them both. Unless… An idea flashed through her mind.

"George, shall we try to find a place to spend the night together?"

"What?" he said with exaggerated surprise over the propriety of such a suggestion.

"Come on, George. You know what I mean. We're both exhausted. Wouldn't it be nice to curl up with each other and go to sleep? At least it would give us a few more hours together."

"What time is it now?"

"It's half past midnight."

She could see he had no objection to the idea. "The problem is finding anything open at this hour. He leaned over the steering wheel to start the engine. "Let's drive along a few streets and see what we can find."

They came to one place just down the road. There was a rowdy crowd inside. George parked the car and got out to see what possibilities were there. She liked how confident and sure he appeared walking into such a place. "He really is amazingly mature," she reflected, suspecting that men well over his lean twenty-four years could not have been more convincingly steady. He soon returned.

"Don't think this is the place for us. That's supposed to go on all night. Some kind of reunion. It's not very clean, either," he said. She did not question his judgment.

"Let's see if there's any place else," she replied.

"Well, I did ask in there if they could suggest anything."

"You did? What a clever fellow. What did they say?" she asked, glad that he had thought to inquire.

"Of course, I would have done the same thing," she silently admitted, amused at herself.

"There are some boarding houses nearby. But chances are still slim that we'll find anything open."

They drove a couple of blocks away from the beach and turned right. They passed several boarding houses, but the windows were dark. The next block down, however, they did see one well-lit window.

"Luck may be with us after all," he sweetly gushed. "Shall we give it a try?" He was already halfway out of the car. This time Indu followed behind him. He rang the buzzer and they both stood silently waiting at the door. No answer came. He rang it again and suddenly a light blinked on in an upstairs room. To their surprise, a head appeared out of a window above them.

A man called down, "You kids need a room?"

"We do, sir," George called up in a calm, reserved tone. "Sorry to disturb you at this hour." Indu was impressed again by his composed manner.

"Do you want a single or a double?"

"A double if you've got it," he answered back, without blinking an eye. It definitely made them appear as guests with "proper" intent.

"I'll be right down," the man said, ducking back inside the room.

"We'd better be real nice to him," George whispered. "I've a feeling we woke him up."

"But the downstairs light was on," Indu protested in their defense. "How were we supposed to know?"

A middle-aged man with a newly-lit cigarette unlocked the door and quickly moved behind the front desk. By his demeanor, he didn't seem too peeved at being awakened, if in fact they had awakened him. He gave them a room key plus one to the front door and directed them to their room.

"You're on the third floor. Go up these stairs, turn to your left, then take an immediate right. It'll be the last door on the left."

Paying the eleven pound charge, George replied, "We'll find it just fine. We appreciate you letting us in at this hour."

Indu unpretentiously slipped a ten pound note immediately back into George's hand. This time she would foot the bill. George started to protest but she shook her head stubbornly. She wanted equality in their relationship.

Before they went upstairs, Indu knew she'd need to return to the house to get her cosmetic bag and contact lens case. The drive to the house took only minutes. George waited in the car. From outside, Indu could see a light shining through the upper bedroom window. She let herself in the front door and quietly went upstairs.

Entering her room, she was glad she had returned. Shakti lay sound asleep. "How sweet of her," Indu thought, "the light has been left on for me."

She turned it off. In the dark, she fetched her things and went back into the hall. Flipping on the desk lamp, she found a brown piece of paper and a pen. Not wanting them to worry about her absence in the morning, she wrote a note to Shakti saying:

Dear Sister Shakti,

Am with George at a hotel around the corner. Will be back here lunchtime or so. Please only whisper this in the ears of anyone who has to know. Thanks.

Love, Indu

She slipped back into the room and placed the note on her own pillow. As an afterthought she also laid the ring of house keys next to it. "It would give everything away if these were missing in the morning," she thought. As she left the house, she pushed the button on the door handle before pulling it shut. Safely locked out, she hurried back to the car and to George.

TWENTY

~

Indu and George quietly let themselves in the front door of the boarding house. The same glowing light which had first caught their eye in the window now helped them see their way through the hall and up the stairs. It was not a fancy place but the stairs and hallway were carpeted and by the low glow of a hall table lamp, she saw decorative chairs, green plants and gold-framed mirrors lining the hall walls. There was a fresh-ness in the air. The room was simple and meticulously spot-less. She was enchanted. There were two twin beds, a sink by the window, a television and a wooden freestanding wardrobe backed against the wall. She went over and opened the win-dow.

"George, we can see the water. It's beautiful."

"But Indu," he said, sounding disappointed, "we asked for a double room. Why are there two twin beds?"

"A double usually means two beds. What did you think?"

"I thought we'd get one big double bed," he said, showing with boyish exaggeration the size that he had wanted.

"So you weren't trying to be discreet after all by asking for a double room," she thought. "Why is your naiveté so sweet to me?"

Wanting to make light of his admitted mistake, she stood with her hands on her hips and said, "Well, I guess we'll just have to cuddle extra close so we can fit on one." He saw her mischie-vous grin. There was no sign of disappointment left on his face. As exhausted as they were, neither hinted at intimacy. In fact, quite the opposite. He sat down on the bed and watched with admiring curiosity as she tied back her hair, washed her face at the sink, brushed her teeth and applied night cream.

"So this is what you do every night," he said, giving her a studious eye when she turned around. A sleepy smile was her response.

They chose the bed nearest to the window that was up against the wall and laid their clothes on the other bed. He hopped under the covers first and she snuggled in behind him. For their last romantic interlude of the night, the glaring lamp light was far from suitable for his tastes. He again got up, found a towel and laid it over the top of the lampshade. The brightness was transformed into a soft, warm haze. Climbing back across to the side near the wall, he nestled close to her, looking into her eyes. She reached her arm underneath to pull him closer for a tender kiss. After a long embrace, he stretched his arm over her head and switched the lamp off. Again snuggling in closely, he was soon fast asleep. She listened to the sonorous movement of his breath, relaxed and peaceful, feeling it slowly lulling her to sleep.

She awoke in his arms the next morning. He was still soundly unconscious.

Feeling the effects of the rich Indian food, she scooted out from under the covers to head to the bathroom. He awoke as she did and with surprising alacrity asked, "Where are you going?"

"To the loo, my love. I'll be right back." With that she slipped out the door, remembering to carry the room key with her.

The bathroom was directly across the hall, petite in size, containing a single toilet and a tiny water spigot in one corner for rinsing hands. She returned to the room, surprised at how awake she felt. George was back asleep and not ready to move. She leaned against the window sill, pushing the window further open. The fresh sea air invigorated her even more. Although she didn't have her contact lenses in, she could still make out the great expanse of water before her and a road leading down to the beach, ending at the retaining wall. She remembered the talk she'd had the day before with George, sitting on the cement bench by the beach. She looked over at him, still deeply in slumber. As she climbed back under the covers, he sleepily welcomed her and again dosed off. Unexpectedly hit with a stomach cramp, she again had to make an immediate move to get to the bathroom.

Roused by her movements, he asked this time, "Are you going for a walk?"

A little shy to admit that she was dashing off to the bathroom again, she simply replied, "I'll be back soon." Then lovingly chastising him, she said, "You'd better be awake by then." He watched as she dressed quickly and blew him a kiss from the door. She went to the second-floor bathroom, amused at herself for being ridiculously shy about her stomach trouble.

Instead of heading back upstairs, she decided, "Why not go for a walk?"

She thought how nice it would be out by the sea. It was seven-thirty. On the street, it was a quiet Sunday morning. She felt light and happy as she walked to the beach, although she did regret not having her eye glasses or her contacts. But she could see well enough for just a short walk. She rested her arms on top of the cement wall and stared out at the water. The collision of the waves onto the beach made a spectacular roar, pierced now and then by a beckoning gull overhead. She closed her ill-focused eyes and let her ears paint the picture of the morning beach. When she opened them again, bright rays of sun were beautifully filtering through a formidable gray cloud front moving in over Liverpool. Her attention drawn back to the pounding surf, she curiously wondered how far the sound would carry past the cement wall. She began stepping backward, one foot slowly behind the other. At ten steps back, the once overpowering sound became muffled, reverberating instead off the sea wall.

Greatly entertained by her experiment, she thought how important it was for everyone to spend time alone, time just to explore their own world, inner and outer. It brought a calming strength to her heart. Still, she did not want to be gone too long from George. Their minutes together were ever limited and precious. His departure could not be postponed for much longer. Walking at a rapid gait, she made it back to the boarding house in five minutes.

Far from being loquacious, George nonetheless greeted her with the news that he was awake. Seeing his half-open eyes, she was wary believing him. Pulling off her clothes, she hopped back into bed. His body felt warm against her own, which had been cooled by the morning air. He wrapped her in his arms, softly kissed her on the cheek and began to dose off again.

Not about to let him drift back out of consciousness, she deploringly threatened, "I guess I'll have to go for another walk."

She watched as he groggily opened both eyes and peered up at her. "Oh, stay," he said, gently stroking her arm. "Stay and keep me company." Her heart melted, profoundly touched by his words.

"Oh God, I don't ever want to have to leave you, don't you know?" she thought. "But is it possible that you're feeling the same thing?" She knew that he loved her, but it was beyond her wildest hopes that he should love her as intensely as she did him. In reply to his plea, she snuggled in closer. He nuzzled his head next to hers. Even with this loving exchange, there was no desire for anything more passionate. Feeling his gentle caresses and returning the same loving touch was enough.

By eight o'clock, they both knew it was time to confront the day ahead of them. "'Bout time I give a quick call to my mom. She may be wondering on my whereabouts. She rather expected me back last night."

"Oh, George," Indu sincerely lamented, "she's going to want my head for keeping you so long."

"No, she won't. She may want my head, though." He was dressed and out the door a moment later. Indu curled up by herself and waited for his return. After fifteen minutes he came back. His cheery mood had changed to one of agitation.

"What did she say?" Indu asked, immediately aware of his ruffled stated.

"It wasn't so much what she said as the tone of voice she said it in. She was very upset that I hadn't called sooner. I know I should have. She didn't really ask anything directly. She just began expressing anxiety about something totally unrelated."

"Which was what?"

"About selling the Morris and the insurance problems with it. It's her way of saying that she wants me home as soon as possible."

Indu sat up in bed, worried to see him standing so distraught in the middle of the room. "I'll be in London on Friday," he said abruptly.

"That's good news at least," she thought. "We can meet somewhere…"

But before she could inquire about their next rendezvous, he sat down on the bed and solemnly said, "I don't think we should try to meet."

She was stunned. "How can you not want to see me?" she thought.

Confounded, she cautiously guarded her deeply hurt feelings by deferentially agreeing. "Well, okay."

But it simply didn't make sense. She sat thinking, "It would have given us one last chance to see each other." Her heart ached that he would choose not to see her.

"Just out of curiosity," she had to ask, "can you tell me why?"

"Indu, Alison is probably going to be with me then. It just wouldn't be fair to her. You know I have responsibilities to other people, too." There was no sound of apology, no sound of regret in his voice. Nothing he was saying made sense given that they'd just spent the last twenty-four hours so close and so in love.

Indu silently pondered his answer. "Is he reacting out of guilt to something his mother said? Did she question his involvement with this strange American lady? How can he flip so suddenly from tender to terse?" No words from anybody had ever hurt her more. "He's giving up our last chance." So wounded was her heart, there was not even a spark of anger. She didn't try to dissuade him. She got up, got dressed, brushed her teeth. While standing by the sink, his eye caught hers in the mirror. He stood closely behind. At any other time she would have reached around to hug him. Instead, the expression of love she might have made recoiled inside of her, pulling her emotionally away. She turned to collect her cosmetic bag. He stepped back.

ℰ *** ℭ

Over the next couple of days, she told me, the feeling of withdrawal was only to intensify. At that moment, though, all she knew was that most likely it would be the last time she'd ever see him. "I had one consoling thought," she told me as she described this very difficult parting. "The night before I'd noticed George had set the little Buddha on the nightstand. As I glanced over the room just before leaving, I saw that it was gone, no doubt tucked back in his pocket. It was at least some comfort to think, 'He's been blessed by a Guru. If our connection has done nothing else, it has given him that.'"

Ickwell

℘ * * * ℂ

When the door clicked closed behind them, she knew that the last private moment they might have had to embrace one final time was gone. But pressure to get home was squeezing in on George. She could clearly see it. She did not care to delay his departure one minute. She hurried down the stairs and to the car.

The sign in front of the boarding house read, "Donne's Hotel." She made a mental note of it.

Trying to lighten the heaviness between them, she commented, "It was a cozy little place to stay."

"I don't know," George dryly replied. "It wasn't exactly up to my usual standards."

She felt quite sad as they backed out of the drive. The fact that they had stayed there together had made the place enchanting to her. She was not referring to its elegance or beauty. She thought, "So I'm sentimental. I can't help it. And I suppose I shouldn't feel upset because you're not sentimental." Trying to keep her spirits undaunted, she asked him what he would do the rest of the day once he got back to his aunt's home.

"My aunt is riding her horse in some show this afternoon. So we'll go out, take a picnic lunch and watch. She's quite a good horsewoman," he said, with pretentious enthusiasm.

She couldn't help thinking, "All right, am I supposed to be envious that you're going off to have such a good time?" She almost did envy him because she knew the heaviness in her heart was only bound to increase after he left. The drive to Reliance House took four minutes. He parked two houses down from the front drive.

Determined not to shed a tear or show her anguish, she spoke as lightheartedly as possible. "Well, since you don't want to see me in London, I hope that we see each other again sometime." Without saying more, she gathered her things, leaned over and gave him a fast kiss on the lips before reaching for the door handle. He stopped her before the door was open and pulled her close to him for one last hug. She intrepidly fought back tears.

"Goodbye," she said, surprised at the steadiness in her own voice. Without hesitation, she got out of the car and walked around to the sidewalk, continuing toward the house.

She heard him start the car and she turned to wave as he drove past. He had rolled his window down and for a moment, their eyes held each other once again. She watched as the white car turned and disappeared at the next corner. He was gone.

She approached the front door and was grateful to find it unlocked. Walking into the house, she was relieved to see it deserted. She knew everyone must still be down in the meditation room. It was no small blessing. To have to explain why she was carrying her cosmetic bag would have been awkward and she doubted her emotional state was reliable enough to get her through any social interaction without revealing her true condition. Heading up the stairs, she was about to turn at the first landing when Uma came in through the front door, just thirty seconds behind her. Indu hurried upstairs to her room without being seen.

She closed the bedroom door and laid her things down. Walking to the window, she looked out at the sea again. A deep sadness gripped her all over. She watched the feeling move like a sudden wave flooding from her head to her feet. As the tears welled in her eyes, she felt thankful that George hadn't seen them. His last memory of her would at least be with clear eyes and a smiling face. No longer needing to keep up a brave front, she let her sorrow flow in a stream of tears. The relief was tremendous. Something told her not to get too immersed in the sadness. "Just let it come and go. Everything is in divine hands.

If we are meant to see each other again, then we shall. Who am I to fight God's will?"

With those thoughts, a peacefulness came to her heart. Her spiritual path stood resolutely before her and remaining as detached as possible from her own personal sorrows and desires, she would tread it with unwavering devotion. She stood entranced by the glitter of the late morning sun on the cool, blue-green Irish Sea. She decided to meditate but first to take a sponge bath. After changing her clothes, she sat on her bed facing toward the window. Her breathing became slow and rhythmical, her heart beating with an even, steady pulse. Not a trace of anger ever emerged. She still loved George; she would always love him. Whether he could return her love or not did not matter. Hers was unconditional.

Afterward, she lay down to rest, although not really feeling sleepy. She did notice the keys were missing from the pillow. She was glad she'd remembered to leave them behind.

After peacefully dosing for awhile, never falling totally asleep, she sat up and looked at her watch. "It's probably time I make an appearance downstairs," she thought, aware of a clattering noise in the kitchen. It was eleven o'clock.

Margaret and Claire were in the kitchen preparing for the buffet lunch when Indu entered. Margaret warmly greeted her. "Here's the dear. We thought we'd lost you to the grave. Of course, you know I'm only joking. I think it's quite good to sleep in sometimes."

Indu gave them both a shy, appreciative smile, truly relieved to hear that they actually thought she'd been upstairs all morning sleeping. It was exactly what she had hoped. Changing the subject, she asked about the others.

Margaret answered, "They're still downstairs getting oil put in their noses. I can't believe I did it a second time. At the Foundation I thought it just felt too weird. Today, I think I almost liked it. Isn't that funny?"

Claire agreed, "I liked it this time, too. It did feel relaxing. How about you, Indu? Do you do it often?'"

Indu replied hesitantly. "There was a stretch of time when I did it every day." She didn't like to talk about her spiritual practices and oil *neti* was one of the more powerful ones.

"Every day!" Claire gasped. "Why did you do it every day?"

"As I remember," Indu spoke, not really sure what answer to give, "it was during a period of my life that was quite stressful. *Neti* does have a strong effect on the nerves. I found it helped me stay grounded."

To herself she thought, "That's certainly a plausible response, and not too far from the truth, now that I think about it. I only left out the small fact that Guruji had told me I should do it every day. I would certainly not have done it otherwise. No doubt he recognized the need for it." She had concealed this last fact because certain exchanges between Guru and devotee were hard to explain. It was a relationship far too perplexing for anyone to understand. That such a trust should exist between any two human beings was no ordinary phenomenon.

Indu was glad when Margaret changed the subject again, this time to George. "I just want you to know," Margaret said, "I think he's a very sweet fellow. And there's no doubt he's meant to be on a spiritual path. It's easy to tell just by the resonance in his voice. That's the first thing I notice in any spiritual seeker."

It was exactly what Indu had told George. She was glad Margaret had noticed, too. It only confirmed her own inner instincts—that George was a great spirit on his way to realizing his true nature. "Maybe that's why I have such unconditional love for him," she reflected to herself. "Somehow all I can see is his shining spirit pouring out from behind his mask of confusion, doubts and questions. Maybe that's why I can tolerate the turmoil between us." To Margaret, she only quietly nodded in modest agreement.

Margaret continued, "One other thing which absolutely gives it away, about him being a spiritual man, I mean... It's in his eyes. They're so beautiful and clear." The "windows of the soul," as Indu had thought earlier. Turning and looking at Indu, Margaret suddenly burst out laughing. Although puzzled, Indu amiably smiled back at her. Margaret quickly explained, "My dear, you should see the color of your cheeks. They're as red as cherries."

Indu raised her hands up to her face. Just talking about George had made her unconsciously blush. She laughed and confessed, "I'm afraid I'm rather fond of him."

"Oh my," Margaret sighed. "I remember when I first met Paul. I couldn't eat for weeks. My appetite simply disappeared. I couldn't understand it. I didn't even know I was in love. I thought I was too old for that sort of thing."

Indu thought, "So she lost her appetite, too. That really must be a sign of falling in love. My God, am I ever in love! How is it that the stomach automatically knows? Mine certainly is a smart one." None of this did she intend to mention in the present conversation. Margaret's last comment, though, pulled her from her reverie.

Indu turned and asked, "What do you mean, too old? How can anyone be too old for love?" She was genuinely interested to hear Margaret's story.

"Well, I'd already had one marriage. As far as I was concerned, that was enough for me."

"I just assumed you and Paul had always been married," Indu replied.

"No, no. We met ten years ago. The minute I saw him I knew something was different about him, but I couldn't figure it out. Finally it became so obvious that we were meant to be together, everything just suddenly clicked. But I think he realized it before I did. Seeing now how well we work together, there's no question that in lifetimes past we've been together."

Indu wondered if it would ever become that clear for her and George. "There's heavy karma between George and me," she thought. "I just don't know what to make of it."

She got up and began to help get things ready for the group feast. As the others came into the kitchen, no one questioned her about her late night or absence from the program that morning. Even Shakti was too preoccupied to say much, except to gaily raise one finger to her lips to show she'd kept the secret, at least as best she could. As delicious as everything looked, Indu wasn't even tempted to fix a plate for herself. Instead, she kept busy doing dishes and cleaning the table. After lunch, there was to be another rebirthing session.

All together downstairs in the yoga room, Indu let thoughts of George drop as she concentrated on the breathing technique. She did love these sessions, reaching out to people without them knowing who she was and having them accept her, allowing her to touch their head and abdomen in a trusting union of their breath and hers. Again, probably from lack of eating, she felt intoxicatingly dizzy and her hands vibrated with tingles. This session concluded Guruji's weekend workshop. The following day, they would return to London.

As she was leaving the meditation room to go back to the house, she passed the table with Guruji's booklets and cassette tapes. One booklet in particular caught her attention. It was entitled, "How to Select a Guru?" She saw there was only one copy left. She knew from her talk with George that it would be a good one for him to read. Hoping no one would mind if she appropriated it, she removed it from the table along with three others: a beautifully transcribed meditation taken from a cassette tape of Guruji's, a collection of mystical essays Guruji had written over the years, and a booklet on *Nada* Yoga or the science behind the ringing sound in the head.

"It's the least I can do," she thought. "I'll send him these words of Guruji's which contain divine nectar and divine truths. They may not help him now, but maybe sometime in his life he will find them and they will fill him with inspiration and help him in his spiritual quest, for I am certain he will be a devoted seeker on the path to God realization." She carefully noted the amount she owed their publication department.

Returning back to her room, she sat cross-legged on the bed and suddenly had a strong desire to write a letter to George, or rather, things she wanted to say to George began running through her head and she simply began writing them down.

℘ * * * ℃

At this point, she got up from her armchair and returned minutes later with a gray folder. Inside was a pile of photocopied papers and a small stack of letters held together with a rubber band. The papers were copies of letters she had written to him, revealing that there was much more to her story. Fortunately, it was her habit, since she kept no diary, to make duplicates of the letters she wrote and in this way keep a record of some of her feelings and thoughts. On top of the pile was a handwritten copy of this first letter written to George. I asked her about their correspondence. She assured me that although the letters were very private and dear, she did want me to see them. In fact, without these letters, it would be challenging to complete her story. But for the time being, she handed me this first one to read. It was short:

Dear George,

Was actually able to get back into the house without anyone seeing me. Was grateful for that. Probably only Shakti and maybe Uma know of our all-night outing. Everyone was

327

still in the meditation room, so had some time alone—to think, to reflect. Then took a sponge bath and meditated on the Irish Sea. Finally went downstairs to the kitchen where Margaret and Claire were preparing lunch. Had a nice visit with Margaret. She told me she liked you a lot. Do you know, one funny thing happened. She noticed just talking about you made my cheeks turn red. Could only agree with her that love does do strange things. She told me how she lost her appetite when she first fell in love with Paul. Didn't tell her that mine had been gone for over a week. After lunch, there was another rebirthing session which brought Guruji's workshop to a close.

Must admit, just after you left, my heart was filled with intense sadness. But I watched it and suddenly it dissolved into a peaceful feeling. What came through clearly as I stood looking out the window over the water was that if we are ever to meet again, divine intervention will be needed. You're being pulled in one direction and I'm moving in another. Only if the Law of Nature allows it can we bring our two lives together. If it is not meant to be, then so it is destined. I will take this chance to say how lovely it was to be with you this weekend. In fact, cannot begin to describe how deeply my heart was moved to see you. Such feelings, which are themselves so unexplainable, cannot easily be expressed in words.

Will have love for you always, Indu

Wanting to inscribe something on the front page of the booklets, she had thought how to express her heart in the fewest possible words. The inscriptions she had also noted in the margins of her paper. She had written in one: "Blessed are the rare moments in life when by a glance Two meet again." Feeling their past connection had been a strong one, she had written in the other: "In loving memory of what was before and what has come to pass."

ॐ * * * ॐ

Setting the letter and booklets aside, Indu went downstairs to find Paul to ask if he had a large envelope which could hold the booklets. She wanted to mail them the following morning before departing from New Brighton. It seemed the best way to end this chapter of their most extraordinary relationship. She might never see George again, but at least she would end it lovingly.

Fortunately, Paul had a small folder just the right size. As a last thought before sealing it, she pulled out the three small pictures of herself and chose the silly one, writing on the back, "Just so you won't forget."

TWENTY-ONE

~

Back in London, Indu woke up Tuesday morning feeling drained and tired. She consoled herself that it was not surprising given the long day's travel the day before. She had gotten the package off to George from New Brighton. "It should arrive in two days," the clerk had said.

"So by tomorrow he should have it," she thought as she got up and prepared for the day. She dragged herself through the London streets following behind Guruji, trying hard to forget how much she was missing George. Mentally, she kept telling herself that it was much better to work through their karma without having to marry. She had heard somewhere or read in a mystical book that concentration on the ringing sound in the ear was useful for burning off one's karmas. She didn't really understand what that meant but she did know she was going to need as much help as possible to get through her present karmically-distressed state. The entire day she listened intently to the inner ringing sound, struggling with the confusion between her emotions and her mind.

"I must simply accept the fact that I may never see him again," she lectured herself, but she couldn't shake the heaviness in her heart. Valiantly, she tried to give the appearance that her life was continuing just as it had been. None of the others commented about any change in her mood or behavior. Naturally, they teased her, wanting to know what the prospects were for her and George. With as much levity as she could manage, she replied, "Heaven only knows," and left it at that. By the end of the day, she had to silently admit that pretending not to be in love was no easy job.

That night after evening program, they were all together in the apartment. Guruji sat in his corner chair, Uma was in her room, and Shakti and Mangala were in the kitchen. Indu sat down on her bed in front of Guruji and tried not to think of anything. That was what he had taught her: "When problems stand before you, simply be the neutral observer." She had been trying to be a neutral observer all day, although having only marginal success. Now before the Guru, she was determined to keep trying.

Guruji interrupted her concentrated effort with a question. "Did you find a copy of that Tibetan bowl record?"

Guruji had asked her that morning to purchase a copy of the record that they had heard in Nhoj's room, but none of the record stores she had called had had it. When they'd passed a record store that afternoon while shopping, she'd stepped inside to inquire but without luck. "So far, Guruji," she replied, "I haven't been able to find one, but I'll keep looking."

With a steady eye on her, he said, "Why don't you ask that young man to make a tape recording from his record?"

"Yes, I can do that," she agreed, imagining she could write a letter right away to Nhoj asking if he'd do them that favor. "I'm sure Nhoj will be happy to mail us a copy," she said to him, trying to sound positive.

With his twinkling eyes dancing before her, a phenomenon which she had learned to watch for since it meant mystical intrigue was afoot, he stated, "Well... Or maybe someone can bring it."

She nodded silently as she shrugged her shoulders to say that anything was possible. To contradict her Guru by giving a skeptical response was something she didn't want to do. She knew that skepticism was a futile play of the mind, and Guruji operated at a level far beyond that. Still, she could not suppress the doubtful thought, "I'm afraid the odds of someone bringing it are slim, especially if it's George you have in mind."

The others then came back into the room and there was a general motion for everyone to go to bed. It was a quarter past ten. Indu stood as Guruji got up from his chair. He disappeared into his room and she went over to sit on Shakti's daybed. Unexpectedly, he reappeared in the doorway, his eyes penetrating right through her, and said, "Why don't you call the Foundation about the tape." With that, he went back to his room.

"Why the special emphasis to tell me to call?" she wondered, the significance of which was not lost on her. She never took anything Guruji said lightheartedly. She sat pondering what to do. Here she had a bona fide excuse to call the Foundation wherein she could naturally ask to speak to George. But truly, it was the last thing she wanted to do at that moment. She didn't want him to think she was pining after him. Quite weary from the emotional burden, she began feeling angry with herself for being so unbearably attached to him. He had said he didn't want to see her and she didn't want to try to change his mind. The more she thought about it, the angrier she got. She'd already made her last contact through her letter. Now it was up to him to decide what he wanted to do.

"I will call. I'll call and talk with Nhoj. But I'll do it tomorrow," she thought. "I'm in no mood to do it tonight. Besides, it's too late."

The voice of procrastination suddenly jarred her attention. This was not her usual way whenever Guruji made a suggestion. He had come back out especially to tell her to call. If he'd meant tomorrow, he would have waited until tomorrow. She chastised herself, "How could I have almost made such a mistake? Regardless of my personal feelings, I must call tonight, or at least try."

She collected £1.50 in change, got the number from her purse and walked down the stairs to the phone. As she dialed the number, she wondered if anyone would even answer at such a late hour. The phone rang twice and someone did pick up. It was Nhoj.

"Nhoj! You're exactly the one I was wanting. This is Indu." She couldn't believe it. Of all the people, how was it that Nhoj had answered her call? The thought "Never underestimate the Guru" teasingly taunted her. She could feel some divine mischief. Her resistance now melted, she was more than willing to play along and see what would happen.

"Indu, it's good to hear from you. What is it I can do for you?"

"Well, I'm calling for Guruji," and she explained about trying to get a copy of the Tibetan bell record in London without success.

"Of course, I'll be happy to make a recording of it for him. No problem."

"That would be very kind of you, Nhoj. Do you have the address of where we're at?"

"Sure, we have it here. Listen, Indu, since I've got you on the phone, could you chant again the *Gāyatrī* Mantra for me. For the life of me, I can't remember the melody to it."

It had happened to her before that when something unexpected was requested, her mind would go blank. And her mind was blank. Had her anticipation of talking to George short-circuited everything else? She didn't want to believe it. She took a deep breath, determined to give it a try. What came out was close but terribly off-key.

"Nhoj, I'm sorry. I seem to be a little tone deaf at the moment. How about I figure it out on a keyboard and send you the notes?" she said, hoping to smooth over her embarrassment.

"Gee, that would be great. Say, do you want to talk to George?"

Nhoj had picked up on her anxiety and had correctly guessed the reason for it. She wished it hadn't been so obvious but there was nothing she could do.

Looking down at her dwindling pile of change, she replied, "Only if he's close by because I only have thirty pence left."

"Well, he's not far. Hold a second." The line went quiet.

Just then, Muniji peeked around the corner from his room and put a bag of ten pence coins in her hand. Before she could protest, he had slipped back into his room and closed the door. "Guess I'm going to talk to George whether I want to or not," she thought. Moved by Muniji's kindness, her anxiety began to wane. It was simply in the divine planning that she talk to George that night, come what may.

His familiar voice was there on the other end.

"George... funny thing... Guruji asked me to call to request a copy of Nhoj's Tibetan bell record and Nhoj actually answered." She paused. "So, how are you?"

"Well, I just got back today. Stayed on an extra day with my aunt and mother. I picked up Alison at the station this evening. Things are still a little rocky. But the visit in Chester was really lovely. Got back there before noon on Sunday and everything was fine."

"I'm really glad to hear that. I mailed you a few of Guruji's booklets before I left New Brighton. You'll probably get them tomorrow."

"You did? I'll be sure to watch for them. Indu, I'm planning to come into London on Thursday to have a cassette deck installed in my car. I haven't made a schedule yet, but do you think you'd have time to visit in the evening?"

"Sure," she said, amazed. "What time will you be coming in?"

"Probably late in the morning."

"In the morning? Then why don't we try to meet earlier, that is, if you have time?"

His voice becoming warm and resonant, he replied, "Well, that's what I wanted but I didn't know if you could take the whole day off from the group."

So he does want to see me, her heart rejoiced.

Remembering Guruji's twinkling eye, she replied with fair amount of certainty, "For some reason, I don't think Guruji will object."

"Really? Then why don't I call you tomorrow evening when the details are set."

"You know, I don't know if Nhoj can make the tape that fast, but if it's ready, maybe you could bring it with you."

"That's a good idea. I'll call tomorrow between seven and seven-thirty, before your evening program."

"All right. Talk to you then.

"Goodbye."

"Goodbye."

࿐ * * * ࿐

Through her years with Guruji, Indu told me, it had always been in subtle ways like this that he had shown her a level of understanding beyond physical limits. It was not to be elucidated through words. He would never ask her specifics about the call and she would never comment on the depth of his wisdom, yet both would know that their bond as Guru and devotee had once again been confirmed.

An uninitiated person often questions the prudence of blindly following the words or indications of a spiritual teacher, particularly when it means repressing their personal planning. But trusting in an Enlightened One had shown Indu time and time again that divine planning far surpassed her own. Initially, though, comprehending the magnitude of this divine operation had come as an astounding revelation to her.

To illustrate man's shortsightedness in this regard, one evening Guruji told the parable of the frog king Shrimad Manduka, king of a vast water well. His kingdom included his parliament, his army, and all the citizens of his empire. One day, two guest frogs came from outside the well and told the king of the ocean. The frog king could not believe that any body of water existed greater than his well. Accusing the guests of being heretics, he banished them from his well kingdom and threatened imprisonment if they returned. "Even the universe," he claimed, "could not be more vast than my well."

After finishing the story, Guruji had said, "It is like the universe in the planetarium."

When she heard him say this, Indu had been startled, suddenly grasping the reason Guruji had insistently taken them to the Hayden Planetarium in New York City. The illusion of being limited within the boundaries of the body was just as ridiculous as believing that the universe was confined within the dome of the planetarium or that the breadth of a water well was greater than the ocean. Fireworks illumined the night of her soul as this realization came—that the mind sets absurd limits to human existence, substantiating only dimensions within time and space, the realm of thought.

"But the ocean is greater than the well and the universe is greater than the dome of the planetarium and we are greater than the boundaries of body and mind," she marveled with me. This was Guruji's great lesson. "It's only in our ignorance that we imagine otherwise." Divine Nature wants us to recognize the absurdity of our self-imposed limitations.

ℰℴ * * * ℭℬ

"So George will bring the cassette tape on Thursday," she thought, reverently acknowledging Guruji's wisdom as she climbed the stairs back up to the apartment. She would see George again after all. Still, their conversation had been short, and she couldn't begin to discern how he was feeling about their relationship. The following day, anger finally did surface. It was harbored in her heart from his comment in New Brighton about not wanting to see her. She suspected some of it stemmed from her own anxiety about their next meeting. Regardless, at the time of his call that evening, the anger was still there. He said he'd arrive at ten o'clock the next morning.

"Shall I come pick you up?" he offered.

"Is it on your way?" she asked.

"Actually, it's not even close."

Defensively, she suggested, "If that's the case, why don't we meet at a tube station somewhere?"

"Okay. How about the West Kensington station at eleven o'clock?"

She had no idea where it was but agreed to it anyway. To prevent confusion in her mind, she asked, "Which line is that on?"

"It's on the District Line."

Had she known it was on the other side of London, she might have reconsidered his offer. "Wherever it is," she thought, "I'll simply leave at ten o'clock. Surely I can find it in an hour."

They both carefully skirted any discussion of their personal feelings. It was clear that they did want to see each other again, and that there was a lot they needed to talk about. She could only imagine that he detected a cautious reserve in her voice and therefore asked, "How have you been feeling?"

At that moment there was only one answer she could give. "I am feeling a little angry."

"Is it because of Alison?"

"No, George. I'll explain tomorrow."

"Indu, I did receive your package." There was a short pause. "Thank you."

So he had read her letter. No wonder he had not suspected her anger to be from anything he had said that weekend. Even she was surprised how subliminally it had crept in, juxtaposed with her love, both coexisting with mutual force in her heart, neither contradicting the other. Her love for him was as intense as ever, with her desire to see him increasing by the minute. When she hung up the phone, the mix of her emotions, with the anger stemming from love and loving in spite of anger, left her stomach in queasy distress.

That night after the evening program was over, she deliberated as to when the best time would be to approach Guruji with her plan to meet George. It would be the first occasion that she had ever chosen to be separate from her Guru for the whole day. Usually having to travel great distances and make special arrangements to him, she would carefully, even religiously cherish every minute she could spend with him. But she knew she needed to see George, and she prayed she could do it with Guruji's blessing.

As odds would have it, though, a London devotee followed them up to the apartment after the evening program and made the grand invitation to take the entire group on a trip the next day to see Stonehenge, located two hours south of London by car. As much as she desperately wanted to see the great prehistoric stones, she would have gladly relinquished the chance if it meant she could see George one more time. The discussion over the trip went on for half an hour, but it was resolved that a luncheon invitation instead would be accepted and the Stonehenge trip postponed to the following week. With that decided, Guruji had gone directly to bed. If in the morning he requested her to attend the luncheon, Indu knew that she'd have no way to inform George, who would be leaving the Foundation very early.

That night she thought, "But everything is in divine hands, so no use worrying about possible complications. It's a redundancy if ever I've heard of one!" She laughed at her inane anxiety.

The next morning she was dressed and ready by eight-thirty. She sat counting each moment until Guruji emerged at nine o'clock from his room for a small group meditation held each morning. He sat down in his corner chair and immediately handed Shakti a book to read aloud.

"This is just what I suspected," Indu thought. "Not until the minute before I have to leave will I be able to talk to Guruji." After the reading, a period of silent meditation followed.

Indu tried hard to surrender all desires, praying that her love for George and her love for her Guru should not be in conflict. "Two kinds of love, so different, so intensely present in my heart: one ethereally divine and the other exquisitely personal. Can I possibly be true to both?" She searched deep in her heart to understand, watching during the meditation how the pulsations immersed her consciousness in a sublime pool of love.

It was ten o'clock when the meditation ended. Guruji stood up and Indu knew it was time. Whatever preference he had would sway her decision. He stood looking at her, seeing her hesitation, knowing she had something to say. He smiled, waiting patiently. "What are the words I should use?" she thought, racking her brain. "How can I tell him that I want only what's best—for him, for George, for myself?"

"Guruji?"

"Hmmm," she heard through his smile.

"George is going to be in London today…"

But before she could convey anything further, he waved his arms in front of her and exclaimed, "Call, call, call."

Taken aback by the urgency in his voice, she quickly tried to explain. "Guruji, I did call him, Tuesday night. He's bringing the cassette tape."

Standing as quietly as he had been before, he replied with a whimsical gleam in his eyes, "Good."

"So if it's okay, I'll meet George this morning at eleven o'clock." She said this as she glanced down at her watch. "It's already quite late. I should probably be leaving very soon."

"Leaving?" he asked with surprise. "Isn't he coming here?"

"We're planning to meet, Guruji, at the West Kensington tube station." In saying so, she revealed that the plans had previously been made. Although his manner became suddenly austere, still his eyes were playful. Truly curious what the outcome would be, she watched him steadfastly.

"No, no," he began saying. "He should come here."

"He did offer, Guruji, but it seemed simpler to meet at West Kensington," she said. The other three women stood listening to the exchange.

"It's not a good idea," Guruji said with firmness. With those words, Indu was ready to give up the entire scheme.

Shakti jumped in with the question, "Indu, would George know to call here if you didn't show up?"

"Yes, probably he would," she replied, knowing that she and George hadn't verbally made any back-up plan. Everything had been decided so quickly on the phone.

"You see," Guruji said, "you don't know London. You'll get lost."

Indu thought for a second and then responded, "I have a map of the Underground and my tube pass. I think I can find my way." It was true, she had little experience navigating the London transit system, but she had been counting on extra time and common sense to get her there. The others rallied behind her. It seemed they all wanted her to be able to see George one more time.

"She'll be okay," one said.

"I'm sure she can find it," said another.

"He'll call here if she's late," the third one added.

Through all of this, it was clear that Guruji was not upset by her desire to be with George. He finally gave his blessing by saying, "Go ahead and try to meet him."

She walked quickly to the nearest Underground station in Belsize Park and got on the Northern Line heading south. "Shouldn't be too hard," she thought while sitting in her seat studying the map.

"I'll catch the Piccadilly Line at Leicester Square, go to South Kensington station and change to the District Line going west to West Kensington." What she hadn't known was that at her point of entry onto the train, the Northern Line would later divide into two southbound routes: one going through Leicester Square and the other going east through Bank Street. Already she had made one mistake.

She'd gotten on the Bank Street train, which was taking her in exactly the opposite direction from West Kensington. After realizing her error, she quickly analyzed the map. "Still, there's no harm," she told herself. "I'll change trains at King's Cross, catch the Victoria Line to Victoria Station and from there I can also pick up the District Line." But at King's Cross she managed instead to board the Metropolitan Line still going east. She'd gone all the way to Moorgate, three stops later, before realizing again her mistake. She was now even further from West Kensington and it was 10:40 a.m.

"Good grief, was Guruji ever right," she moaned, knowing there was no way she could make it in time to meet George. Fortunately with her train pass she could have changed trains a hundred times without having to pay extra fare. The only recourse that she could see was to get on the Circle Line going either direction, since it literally made a circle around London, and change to the District Line at Gloucester Road, which was diametrically opposite from Moorgate on the circle. If she had known that the Circle Line alone was going to take forty-five minutes, she might have opted to surface and take a taxi, gladly paying extra. But blinded by naiveté, she began the long trek around the loop.

Stop after stop, she watched the minutes passing. If she didn't make any more mistakes, she was still going to be extremely late, and she was helpless to do anything to let George know that she was coming. With a long delay at Paddington, she felt sure she had never been in a more agitated state. She tried to console herself that if George wasn't there, she would wait an hour in case he returned. If he didn't, then she'd take a tour of London or go shopping instead. She reminded herself again and again, it's all in the hands of destiny. The thought comforted her heart but did not do much to mitigate her agonizing restlessness. At Gloucester there were four different trains running on the District Line.

"At least this folly has taught me how to use the Underground," she thought as she carefully examined which train on the District Line she would need. One went east to Upminster. "God forbid I should get on that one," she bemoaned, carefully paying heed. Another went south to Wimbledon which also would do her no good. Both the Richmond and Broadway trains went west. Finding the platform for the Richmond-bound train, she boarded and soon found herself at West Kensington. It was five minutes before noon.

The doors to the train opened and she stepped onto the platform, looking furtively for George, but he was nowhere in sight. "It will be a miracle if he's still here," she lamented. If George hadn't phoned before eleven-thirty when Guruji was departing for the luncheon, he would have had no way to know whether she was coming or not, since no one in the group would have been there to take his call. She followed the "Way Out" signs, feeling relieved just to get above ground. She walked up the steps, showed her pass to the attendant at the gate, and then suddenly saw George. He came walking toward her with a big smile. Before a word was spoken, they were in each other's arms.

"I'm really sorry for being late. Thank God you waited. I was sure you would have gone by now."

"I finally called Muniji's house and Uma told me you were coming to West Kensington, so I knew to wait."

"What time did you call?"

"It was 11:40 a.m."

"They were still there?"

"It was very lucky. Uma said they had been on their way out the door when Guruji heard the phone and had sent her back upstairs to answer it."

Indu made the silent prayer, "God bless Guruji for knowing."

Looking into George's face, she could only think how much she cared for him. Seeing him walking toward her after all the trauma on the train had been one of the happiest moments in her life. If there had been awkwardness on the phone, anger in her heart or confusion in his, something magically happened when once again their eyes met. Walking hand in hand, they left the station and ventured onto the streets of London. And so began their third and final meeting before the long separation which would test the power of their love.

TWENTY-TWO

~

Their first stop was to take George's car to the shop where he would have the stereo installed. On the way there, George drove down a small side street and pointed to a red brick building with white wrought-iron balconies.

"That's where I lived for four years while I was finishing my degree in hotel administration. I shared a flat with Oliver, the chap we're going to have lunch with today. He finished the same degree and has quite a nice job with a private business club."

Indu was impressed with the neighborhood: clean, groomed and quaint. She liked thinking he had spent four years in such nice surroundings.

George was saying something about Nhoj. "...and I came into the flat, headed straight for the loo and found Nhoj soaking in the bathtub."

"Nhoj was in your bathtub?" she asked, knowing she had missed part of the story while being preoccupied with perusing the area.

"He was. He'd somehow climbed up to the balcony and come in through the window. Hadn't seen him in over a year and he suddenly appears in the bath. Can you imagine?" he said, shaking his head as though still in disbelief. "God, I really love him. Do you have friends like that?"

"What? Friends that appear in my bathtub?"

"No, silly. Friends that you maybe won't see for months and months and then unexpectedly or not, you see them again and you feel just as close as ever."

"I have a couple who are like that. I think that's when you know it's a real friendship. And they are pretty rare," she said. But she couldn't help thinking to herself how it was even stranger to feel that unbelievable closeness with someone whom one didn't even know. She was thinking of George, whom she'd met less than three weeks before.

After turning a few corners, they pulled into a whitewashed garage and circled around to the back. "Do you want to come in and help me choose the most reasonably priced stereo system they've got?"

"Don't think I can be of much help, but I'll come in with you."

A clerk inquired if they needed assistance. George replied in a most serious voice, "I need you to sell me a tape deck and I want to know what's your best deal."

"We've got a Quasar on sale right now, sir. It's this one over here."

Indu liked the respect the clerk showed George and wondered if it was just the British style of business or if it was George's straightforward, genteel manner that commanded it. After looking at several different models, George settled on the Quasar. She was surprised he could make the decision so quickly. Two walls of the little shop, from top to bottom, were nothing but tape decks, from the simplest to the most advanced in audio equipment. George had taken it all in within five minutes and then made his choice. She silently admired his discriminating decisiveness.

"You can pick up your car at six o'clock this evening, Mr. Acroilus."

When Indu heard this, she realized that meant they had five hours on foot. She wondered what they'd do for five hours. Of course, the car was hardly needed for getting around London. Between the buses and the Underground, every part was easily accessible. "The Underground," she thought with a shiver. But this time she'd have George with her.

As George walked back to get something from the car, she noticed a small hole in the shoulder of his sweater and thought, "I could have that fixed in five minutes, just a little blue thread and you'd never see it." It was the same sweater he had been wearing at the Foundation when he'd appeared out of the darkness of the night to fetch ten cups of tea. She laughed at her mending instinct. "What is it in a female's psyche that makes her want to mend a man's clothes, as though a man needs someone to take care of him? Typically female," she mocked herself, almost in dismay.

They set out on foot, hand in hand, immediately jumping into a serious discussion, talking in general about relationships and about marriage. George was saying, "In the marriages I've seen, I mean the really good ones, the couples tend to always do things together. That means there has to be a strong tendency for both to agree on the same activity."

Indu figured he was alluding to the obvious differences between them, in background and culture. "I don't think a marriage has to be that way to be a good one," Indu countered. "Two people should be able to love each other and still do things alone. For instance, I'm always going to have an interest in staying connected to Guruji's ashram in New York. Would it be fair for me to expect my husband to have the same interest, with the same intensity? And suppose he enjoys horse racing and I don't? Does that mean I have any right to deny him the pleasure of going just because I refuse to sit in the stands and be bored silly?"

"How can you be bored at a horse race?" he emphatically exclaimed.

"George, I've never been to a horse race. I'm just using it as an example, you nut. If two people love each other, really, truly love each other, whether they do things together or not isn't going to increase that love. In fact, it's almost a declaration of its strength by letting the other go off and do whatever makes him or her happy without feeling neglected or abandoned."

"That kind of marriage would take two strong, independent people," he announced.

"Yes, it would," she heartily agreed. "And what would be important would be for them to discover something that was commonly enjoyed, something they'd take great pleasure in doing together. That kind of marriage could never get dull because instead of growing apart, they'd continue growing closer and closer."

"Mmmm. Sounds good to me," he said, giving a quick turn of his head to show two ruddy cheeks and a smile.

So far they had both artfully avoided any particulars about their own relationship, but there was no question they had both been giving the topic serious thought. They dropped the subject for the time being as they hurried down the steps of another tube station. Oliver worked at a club not far from Berkeley Square. It was a lovely part of London. After a ten-minute train ride, they emerged again into the slightly overcast September day.

Walking in the direction of the club, Indu began to explain why she had felt angry when they had last talked on the phone. "I couldn't disagree with you, George. You do have responsibilities to other people. And God knows, if you don't want to create more karma for yourself, you'd better be darn careful how you meet those responsibilities. But what slowly gripped me was the utter uselessness of us even trying to stay in contact. It just didn't make sense. If we didn't want to try to beat all the odds to see each other when we're in the same city, why would we even want to try to stay in contact when living on separate continents?"

"But Indu, I know that. I felt the same thing. It was so confusing on Sunday. I didn't know what to do," he said, regretful despair shadowing his words.

"Do you know what I've been trying to do for the past three days?" she confessed, their steps perfectly synchronized, her hand linked in his. He shook his head "no." "I've been trying to burn up the karma between us by listening to the *nādam,* the ringing sound in the ear. Somewhere I heard that it has that power. I don't know if it's true or not. But I just wanted to be finished with whatever karma we have. I would never have called Tuesday night except that Guruji said I should. But George, I can't deny what I'm feeling today." She squeezed his hand. "I would if I could, but I can't."

As she said these last words, George stopped in front of a prestigious-looking facade inset with a polished wooden door framing a beautifully ornate beveled window. This was the club. He held the door open for her. A concierge politely addressed them before they'd taken five steps into the hallway. From their attire it was obvious they weren't business clientele. In a most assured manner, George made the request that Oliver Winston Chadbury be informed of their arrival. "He works in this establishment." By the nod of the man's head, George knew no further elaboration was needed. As they stood at the bottom of the stairs waiting for Oliver to descend, George said, half under his breath, "For some reason, hearing what you've just said has rather frightened me."

Indu wanted to ask him what exactly he meant by that, but at that moment a smile lit up George's face as he saw Oliver at the head of the landing. Indu looked up the staircase to see an equally broad grin on the face of an admirable-looking fellow. In a few agile steps, Oliver descended the remaining stairs and with unabashed exuberance wrapped both arms around George's shoulders for a quick hug. In contrast and in true gentlemanly fashion, he extended his hand to make Indu's acquaintance. She liked him right away, although she curiously observed the striking difference between these two obviously close friends. Oliver was several inches taller than George and seemingly several years older. His deportment was reserved and distinguished, not totally unlike George's only heightened by a self-assured finesse, further accentuated by his light gray suit and black leather Oxfords. George was clearly the more carefree and unencumbered of the two.

She walked next to George, listening to them banter back and forth.

"It really is grand of you, Oliver, to give up your meal ticket for the day to have a sandwich with us. Tell me, what savory delights did you renounce in this honorable sacrifice?"

"Oh, some kind of paté consommé julienne, egg croquettes, veal daube, and chocolate mousse," Oliver replied, rattling off the menu. George made an exaggerated grimace. Indu finally understood that working at the club entitled Oliver to the same elite luncheon menu as that served to the patrons, and instead he was settling for a deli sandwich just to enjoy George's company. Oliver led them to a small walk-through deli not far from the club. Indu ordered a cream cheese and cucumber sandwich with cole slaw, George a tuna sandwich and slaw, and Oliver something equally unpretentious. With their three white paper bags, they entered Berkeley Square and settled on a park bench that easily accommodated the three of them, George in the middle.

Indu sat listening as the two former flatmates discussed mutual acquaintances, who had married whom, as well as the health and occupations of their respective family members. Realizing she'd forgotten to pick up a fork for the cole slaw, she wondered if Oliver would be totally shocked if she ate it with her fingers. It was too much trouble to walk back to the deli and yet hunger made the slaw appear temptingly tasty.

"If George looks too aghast at the impropriety of it, I'll simply forego the slaw," she thought. "Otherwise I do hate to waste it."

To her great surprise, a few minutes later George turned toward her and, seeing her trying to daintily eat the shredded cabbage with two fingers, he helped himself to his own, using the same manner of conveyance.

"Forgot forks, didn't we?" he said after enjoying a mouthful. Oliver seemed undaunted if not amused. It was almost as if he admired that she and George could be so practical about it. She also liked that Oliver was tactfully avoiding any question regarding the exact nature of her friendship with George. In the course of conversation he did politely verify her American nationality, which he had easily guessed, and inquired as to what had brought her to their country and whether she'd enjoyed her stay thus far. He then wanted to hear all about George's future plans. At one point when the talk was not even tangentially related to her, George raised his hand and seeming unconscious of any outward display of affection, gave three long strokes down her back while still carrying on his end of the conversation.

Fully aware of the message it must have conveyed to Oliver, Indu wondered, "Is it George's sweet way of telling his friend that I'm not just a passing acquaintance? And whoever commented on George's inhibitions about expressing intimate feelings in front of others was certainly wrong." His caress gladdened her heart.

Oliver's lunch hour was almost up, having passed quickly for all of them. George whipped out a camera from his knapsack and leaped out in front of the bench.

"Come on, you two, slide in a little closer. I don't have a wide angle lens on this thing." He had meant it as a joke to draw her and Oliver's attention to the enormous gap left between them. Indu looked at Oliver, who was looking at her. They both slid in toward the center although still leaving a respectable distance. She was a virtual stranger to him and he to her, but their mutual love for the friend before them, kneeling with a camera, would forever make them more than just strangers. The moment captured on film, they deposited their empty bags in a nearby trash bin and exited through the black iron gates of the park. Respectfully nodding to Indu, Oliver parted from George with a brotherly hug and handshake. They both knew it might be a long time before they'd see one another again. She and George watched as the back of Oliver's business suit disappeared into the crowded street. Indu was touched by the strong bond that obviously stood between the two men she'd just seen part.

The look on George's face was forlorn. He turned toward her and said with unabashed despair in his voice, "I hate saying goodbye." He gazed sorrowfully into her eyes. "Do you know what I want to do right now?"

"No," she said, thinking she'd do anything to make him look happier.

"I just want to put my head on your shoulder. Do you mind?" They stood silently outside the large rectangular park, in the middle of a bustling afternoon crowd, his head drooping tiredly upon her shoulder, their hands clasped at their sides.

"It's so strange, Indu," he said, looking up at her. "Usually I'm very happy about my life. But sometimes, like now, I feel so in limbo. Just look at Oliver. We graduated at the same time from the same program. He's out there doing something with his degree, climbing the ladder to success. Does it strike you as strange that I'm not doing the same?"

"Do you want my honest observation?" His beseeching eyes said that he did. "I don't know Oliver from Adam. But he didn't strike me as particularly happy. I mean, he was happy to see you, but in hearing him talk about things in his life and the few comments he made about his work, I didn't get the impression that he was overjoyed about anything. He's simply doing what he thinks he should be doing. Is it your fault that your spirit already knows it can't be happy doing what Oliver is doing, scrambling hard and fast in the nitty-gritty business world? George, my spirit wouldn't be happy either. Maybe there's a fire in us, or a restlessness that makes us want to go and see, to search and explore, to find out and understand something that lies ahead of us. It's not meant for everyone to climb the same ladder. And believe it or not, you have your own ladder in front of you and you're climbing it in your own way, and so am I. You can't measure your life against another's. Everyone's destiny is different. And as I said before, I like you just the way you are."

The smile that broke across his face made her breathe a sigh of relief. He kissed her sweetly on the cheek. "Sometimes I guess I start worrying about how my life is going to turn out. Fortunately, it doesn't happen very often. No doubt, someday I'll settle down and find a way to bring in a decent income. It's just I'm not ready for that now. I'm just not ready."

"Certainly not. You've still got Germany and Greece to explore and who knows what else in between."

"Zimbabwe."

"Zimbabwe isn't in between Germany and Greece!" she teased, wondering what Zimbabwe had to do with anything.

"I didn't tell you yet, but I've been offered a job at a boy's school in Zimbabwe. Do you remember I told you about the pastor, Jim, who saved my neck any number of times when I was in school? Well, through a connection of his, I've been offered this job."

"Are you going to take it?"

"Haven't decided yet. I have to let them know by October. It would definitely be a good experience. I'd only be committed for four months. But the nicest part about it would be seeing

Jim again and having time to spend with him. He's the pastor at a nearby school down there. He's been a great spiritual teacher to me and I have this feeling there's a lot more I need to learn from him."

"And what do you think you'd be doing after that?"

"Well... I may be heading back to London. You see, I got a bit of a blow this week, which may partly explain my pangs of melancholy."

"Did something happen?"

"A letter was waiting for me at the Foundation when I got back on Tuesday that bore some rather unfortunate news. You see, I took a board exam in June to get certified in hotel administration, and I didn't pass."

"Oh, George, that's a shame. What does that mean exactly?"

"It means I can give it a second try in June of next year and if I fail again, they'll give me one last try in June the year after that. But then I'm up a creek. Actually, I can still work in the business but there won't be so many doors open to me. It just makes it that much harder. But probably I should give it another try which means being back here in June to study my head off and sitting for the darn thing again. Then, it's another two months' wait before I know anything. What I dread is telling my parents. I know they're going to be disappointed."

Indu could see that the next ten months were going to be a challenge for both of them. They walked hand in hand for several blocks as they talked. When they saw the Connaught Hotel straight ahead, George pointed to a corner window on the fifth floor and matter-of-factly informed her that he had met Paul Newman in that room and several rooms down from that he'd met a famous princess.

"And what, pray tell, gave you such exclusive privileges?" she asked, admittedly impressed by his name-dropping.

"When I was finishing my degree, I did a special rotation in this hotel for six months. The fifth floor was all mine and it was my job to keep everyone happy."

"You must have been good at that," she said, giving an earnest accolade.

"Well, I didn't always succeed. One night Paul Newman called me in and said, 'I'd give my right eye for a bottle of Château Haut-Brion.' I told him I'd check into the matter but the hotel had nothing even close to it in the cellars. I went back and told him, 'Mr. Newman, we don't have that particular fermented grape in the house. But besides, what would I do with your right eye anyway?' He at least got a good laugh out of it."

"You're a true nut. Let's go inside." She was by nature a lover of sumptuous beauty, not that she wanted any of it in her life. She simply liked admiring the plush carpets, the formidable chandeliers, the velveteen wallpaper, the stately furniture and the ambiance of an orderly and traditional setting. The Connaught did not disappoint her. It reminded her of the Waldorf Astoria in New York City where she had stayed one time. This hotel had the same distinguished elegance. George entertained her with descriptions of the duties of the different uniform-clad young men who scuttled past them. Nhoj had also worked there for a short time, a period which had given George total enjoyment. Indu stepped into the ladies' lounge and admired the long marble counters and mirrored walls. She joined George again in the lobby and arm in arm they made their exit.

In that fashion, they strolled several blocks more until they passed a red phone box. George said, "I need to call my mother at some point this evening. Let me go ahead and try now." Thinking he looked adorable standing in the red booth calling his mother, Indu pulled her camera out of her purse and snapped his picture. He actually turned toward her just as the shutter clicked and then put the phone back on the hook. He emerged with the news that she wasn't home. Seeing a man walking toward them, the idea suddenly came to ask if he'd kindly take her photo with George.

The man's reply was a surely, "No, I will not," as he walked briskly past them. George was about to console her when she saw an elderly couple coming down the sidewalk. The gruff refusal had far from discouraged her.

In the same sweet manner she asked them, "Excuse me, would you mind taking our picture together?"

"Why dear, not at all," the woman said. "Harry, maybe you'd better do it. Your hand is steadier than mine."

"All right. Let's see how that camera works," he readily consented, accepting the camera from Indu's outstretched hand.

"It's very kind of you both. George, shall we stand here?"

ဢ * * * Ꮳ

A charming white church with a soaring steeple stood at the end of the street behind them. As a landmark, Indu had wanted it in the picture, too. George had tucked his arm around her waist and she had slipped hers around his. This would be their second picture together. She showed it to me. Even more striking than in the first was their uncanny resemblance to one another.

ဢ * * * Ꮳ

Returning the camera, the man asked, "Are you on your honeymoon?" Indu was surprised that the man had even thought so. Even more surprised was she by George's answer. With a punctilious air he immediately responded, "No, not yet." Indu gave a glance in his direction and then engagingly smiled at the couple.

"And where are you from, do you mind if I ask?" the woman said. Indu thought it was nice that they should be so curious about this young couple who had accosted them for a picture.

"I'm from the States," Indu said.

"And I'm living here in London," George pronounced right after her.

'Lovely, lovely," the woman softly bubbled. "We're just visiting here in London, also. My husband is an artist."

"Really," George said with admiring interest.

Taking hold of her husband's arm, the lady bid them farewell and the couple went on their way. Indu and George walked two more blocks until they found Hyde Park graciously stretched before them. Dodging through the heavy late-afternoon traffic, they crossed the street and continued strolling along a grass-lined asphalt path. A cloud burst sent down a cooling momentary shower, clearing the air and brightening the colors. Protected from most of the drops by tree foliage, George took the opportunity to tell her about the time he'd been riding his bike through the park, zooming down one of the winding paths. Without any forewarning, he had hit a pile of pigeon droppings and gone flying into the mess of them.

"The whole side of my clothes was covered with it. I looked horrific. And I was on my way to work, and late on top of it all. That was not one of my better days." Indu laughed at how he told the story.

The path sloped downward toward an expansive duck pond. Walking to the far side, they took the third bench from the end, which was the first vacant one available, and sat to rest and watch the ducks. It should have been but another pleasant moment in their day together, but the reality of their separation looming in front of them put them both in sober, reflective moods. Indu kept repeating over and over in her mind, "What is the strange connection between us? What is it? What is it?"

She turned to George and was astonished at her own boldness in saying to him the same thing that he had said to her in New Brighton. Only instead of asking it as a question, she made it a statement. "George, we're going to be parting soon and there's only one thing I can think to say as that time comes closer."

"And what might that be?"

'Please consider marrying me." She said it still with the thought of wanting to test their karma. She desired no answer from him. Over the next ten months, however, when they would virtually circle the globe between them, she knew they would have to give serious consideration to such a possible prospect. After all, if there was no possibility of marriage, then they might as well make this farewell final and not try to keep track of one another from Europe to America, from the Greek isles to the isles of Japan, and from Africa back to the States. What was the point if their intentions toward each other were not serious? That was what she was trying to say. But it was not a particularly romantic moment. Standing before them were too many practical considerations which made marriage an intimidating subject, especially for George. He hadn't even intended to marry before he was thirty years old. By that standard, he still had six years to go.

"Indu, I just don't know anything right now. I can't even think about it." He gazed blankly at the ducks on the pond.

"I don't want any commitments made now, either. I just wanted you to know that it's in my mind, also. I know this next year is going to be a long haul for both of us. And I suppose anything can happen. Just... if ever you have nothing to do, you might think about it now and then." She said the last half in jest. His return was only silence tinged with resistance. Any kind of expectation seemed too much for him just then.

It did bemuse her. They'd talked impersonally about happiness in marriage, he had joked that they weren't on their honeymoon "yet," they'd been hand in hand from the moment he'd met her at the tube station. But the actual discussion of their marriage left them both heavy-hearted. They had, after all, only just met. The subject was dropped. They both sat silently and watched the ducks and toy boats float past on the pond.

TWENTY-THREE

~

George glanced down at his watch. "Indu, it's probably time that we go back to the car." It was close to five-thirty. They had sat on the bench for a long time quietly holding hands. The sun was low in the sky with a hint of evening glow. They walked back across the park, down several city blocks, and soon found themselves on Oxford Street. Heading toward the nearest Underground station, they past one of the biggest record stores in London.

"Indu, let's run in here for a few minutes. I'd like to see if they have Eric Clapton's latest album." She had no objections. She hadn't known he was an Eric Clapton fan. They entered together but immediately went different directions. She was curious to see what they had in rhythm and blues. One thing her life near Kansas City had fostered was an appreciation for certain blues artists. She found a cassette entitled *Best of the Blues*, which had tunes from Muddy Waters and the Nighthawks, both of whom she'd seen in concert. She decided to buy it mainly because it reminded her of home. She met George over in the rock 'n' roll section. Her eyes landed on a cassette which had been one of her favorites.

She held up the album to show him. "Have you ever heard this one?"

"I've heard some of the songs from it on the radio. Is it one you like?"

"It is. And I'm going to buy it for you."

"I wonder if George will really like it," she thought as they stood in the check-out line.

Several doors down was a drug store. George stopped suddenly in front of it. "Indu, I also need toothpaste."

"Okay, let's go in." It didn't much matter to her what they did in these last few hours, as long as they were together.

What she couldn't get over was how natural it felt to be with him, whether they were strolling through Hyde Park or through a drug store. There was an ease between them. Anyone observing them would have thought they'd shared opinions on toothpaste brands or shampoos many times. It had not been a thought in her mind, but when they passed a display of contraceptives, it suddenly seemed a practical item for them to consider.

She waited until they had walked passed and then asked, "George, I don't know what your feelings would be about this, but if there's any chance we'll be spending the night together, then it might be a good idea to purchase contraceptives while we're here."

Appearing startled, he replied, "I hadn't thought we'd be spending the night together." His amazement seemed more from the fact that she was planning ahead for something that might not even happen.

"Well, we may not be. But we didn't plan to be in New Brighton and look what happened. At that time, it was okay. It was a safe time in my cycle. But that was five days ago and it sure isn't safe anymore. Seeing as it's our last night together, I don't want to take any risk. It's better to have them on hand. By the time we actually know whether we can be together tonight or not, the stores will be closed."

A gentle, thoughtful expression came across his face. He slowly nodded and said, "Whatever you think is best."

Without hesitation she went up to the counter and began to examine the different boxes. She had expected George to go ahead and pay for his things at the front of the store. It was a pleasant surprise when he came and stood next to her.

"George," she whispered, "is there anything here that you usually use?"

He shook his head and whispered back, "I never have."

She was stunned. "George, you've never worried about birth control before?"

"Of course, I've worried about it. It's just I've never done anything like this before."

"Like what?"

"Being with someone to buy birth control. I don't like condoms and every woman has her own method."

"So you've always left it up to the woman to take care of it?" she said with a slight reproving tone.

"I suppose I have," he said, accepting her reproach.

She really wasn't upset or terribly surprised by that fact. In her own experience, the burden had almost always fallen on her as well. "The woman simply has more at risk," she had bemoaned to herself.

Curious though, she asked, "What did you and Alison use?"

"Alison had a diaphragm."

"Mmmm. That's what I usually use, too. But I didn't even bring it on the trip. You can see I had no intention of meeting anyone," she said, flashing a warm smile at him.

"Well, like it or not," she thought, "condoms it will have to be... and spermicidal tablets for me." Just as the final decision was made, the pharmacist came up behind the counter and offered to take care of their purchases. She handed him the two small boxes.

"I can ring up the toothpaste, too, if you like," he said.

George gladly handed it over and paid the amount.

Indu rationalized silently, "It seemed natural to imagine spending the night together, but maybe he wasn't thinking of it at all. Still, better to be a little embarrassed now for making an amorous overture than be in a compromised position four weeks from now." She had no regret about her forethought.

They walked further down the block, hand in hand, when he stopped again in the middle of the sidewalk. Indu wondered what it was this time that had caught his attention. Placing his hands on her shoulders, he turned her around to face him. Without saying a word, he brought his cheek to hers and held her in his arms. Gripping the packages in her hand, she wrapped her arms around him. The sound of traffic, of a hundred pounding footsteps, of voices whirling past, all melted into an unobtrusive drone. A yellow-golden light reflected off of everything as the sun touched down on the unseen horizon. Her heart flooded with love for him.

After a long precious moment, she had to ask, "George, you realize we're hardly alone. We are in fact standing in the middle of one of the busiest parts of London."

"I know and I don't care. What are they seeing anyway? Nothing that's so terrible. Besides, in a way it feels as though we're in our own world, removed from everybody. It's not so awful that I hug you here, is it?"

"Couldn't think of anything nicer than getting hugged in the middle of a throng of people," she reassured him. "It feels as though we've stopped the world..." Her voice trailed off softly.

They were standing in a separate world, but it was a world that would soon be torn apart by circumstances, intruded upon by obligations and responsibilities.

After only a short tube ride and brisk walk, they were back at the garage. A tremendous sound could be heard vibrating through the closed doors of George's car. George's face beamed as he opened the car door with a grand swing of his arm. The music came blasting out of the speakers which had been set in the lower front corners of the doors.

"It's got a new stereo, all right," Indu said, raising her voice over the stereophonic noise. She had to admit she was impressed. He leaned in to shut it off. The silence was startling. They walked in to pay the bill. She stepped around to the restroom to brush her hair. George had suggested on the train that after picking up the car, they might visit family friends of his. He was under some obligation to go see them and this would be his last chance. She had said that she didn't want to interfere with any personal business that he might have. But by the way he talked, he seemed to have an eagerness for her to meet someone connected to his family.

"Maybe if they can see what a nice person I am, they can pass that information on to his mother, who no doubt must be very concerned about the unorthodox American woman her son has gotten involved with," she thought with amusement. Still, she was pleased that he should want to take her with him.

They hopped into his car and she immediately pulled out their new cassette tapes. "So, which one do you want to hear first?" she asked.

"How about the one you got for me," he said.

It was exactly what she had hoped he would say. She wondered if that wasn't why he had said it. It was great fun winding through the streets of London with a familiar rocking rhythm pulsing through his speakers. She lip-synched some of the words as she exaggeratedly bobbed to the rhythmic beat. She was happy to see him smile at her comical effort. It was nice for a time to forget that only hours were left for them to be in each other's company. But as time went on, it would become harder and harder to ignore the fact.

George stopped on the way at a liquor store to buy a bottle of wine. He knew the propriety of taking a house gift and she admired the refinement in his social education that it reflected. Watching him make the selection, she could also see that he knew more about wine than she did. Either as a requirement for those in hotel administration or as part of his cultural heritage, he had found it to his advantage to know the distinguishing features between a Bordeaux and a Burgundy, or between a port and a sherry, as well as vintage years and non-vintage years, and that Chablis was the best-known white Burgundy and Chianti the best-known Italian red wine. He settled on a Cabernet made from French Bordeaux grapes. She wondered if he'd ever tried a wine from California but didn't ask, suspecting he might laugh at the suggestion.

Her own discriminating tastes could tell a white wine from a red one, and whether it was sweet or dry. But that was it. In her middle-class American upbringing there hadn't been much of a necessity to know more about fermented fruit. It was one of the few times that she felt terribly self-conscious with him, painfully aware of the rude gap in her education. Fortunately, the fact went unnoticed by him.

They reached the house a few minutes later. George lifted from the backseat a heavy photo album which he intended to show the family.

"George, do you mind if I glance through it before we go in? I'm too curious to wait."

"Sure, why not? They're not going to know we're here anyway." He had parked a short distance away from their front door, which was set fairly close to the street.

There was a picture of George with a beard. She preferred him without one.

She saw other pictures of his family on holidays and several of Oliver visiting their home in Mombasa. Glancing in his rear-view mirror, George saw a car drive up behind them.

"What's this?" he said, pulling the latch to open his door. "Indu, they've just pulled in behind us. They weren't home after all."

She turned around to see a lovely middle-aged couple walking to embrace George. She got out, feeling surprisingly relaxed as the introductions were made there on the sidewalk. From their affectionate greeting, she could tell they considered George a member of the family. Their twenty-one year old daughter was also with them. Lydia was her name. She welcomed George with a warm hug and smiled pleasantly at Indu.

"So, come in, come in," Mr. Wilson said.

Just after walking inside, George presented the bottle of wine which was graciously accepted with just the proper amount of fanfare. The smoothness of all the interactions fascinated Indu. There was no pretentiousness, no awkwardness, no stiffness.

Their home was attractively decorated and one in which they evidently often entertained. They brought out just the right little nut dishes to set on the tables near everyone, beautiful long-stem wine glasses and black lacquered coasters. They un-corked George's wine bottle, distributed the nuts and sat down on the couch after seating George and Indu in chairs on either side of the fireplace. George told them about the jugglethon and how in each town he and Nhoj were made to feel like he-roes, meeting the mayors and being interviewed on local radio broadcasts. He described it "as a great experience all around." When asked about his future plans, he sadly told them about failing the exam. Indu watched as their faces went from proud elation over his juggling success to deep concern over his exam mark.

"That's a pity, George, just a pity," Mr. Wilson said. "You've invested five years of your life toward that profession; to be stopped by an exam simply doesn't make sense. You are planning to re-sit it, aren't you?"

Indu could see what Mr. Wilson was doing, trying to sympathize, philosophize and advise without saying too much to make George feel uncomfortable. George agreed that it was to his advantage to try again and that most likely he would, next June. They inquired if his parents knew the news and he admitted that they didn't, cringing as he said it. Indu understood now just how serious the failed exam was. Until he passed it, everyone near and dear to him would not only be disappointed but left with great concern about his future prospects. To have one's career adrift for an entire year with the pressure of leaping the last hurdle still hanging over one's head was not what they would have wanted for him.

The subject changed as Lydia came in. She was wearing a different outfit than when Indu had first seen her. The best way to describe her appearance was downbeat preppy: pink sweatshirt with pink and dark purple striped pants that tapered at the ankle, worn with cute little heels and a string of pearls. She chose to sit in a chair next to Indu. While her parents were telling George about family news, Lydia and Indu discussed career goals. Indu gave a brief outline of her work, omitting any mention of her pending trip to Japan. Lydia elaborated a bit longer on her ambition to be a nurse and to go to India. Indu was honestly intrigued by her predilection for India.

In the process of getting up to answer the phone and to re-fill wine glasses, the seating was changed so that George and Mr. Wilson were on the sofa and Mrs. Wilson in a chair directly to George's right. It was appropriately more intimate that way. Mrs. Wilson was telling how she and her husband had lived in China just after they were first married.

Indu could feel her internal movie camera rolling into place. She liked the scene before her, George sandwiched in between the Wilsons, and Mrs. Wilson reminiscing about the worldly travels of their earlier years.

"Could that ever be George and me twenty-five years from now?" she thought. "Wouldn't our story of meeting and possibly living in Kenya be equally as fascinating as theirs?"

Indu said nothing but politely listened, again refraining from any mention of her upcoming trip to the Orient. For some reason, she had no desire to impress them and they were equally reticent to pry too deeply into her background, although curiously aware that "Indu" was hardly a typical Anglo-Saxon name.

When the moment seemed suitable, Indu picked up her purse and excused herself to visit the quiet sanctity of the bathroom. It was in truth the only reason she went, just wanting to break away. She followed their directions to the first door on the left at the top of the stairs. The voices became a murmuring hush as she reached the top landing. Surveying her appearance in the bathroom mirror, she was relieved to see that everything looked normal. Deciding to use the facilities after all, she then coiffed her hair, applied fresh lipstick and walked slowly back down. Entering the living room again, she made immediate eye contact with George. It was a whole dialog of its own.

His eyes asked, "Is everything okay for you?"

Her eyes answered, "Everything is fine. They're a nice family."

To which his eyes replied, "I thought you'd enjoy meeting them."

She was comfortable in her position as mysterious-girl-friend-from-foreign-country mainly because she couldn't imagine anything more natural than being with George.

No sooner had she sat back down then the discussion turned to politics, a topic Indu generally avoided. Lydia, however, was quick to bring criticism against the current American president, obviously unaware that her opinion might be offensive to Indu. Remaining neutral on the topic, Indu nodded complaisantly all the while thinking, "If she were an American, she'd be a left-wing Democrat, without any question."

Lydia's father, on the other hand, being more astute that his daughter's critical remarks could be construed as a personal insult to Indu, jumped in with some buffering statement. Indu accepted it as a kind gesture on his part.

George then made a motion to leave, which was met with sighs of dismay. Mrs. Wilson insisted that he should first see all the redecoration that had been done since his last visit. Upon her saying, "Come up and see your old room," the story came out that many times throughout his student years he had stayed with them, and that their daughter was much like a sister to him. Indu liked the thought that a teenage George had lunged up and down the very steps they were then climbing. Mrs. Wilson described how the heaviest chore had been stripping off the old wallpaper. Indu again tactfully refrained from boasting that putting up wallpaper was an enjoyed pastime of her own and that she was actually quite skilled in the whole procedure.

As farewells were said at the door, George guaranteed that his mother would be in touch with them soon. Hugs and handshakes were exchanged all around.

The visit could not have been a more cordial one. Back in the car, they headed off to Hampstead and Guruji. It was already eight-thirty. George's knowledge of the London streets was indisputable as he threw his car back and forth between gears, adroitly maneuvering the Polo down one street after another. Crossing over a bridge, he pointed to a park on the left bank, saying it was there that he'd first met Nhoj. It struck Indu how significant that meeting had been. For without Nhoj and juggling, a whole new scenario would have had to have taken place for their own union to have occurred.

On the way, she decided she'd better forewarn George about the unconventional standards under which they were living at Hampstead. He professed it made no difference to him whether he sat in a mauve and crème color-coordinated living room or on a mattress on the floor butted up against the wall. She couldn't help worrying that the dichotomy would nonetheless be startling.

Guruji's evening program was still going on downstairs in Muniji's temple. Indu and George slipped in as inconspicuously as possible. A passage from the *Yoga Sūtras* of Patanjali was being chanted. A cassette tape was then played of a professionally recorded guided meditation, written by Guruji and narrated by a devotee who had once been a dramatic actress. After the meditation, a platter of sliced fruit was passed around and then most of the group trailed upstairs to the apartment.

Guruji sat in his corner chair and visited with the same man who had extended the invitation for the Stonehenge trip. George got into a serious discussion with a woman named Parvati, an intense devotee of Guruji's who was herself originally from London, although she had spent much time in the States and India. Sitting across the room from them, Indu could detect that their talk had something to do with being a disciple. She gathered Parvati was being a little overbearing just by the defensive tone in George's voice. Deciding he needed "rescuing," she went over and suggested that George might like to see Parvati's pictures of Guruji's ashram in New York taken just prior to her departure that summer. George welcomed Indu's intrusion and did in fact find the proposition appealing. It would be his first glimpse of the place from which this Guru and his followers had originated. Indu enjoyed seeing them again, too. They were some of the most attractive shots of the ashram she had ever seen, of the flowers and the fruit trees, of the children, of the gravel drive leading down to the Lake House, of the lake and the arched bridge leading to a small island used for special occasions.

As he handed the stack of photos back to Parvati, he commented with a shining glint in his eye aimed at Indu, "Now I have
the feeling I need to go and see this place." Indu could only
hope that maybe one day he would. At that moment, though,
the Guru was right before them and she couldn't help but
notice that George was guardedly keeping his distance. She
surmised he must still have many questions about the whole
Guru business, preferring for the present moment to observe
this man in orange rather than be actively engaged in conversation with him.

Indu did, however, go over and sit near her beloved teacher.
Guruji leaned toward her and asked if she and her friend had
eaten. It was not an unusual question to come from him. She
admitted that they hadn't but that she and George were planning to go out yet again that night to get something to eat.
In her heart, she was naturally hoping to find a nice place to
spend one last night with him. But she had no idea exactly how
to work the logistics of it. Whether aware of it or not, Guruji
solved the problem. On hearing of her plans to go back out, he
quietly arranged for Mangala to give her the set of keys to the
apartment and to the downstairs side entrance. With such a
request coming from him, the keys were handed over without
any scrutinizing questions. In so doing, he had made it possible for her to respectably depart with George at that given late
hour and to respectably return at whatever hour in the morning she so chose. Further demonstrating his approbation of the
whole matter, he gave every indication that they should hurry
on their way.

Finally coming over to Guruji, George knelt down by his chair.
It seemed he wanted to thank Guruji for something: for the
lovely ten-day retreat at the Foundation, for accepting him—a
simple juggler—into the intimacy of his spiritual group, possibly even for whatever part Guruji had played in bringing Indu
and him together. But expressions of such thoughts do not lend
themselves easily to words. George looked momentarily awkward. How to say anything to someone for whom you have a
deep respect but of whom you have little understanding?

Acting in the most ordinary fashion, Guruji overrode any need for words and simply patted George's head by way of final blessing. George folded his palms together and bowed his head. It was the most genuine expression of reverence she had seen in him yet. It lasted only a second, but it conveyed everything above and beyond what words could have. Standing up, George gave a farewell hug to Uma, saying that he hoped he would see her again, too, sometime, somewhere. After a quick exchange of best wishes between everyone, he and Indu quietly let themselves out the door.

TWENTY-FOUR

~

As they passed the phone on the second floor, George remembered he hadn't yet contacted his mother. He would be leaving
the Foundation on Saturday and meeting her at the home of
his grandparents who lived south of London. His mother was
waiting to hear what his schedule would be. Indu watched as
his concentrated frown suddenly changed to a gleeful expression when his mother's voice came over the line. She found it
heartwarming to see him in the role of son. Having looked at
his mother's picture, she wondered what kind of woman she
was. One thing was sure; he was a son who loved his mother
greatly.

She listened as George told his mother about the new stereo,
about seeing the Wilsons, and about spending the day with his
friend "Indu." She then heard him cryptically reply, "No, no,
she isn't." He changed the subject to the upcoming weekend
plans.

"Now, what was that about me?" Indu thought. "He sure skirted the issue with polished finesse. He obviously doesn't want
to tell her too much, especially with me standing here, all ears."

The last thing mentioned was the exam mark. Indu watched
the painful strain on his face as he broke the news to his mother
and the even deeper agony as he took in her sorrow and disappointment. From George's next remarks, she could tell that his
mother had recovered quickly from the initial blow and was
immediately giving words of encouragement, knowing well
that her son's disappointment must be as great, if not greater
than her own. In saying goodbye, he left it that he'd have more
to tell her when he saw her that Sunday at his grandparent's
home.

Setting the receiver back on the hook, George leaned against the wall as though needing support. "I hated to tell her the bad news but I didn't want her to hear it from the Wilsons first."

"It sounded like she took it pretty well," Indu said, sad to see him distraught about it again.

"Of course, she has to try. It's a fact of history now. No amount of admonishing is going to change a thing."

"But George, you did the best you could."

"I don't know, Indu. I don't know that's true. I probably could have studied more, gotten psyched up for it more. If I'm ever going to pass that financing part, I'm going to have to do a lot more book work."

"So you'll do it. You've got a whole year," she said. That remark was met with a feigned look of disgust. But she could see that his sense of humor was slowly returning. She liked that about him. He wasn't one to stay down too long.

Taking hold of her hand, he led her down the stairs and to the car. With the engine running and in gear, he asked with an air to please, "Okay, Miss Glowworm, where are we off to now?"

"Glowworm? Doth thou take me to be a firefly in disguise, kind sir?" she replied, parodying a damsel of centuries past. Oddly, if she gave her imagination any room to wander, she could easily see herself with George in a past life from that era. Had she been the princess and he the court jester, or had she been a peasant and he a gallant knight? Whatever it was, they had been absurdly in love, much like they were now.

"'Twas only making reference to your shining light, me lady, wondering if 'twould be my beacon in the dark of night," he poetically countered, carrying the parody quite well, she thought.

She dropped it, though, and asked point blank, "Do you want to try to find a place to stay together tonight?"

He leaned over with a kiss, after which he said, "If we can find a place, I think it's a lovely idea."

Just one corner up she knew there was a lodging called the Post House Hotel. It seemed the most logical place to start. George followed her directions and soon had them parked in front of the office. They went in together only to find that no rooms were available. The clerk didn't sound too hopeful. "At this time of night, in this part of town, at this time of year, usually everything is booked well in advance."

Indu still felt sure they'd find a room somewhere. They stopped at another less attractive place only to receive the same report. That clerk pointed them down another street where he said several other hotels could be found. Sitting in the car, Indu promised herself and any of the gods listening that she'd take any room at that moment, no matter what the cost. There was no way she was ready to part from George yet. After searching in vain for fifteen minutes, knowing the hour was quickly approaching midnight and finding nothing that resembled a boarding house or hotel, they stopped and asked a couple walking across the street if there was any place in the area where they could stay.

"Best place to try would be the Holiday Inn three blocks to the left," the gentleman replied with a tinge of skepticism. Indu was amused to think a Holiday Inn was so close at hand. How many times in years past had she watched for the bright green, pink and yellow neon sign of one of the most traditional motel chains in America? Her family had stayed in none other. Even in London, she was again to search for its brightly lit sign. They did find it, but the sign was missing. Only the name in green neon was visible across the front facade. She immediately saw that the international chain had been upgraded from motel to hotel, and a rather luxurious one at that. They parked the car in the circular drive at the front entrance, walked past three pillars of water shooting up from a beautifully lit fountain, and entered a modernly decorated, high-ceilinged lobby.

Indu made the inquiry at the desk, knowing full well if a room was available that there would be no way George could afford it. Practically speaking, she couldn't afford it either. But a certain piece of plastic could at least absorb the shock of the expense, leaving her free of financial worry until she returned to the States. Besides, she had made her promise and she was going to stick to it.

The clerk stood shaking her head. "We have no rooms available at this time." Indu simply couldn't believe what the fates were trying to ordain. A glimmer of hope appeared when the clerk suggested that a cancellation might have recently come in. A Sanskrit mantra filled Indu's mind, leaving no room for any other thought. To say she was praying for a miracle would be very close to the truth. Except for the totally skeptical, who hasn't at one time or another believed that miracles could happen? And on this night, one did.

"My, my, you're in luck," the clerk said. "I do see one cancellation here. It's for a double room. Would you like to have it?" The words fell like precious gems into Indu's hands. Only as a formality did she ask what the rate would be. "It's £73 per night," she said, almost apologetically. Indu instantly converted pounds to dollars. It would be just over $100. Without even looking at George, she slid her credit card toward the clerk and said they'd take it. She hesitated to glance at George's face, feeling certain that his abysmal silence could only mean he was absolutely stunned. When she finally did look his way, she found her suspicion was accurate. A similar expression would have probably crossed his face had lightning struck at his feet and missed him by an inch.

"George, don't say anything," she lovingly advised, although aware he was hardly in a loquacious mood. "This is something I want to do. It's the only way we can be together. I'm not going to give up that chance. Please just smile and say you don't mind."

Before he could say a word, the clerk was back with the credit card slip, asking her to sign on the dotted line. "And here is your key. You're in room 255. I hope you'll enjoy your stay." Indu thanked her and George nodded his head agreeably.

Taking his arm, she steered him toward a glass-paneled elevator. As the doors closed and they were lifted up, gaining an aerial view of the lobby, he murmured, "I didn't know you could be so impulsively crazy." He lifted her hand to his lips and kissed it.

They easily found their room and gave exulted squeals once the door was closed behind them. Within a minute, George had the room service menu in his hand. "Let's order something scrumptiously delicious and it's my treat." From under the 'Midnight Snacks' listing, they phoned in their order for the fruit, cheese and cracker platter, cold veggie plate and two Perriers.

They had no problem passing the time while they waited for the food to be delivered. They were alone again at last, and their arms and lips wasted not another moment in finding each other. But nourishment of a more essential nature was sorely needed and once the food was delivered, their stomachs got priority. Placing the food-laden tray in the middle of the bed, they sat cross-legged opposite one another and started satiating the gnawing hunger which had grown disproportionately since their lunch with Oliver. The extravagance of the whole affair again crossed Indu's mind. But their indulgence was giving them eight more hours together, and it was worth every penny as far as she was concerned.

Unable to take another mouthful, George laid back on the bed and announced, "Now I feel like soaking in a hot bath."

Indu leaned over and kissed his forehead and then swung her legs off the edge of the bed. Starting for the bathroom, she proclaimed, "That's a marvelous idea."

"Hey, where do you think you're going? It was my idea first," he teasingly quibbled as though wanting first dibs on the tub.

Tilting her head around the corner of the bathroom door, she announced the enticing news, "There's room for two."

He came bouncing off the bed and into the bathroom to inspect the tub accommodations. He set the stopper and started the hot water running. Before leaving the apartment, Indu had slipped her toothbrush, toothpaste and contact lens case into her purse. George duly noticed. While she was brushing her teeth, he came up behind her and rested his chin on her shoulder, saying, "You certainly are a woman of forethought. What else did you pack in that bag of yours?"

After she rinsed her mouth, their eyes met in the mirror and she mysteriously replied, "A couple other little things which may or may not be needed." The mystery did not elude him.

He kissed her on the nape of the neck and then said in his most distinguished voice, "Madam, I've drawn the bath. If I may be of any further assistance, do let me know."

She responded, "It's very kind of you to offer, but I'm just wondering who will be the first one in."

With that, the contest was on. He won by only a slight margin. Sitting at opposite ends, they took turns sudsing each other, somewhat shyly approaching the lower areas. She didn't feel self-conscious about him seeing her with two-day-old stubble on her legs and only petite, rounded breasts. He admitted that he did feel a little self-conscious. She couldn't imagine why. His body was broad, muscular, tan and gorgeous, but she liked that he had told her. Letting the water drain, he turned on the shower to get one final rinse. She remembered thinking how different he looked with his hair slicked back with water. Staying arm in arm, they turned so she could also stand under the shower's spray but keeping her hair as dry as possible.

Standing dripping wet in each other's arms, what might have been a deeply passionate moment was only another profoundly romantic one. They gazed longingly into the tired eyes of the other, feeling the magnetism that had kept them from parting that night. What attachment was it that could bind two hearts across continents and oceans? They knew they would soon be putting it to the test. After a loving kiss, they stepped out and dried themselves and seconds later were snuggled under the covers. George reached over to set the bedside lamp on "low." Next to it, Indu had placed the two boxes.

Wrapped in his arms and lost in his lips, time drifted into eternity. She knew nothing but the love she bore for him in her heart and she felt nothing but the love he returned through every caress, every stroke, by the gentleness of every kiss, by the way he would nudge his nose against hers, against her cheek, against her chin, all the while holding her firmly, bracing one hand at the back of her head and one on the small of her back. The desire to be coitally entwined was there, to be moving as one rhythm, one breath. But something in her hormones was missing. In the exaltation of her love, her body had not thrown whatever switch was needed to make it logistically possible. But it didn't matter to her. And although his "on again, off again" readiness was not a problem this time, there was no urgency on his part to do anything about it. The little boxes were never opened.

Emerging from a passionate embrace, cuddled in each other's arms, he fell soundly asleep. Stretching one arm to shut the light, she curled up against his side. An amusing thought drifted across her mind. It was the third time they'd met intimately under the covers, and still their love affair remained in its virgin state. Their love, being carnally innocent, was even more endeared to her heart.

A streetlight from the window cast a salmon glow over the room. Nestled with her head upon his outstretched arm, she watched the rhythmic heaves of his chest, so beautifully arrayed with dark curls of hair. How secure she felt with him; how she hated the thought of parting. She wanted only to watch him sleep, but found her own eyes growing too heavy. So it was that their last hours together were to be spent cradled as one in deep and undivided sleep.

It was seven o'clock in the morning when their eyes met again.

"George, what was it that your mother asked about me last night on the phone?" She didn't know why it was the first thing in her mind.

"She asked me," George replied, blinking hard several times to jog his memory, "she asked me if you were East Indian. I had only told her before that you were American. I think she'd been wondering about your name. I hadn't tried to explain anything to her about it. But what she really meant by the question was that she was wanting to understand who you were. She doesn't interfere, but she does like to know with whom I'm spending my time." There was a long pause as they looked at each other's sleepy morning faces. "Now I have a question for you," he said, enunciating each word slowly.

"You may ask me anything you wish," she declared, planting a smacking kiss on his cheek.

"Do you find you're sexually attracted to me?"

It was an unexpected question. She knew that of all the times that they had embraced, kissed and cuddled, she had not once felt aroused. She wondered how to explain to him that the very fact was significant to her. "Surely he doesn't think there's anything about him that's unappealing to me," she thought in disbelief. "I adore every inch of him. I don't think I could adore him more. Can he really have any doubt?" But obviously he did. She decided to take the most direct approach.

With as much vehemence as she could manage, she replied with four straight "no's" and then explained. "George, I love you, not your body." It was the first time she had said those words, that she loved him. But she didn't give him any chance to reply. "Don't you see, George? Don't you see what it means? What I feel for you is not coming from any physical desire. That's not to say physical desire won't come sometime. I have a sex drive like anyone else."

"You have?" he repeated, clearly wanting her to elucidate further.

"Of course, silly. Who doesn't? Mine just comes and goes, like it's on its own clock. Maybe because of the circumstances, or the intensity, there hasn't ever been a chance for the alarm to ring. Maybe it isn't the right time. But the attraction between us, I don't think it's contained within any physical boundaries."

It sounded so mysterious, and yet everything about their relationship was exactly that, and neither one of them truly understood what had happened nor what the outcome would be. What they did know was that their last hour together was already upon them. George sat up in bed. "Good grief," he moaned.

"What is it?" she asked, not liking the sound of distress in his voice.

"The first thing I have to do is call Alison."

"You have to call her now?"

"Indu, she was expecting me back last night."

"What are you going to tell her?"

"I'm going to tell her that I spent the night at the Wilsons'."

"George, you're going to flat-out lie?"

"I don't want to hurt her by telling her the truth. Sometimes the truth is crueler than a lie. She may find out about it later, but by that time we'll have had a chance to talk. To just hit her cold with it now, I can't. And I have to call her because otherwise she'll worry all morning."

Indu didn't like it. She understood his premise, but deception was deception. She sat on the bed, listening to his conversation. She felt bad for Alison and she felt hurt herself. The fact that anything so precious to her should be viewed as unforgiving by anyone pierced deeply through her heart. Why had she let herself and George be blind to the commitment he had with Alison? "Because," she told herself, "this was our only chance." But the thought did little to ease her conscience.

Apparently questioning why he hadn't called the night before to say he was staying over, he came back with the perfect answer. "I was out till very late with Lydia and some friends of hers. I thought calling you first thing this morning would be just the same."

To hear him telling such an untruth sent a shudder down her spine. Granted, to tell Alison at that moment that he'd spent the night with another woman would have sent shock waves bouncing off the telephone wires. The timing of her own relationship with George was not the best. But a thought came which did comfort her: "When God hands you a rare and precious gem, do you complain if it's presented on a tin platter instead of a silver one?"

George set the receiver down and looked over at Indu. "Please don't think anything terrible of me."

"I don't, George. It makes me sad that it has to be this way. And I can only pray that you will never, never have to do that to me. I really think I would prefer the cold truth."

"Indu, I hope in my whole life never to have to do that again. And the odds are great that she's going to find out anyway and then she can accuse me of unfaithfulness and deceitfulness. But I'm going to clear things with her just as fast as I can."

Without further delay, they gathered up their belongings and checked out of the hotel. Whether they ever saw each other again or not, Indu knew she would never have any regrets that they had met. She only hoped George could say the same. He parked across the street from Muniji's house. The moment had come for their final embrace.

His last words described exactly what her heart had been silently crying all along. "My God, how am I going to live without you?"

She could only answer with another question, but it was beyond the power of her voice to utter it. Her eyes did it for her as she gazed for the last time into his. "Why do we even have to try?"

Four days had passed since that final farewell. It was Tuesday, September 11, at seven o'clock in the morning. The sound of Muniji calling her name pulled her suddenly from a dream. He poked his head into the apartment to announce that there was a phone call for Indu. At such an hour, it surprised everyone.

As she quickly pulled on clothes, she said out loud, "Goodness, it must be someone from my family." In her heart, she prayed that it was George.

She rushed down the stairs, picked up the receiver and gave a breathless "Hello?"

It was George. "Thank God it's you. Where are you?"

"I'm in Dover about to get on the ferry to cross the Channel. I tried to call last night but you were out."

"No, we were down in the temple until late. Is Nhoj with you?"

"Yes, and Alison, too. Everything is completely packed up in the car. I have a terrible cold. How have you been?"

"I'm okay. You do sound a little different. Can you thank Nhoj again for the Tibetan bowl tape? We've been listening to it and it's beautiful. When will he be back up?"

"In three weeks."

"Tell him I'll write a letter to him. And I've also been thinking about Alison. I don't know how you can convey this to her, but I've been sending her lots of love."

"Everything has worked out just fine with Alison. She's sitting now in the car listening to the stereo. I found out when I got back that she'd read your letter from New Brighton."

"Well, that's all right."

"I was furious."

"George, I really can't remember what I said."

"You know I've been reading Guruji's books. I didn't see your inscriptions until just a couple of days ago."

"Ah, well…"

"I've written a letter to Jim accepting the job in Zimbabwe."

"When is that?"

"January 10 to April 7."

"Then, depending on how things go, maybe you can come to the States."

"I can't say right now. We'll just have to see what happens. Indu, they're just announcing the final call for the ferry."

"I don't want you to miss it."

"No, I don't want to miss it either. Where will you be when you return to the States, at your parents' home or yours?"

"I'll be at my parents' for two days and then at mine in Kansas until October 9."

"I'll call you again."

"It's cheaper to write."

"But I want to hear your voice."

"Yes, okay. I love you."

"Until we meet again. I love you, too."

"Goodbye."

"Goodbye."

PART II

~

THE LETTERS

*Praise everyone. If you cannot praise someone,
let them out of your life.
Be original, be inventive.
Be courageous. Take courage again and again.
Do not imitate; be strong, be upright.
Do not lean on the crutches of others.
Think with your own head. Be yourself.*

Excerpt of Message from Haidakhandi Babaji
www.babaji.net

See epigraph of Part III for continuation of message.
Reprinted with permission.

TWENTY-FIVE

~

We both got up and went into the kitchen. Several hours had past since she had first begun her story. It was late afternoon. She put water on to boil in a stainless kettle and removed a brown ceramic teapot and two cream-colored mugs from the cupboard. She took her tea with milk and sugar and I took mine without. Sitting down at the kitchen table, I was ready to hear what had next happened. I knew that the parting in Hampstead was not the end of her relationship with George. But there might never have been another reunion, she told me, had Guruji not suggested that she travel to Denmark.

Guruji's invitation had come in May, eight months after she and George had parted in London. At that point, it had been two months since they had even exchanged letters. They had tried to stay in contact only to encounter again and again dishearteningly unfavorable odds.

"But you wrote to each other," I said, wondering how their immense love could possibly have been defeated.

She nodded in agreement and once again pulled the photocopied papers and bundle of rubber-banded letters from the gray folder she had carried with her into the kitchen. George's letters were in classic blue airmail striped-edge envelopes. It was most fortunate she had kept copies of her own.

These letters would now give the clearest picture of what had happened between her and George over those eight months when their two lives had been hurled around the globe, forcing their love to survive on nothing but the memory of their short time together. She had the letters arranged in chronological order. The top one, although the first he had written, was marked in red ink, "Received November 5." It had been

written in September, just four days after his phone call from
the ferry dock in Dover.

I immediately saw why the odds might have been complicated.
Over a decade before the advent of email, aberrant delays in
oversea postal deliveries had perilously weakened their main
line of communication. She went on to explain that the letters
would show how they had both battled gallantly to make sense
of that three-week period which encompassed the substance
of their relationship. But as more and more distance and time
separated them, the more intangible that union seemed. Was
the magic they had felt in each other's arms real? Was it meant
for them to be together? These were the questions to which
they tried to find answers in their letters.

To keep the proper sequence of events, Indu began reading the
first photocopied letter. It was one she had started the very day
following George's departure from London.

℘ * * * ℘

[Indu's Letter #1] London, September 12

Dear George,

Have decided to start an ongoing letter, since I keep thinking of things to say to you. Not very important things, just
a thought here and a thought there. No great revelations.

First chance tomorrow morning will be picking up the pictures taken at Ickwell. I think you'll be in at least half of
them (juggling, Cambridge, and us). Will find a nice bench
somewhere and enjoy again those days when we first met.
Copies will be included with this letter.

Am still marveling about our entire encounter. So many
odds were against me coming to England in the first place
(job, money, etc.). Then I was totally involved with Guruji
and you with Alison (so it seemed). We had so few weeks

to even try to make it work. Now we have thousands of miles between us, careers pulling me to Japan and you to Africa. We feel some attraction between us but it certainly isn't the kind described in the book *The Joy of Sex* (but poets over the centuries have been attempting to put into words the emotions that we felt). It's entirely mystical as far as I'm concerned.

And such a conflict is going on between my rational and intuitive minds. I know you were aware of it since one minute you'd hear me saying something about marriage and the next saying dubiously, "Well, hope we see each other again." Intuitive mind is seeing us together and rational mind sees all odds against it. It's a divine comedy!

'Tis almost midnight. Wishing you sweet dreams.

[Indu's Letter #1-continued] September 13

I know you've been concerned that the intensity of our spiritual pursuits is so different. But what really matters is not what was in the past but what is to come. Divinity isn't a product that accumulates with time. It simply is. Last week Guruji took us to meet a great swami. He's 106 years old and has been blind since the age of five. Guruji sat so humbly in his presence and tears often came to his eyes. Guruji had him initiate us and I have never felt more unworthy to receive such a blessing and unworthy to have such a Guru as Guruji. But Guruji says that we never need to feel unworthy because we are all divine beings, only we have forgotten our divinity. I once read somewhere, "Mortal man is nothing but a divine fool." Ignorance is what blinds us, and any spiritual study and practice will begin to remove that ignorance.

In our relationship, what matters is from this point on. Can we continue to love each other unconditionally, to help each other's spiritual growth, to merge together and yet allow the other to stand independent? In an ordinary marriage, to have all these things is virtually unheard of. I am probably not capable of doing all these things all the time (I am after all a divine fool) but it would be my goal, my deepest desire.

[Indu's Letter #1-continued] September 14

Tonight, during our evening *satsang*, Guruji guaranteed $5,000 cash to anyone who did not feel a total transformation in their life after chanting Patanjali's *Yoga Sūtras* one hundred times. He said not to worry about the meaning. The vibration alone is the power behind them. If one chapter is chanted every day and there are four chapters, it would take 400 days. I'd think after one year of chanting the *sūtras* you'd get not just transformation but total enlightenment!

Have you tried oil *neti* again? If you can't find almond oil, then sesame is good but the oils should be pure since they are going to the brain. I've decided also to start doing it again every day. Have a feeling this next year is going to be pretty challenging since major changes may be taking place (i.e., changing jobs, family affairs and who knows—marriage?). *Neti* has a very stabilizing effect.

Have also thought about your experience during the last rebirthing session in New Brighton when you felt powerful sexual energy stirring. Don't think I mentioned at that time although you may have realized this, but most likely it was *kuṇḍalinī* awakening. Ordinary sexual feelings (those with obvious source of arousal) can be used to rouse *kuṇḍalinī* also; this is the science of tantra. In a book written by one enlightened Master, he describes how during meditation he would get an erection which would last a very long time. For weeks in his meditation this went on. He knew just to watch it. It's a beautiful story. Will try to find a copy of it for you.

Well, I only have two days left before returning to the U.S. Guruji has definitely indicated that it's time for me to resume my worldly life. I've been with him now almost constantly for the past two and a half months. An awful lot of growth has taken place in that time as well as soul healing.

[Indu's Letter #1-continued] September 15

One *sūtra* which I read today described exactly what I was trying to say on the beach in New Brighton about self-discipline.

TATAH PARAMĀ VASHYATENDRIYĀṆĀM
(Patanjali's Yoga Sūtras, Ch. II, #55)

It suggests that real self-discipline on a spiritual path comes naturally and without force. The desire to understand the meaning of life and one's self is a very compelling factor. Suddenly you find yourself wanting to study Sanskrit or wanting to meditate or do hatha yoga or practice *trāṭakam* (gazing at something steadily). It's all a great experimentation.

Have looked at the Ickwell pictures many times. Wish they were clearer. But still they bring back such lovely memories.

[Indu's Letter #1-continued]
30,000 feet above Atlantic, September 17

We'll soon be landing at Newark Airport in New Jersey. Gurujj, Uma, Shakti and Mangala saw me off at Victoria Station. I took the British Rail to Gatwick Airport and they headed to Heathrow to see off that other swami I told you about. He's returning to India today. It was hard saying goodbye to them all, although I should be used to it by now, having said goodbye so many times. Just found out I'm sitting next to newlyweds. They went to London for their honeymoon. Couldn't help thinking that's not a bad idea. Love is definitely in the air.

Hope the juggling convention was fun and you learned even more tricks. So now you're on your way to Greece. Well, I bet by now you're tired of reading this letter. It has after all taken me five days to write it. Please do write me. I am wondering how you're feeling—about everything. Should we consider for a moment taking this even one step further? Now that's my rational mind speaking. I'd like to advise you to ignore it in the matters of love since it is basically ignorant in that area. But it will still pop up anyway every now and then. Landing is in forty-five minutes. Will probably not write further until back in Lawrence, Kansas.

[Indu's Letter #1-continued] Lawrence, Kansas, September 22

Greetings from Lawrence. Landed at Newark Airport and called my sister. She said just from the sound of my voice that she could tell I'd met someone special. She knew your name before I'd hung up. Had been debating whether to mention to anyone about meeting you since so many things in our relationship are still unknowns. But now the cat is out of the bag. I'd make a terrible spy. Figured then I'd better level with my family that there was a possibility I'd be heading to Greece next summer for an indeterminate amount of time. After seeing your picture and hearing a few stories about you (all true), they voiced not a single objection. They also commented on the striking resemblance between us (for that matter, so did Uma and Shakti). They said if I would be happy with you in Greece or wherever, they would be happy. This comes at a rather difficult time for my parents. After thirty-four years of marriage, they have decided to get a legal separation. This is not sudden news to me. I am certain they will be happier apart. I hate to mention any family problems to you but for some reason it only seems fair that you should know (since from your

398

noble line it may make me totally unsuitable for matrimonial consideration!).

Spent three nights and two days in Tulsa going over the family situation. Despite the rather serious mood of the visit, I really felt optimistic that things would work out for the best. Had my first day back at work yesterday. Rumors had been flying that I had gone off to get married. I laughed and said possibly later. Got back all my pictures from the trip today. Wish so much I had taken one hundred of you. On the last three rolls of film, I only had two of you. So if you happen to have any good shots, it would make me extremely happy if they would fly to the U.S. or Japan (am enclosing more silly shots of me).

The day before I left, I took a guided tour of London on a double-decker bus. Could not believe it when we passed by the Connaught Hotel and a few minutes later drove around Berkeley Square. I definitely felt an arrow pierce my heart. Took a picture through the bus window of the bench where we sat for lunch. Well, my love, it seems it's time to say farewell, at least for the moment. I hope you enjoyed reading this as much as I enjoyed writing it. I feel you have been with me in spirit.

Love, Indu

P.S. Enclosed in this letter is one bear hug and a big kiss which you get every time you even look at this letter.

P.P.S. I may never get this letter mailed. I keep thinking of things to add. While washing and folding my yoga clothes, it crossed my mind that possibly next summer we might go to the ashram together. It was a pleasant thought. But then it hit me that that was an extremely long time to wait to see you again. Am afraid my heart has only grown fonder as the distance between us has grown wider.

So today, began inquiring into travel to Greece in December. Now if this does not feel right to you, please let me know as soon as possible. For instance, if Alison should be there or whatever. Turns out it's extremely difficult and expensive to fly from Japan to Greece and then to the U.S. (around $2,600). But round trip from Kansas City to Athens is $879, which seems cheap compared to the other. Ordinarily, I couldn't afford it at this time, but I have some money invested which is just waiting for a special need. I know full well that if we both don't make a strong effort, we will have only fond memories of a time-enduring romance in England—meaning that the feeling I have now most likely will not die, even if I never see you again. Alas... So, my love, let me know what you think. My boss is in Japan now until October 4 and before I leave on October 9, I should clear this with him. Of course, it will be a short visit, about two weeks (Dec 15-Jan 3). But well worth it if you also agree.

Now I also realized I did not tell you my Christian name. It never even crossed my mind and you never asked, but just for your information, I was christened Elizabeth Susan in the Episcopal Church. Family calls me Liz. As far as genealogy goes, I'm the eighth-generation-removed granddaughter of King George III (on the illegitimate side). Not exactly a claim to fame!

Now I promise I'll mail this epic of a letter.

ℰℴ * * * ℭ𝔞

She explained to me that after mailing her first letter, she waited an agonizing week, hoping each day that a letter from him would arrive. But none did. With a heavy heart, she had started another letter to him, although not intending to mail it until she had heard some word from him. It was almost a month in the writing and she mailed it two weeks after she arrived in Japan.

&) * * * CR

[Indu's Letter #2] Lawrence, Kansas, September 30

Dear George,

It's the last day of September. The sun is shining brightly, the air cool, the sky blue and clear. It's a peaceful Sunday afternoon (1:14 p.m. which means it's 9:14 p.m. in Corfu). Decided to start another letter to you. Mailed my last one about a week ago. Possibly you will receive it tomorrow. But still no word from you. Alas, have you forgotten me?

Found an interesting book at the library by Lawrence Durrell entitled *Prospero's Cell*. It's about life on Corfu just before World War II. Of course Saint Spyridon is mentioned. Durrell gives a beautiful description of the landscape, people, etc. Have read that Prince Phillip was born on Corfu. Anyway, have gotten a favorable impression of the place. Can't imagine why I should have picked up such a book.

Again I'm wondering why I haven't heard from you. Possibly it is best for the whole thing to remain a very happy memory. I don't know...

Met up with an old boyfriend this weekend. We spent some time together. It was over two years ago that we ended our relationship. Says he's ready to start a family. Have another former involvement coming for a visit this weekend. Works in Detroit for a bank. Has asked me to marry him several times. Even my mother thinks it's a good match. And have a friend coming over to dinner tonight. We started dating last March and have kept the friendship platonic so far. What I'm trying to convey to you is I'm not at a loss for companionship, if that's all I wanted. But something is missing in all these relationships and I thank God I can recognize that. But what is that something—that something that is special and bonds two people beyond the physical plane? Didn't we feel it, I wonder, something drawing us together yet beyond words, explanations? Well, it's up for speculation. Would love to hear your thoughts on it.

Had a fairly good week back at work. Got caught up on quite a few things. Have less than ten days before leaving for Osaka. Still lots of things left to do. Will probably write Nhoj a note today. He should be back at Ickwell by now.

The campanile bells just chimed. It's two o'clock. Guess I should get to work around the house.

[Indu's Letter #2-continued] October 2

The thought crossed my mind today that exactly one month ago we were together in New Brighton. It seems both a long time ago and yet just yesterday. I think time is playing a trick on me.

[Indu's Letter #2-continued] October 4

Hi. Not much news to tell you. Just got home from work and I'm pooped! Thought I might mention to you about an invention you may not have heard about. It's called "paper and pencil." Even a pen will work. That's a not too subtle hint.

[Indu's Letter #2-continued] October 7

So almost one month has passed since we talked that early morning before you took the ferry across the Channel. Heard from Uma that all is going well in London. This weekend they were back in New Brighton with Margaret and Paul giving another workshop. They've also made excursions to Salisbury Cathedral and Stonehenge. Wish I'd been there to go with them. As for my life, in less than forty-eight hours, I'm off again. Still have laundry and packing to finish up. Am wondering how you are.

[Indu's Letter #2-continued] Los Angeles Airport, October 9

Am sitting in the L.A. airport by my gate waiting to board a Korean Airlines flight. Still have another hour to wait. For some reason, had expected that I would have heard from you by now.

Was actually a little worried that some accident might have happened driving across Europe. So Sunday night, called your parents just to make sure you were okay. Found out they were in Greece, too. Certainly do hope that all is well. Have only slept three hours in the past forty except for a doze from Denver to L.A. Am feeling a little spacey, but it's a nice feeling.

Well, guess we will have to wait until next summer to see each other again. Since hadn't heard from you, I decided not to ask my boss for the time off during the December holidays. Probably just as well.

So, Mr. Acroilus, if you are having reservations about anything concerning *moi*, please just write a short note and tell me. Given the rather unusual circumstances of our three encounters (by the stone, New Brighton, and the day in London) and the circumstances in each of our lives, I don't think I'll be too surprised. Am I having reservations? Well, at the moment, none yet. But then I'm afraid I'm a bit of a romantic.

[Indu's Letter #2-continued] Kimhae, Korea, October 11

Was only just a few hours ago when I wrote the above. It's now seven o'clock in the morning and I'm sitting in a Korean airport south of Seoul. Lost a day flying over the Pacific. Airport in Seoul is fogged out so had to land here to refuel. Have to wait two hours for fog to lift. Fortunately, can still make my eleven o'clock connecting flight to Osaka out of Tokyo. Slept on the plane. Was supposed to have been an eight-hour flight from Anchorage, Alaska, but seemed shorter. Obviously, I missed something.

[Indu's Letter #2-continued] Osaka, October 13

Greetings from Osaka. It's 7:18 p.m. Am already in bed. Traveling is finally catching up with me. Have been here forty-eight hours and am very happy and content. Have a lovely little house to myself. But only a two-minute walk away live good friends of my boss. They have been taking very good care of me, inviting me for breakfast, lunch and dinner, shopping, etc. I met them last March in Lawrence. Went to work on Friday, met everyone in the lab, set up my desk. Unfortunately, Osaka University is two hours from where I live. So every day I must commute by train a total of four hours! But I can use that time to study Japanese.

Woke up this morning and realized that for the first time you were in my dreams (that I remember). Actually, I did not see you, only I was thinking of you. I was with some other man whom I met in this dream, nice guy, but I was thinking to myself, "He's nice, but he's not George." My feelings just weren't the same. So, my love, you have definitely reached my subconscious.

[Indu's Letter #2-continued] October 22

Already ten days have gone by since the last installment. Things have been going full speed. It's now 9:30 p.m. Just had a luxurious Japanese bath and am curled up in my futon. Have had a cold for the past three days. My lovely little Japanese house has no heating system! I'm actually using a toaster oven to heat up the room. If I change rooms, I carry the toaster oven with me. And I am happy to say your letter arrived today. It was a happy sight. Unfortunately, as I mentioned earlier, a meeting in December will not be possible. The reason I was so anxious to hear from you quickly was so I could arrange things with my boss before leaving. Am afraid he wouldn't look too favorably on another sudden request for a trip leave. And also, before you raise the dowry requirement I better tell you I'm $3,000 in debt. It was only that my heart was rich in desire to see you again, and still is.

Have been giving you and me a lot of thought. An interesting thing happened last week. An acquaintance, also from Lawrence and now on scholarship at Kyoto University, was visiting here and saw a picture of you and me together. Her first remark was, "Is that your brother?" Later again she commented on the odd resemblance. Her question has stuck in my mind. Is that what our most recent incarnation was, brother and sister? It does seem to fit in many ways (one in particular!). Pondering on this, something in me began to relax.

And so now, not wanting to be an overbearing sister, I want to say that you are absolutely free to work hither and thither and go here and there till your heart's content, be it one year or five or ten. Wherever you are you will always have my love. Such *strong* feelings I have for you. When I first recognized them, my mind immediately jumped to marriage, but now I also recognize that one's previous brother does not necessarily become one's present husband (although it might not be a bad arrangement). I also remember in your description of our relationship to Nhoj, you said that I was a spiritual sister. It seems you were speaking a greater truth than you may have realized.

As for me, although supposedly destined to marry next year (according to that psychic) am strongly feeling now not to marry at all. Being alone actually suits me quite well. Of course, I will wait and watch what Guruji indicates for my life, since life's main purpose is not getting married or remaining unmarried but spiritual growth. So hopefully any marriage for me will be to that end. That is one of the blessed advantages of having an outer Guru; he can shine a light into the dark unknown and help you see your way.

Now back to us—still and all I'd love to see you again—the sooner the better. But as for our future together, you are right in saying time will tell. It always does.

[Indu's Letter #2-continued] October 25

Overslept this morning. Got up at seven instead of six. Am now riding the 7:46 a.m. train so will arrive at work at 9:45 a.m. Will no sooner get started than it will be time to eat lunch. Found some centrifuge tubes in the lab which should do quite well as *neti* tubes. Have boiled them so they're ready for use. Will mail them same time as this letter.

And now about one's past behavior. One fundamental rule in yoga is not to think or worry about past events. Sometimes I have to force myself to stop thinking about something which happened in the past and is now filling my head with worry or anxiety. I try to suddenly stop the disturbing train of thought. Oddly enough, I feel one hundred percent better and later realize it didn't matter anyway. Do you know the story about Shri Aurobindo? He was a revolutionary leader whose motto was, "See and shoot." But with the aid of his Guru, he transcended that karma and became a great spiritual teacher. So I think there's hope for you!

So now my dear George, I want you to know you are in my thoughts throughout my day, while riding a train surrounded on all sides by people (as now) or walking by the golden rice fields (by my house) or curled up in my futon. Never forget you have my love.

With love, Indu

TWENTY-SIX

~

The letter she was about to read to me was not George's first letter. It was his second. But when she received it, she assumed it was the first correspondence he had sent. She had given him the Osaka address before leaving London. She imagined that he had waited to get comfortably settled in Corfu before writing or had possibly been waiting for her to get to Japan. Nonetheless, she took the letter's tardy arrival as a sign that he had grave doubts about staying in contact. It was this supposition that had led her to emphasize in the last part of her second letter the brother-sister connection and to suggest that she might not want to marry. She wasn't meaning to mislead him about her true feelings, but was only trying to open the door for a graceful exit on his part if that was in truth what he was really wanting. But except for its late arrival, there wasn't anything in the letter indicating that such a desire existed in his heart. Ultimately, after first reading it, she was totally confused as to just how seriously he felt about their relationship. After giving me this preface, she began.

છ * * * ૭૪

[George's Letter #2] Corfu, October 10

My dear Indu,

I've just had a hot bath and am alone and quiet in the house. In front of me is your wonderful well-thumbed letter which gladly greets me with a bear hug and kiss even every time I so much as glance at it. I don't imagine for a moment that

I shall finish writing this tonight so perhaps the end will come in a few days.

The rational and intuitive minds: well, what a delightful struggle they are having in my mind. Intuitive side says, "Reach out and experience this current of love and trust and honesty; drink from that cup which is the first to quench such a thirst." But being the suspicious-minded fellow that I am, my rational mind is quick to raise its head and say, "Yes, but wait a minute; this is only your perception of an extraordinary experience. Might you not be merely caught up in the mysticism of your early yogic experiences?" Well, who knows? Time can only tell. You say in your many-petaled letter that I should ignore any comments that your rational mind might have concerning love, as it is basically ignorant in that sphere. I so wish that my life could be lived intuitively, though at the moment it cannot and that's why my rational mind has such a strong voice.

"Now for heaven sake," says my intuitive mind, "do you suppose that for the sake of wanting to work here and there and everywhere and do this, that and the other; and just because you've always had it in your head that you'll probably settle down and think of marriage at about thirty, that you won't—or maybe are too frightened to—drink from this cup?" And so my head spins. But Indu my love, I know what I've felt with you and if we should spend our lives together then there is no rush to fix it all up. I feel that we will have enough opportunities for seeing each other again and will know, for certain for certain, whether we can both spend the rest of our lives together. That means all the little bitty things like family responsibilities (although we may not be capable of having our own), aims and ambitions.

I think that even if one has embarked on a spiritual path (unconsciously or otherwise), one can feel complete in oneself if in a particular environment. I know this so well, as my relationship with Alison has taught me so. She and I are probably both on some kind of spiritual mission and we both love each other for that reason and some others besides. But what makes Alison blossom makes me shrink. I'm willing to admit that there may be a great deal of immaturity in me that makes me shrink. Still, I do believe that it is a fundamental difference in character/astrology/psyche, call-it-what-you-like that has determined that Alison and I should not spend all our time together. I think that's what you and I have to find out.

Immediately having written that, my mind has been echoing two indignant cries of, "What about unconditional love?" If you love someone, and I mean really love, nothing should matter. Unfortunately, I am only a divine fool and for the moment I feel I can love somebody unconditionally but might not want to spend the whole of my life with them. If I write any more about all this I'll start becoming incoherent, so suffice to say that my spirit craves spending more time with you. I long to be with you again.

I can't tell you what joy the photos and pamphlets and letter have brought me. Time and again I have leafed through them and thought about you and now you even write to say that you're prepared to spend a colossal sum of money just to come out to see me. Indu, I can hardly believe it! You mentioned the dates December 15-January 3. Well, I have an idea. I start work in Zimbabwe around January 18 and was planning to go back to England in early January. Why don't we, airplane tickets permitting, drive back to England together either at the end of December or whenever?

[George's Letter #2-continued] October 11

I'm on a ferry going across to mainland Greece and thence up north toward Albania to a wool fair. I've no idea what it'll be like but I think it's a festival when all the wool is collected together from the shepherds and brought down to a small provincial town. I'm with David and Cathy. David is a cousin who farms on the island and Cathy his English wife. They are both going away to England at the end of the month and have asked me to look after the farm for them.

On Monday, I'm going to stay with them and be shown the ropes. It involves milking Maria, their cow, twice a day; chopping wood; clearing land and looking after plants and crops. I will live in the house with Georgia, the most lovely, old Corfiot woman who has been a nanny with my uncle's family for years. She used to take me out for staggers when I was still in nappies!

Their house is perched on the side of a mountain and built into a rock, and in front is the family chapel and fantastic view across to Albania and the mainland. It's been built in the Venetian style with one large central room and then all the others leading off it, similar in design to our home. Seems a shame to have to go and work on someone else's land when there's so much that needs to be done at our house. Still, I have to do it as they will pay me a little and my financial position at the moment is slightly alarming.

I met a Dane at the Frankfurt convention who told me he was going down to Corfu. So we've met up again and he's been living with me out in the village. We've worked really hard putting together a juggling and magic show which lasts for about twenty minutes. It had its premiere at a hotel discotheque and went down quite well with the guests, but unfortunately the manager didn't book us again. Before leaving England, I met the court jester of Chilham Castle near Canterbury who is a magician apart from his many other talents. He initiated me into various other forms of witchdoctory and sorcery so my repertoire has expanded. I now have the use of a very special handmade-with-my-own-horny-fingers magic bag!

Would you believe it, I've heard that the great English literary figure C.S. Lewis is a resident of Corfu and that he is most interested in setting up some form of meditation center. He's into Zen or something. I've not met him yet but I believe he lives quite close to David and Cathy so when I'm there I hope to find out more about it. There is also a hatha yoga group on the island but unfortunately the women in it are more into the body-beautiful bit than anything else.

I have been doing a fair amount of meditation, the first time for me really, and also some hatha. It's wonderful to live by myself—well, almost, but René the housekeeper is quiet and also fairly yogic—and to be able to discipline myself to do meditation twice a day and postures and study my Greek books. Most sadly I cannot practice any *neti* as in Brindisi the car was broken into and a bag containing the tubes that I got at the Foundation was pinched. I was so furious.

[George's Letter #2-continued] October 13

I went through my finances the other day and found to my horror that I've barely enough money to get back to England. It worried me to think that I had so few pennies in the bank and the thought of returning to England to find some work crossed my mind. Then I thought, "Remain calm, live frugally and diligently and hopefully something will turn up." I heard yesterday that quite a few people leave Corfu in the winter and need people to house sit for them. I would try to make absolutely certain that if you managed to come out for a couple of weeks that I had the time to spend it entirely with you and in our house. I must confess that on several occasions I have caught myself day-dreaming about you being here and the loveliness of the whole idyllic setting. Oh, Indu, what are we going to do? Here I am with olives and goat's cheese thinking of you, and there you are with tea and bamboo parasols thinking of me.

My mother saw Jim in London last week. He says that the school in Zimbabwe is very determined to have me work out there and might be in some position to help finance my trip. Fantastic news considering the state of my coffers.

Also my great auntie said she might help "George, dear boy." What I'd love to be able to do is, after returning to Europe in April, then come over to Lawrence for a while, as I have to re-sit that bloody exam in June. If I pass the exam it'll mean I have letters after my name (tra-la, tra-la) and might be able to borrow money from the bank. However, if I fail, that'll be your job.

I've just read "The Mind and Meditation." Those rare moments, fleeting milliseconds, are indescribable. But a glimpse of non-thinking mind when meditating by myself makes me want to meditate with others and the experience seems to occur slightly more often under those conditions. I think I'm beginning to understand what you mean when you say that your meditations become deeper and deeper. The whole experience becomes smoother and rounder, loses those sharp edges which were anxious streams of ego. I still wonder in amazement how I can realize so clearly in my mind how appallingly I've behaved and said something so utterly ridiculous, and yet at the time when involved in those particular incidences my head was so ego-oriented and so unaware of how I was really behaving.

I read with interest the snippet you sent about the yogi's unbelievable *kuṇḍalinī* manifestation. What control he must have had! I've made a strong effort to exercise more control over my mind in those things. An extremely good place to be as there are scantily dressed nymphs who abound. Somehow, though, I manage to get through the day without thinking too many wicked thoughts.

That's another aspect of our relationship that leaves me thinking just what on earth is all this about? I have always had quite strong physical relationships and now I find myself somehow elevated with you where my perception of the "physical relationship" is entirely different. I don't know too much about *kuṇḍalinī* and all that but it certainly seems to provide some answers. That sounds very skeptical but then I maintain that doubt is an important element in a spiritual life. Sometimes I doubt my ability to live with someone who yearns to wear the orange robes of a spiritual ascetic, as I doubt my ability to grow along the same path and to feel that it might be a natural progression in the course of my life.

[George's Letter #2-continued] October 14

I've just read a miscellaneous snippet in a book, *Orthodox Spirituality*, by a monk of the Eastern church: "According to the 'classics' of the spiritual life, contemplation begins with the 'prayer of simplicity' or 'prayer of simple regard.' The prayer of simplicity consists of placing yourself in the presence of God and maintaining yourself in His presence for a certain time, in an interior silence which is as complete as possible, while you concentrate upon the divine Object, reduce to unity the multiplicity of your thought and feelings, and endeavor to 'keep yourself quiet' without words or arguments. [...] Anyone who is even to a slight degree accustomed to pray is sure to have experienced this form of contemplation, for a few minutes at least. It is marvelously fruitful. It is like a welcome shower of rain falling on the garden of the soul. [Isn't that lovely?] It gives most powerful assistance to the efforts which we make in the moral order to avoid sin and to accomplish the divine will."[17]

[George's Letter #2-continued] October 16

I really must get on and post this letter, though now I'm in town and the few photos of me that I have are back at the house. Still, never mind. I'll post this today and write again soon and send some photos. Hopefully by then I will have got another film back which might have some more, though they're slides, still good for making prints.

Well, my love, I must go now. Never does a day go by when I'm not thinking of you and wanting you to be with me in what I'm doing. It would be perfectly blissful if we could work something out in December, though having said that

I think you ought to think again about spending so much money. It's a hell of a lot for such a short time. I think you must be very rich or something! I must consider fixing a new price for the dowry.

Anyway, enough of this frivolity—just that with this letter comes gentle and tender love all the time.

With my love, George

℘ * * * ℭ

After she read his letter, I wondered how she could have doubted the depths of his love for her. But it's not uncommon for circumstances of life to raise doubts in one's mind even when the truth is so obvious. Her perplexity was further confounded when she received a phone call at the university from her father. It was a fatherly gesture which she found extraordinarily kind. He had called to tell her that a letter from Germany had just been forwarded from Kansas to Oklahoma bearing all sorts of postal stamps.

Being aware of his daughter's affections for someone overseas, he had surmised immediately that the existence of the letter would be of utmost importance. But even if he had mailed it to Japan that day, it would still have taken almost ten days for it to reach her. He had decided it was worth a call just to tell her. He had the telephone number for the university that she had given him. He later told her that as he dialed the numbers he didn't have the foggiest idea how, without a word of Japanese, he was going to locate her. But he did.

The news of the letter eased some of her angst over George's intentions. George had tried to reach her after all, and would have except for an oversight in the postal service which had caused the unbearable delay. But her doubting mind had already brought up too many insecurities to be quickly squelched. Something more would be needed to convince her that George really wanted their relationship to continue. And so she wrote her third letter to him, trying to maintain a reserved tone. After this explanation, she started reading again.

ℰ *** * *** ℭ

[Indu's Letter #3] Osaka, October 27

Dear George,

Just after I mailed my letter to you yesterday, again I thought of something else to write. So, alas, here I am again starting another letter to you. Only wanted to mention to you that Gandhi had to take his law exam to become a barrister more than once before he passed. After that, his law practice was almost nil until he went to South Africa and got involved in civil rights. Also, Einstein did not show much scholastic ability during the major part of his formal schooling. Some geniuses are just late bloomers. And even then, sometimes their genius isn't recognized until they've come and gone (several artists come to mind). So you're in good company as far as retaking that exam. I would say that your name is long enough without adding four more letters to it but I wouldn't want to discourage you from trying … so I won't say it.

Also heard from my family that a letter from Germany has just arrived. Only person I could think it would be from was you. Did you send a letter to Lawrence after all and it's just now arriving? (Am having Lawrence mail forwarded to my parents.) What a strange twist of fate if it's true. Was so wanting some word from you so I could know whether or not you'd be at all interested in seeing me again in December. When I didn't hear anything I surrendered to the fates, feeling awkward planning to come to see you without any invitation or even a tiny indication that you also felt the same way, i.e., in love.

Spent today in Kyoto watching volleyball games between Osaka University and Kyoto University. Several students from the lab were playing so we met for lunch, went to the games and then to a party afterward. Didn't stay very late since had to travel an hour by train to get back home. Interesting watching the team spirit amongst everyone. When someone missed everyone from the side would yell *donmai, donmai,* which was Japanese English for "don't mind." If something good happened, they'd yell *naisu,* meaning "nice," or *lukee,* meaning "lucky." Am now getting ready to take a bath and go to bed. Tomorrow am being picked up at noon to go to dinner at Dr. Miura's house. Socially, weekends are going to be quite busy until I return to the States. Anyway, just couldn't resist the desire to jot these few lines to you.

[Indu's Letter #3-continued] October 29

Funny thing: I've been asked not to come into work tomorrow. They're expecting some government officials (government has strong hold on national universities) to come in to check up on things and they don't want to have to explain what I'm doing there. Officially, I have no connection with the university. So brought some work home with me and will spend part of tomorrow going over it, writing postcards and visiting a couple of temples about an hour away by train, also doing some shopping: peanut butter, bread, cheese, paper towels, etc.

Want to tell you how much I loved what you wrote on contemplation, sitting in the presence of God. It's so beautiful because it takes you away from trying to go anywhere in your meditations, from having expectations of what should happen, simply "maintain yourself in His presence." And in doing that, those moments of no-mind come which are beyond description. There are many things on the spiritual path which I don't have any understanding of how they work. Like a child with a toy. If he pushes button A, door 2 opens; button B, door 3 opens; button C, door 1 opens, and every now and then he'll find more hidden buttons that can open all the doors at once or two at a time. He can't explain how it works but he knows it works. So it is with me. (I was a very mechanically-oriented child.) Even the desire to know can be a hindrance since it's only the mind asking the question.

[Indu's Letter #3-continued] November 3

It's Friday night, 10:15 p.m. Got home from work at eight-thirty. Fixed dinner and watched a little television. Of course, can't understand the dialog but get the gist of the show anyway. Good practice for listening comprehension. But have been surprised by how much violence is shown (not to say American television is without). But the Japanese shows seem to be much more explicit, and whereas American shows abound in romance and comedy, haven't seen that much here.

Well, on my day off, ended up sleeping in, then went to visit the friend who lives around the corner who's been helping me. Then went shopping. Had to take a bus for thirty minutes and then walk for ten to get to this big shopping center. Shopped almost four hours. Bought so many things (food, four big boxes of tissue, several rolls of paper towels, both bulky), could barely make it home. Am too used to having a car waiting just outside the store. Anyway, never did get to look at any work but didn't really matter since am actually a little ahead of schedule.

Will spend tomorrow visiting friends in Kobe (about ninety minutes from here by train) and Sunday morning I'm being picked up at ten-thirty to visit other friends here in Osaka. These are people who have worked in Lawrence under my boss. So should probably get myself to bed early. One thing in your letter has come to my mind, about loving someone unconditionally but not wanting to spend a lifetime with them. Ideally, we should love everyone unconditionally. But as far as spending time with someone, the *Yoga Sūtras* advise, "The mind becomes calm and tranquil by cultivating and developing attitudes of friendliness and fellowship toward the happy-going persons, compassion and kindness toward the miserable, entertainment and joy toward the virtuous, and indifference and neutrality toward the evil-doing persons." [18] (Ch. I, #33) I often think of this as I'm watching my relationships developing with different people. Are they the happy or miserable, virtuous or not so virtuous? Inwardly I give everyone my love but this *sūtra* helps teach us to protect ourselves, our spiritual energy, so we're not pulled down by our relationships. I'm sure you've heard the story of the cobra who became a devotee. Just before parting for a long journey, the Master forbade that he should bite anyone. When the Master returned and saw his cobra pupil close to death, he asked what had happened. After relaying the story how people had abused him once they found he wouldn't bite, the teacher replied, "I said don't bite, but I didn't say not to hiss." So while trying to love all people, there will be some at whom I will hiss and only a handful with whom I'll choose to be close, and it goes without saying that you're one of them. As for unconditional love in a marriage, so often it becomes polluted by the idea that "he should do this" and "she should do that." A very unhealthy dependency then develops. Have every intention of avoiding that one at all costs.

Well, Mr. Acroilus, I'm blowing you kisses goodnight!

ʕ) * * * ʢ

In the next segment of this letter, written two days later, she would make reference to George's letter from Germany, which she had finally received in the mail on November 5. To help keep the sequence of things coherent, she thought it best to slip it in now. It was only two pages long. I was eager to hear it.

TWENTY-SEVEN

~

George's first letter, having traveled nearly around the world, across the Atlantic and then Pacific oceans, was a poignant reminder that even the best laid plans can go awry. Indu had wanted to hear from him. He had written. Yet the letter had taken weeks to reach her. What force had determined its fate? Indu told me that she couldn't help but wonder how it was that these invisible forces influence so many aspects of our lives: our decisions, our reactions, our feelings. We like to think that we can control the course of events, but is that really even possible? "Sometimes," she said, "all we can do is hope to find peace with what comes to us." After this bit of philosophizing, she commenced reading his first letter, the letter from Germany.

ℰ❀ * * * ℭ

[George's Letter #1] In a Frankfurt park, September 15

Dear Indu,

Just looking through my date book I now realize that this letter won't be waiting for you when you arrive in Lawrence, which is what the intention is. Still, you never know your luck; the envelope might fall into the hands of an enlightened postman.

We've had quite a good trip so far driving in convoy until Germany where I lost Nhoj. Alison and I spent the night in a small village, very worried as we thought Nhoj's car (also an old Morris) had broken down somewhere. You can imagine our relief when we walked into the convention hall to see him juggling away.

The days are very tiring, hundreds of jugglers all doing their thing and the hall pulsating with energy that leaves you stunned. They've arranged different workshops: five balls, cigar boxes, devil sticks and diabolo, club passing, etc. Quite the most amazing source of inspiration that makes me feel there's no way I could go anywhere to volunteer myself for "evening entertainment" in my present condition, not even with a little more practice. No doubt, despite all my dear Bohemian dreams, I shall end up in a suit working in my cousin's hotel.

At the moment, we're camped (no Holiday Inn for us, but then those luxuries should only be enjoyed with terribly special people and on immensely important occasions) underneath a motorway flyover on the outskirts of Frankfurt. Quite the most dismal place you could imagine and it's been pouring rain so in the morning you crawl reptile-like out of the tent and squelch through mud to the shower block fifty meters away to "freshen up." Oh well, the rich tapestry of life, I suppose!

Tomorrow is the last day and then on Monday morning we leave for Italy. I think Alison would like to dump most of her bags in Verona and come with me to the south of Italy and then hitch back, but the plans are still uncertain. We haven't been getting on too badly considering I'm in the unfaithful lover bracket. Really, I'm amazed at her optimism and tenacity.

I haven't really had the time to read all the things you so kindly sent me and can't wait to get out to the peace and quiet of the house. I'll see my parents for a few days as well which will be great, and some old friends from Uganda who are staying at the moment.

Well, Indu, I must stop now and find a post office because it's nearly five o'clock and the letter is supposed to be short and sent off in time to welcome you back home. Sometimes during the day, I can almost feel you. I'm sure you're not a dream though sometimes my badly abused little head whirs and fells me so. Good God, what's happened to all my reference points? Maybe it's because I can't rationalize my feelings that I'm in a muddle, or am I in a muddle?

Anyway, all I know is that you're lovely and that I've got nothing to be sad about. Welcome home, and I wish I was there to give you a big hug.

With my love, George

ᴈ◌ * * * ♋

It was an irony that such a sweet letter had not been delivered before she had left for Japan. Although it showed that he was still working through things with Alison, it would have gone a long way to relieve her mounting anxiety. But such had not been the cosmic plan. And even more ironic was the effect it had on her at this time. Instead of bringing happiness that he had been thinking of her all along, what she mainly saw in it, received at such a late date, was that he and Alison were "getting on not too badly." She continued reading the next installment in her third letter. She prefaced it by saying that the November 5 segment was short and written with sadness.

ᴈ◌ * * * ♋

[Indu's Letter #3-continued] Osaka, November 5

It took seven weeks for your letter of September 15 to finally catch up with me. It was a dear letter but I know if I had received it in Lawrence, I would still have cancelled any

421

idea of a December trip and probably would not have even mentioned the thought to you. You mentioned that you and Alison were getting along very well and truly I'm happy for that. As I told you in New Brighton, I don't want to interfere with your relationship with each other (although I know quite unintentionally I have). Possibly you two should still try to make a go of it, although I'm certainly not the one to give any advice since my record in that department doesn't have many gold stars. Our time together does seem like a dream and it's one I will always treasure.

ജ * * * ങ

She interrupted herself again to say that two weeks were to pass before she was to write another entry in her letter. But the ache of being apart from him was only growing with each passing day. She was trying desperately to follow the advice that Guruji had given on the day she had departed London.

"Remember," she read his words which she'd recorded in her notebook, "the mind cannot be controlled. The thinking mind is more powerful than the pounding waves of the ocean. How to stop the waves of the ocean? You cannot. But you can watch, witnessing each thought entering and leaving. The witness is beyond the thinking mechanism. As a witness, automatically the inner silence will come. The mind cannot stop the mind. Always be the neutral observer in everything in your life."

There was great wisdom in those words. But when it came to George, she confessed to me she had found it extremely difficult at the time to remain neutral about anything. A fairly serious case of lovesickness was blurring her objectivity.

"So," she had told herself, "why not simply observe these torturous love pangs torturing?" In so doing one day, she saw her pain in a most comical light and her proud attempt to show reserve in the first few pages of her present ongoing letter seemed equally laughable.

The Letters

On that day, November 15, just before departing for a week-end excursion, she wrote a postcard to George upon which was written:

> Am heading off for a long four-day weekend to Hiroshima. Have a letter started to you. Trying hard to remain a neutral observer in our present romantic involvement (as recommended by all spiritual teachers) but finding it next to impossible. Letter started will sound very noncommittal, but don't be fooled. Will mail it anyway so at least you'll know I tried. Anxiously awaiting your next letter.
>
> Love, Indu

ဆ * * * ᘓ

She now reached for the bundle of airmail envelopes. As luck would have it, after mailing this postcard, she received another letter from George, his third, which gave her unbounded inspiration to finally finish writing her third letter to him.

ဆ * * * ᘓ

[George's Letter #3] Corfu, November 6

My dear Indu,

I heard yesterday that I had some mail waiting for me in town so went in and there was your letter. I sat in the car and read it and thought with increasing despair that you must be thinking that I was behaving so unfairly toward you. Not only (at the beginning of your letter) had you not received the letter I sent to you in Japan, but also it seems you didn't get the letter that I sent to Lawrence before you'd even left England. I felt really quite sick with frustration. I could tell by the way you wrote that you were so disappointed and puzzled, having thought that my feelings were so genuine and then my seeming total silence as if to say, "Well, thanks for the experience but now I don't want anything more to do with you." Well that's not true, as you know. I don't even have to say that.

I suppose over the last fortnight or so I feel my life has stagnated. My willpower has become weaker, meditation irregular and recently almost nonexistent, as I struggle pathetically with Greek and wish that I had something better to do during the day than milking the cow, cleaning the stable and yard and gardening. It's not a new experience at all, as I tend to go through these things (don't we all?) but what I long for most is to be with you—totally selfish. I miss so much being with someone I can love and who loves me and I think this is something that has dogged me for ages. It has brought many relationships to an end because I've realized that I no longer need what that person has been giving me. Rather like a child growing out of a toy. I don't reproach myself but can see that in every relationship the "need" is different. One day the need will be to give totally and unconditionally but I've still got so much to learn before then.

I've had a lengthy talk with Melinda, my sister, about this. I have often said to her that sometimes I doubt whether I should become involved in relationships, as ultimately they all end in pain and sorrow. Yet despite the grief, there has also been happiness for me, but after the oil has been burnt I see the pain still with the girl, instead of a love that should be there. I know we grow through these experiences but sometimes the end is hard to bear. But with you, Indu, I feel all that has been transcended. We have something greater "going on." I don't know what it is either, but that love will always be there. The brother/sister reincarnation theory is interesting, though I don't believe that previous incarnations also have a genetic effect. I think that we might have similar features due to our respective genetic inheritance rather that past lives.

I must tell you about a dream I had last night which was a result of receiving your letter and also the result of being able to put into perspective the relationship that I think I have with you. It is also the first time that I've remembered dreaming about you and it was quite powerful. I shall recall the sequence of "visions" and the emotional feelings that went with each picture.

A large, predominantly white, fairly low-ceilinged building with polished stone floor and pillars. Similar to an airport-type building but it wasn't an airport but more a conference center. I remember standing and waiting for you, shades of waiting at West Kensington tube station, "Where's Indu, where's Indu?" Then there you are walking toward me dressed as you were at Ickwell. We hugged each other and I saw your face while you were embracing me, looking whimsical. I felt anxious about (in retrospect now) what our relationship would reveal.

The next part is slightly more obscure in my mind, as a picture form, but the impression it left me with is quite clear. Again a large room with quite a few people and you are with a group. I have a strong feeling that Uma is there somewhere. All the time we are apart and I'm looking out for you and you're involved in something, not anything particular but with a group of people. You were then always apart from me and I felt like an observer of what you were doing. It was something that I was not directly involved in. You were always full of joy and happiness and smiling. My dominant feeling was of anxiety as to what I would see from you and what you were up to. Well, that was the dream…

Quote from your letter: "…Of course, I will wait and watch what Guruji indicates." And:

"…that's one of the blessed advantages of having an outer Guru." I remember you speaking at length in London about having a Guru and you sent me the "How to Select a Guru?" pamphlet.

The dream, what you've written in your letters and what we've had a chance to talk about has made me feel that if I were to seriously, seriously consider altering my life in order to spend more time with you, which would only involve coming to America to work, I would feel incomplete. This is because despite the fact that you say "any marriage for me will be for that end" (spiritual growth), actually your outer Guru would determine the events and personal decisions in your life, and not what you worked out with your husband.

I've thought hard about whether I could also place myself in that position in order that both our lives would be guided as one by Guruji. I'm just not able to come to terms with that, and marriage for me would be incomplete togetherness if my spirit could not accept your Guru.

In ways, Herman Hesse's novel *Siddhartha* helps me to understand how I feel. Govinda, his greatest friend and companion, hears the teachings of Gautama, the Buddha, and takes the monk's robe, whereas Siddhartha's spirit compels him to leave the devotees of Buddha and to follow his own will. Indu, I have never had a Guru as you have. The idea is strange and alien to me, and I feel I must continue on my own way, though pausing to listen to Gurus and saints alike. Whether through my own need, insecurity, whatever, I feel, no, there's something amiss: that is, that I would be having a relationship with a divine girl but who is not just Indu, as I would love her to be, but with her Guru as well.

I love you for what you are now and don't want, through a change in our relationship, to find that my feelings would change. I've just reread the last two pages of this letter, all the time thinking I hope it won't change anything. I feel strangely vulnerable; maybe I have misunderstood some basic part of you and the relationship you have with your Guru. But still now you can put me right. But don't tell me that like Shri Aurobindo I can transcend my karma with the help of a Guru and become a great spiritual teacher! (Thanks for your confidence in me.)

I'm so sad about December—still, never mind. I think there's a chance that I may come over to America after I finish work in Zimbabwe in April. I know that you don't have a holiday then, but come July I have to be back in Greece to work. However, a while in Lawrence in spring might change all that. Greece is a police state in reality and I'm a little worried about working here for a long period of time, as they might suddenly decide that I must do my two-year military service despite the fact that my passport has a stamp exempting me from doing it. A lawyer will tell you one thing and an arresting military policeman another. Rather precarious!

I gave an old man a lift to his village yesterday as he'd missed the bus and had a great bandage wrapped around his leg. He knows my cousin, and thought I was a son or something and kissed my hand and crossed himself several times. Quite embarrassing! Anyway, we reached his house and he asked me in and sat me down to a glass of wine, cheese, bread, tomatoes and a boiled egg. Such a dear old man and he lived in a lovely, old house with white-washed stone floors and walls. Then he wrote a note to David (the cousin) and he gave me a plastic bag full of peppers and aubergines (eggplant) and a bottle of homemade wine. We embraced, a kiss on both cheeks, and off I went. His father was a priest and the old man never stopped crossing himself and invoking the names of the saints. He was also called "Spiro." Most Corfiots are, as St. Spyridon saved Corfu three times from certain disaster: the Turks, a plague and something else I can't recall.

I've just spent a lovely hour or so in meditation and doing *trāṭakam*. You see, my love, your letter has brought me peace of mind once again and restored my spirit. I did some breathing exercises, gazed into a candle and brought you close to me. I've now had a bath and am feeling good. I've also just reread the "How to Select a Guru?" pamphlet. Although what I've already written might appear harsh and insensitive, I still think that I do have an outer Guru, though not in the same form as you, and I have a special and deep relationship with that Guru, though he has no name. I wonder if you know what I mean. A place, a feeling, even you are my Guru.

I will mail this letter tomorrow. Letters take awhile from here. First to Athens and then on, I think about ten days, to Japan. Enclosed are a couple of photos taken last year here. I hope you like them. I carry you in my wallet and my heart.

Indu, I can't express in words how much I miss you, so soft and lovely and gentle. Your hair, eyes, lips and heart. I close my eyes and can see you so clearly, even on that day when you wanted the yoga mats and we spoke for the first time. So now I must go to bed and leave you with all my love, a longing hug and gentle kiss.

With love, George

ஒ * * * சு

And so on the very same day that this, his third letter, had reached her, she finished writing her third letter to him, one which she had started over three weeks before. The "watching" technique had helped her tremendously in overcoming the doubts and anxieties she'd felt earlier. She could see from his letter that he, too, had been having a difficult time wrestling with similar disturbing feelings. In the last pages of her letter, her only desire was to reassure him that her love was unconditionally given.

ஒ * * * சு

The Letters

[Indu's Letter #3-continued] Osaka, November 1

George, my dear George! Your letter arrived today or I should say it was waiting for me on my desk when I came in this morning. Have probably read it at least ten times already today. You'll probably notice a difference between this part of the letter and the first couple of pages. My mind was saying, "Hold back and don't overwhelm the poor fellow," but my heart has won out, as I mentioned in the postcard. But even so, in rereading the first part can still easily see my deep feelings for you coming through loud and clear. And I was trying to tone it down. I was also trying to do the same thing in the last letter toward the end. That was the reason why I emphasized the sister part and the Guru part. Not to say I don't have strong feelings about both. Understanding our past incarnations can greatly help in understanding current relationships. Uma shared with me one example.

Two close disciples of Guruji had a long history of difficult, strained interactions. Neither could figure out what the problem was—both devotees, both women, both near the same age. Finally, when one of them was with a famous seer, she asked him what her previous incarnation with this other woman had been. It turned out that they had been lovers, a man and woman, and by some unfortunate circumstances had been pulled apart, leaving painful feelings for both. As an experiment, without telling the other woman about what the seer had said, this devotee changed her whole approach in interacting with this woman and oddly the long-standing rough edges began to smooth.

As for our resemblance being an indication of our past life relationship, I can only recount an unusual exchange with Guruji. With a degree in zoology and plenty of genetics under my belt, I know what I have said sounds absurd. But when I was nineteen years old, I was standing next to a fellow at the ashram who bore a good resemblance to me. Guruji asked if he was my brother. I denied it, but Guruji shook his head, saying some previous incarnation was there. I actually did feel some pull toward him but it remained just a friendship. As for you and me, our bloodlines aren't really that similar, so it would be pretty miraculous for genes to make sense of it all. But our resemblance is not just physical. There's another element there but beyond words, so I won't try to expound on it.

Couldn't help laughing at your dear rational mind cranking away trying to figure out what the hell is going on! I.e., "dream... result of being able to put into perspective the relationship I think I have with you." You never did say what exactly that relationship was! Also, "...don't want through a change in our relationship to find that my feelings would change." My love, our feelings for each other are eternal, regardless what our relationship is. I think that night at the stone proves that better than any words I could write down now. Please give your poor sweet mind a rest and know I'll love you no matter what happens.

Also, your dream intrigued me. It describes so closely my feelings when I first met you. Actually, when I first saw you walking past me at Ickwell, juggling away, totally oblivious to my presence, it was like a cannon exploded and the ten-pound iron ball landed in my stomach. My first thought was, "Oh, no...!" Talk about anxiety. I spent the next week "looking out for you." And you were always with other people, "involved in something" and looking happy. I was fascinated by the chemistry between us but did not feel I could join your "group." Was anxiously watching what "I would see from you!" Wrote it all down while still in London. You'll probably get a tremendous laugh out of it when you read it.

It is really too much for me to expect anyone to understand my relationship with Guruji when I can barely comprehend it myself, which also makes it difficult when trying to explain it to someone else. The closest I can come is to say there is a deep trust. But don't think that the Guru "determines" anything. He gives nothing but challenges and tests, incredibly tough ones, too. Just imagine trying to teach someone to drop the ego. It's just like teaching someone to die, because that's how attached to the ego we are. In July, Guruji asked many people to go to England, but privately once, he turned to me and said, "How about you?" I said nothing but just looked at him. It was the worst possible time for me to go. Dr. Miura was arriving from Japan the week before Guruji was planning to leave. I had personally made the arrangements for Dr. Miura to stay until September 3. Was just finishing one seven-week leave of absence spent with Guruji at the ashram and here Guruji was suggesting that I ask for another five weeks. Furthermore, I had no money for the trip. When I told my sister about it, she immediately disapproved, saying something about job responsibilities and career goals. But I put everything on the line.

I wrote my boss saying I would resign from my job, asked my father for a thousand-dollar loan (actually he offered when he heard I was in a pinch), flew back to Lawrence from New York for one week, mainly to get my passport and prepare to be fired by my boss. Instead, he discusses sending me to Japan with a thousand-dollar expense account and gives me another five weeks' leave. Spent that one week working hard and fast at my job to get everything ready. Then I came to England to meet you! You say you love me for what I am now. I am what I am now because of the challenging years with Guruji. What you love is not me but my (modestly) shining spirit which has gained incredible strength through devotion to Guruji. You worry what my relationship with my husband would be like. I guess I don't really want a husband nor do I want to be a wife, but soulmates: two people on spiritual paths, and not necessarily the same path, but helping one another along the way. I certainly never meant to imply that Guruji should be your Guru also. I never meant for you to think so. Please always follow your inner voice and whatever Guru you have. I actually feel that the stone at Ickwell was a divine Guru. I often remember that warmth we felt coming from the top. How magical that heat felt, protecting us even from a four-foot, double-barreled shotgun.

As for your life on the farm, time being alone is invaluable and so I think it's good you have this time now. You know you can meditate while doing just about anything. Just keep working and all the while continually watching the mind. For me, it's rather a fun game. Of course, sitting in quiet meditation is also needed, but I find "active" meditation very beneficial. Mantras are very useful for quieting the mind. Just imagine concentrating on *OM* while milking the cow. *OM* 1, *OM* 2, *OM* 3, *OM* 4, *OM* 5... I think a cow only has five teats!

Realized that this will probably be the last letter I will receive from you while I'm in Japan since I have less than three weeks to go. Am glad we have some way to get letters back and forth but wish it didn't take ten days between Corfu and Osaka!

If you can get ahold of a copy of *Autobiography of a Yogi* by Yogananda, I strongly recommend it. If you can't, I'll try to send a copy from the States. Describes Paramahansa Yogananda's experiences while on his spiritual journey. Also loved Tolstoy's *War and Peace* which is an incredibly spiritual book. Tolstoy was also searching for life's meaning and purpose.

Loved the pictures. Please send more current ones, too, if you have any. Am enclosing a couple of me although not very good ones. They were taken this past weekend visiting Hiroshima area.

Must now tell you that you are lurking in my thoughts constantly throughout my day. It's obvious I'm rapturously in love with you. Missing you with all my heart.

Love, Indu

TWENTY-EIGHT

~

A full week passed after mailing her letter to George before Indu realized she'd neglected to say anything about his possible visit to the States in the spring. He had only mentioned it briefly in his letter but she couldn't believe she'd blunderingly forgotten to even acknowledge it. She worried what George would think not receiving a word of excitement or hopefulness from her on the possibility of seeing him again. Using her last aerogram, she wrote a "shorter" letter which she hoped would assuage any doubts he might have regarding her feelings toward such a venture. This was the next one she read to me.

$\wp$ * * * $\wp$

[Indu's Letter #4] Osaka, November 27

Dear George,

This will be my last letter from Japan. Will mail it just before leaving. Realized I did not say anything about your visit to Lawrence in April. Nothing could possibly make me happier than to see you in four months. Already three months have passed since our days at Ickwell. Yet I feel I've known you for so much longer. Am really afraid to get my hopes up in case you can't make it then. Am also sad to say that my parents will probably be in the middle of getting their separation. So it's not exactly going to be the best time to meet my family although they're all greatly looking forward to meeting you, particularly my sister. As I mentioned in my earlier letter, she was first to pick up on the fact that I'd met "someone" in England. Am sorry my family situation isn't better. Karma definitely is there. Also, am not sure if I'll be able to even take off a few days from work since will be also in the middle of a big project running on a tight time schedule. But so far already we have overcome tremendous obstacles in the path of our (re) uniting: 1. Atlantic Ocean; 2. our innate shyness; 3. your relationship with Alison; 4. shortness of time together; 5. God knows how many miles between us; and still our love for each other is there.

[Indu's Letter #4-continued] November 29

One thing I must admit, and that's that I still feel a little funny about stepping into the middle of your relationship with Alison. Am wondering how things were left between you. Was she terribly angry with me for falling head over heels in love with you? I really liked her very much, although even at Ickwell before you and I had our marathon chat, I felt there was something strained in your relationship with her but I couldn't quite put my finger on it. But then maybe it was just my incredibly biased perception of the whole thing.

Was reading a commentary written by Roy Eugene Davis over the *Bhagavad Gītā* today. He was a disciple of Paramahansa Yogananda. He expressed so beautifully many of the things I wanted to say to you about the spiritual journey and the Guru. "It is not enough to follow blindly what is written in scriptures or what is spoken by a spiritual teacher. We must use reason and intuition to know the truth for ourselves. Then only will we be completely satisfied. It has been said: 'He who has no personal knowledge but has only heard of many things cannot understand the meaning of scriptures even as a spoon has no idea of the taste of soup.' [...] Here is the key; we must combine devotion to the teacher with the unrestricted right of free examination and inquiry. There must be no such thing as blind obedience to authority. Death of the intellect is not a condition for spiritual insight. [...] Intellectual apprehension is only the beginning. The initiate must tread the inner path. Faith comes first, then knowledge, then direct experience. [...] A Guru is one who rests in the inner awareness of his divine nature and whose only purpose in life is to awaken souls and show them the way to freedom."[19] Also from his book: "It is said that a little learning results in dogmatism, a little more to questioning and more still to prayer. We learn that we are sustained by something greater than we are." [20]

I could probably write another three pages of quotes but probably easier for you to read the book. Will get a copy to you. These aerograms are unfortunately too small for my style of letter writing! Probably five days after you receive it, I will be back in Lawrence eagerly awaiting your next letter!! Your picture is in front of me now (which is actually not too unusual.) Can't help thinking how wonderful it will be to see you again!!! With hugs and kisses ... and hugs and more kisses.

Love, Indu

ℰᗡ * * * ℭᘔ

Before starting the next letter to him a week later, she had sat with a calendar before her and had carefully calculated: it was then December 6; if she started a letter and mailed it from Lawrence on December 16, he should receive it in Corfu by December 27, at least five days before his departure for England. And she felt sure that a letter from him would also be waiting upon her return, or arriving soon afterward, since his last had been received November 19. Having to wait a whole month between letters was the greatest test of endurance for her patience. But determined to keep her chin high and spirits up, she began another multi-segmented letter to him, one that would see her from Japan back to the States. After these comments, her reading continued.

ℰᗡ * * * ℭᘔ

To my dear George,

Can't figure out why I like to write to you so much. Usually I'm a terrible letter writer. Guess I'm just terribly inspired! Am sitting at my desk at Osaka U. on my lunch break. I find myself again and again mulling over our days together in England, how we virtually avoided each other during those ten days at Ickwell (at least I you). I was deathly afraid for you to find out how strongly I felt about you since I was quite sure the feelings could not be returned. Even when we hugged for the first time by the stone, I had no idea it would go any further. I was just happy to have one chance to hold your sweet head! Felt my heart expanding with joy. Was truly surprised when I realized you felt something, too. How strange life can be. As you know in my last two letters (before aerogram), I was still trying to somewhat conceal my deep love for you, still a little afraid, I guess, that it would not be returned, trying to protect my poor vulnerable little heart. Am wondering what it will be like to meet again after seven months. My heart tells me it will seem like only seven hours have past since our parting in Hampstead. How clear that moment still is in my mind!

[Indu's Letter #5-continued] December 7

One week from today will be flying over the Pacific Ocean. Will finish everything up at work on Monday and Tuesday and spend Wednesday and Thursday packing, cleaning the house, last-minute shopping. Am trying to ship two futons back to the States but have found it's going to be very expensive. Still trying to find a cheap shipping company. Must admit am looking forward to returning. Mainly because it means I'm that much closer to April! Am hearing lots of Christmas carols in the stores and train stations. It rouses such a feeling in me; no specific memories but just being with family (or ashram friends) and happy. Maybe more intense now since am overseas. What are your Christmas plans? Will you be in Corfu with family? Who knows, maybe next Christmas we can be together.

Was also wanting to mention that if, by chance, we do decide to trot through this life together, would not mind at all living outside the U.S. (i.e., Greece or England or wherever). Since am planning to devote serious time to writing, I can do that anywhere. Although must say the job I have now is quite a good one. But please don't feel you must come to the States if we are to be together. Anyway, we can discuss it when the time comes.

Received a nice note from Nhoj. Got a good laugh out of it, too. He said he enjoyed having us all at Ickwell, "It made everything so beautifully zingy," according to him. Also said he hadn't heard from you since Germany but had a funny feeling I had!

Every year on this day I always remember it was the day Pearl Harbor was bombed. And to think I'm now in Japan. Wonder where my spirit was in 1941. I feel it too strongly to have any doubt that the soul incarnates again and again on its journey toward spiritual enlightenment.

[Indu's Letter #5-continued] Evening, December 7

Wrote the above at work during lunch. Was glancing back over the notes I made in England and in the U.S. about our relationship. Here are two excerpts, too silly to really call poems, now presented here for your pure enjoyment.

(Written September 13)

> *Oh, George, Oh, George, on this day*
> *what are you doing? So hard to say.*
> *So often it seems I am thinking of you.*
> *Are you thinking of me? I hope it's true.*

Was actually expecting you to call me in Lawrence sometime since you hinted you might during our last phone call, so somewhat sadly wrote the following on October 7:

> *Time is at a stall*
> *Why, why, why don't you call?*
> *Is it not to be after all?*

Now that your literary horizons have been duly broadened will give you another quote from that book on the *Bhagavad Gītā*: "The masters of India, in teaching the concept of celibacy, did not mean total abstinence from sexual intercourse. What they stressed was right use of all energies and right direction of thought. A person in the world who lives a normal life but who meditates and works with the realization that the One Life is working through and as him, is a true sage."[21]

[Indu's Letter #5-continued] December 9

Am on my lunch break again. Am afraid I'm fighting exhaustion. Today and yesterday energy level has been extremely low. Am trying to eat well and have been taking a special vitamin every day for the past month or so (supplied by a Japanese friend working for a pharmaceutical company in Tokyo). Have no doubt it's partly emotional. I remember after we had lunch with Oliver in Berkeley Park and had said goodbye, you just stood and put your head on my shoulder, saying how difficult it was having to part from friends as you prepared for your trip to Greece (and I suppose all the other details involved). Well, now I have the same feeling. I just want to put my head on your shoulder.

During the past two months, have met so many old friends and then turned right around and said goodbye again. Realized I've actually been doing this since July! Although it's been very nice, it does have a strange effect on the psyche. It's like being on an emotional roller coaster! Will be so re-

lieved when am finally on the plane heading home. Hope I
don't collapse before then (only four more days).

[Indu's Letter #5-continued] Seoul, Korea, December 14

Am happily sitting in the Seoul airport (albeit a little tired).
Only slept two hours during the night. Stayed up cleaning
the house and packing. Was picked up for the airport at
seven in the morning, departed Osaka at eleven. Arrived in
Korea at twelve-thirty. Was treated to a delicious tempura
lunch by the airline (Korean Air). Have browsed through
the duty-free shop and am now waiting for my six o'clock
departure. Ironically enough, I then fly back to Tokyo! Wait
an hour or two there and then on to Hawaii and Los Angeles. Haven't the faintest idea how I made it through this
past week. Can't remember feeling more stressed. Won't
bother you with all the details. It's just so nice now to be
sitting looking out over the runway at some mountains and
a somewhat hazy sunset. By the blessing of the divine this
trip has been a success in every way. My main problem was
my physical strength. Am greatly looking forward to the
holidays and a good rest.

Am sorry to say you probably won't receive your Christmas
present until January. Was extremely short of yen so had to
mail it by sea mail. Since I knew you would leave Greece in
January, mailed it to your parent's address. I hope you like
it. It's a wool sweater. The size is "free" which means one
size fits all. Sorry it won't arrive in time for your Christmas
holiday but hopefully this letter will. Plan to mail it tomorrow as soon as I arrive in Lawrence.

[Indu's Letter #5-continued] Tokyo, December 14

Considering I've been en route to U.S. for the past thirteen
hours and am now only in Tokyo, it sort of feels like I've
been on a treadmill, but not complaining. Have been wondering how the food shortage in Africa might affect you in
Zimbabwe (or your parents in Kenya). Have spent time on

the airplanes reading three English newspapers and one news magazine. Have felt a little removed from the world news for the past two months, although kept up on the big headlines (Indira Gandhi's death, Reagan's re-election, Urban Carbide gas leak in India, food shortage in Ethiopia). Reading about so much suffering makes my own difficulties seem quite insignificant. Am feeling a little disconnected from lack of sleep so will write on after reaching Hawaii (and having a nap)!

[Indu's Letter #5-continued] Lawrence, December 16

Had to go through customs in Hawaii, which took over an hour. Had not slept at all on the plane so still felt extremely groggy. Just sat in the sun for about twenty-five minutes and then reboarded again. Wish so much I could have stayed a few days. The hot sun felt so good. When finally arrived in Kansas City, found my mother waiting for me. She had driven over five hours just to meet my plane. We had a good visit, went to see a movie. She went back this afternoon. Feels wonderful to be back home but still have so many things I have to do: laundry, round up dry cleaning, write Christmas cards, wrap Christmas presents. At least tomorrow when I head to work it's only a three-minute car ride and not two hours by train!

Am afraid any letter you may have sent has already been forwarded to my parents' home. Asked the post office to deliver mail here until December 22 when I will also head home. Probably returning December 30 since should really be at work on January 2.

Have loved writing this to you over the past week, even though I wanted terribly for you to wrap your arms around me and just hold me. At least I could hold you in my heart. I feel our meeting each other is nothing but a divine blessing. Showed my mother the pictures you sent and again she laughed at our resemblance. Said she'd be very happy if we had a Greek Orthodox ceremony (if we do decide to marry,

440

that is!). Found out there are two Greek Orthodox churches in Kansas City. Just thought I'd mention this for your general information!

Seems so long since I last heard from you, almost a month. Hope all is going well with you. Am enclosing my Christmas card. Had them made in Japan. The picture was taken in Hiroshima with the couple who lived around the corner and looked out for me. By chance, he was giving a lecture at Hiroshima University the same weekend I was there.

Am praying these next three months go by quickly. Unfortunately, I'm not a perfect yogi who can remain in the present all the time. My mind keeps jumping to April.

With my deep and tender love, Indu

℘ * * * ℭ

For the next week, Indu told me she had anxiously opened her mailbox, hoping and praying his letter would be there. At that point, she had sent him three letters in a row: her third in November in answer to his third letter which had been written on November 6, the aerogram, and the one she'd just mailed. But nothing came from him that week. So it was with an extremely heavy heart that she had headed home for the holidays. Now in retrospect, it was easy to see the "perfect storm" brewing. If she had been rested, if her boss had given her even a few words of praise for the nine manuscripts she had completed in Japan, if she had had a peaceful and joyous holiday with her family, her frame of mind would have been different, quite drastically in fact, than it was when she finally returned to Lawrence and found George's fourth letter waiting at the post office for her on December 31.

But her fight with physical exhaustion was cruelly compounded by emotional fatigue during those two weeks after her return. Not a single word of congratulations or recognition came her way that first week back at work. Was her boss assuming she'd simply done what was expected? Did he not realize the enormous effort she had put out as an emissary coordinating work between Eastern and Western universities, obliged as well to greet socially so many of the scientists who had worked with him in Kansas? Then sadly, the following week, she had found herself sitting in a lawyer's office with her father, discussing the legal framework of her parents' marital separation. Christmas day had been nothing but a family conference on the marriage breakup.

Back in Lawrence, she had been alone to ring in the New Year. Although she had friends, they had either been off with family or coupled up at parties. On the edge of a physical and emotional breakdown, she had opened George's letter on the last day of December, a cold and icy day, her heart clouded by serious depression.

I confirmed the obvious. "So trouble's ahead."

She smiled and nodded as she began reading this fourth letter from him.

ℰ * * * ℭ

[George's Letter #4] Corfu, December 3

My dear Indu,

"The mind does nothing but talk, ask questions, search for meanings; the heart does not talk, does not ask questions, does not search for meanings. Silently, it moves toward God and surrenders itself to Him. The mind is Satan's lawyer; the heart is God's servant." —Nikos Kazantzakis, *Saint Francis.*[22]

I'd just read that and thought, "Well, haven't started a letter to Indu yet so why not start?" A really lovely book. Another lovely letter from you; I read it and glowed and felt so close to you. You know you have a clarity of thought and expression that I'm sure has come from a self-discipline that I dodge nimbly. After all, Satan's lawyers know their craft. My lawyer is a special rogue. He pits my heart against my mind, knowing that my reason has been carefully conditioned till finally my heart utters a great shriek of despair. At this point I always find refuge and it seems that my heart has won the battle, Pyrrhic though the victory may seem— as soon enough Satan's lawyer is mocking me again. That elaborate metaphor has quite exhausted me so I shall hug you so tightly and say goodnight though it's so miserable to have to do it on paper.

[George's Letter #4-continued] December 4

Well, things are beginning to move now. Since the beginning of November, I've been working for an Anglicized Greek in the village. He pays me very badly and I spend the day doing odd jobs which have included digging the garden and planting spring vegetables; helping his son with English and French; anti-rust painting his aged Volkswagen Transporter; sanding down and varnishing holiday villa furniture and most recently clearing rubble out of a stripped apartment. At the moment, I'm also trying to do some serious classical guitar practice which requires fairly decent-length nails. Needless to say there's not a hope in hell of that! I work with a Scot called Jan who talks a lot, which is quite tiring but she's quite sweet and has a good heart. Mr. Beloque is going away for Christmas and between Jan and me we shall look after his house. However, Jan refuses to stay alone in the house as she's frightened of mice which might tie me down a little.

My very good French and Italian friends who live on boats will be here over Christmas and we want to all go out to my house and have a party so I must sort something out with Jan.

I don't think I've told you much about them. They have been planning to work in the Adriatic during the summer season as a "sea theater" troupe. Operating from tourist villages, they would offer fishing, water skiing and scuba diving; yoga and breathing exercises, macrobiotic diet; and then in the evening an extravaganza that would include mime, magic, music, dance and slideshows with animation. They're all very talented and lovely people and have shown me great kindness and generosity. The French couple, Arnaud and Marie, and their five-month-old daughter, Lisette, are also lovely. They've lived for four years on their boat, *Bonhomie,* and spent two winters up the Nile. Their large cabin is beautifully decorated with brightly-colored, warm Egyptian rugs. So cozy!

[George's Letter #4-continued] December 5

Indu, I miss you so much! I do hope that I can come and visit you in Lawrence next year. I can't remember whether I mentioned to you my plans, as you made no comment in your letter, but I would love to come over in May and spend some weeks with you. I shall have to study for my exam in June so the fact that you'd be working during the day is no problem. I don't know if it might be difficult for you, whether you have room in your flat or whatever. Anyway, I'd love to come.

I should be driving back to England around January 3 with—if there's enough room in the car—Jacque, Marie and Lisette, who shall go as far as France. You remember me speaking about Jim, the school chaplain and my spiritual mentor? Well, he'll be in England and we both hope to fly out to Harare on the same flight, which would be wonderful. In the few days that I have in England, I must go and dump my surplus belongings in a warehouse and try to sell the car, as without a steady job and possibly being abroad a lot, it is a bit inconvenient to have right now.

I shall try and take the absolute minimum to Zimbabwe, as when I finish in April out there, I'd like to go back to Mombasa for a couple of weeks by way of Zambia, Malawi and Tanzania—bus and train.

I was sent a formal contract by the headmaster of Ruzawi School the other day and a glossy prospectus. It's a school set in beautiful countryside: 216 boys, 30 staff, breakfast, lunch and supper, every other Sunday off and a five-day break in the middle of term. Paula, Jim's wife, wrote me a hysterically funny letter filling me in with all the news and what's what. They will be living about twenty minutes away at another school though Jim spends every Thursday there, and they both come over on Sundays for a service. I'm so excited at the thought of being back in Africa again—in just over two months.

You must be anticipating your return to America now—only three days to go—and winding everything up in Japan and saying goodbye to friends. Though you described the first two pages of your letter as being noncommittal, I thought it was great to hear about what you get up to during the day. It intrigues me to find out that "tissue paper" and "paper towels" are most important on your shopping list and that you require boxes of them. Goodness Indu, you are taking *neti* seriously! I'm ashamed to say that I don't think I ever thanked you for sending me those centrifuge tubes which I've used successfully with almond oil, which states quite clearly: "Not to be taken internally." Thank you, my love! Well, it's getting late now and I'm feeling tired so I will stop for today. So here's a tight hug and tender kiss goodnight.

[George's Letter #4-continued] December 6

I'm off into town just now to buy some new parts for the car and see what's in the shops for Christmas. Faced with an awful dilemma of not having enough money to get back to England (without borrowing, which I hate doing) and at the same time wanting to buy some Christmas presents for family out here. I think I'll sell my tent. (Later in bed) Well, no luck in selling the tent but it's St. Spyridon's day on the 12th so maybe I'll do some street performing and put out a hat.

How I laugh to myself when I think what I wrote in my last letter about my relationship with you and worrying about how it might change, etc., etc. It's one of those occasions when I think, "God, didn't I realize that then? Has it really had to be pointed out to me for me to see?" But you know it's because my mind tries so hard to rationalize everything and give it logic. It's funny really because I can't see much "logic" in finding myself having such a relationship with you. I should hasten to say, though, that it's old logic that I use as a comparison. In previous relationships, the logic has been focused on quite material things: "do we like playing the same life games?" sort of thing. I mean you haven't ever said to me the sort of things that I've previously been able to relate to, e.g., reincarnation, mantras, Eastern spiritual teachers, *neti, kuṇḍalinī,* etc. So now you see the points of reference in my life are changing. My logic is changing; the mind is being dropped and the heart opened. Just as Nhoj said: "Work on the heart *chakra,* George." Quite honestly when he said it I thought, "How dare you" (frantically defending myself). But it seems that unbeknownst to me, that is what has (naturally and spontaneously) been happening. He's such a dear friend.

Now it seems to me that part of this change has been brought about by you. When I talked in my last letter about the relationship I think I have with you, I was referring to the understanding I have with myself about why I'm having that relationship. In my dream, I can see so much of my ego there: "What's she doing? Will I like it? Will it please me and make me feel good and safe? Will she embarrass me? Is it all a bit sweet and rather limp?" I think I feel these things because my perception/logic has been beaten into shape by my ego. It's a little frightening to think, "What do I really feel and what do I feel because of my ego?"—and more especially, "Can one tell the difference between the two?"

[George's Letter #4-continued] December 7

Was just thinking this evening as I was bringing the donkey back to the stable, wandering through the olive groves, how so much of our communication is unspoken. I remember an occasion in New Brighton when I was saying a warm hello to the dog, immediately I felt something from you. I don't know quite what, a strong presence and then you said something about the sensitivity of your skin around animals and then I washed my hands. I'm interested to know what all that's about. Also, you've said that I seem to know when you're about to say something but then hesitate. I don't remember chatting and chatting at the standing stone but we managed to pass away seven hours or so. I love that type of communication, unsaid understanding. And yet, O ye of little faith, though you hadn't received word from me in Lawrence, had the audacity to remind me of "pen and paper"! You poor thing! How I would have felt as you did, but then, in a way, I did as when I read your letter I was in despair to think that those were the thoughts in your mind. And yet, I had written, and lovingly, too.

[George's Letter #4-continued] December 8

Shhh! At the moment I'm proctoring an exam and the atmosphere is charged with anxious, clammy-palmed, adolescent students of English. Actually, I feel as though I'm cheating in an exam as I shouldn't really be writing a letter but rather remaining vigilant for slips of paper concealed under watch straps. *Cave*!! [Latin]

[George's Letter #4-continued] December 12

Well, today is St. Spyridon's Day and a public holiday in Corfu so I'm at home. Have just written a lengthy epistle to my parents, giving them all my news and wishing them

Happy Christmas. It's the first time that we've all been in different places during December, Melinda in Australia and me out here. Sad really but still, I wonder where you'll spend Christmas and what you'll get up to. The other night I finally finished *St. Francis*. I'm glad suddenly to have had the world of Kazantzakis opened up to me. His writing is so beautiful, lovely prose and imagery and moving story. In the English bookshop yesterday, I saw five or six others and wished that I had the space to buy them and take them to Zimbabwe. Actually, I've decided not to take many books with me out there as I've no doubt that Jim will have a few that will occupy my time.

[George's Letter #4-continued] December 13

Last night I went to see my friends on the boat and we all took off to town to do some street theater. So totally different from England; people immediately stop to see what's going on even if you're not doing anything. There were four of us: two were wearing masks, one dressed as a doddering old man and another a ravishing maiden complete with "crimson gash" and long black hair. I've been given a terrific clown suit with shoes that are about eighteen inches long! Generally it was accepted with sympathetic tolerance and we made enough to go out afterward and have a good meal. Good fun evening.

Today I received another letter from you. You do spoil me. I think it's perfectly natural for you to feel funny about stepping into the middle of my relationship with Alison. Certainly in every relationship I have there is always a seed of doubt no matter how wonderful and rosy life and love appears to be. It's because I've never really committed myself. For me, it's natural that other people also might feel the same way. So being aware of the seed of doubt in other relationships can only make one feel a pang when, by stepping into a relationship, one is aware of watering that seed. I think it's compassion and not guilt.

But with Alison, she throws herself wholeheartedly into every relationship, something that is difficult for me. When I first met her in Kenya, I failed to realize the seriousness of the type of relationship that she was pursuing. I totally and utterly admit to letting the physical aspect of a relationship get the better of me and then found that Alison was (and still is by character) a very tenacious girl. This is where it always boils down to the daily life/interest/culture bit again, and where I think the seed of doubt is nurtured. Despite loving Alison in many ways (she has wonderful talents), there are a lot of things about her I am unable to handle, aspects of her character that are her and that shouldn't change though they are aspects that I find difficult, e.g., being slightly more introspective than she is and not really feeling that I'm allowed to be. Obviously at Ickwell, it was difficult because there were a lot of people around and I wanted to "watch and listen" whereas Alison was so excited and wanted to "do and talk."

What you said about marriage is so true—the relationship does become polluted when roles are acted out, and that ideally a marriage should be a spiritual bond that allows freedom for development. Though we seem to have known each other a long time, I don't actually feel that I know you as a person, flesh and blood, ups and downs, moods and passions. I suppose that I'm looking not only for the perfect painting but also to understand and feel every brushstroke, mood of color, and delicacy of detail. It sounds incredibly idealistic (probably unattainable) and I consider myself naive to think that I won't mellow out a little! Afterthought: I'm probably being protective.

Also I think the reason that I've never really committed myself to a relationship is that I have the most amazing mother and sister who shower upon me all the love I could possibly need and who have quite wonderful qualities. But as I was saying earlier, my points of reference have changed and so therefore has my idea of what I'm about and doing in a relationship. My spiritual relationship with you is timeless and therefore cannot be considered in the same light as "my other relationships" are. Oh Moonflower, my love.

To tell you the truth, your aerogram alarmed me a little, probably stupidly so. I think it's because your passion overwhelmed me and by intuition I get nervous when "they're as keen as mustard." That only means to my mind that I'm now a little responsible for someone's feelings. But at the same time I feel that my buzzing little head has got everything muddled up and that with the clarity of your thought, all shall be put into perspective again when I next hear from you.

Well, I must get this off to you now, otherwise I'll just go on adding a little every day. By the way, my address in Zimbabwe is as follows:

Ruzawi School, P.B. 5535 Marondera, Zimbabwe

If you were here with me now, Indu, I'd stroke your beautiful thick hair and kiss you so gently goodnight.

With love from George

TWENTY-NINE

~

Any relationship takes an enormous amount of giving: giving of love, of time, of patience. It requires acceptance of short-comings, sharing of feelings and bending flexibly when compromise is needed. Generally speaking, to keep a relationship alive takes strength and energy, neither of which Indu had as she prepared to write what she expected might well be her last letter to George.

What she had needed to hear from him was that he loved her, without reservations and doubts, just as she loved him. Of course, his love had been expressed in many ways throughout his letters: "I'd love to come see you," "I can't express in words how much I miss you," "I long to be with you again," "This letter comes with gentle and tender love all the time," "We have something greater 'going on.' I don't know what it is either, but that love will always be there." Still, in his letters there was vagueness as to the direction in which that love was going to take them. And if he made an allusion to marriage, then he invariably circled the words in a shroud of doubt as to their implicit meaning: "I love you for what you are now and don't want, through a change in our relationship, to find that my feelings would change," "I know what I've felt with you and if we should spend our lives together then there is no rush to fix it all up."

What she got from his December letter was that he was frightened to commit to what was between them; that he had "seeds of doubt" as to whether he had found the "perfect painting" or someone as "amazing" as his mother and sister. She was angry that he was still feeling so muddled. She was angry that she loved him so much. The final blow to her heart was a marriage proposal from another friend which came long distance over the phone on New Year's Day. Not that it took her by surprise.

Mark had asked her before in his zestful way and she had convivially declined. They had never been romantically entangled. They'd sailed together on the lakes of Kansas, seen a couple of movies together, and spent one intimate night whereupon they'd but tiptoed across the boundaries of platonic friendship.

"Elizabeth," Mark had said, "I know you want to be a writer. You know I've got this word processor here which I'd let you use if you'd marry me. I'd even give you two years to come up with a book before I'd send you out to get a job."

"Gee, Mark. That's awfully tempting. I'm probably quite foolish to turn down such a shining offer!"

"Well," he had replied, "I'll give you until the end of this decade to think about it. Happy New Year."

It did get her thinking, though, about how long she'd have to wait before George would seriously ask her to marry him. He may have felt that there was no rush, but she was ready to settle down and she loved him deeply. Had Nature made these two desires coincide: to be with the one who is dearly loved and to raise a family with him? Was her desire to settle down connected to her biological clock, which was well advanced and ticking? Although her heart told her otherwise, she sadly wondered if maybe it was true that her karma with George had been completed by their meeting alone.

The letter she started to him was not a happy one. She felt no patience for him to still be confused about what he was doing in their relationship. However, not wanting to act impulsively and also being fully aware of her own stressed condition, she did wait one month before writing the last half of the letter.

She told me that her thought had been this: "If he loves me, he will have to accept my highs with my lows, my clarity of thought with my emotional needs. It will be a real test of the karma between us." She sat back in her chair and began reading.

The Letters

ဢ * * * ᘓ

[Indu's Letter #6] New Year's Day

Dear George,

Received your letter yesterday. Returned from Tulsa December 29 (Saturday night) and first thing Monday morning I went to the post office to pick up my mail in hopes there would be a letter from you. Even had to scrape a quarter inch of ice off my windshield and venture out onto slippery roads to do it. And alas, there was your letter. It had been six weeks since I'd last heard from you. I wish I could say I glowed after reading it but I didn't. In fact, I felt a bit frustrated. Still you say you are feeling muddled about our relationship. Well, my love, (and you will always be my love regardless of what happens), this letter is not going to give you one bit more clarity. In fact, I don't want it to. I don't want to even try to convince you that there is anything worthwhile in our relationship.

My friend Mark called this morning and again proposed marriage. It's almost an absolutely perfect match. We've known each other over three years. He has been practicing a type of Buddhist meditation with which I am familiar; he totally accepts my yoga practice and relationship with Guruji. Although he's never met Guruji, he's quite eager to. Our family history is similar in that he's the son of an Episcopal minister and I'm the granddaughter of a Methodist minister and baptized Episcopalian. He likes sailing (as do I) and even owns a catamaran. We both keep cats as pets. He's now making over $30,000 in his present job as a banker in Detroit and would easily be able to support the career of a budding writer (if that is what I am to be). He's also planning to eventually move out to New York which would put me close to the ashram or a quick transatlantic flight to

England. And furthermore, I like him very much and feel love could easily blossom.

Why I'm telling you all this I'm not really sure. It's certainly not to try to make you jealous. I don't like playing that game. Actually, it's to try to make you feel the opposite, whatever the opposite of jealousy is. Could it be relief, relief to realize you are not responsible for my feelings? You are responsible only for your own feelings, and I for mine.

You often say in your letters that you miss me. But it makes me wonder, what do you miss? What is it that you need that I can give? Am I to be another toy of which you will eventually grow tired? Will another woman be able to so easily step in between our relationship as I did between yours and Alison's? I'm not saying this to be callous or cruel. It may even be for your own protection. After all, am I not possibly destined to wear the robes of an ascetic one day? I sensed from your letter that next summer you would also be interested in doing a little "sea theater" with your friends in the Adriatic and not contemplating marriage, even with the most divine woman (so I have a little ego left!). Why did we ever make the connection that we did? Why didn't I just greet you in my friendly way and walk past you when we had that encounter on that last day at Ickwell as you were inspecting something under the hood of your car at the already late hour of 6:00 p.m.? Why did we ever discuss the existence of that stone in the first place? If we hadn't, then there would have been nothing really to talk about and no excuse to have a few minutes alone together (if you can call seven hours a few minutes).

My feelings for you have not changed and I don't mean to sound like I'm angry with you. You are twenty-four years old with still many things you want to do before considering settling down. I also know my life has its own momentum and is not waiting to latch onto someone else's life and follow their direction. Nor do I want someone to latch onto mine and follow my direction. Nor do I want to be with someone who is going to be standing from afar and judging my actions to see if they're embarrassing or "a bit sweet and rather limp." Sorry, not meaning to use direct quotes from your letter but that is the way it hit me. So what exactly am I saying, or trying to say to you?

You brought up the fact that Alison would throw herself wholeheartedly into a relationship whereas you were much more cautious. I must tell you now that although Alison and I are quite different in nature, we do have this one trait in common. My whole heart is involved when I am in a relationship, and being a Taurus I have also found myself to be rather possessive (although I have been trying to work on that). Frankly, I don't want to be in a relationship unless the other person is also involved totally.

As for my life, it looks as though I will be resigning from my job sometime between May and June. After returning from Japan, I felt stronger than ever that it was time for me to move on. To stay here will only stifle whatever creative energy I feel moving through me. Have already discussed this with my parents in regards to the house and it was agreed that whenever I'm ready I can go ahead and put it up for sale (probably April). After contemplating this phase of my life I can honestly say I'm not sure what will come next. Many possibilities are open. I am waiting for divine guidance.

I do love you and although you have never said it in your letters, I feel in a way you do love me. But possibly our time is not ripe yet. And this letter is not just my mind trying to be analytical about the whole affair. This is truly from my heart. I was hesitant at first to reveal my true passions to you and my intuition was not incorrect since after receiving two to three letters from me in December, you state you began to feel nervous. Obviously it says to me you are not ready or willing to receive such a love as mine.

Again, I don't mean for this to sound abrasive. It is just something my heart is slowly coming to accept. I have no intention of mailing this letter right away but will wait for at least a month and see what I feel and what I hear from you.

[Indu's Letter #6-continued] February 3

One month has passed. Haven't heard anything from you. I wonder if your silence is as intentional as mine has been. In sending you the New Year's part of this letter, I suspect you will either be terribly relieved or quite angry. The fact that I don't know which way you'll feel tells me that the months that have passed since we last met have been too many. That's not to say the connection I feel between us is diminishing, only growing more and more ethereal.

Not sure what more I can say now. About the aerogram, had bought a dozen of them when I arrived in Japan. Had used all but one. When I realized I hadn't said anything about your possible Spring visit, didn't want to wait a month or more before acknowledging it, that is to say, encouraging it as much as possible. Figured the aerogram would be the easiest and fastest way.

Must admit this past month—actually the past two months—have been very strange for me. Have been functioning quite well considering I've been in my third major depression of the past ten years. The first one ended up taking me to the ashram at the age of seventeen. Now you know the secret of why I study yoga. If I didn't, I would have committed suicide long ago. First started contemplating suicide at the age of seven which coincidentally was the first time I heard about Guruji. These periods are really quite enlightening for me. Everything they say does seem to be true: "The night is darkest before the dawn." When we're willing to walk through the portal of the "valley of the shadow of death" and "fear no evil,"* we end up on the other side, in the Beyond. That's the cosmic joke.

Probably because of my present state of mind and because so much has happened in the past five months, I am feeling quite distant from you. Well, you wanted to know my ups and downs, moods and passions, to understand each stroke of this painting. Possibly now you will view it differently. But you know the story about the seventy-five-year-old man who had been looking for the perfect woman. His friend asked him in disbelief, if he'd never met anyone in the past fifty years whom he liked? He admitted he had. His friend asked why he hadn't married her, then. He replied that unfortunately, she'd been looking for the perfect man.

Hope life in Africa is treating you well. Very hard to say what the future holds. But know you have my love.

May the moon brighten your way, Indu

P.S. Also, I did send a letter Dec 18 to Corfu. Am wondering if you got it before you left.

[Indu's Letter #6-continued] February 9

P.P.S. Dear George,

How I would love to hear from you. Had decided not to mail this letter until I'd heard something from you. A couple days after writing the February 3rd installment, I had a dream. Can't remember any details except that you were there, so clear and close and looking at me. Any distant feeling I had been having vanished. Suddenly I found myself feeling closer to you than ever before. Oddly enough, I think it's fairly safe to say the depression seems to have

---

* Ps. 23:4 (AV).

lifted. Believe me, after two months, it's wonderful relief. Not sure what connection it might have to the dream.

Read a book a week ago by Swami Muktananda, *Mystery of the Mind.* How mysterious the mind is. Meditations have been invaluable to me working through this whole thing. Have read so often the Masters' teachings that we will reach many plateaus on our spiritual journey. At times we will feel not only that we are not progressing, but we are regressing. And then suddenly something breaks through the block and we're off and flying again. These blocks must be worked through. Often they're very deep in the subconscious, even relating back to past lives, unfinished business so to speak. It is at these times persistence in inner practice is imperative. It's so funny trying to put it into words; it's so elusive.

Anyway, have decided to go ahead and mail this letter. Mark called again today. Wants me to fly up to see him. Haven't mentioned about meeting you yet. Yet what can I say? "Have met someone whom I haven't seen in five months and don't know when I'll see him again, but if I don't marry him then you stand a really good chance!" Talk about sounding muddled! Ah, the intricate web of life. As you can see, I'm back to my philosophical self, at least for now.

Love from your moonflower, Indu

℘ * * * ℭ

It had crossed Indu's mind several times during the completion of this letter and the passage of her depression that very possibly George had not received the last letter she'd sent him in Greece. She assumed if he had that he would surely have written by the early part of February. As it was, his last letter had ended with an installment made nearly two months ago on December 13. What was he thinking? What was he feeling? Would he feel she had betrayed the love they had shared by even mentioning the prospect of marriage to another man? Would he understand that the belligerent tone of her New Year's letter was really a crying plea for him to come to terms with what it was that he was "about and doing" in their relationship? She wanted the uncertainty of their karma to be finished. But she could not rid her heart of the feeling that their meeting had been a divine gift, a meeting of extraordinary dimension.

After telling me this, she picked up another photocopied paper, not a letter but a passage she had copied from a booklet that Guruji had given her, part of an essay by Pir Vilayat Inayat Khan, head of the Sufi Order. It was with her papers because she felt the quote beautifully described the pull that she'd felt to be with George: "Something irresistible draws one toward a being when one feels tremendous fate in the meaningfulness of one's relationship. And this may in turn attain tremendous proportions when the marriage [or in Indu's case she substituted the word "relationship"] is one made in heaven and it is celebrated by the rejoicing of the angelic beings who rejoice in the coming together of two beings because of all that this involves in the universe. Each part of the universe is seeking each other part of the universe in the fulfillment of itself. When this quest, this nostalgia for an encounter is between two people who are meant for one another, the repercussions that it has in the universe are just tremendous."[23]

Before continuing with the letters, she related the decision she made to call George in Zimbabwe.

ဆာ * * * ౿

She had wanted to know what George was feeling, and what the reason was behind his long silence. Late in the night of February 11, the idea to call him in Zimbabwe came to her as the obvious answer to all the questions whirling in her mind. He had not sent her the phone number but she did have the name of the school. Calling the operator, she got directory assistance for Zimbabwe. They informed her that Ruzawi School had two different numbers but they could not connect the call and it was not possible to direct dial into that country. A Zimbabwe operator would be needed.

Indu sought the help of the U.S. international operator. "For some reason," the operator said, "at certain hours the Zimbabwe operators simply are not answering the phones. We've been having this trouble for the past three weeks. If you'll leave the number with me, I'll keep trying and when the line is open, I'll give you a call and connect you."

Indu was grateful for the operator's kind offer and accepted it as a sign that she should try to contact George. Four hours later, at 5:15 a.m., Indu was awakened by her ringing phone.

"I've connected with the party you requested," the operator told her. "The line is ringing now." Indu thanked her for her help and then suddenly felt a wave of apprehension rising in her stomach. There was no time for second thoughts. Barely awake, floating in the twilight of a dream, she heard a voice at the other end.

"George Acroilus, please. I'd like to speak to George Acroilus," she heard herself saying.

"One moment," the innocuous voice said. "I'll try to find him."

Her heart pounded with a force which marked the passing of each second. Barely fifteen seconds had passed when his dulcet and deeply masculine voice responded over the receiver.

"Hello?" he said, sounding curious.

"George, it's Indu."

"My God, Indu! I had no idea. How are you?"

"I'm fine. Was wondering if you'd written recently."

"Indu, I did write something to you but it wasn't nice, so I crumpled it up. It just seemed too superficial. Do you have my address?"

"Yes, but I haven't mailed anything either. I have written to you, though. It's quite a strange letter and I've hesitated a long time about mailing it."

With undeniable surprise, he replied, "Really! Well, did you think I had gone off to Africa and disappeared? Has it bothered you that I haven't written?"

She hedged a little in her answer by saying no, it hadn't bothered her. She hated to admit how much it had. It was almost a matter of pride. "No, it hasn't exactly bothered me although I was beginning to wonder. But after all, I haven't written, either."

"Do you know I haven't written anyone, including my mother? I've been quite happy here and am really enjoying the work. I feed the whole school. I'm officially the culinary administrator, or some title like that. In fact, I was just eating lunch when I got your call. It's 1:35 p.m. here."

"Well, it's 5:35 a.m. here," she said with due emphasis.

By his next question, she realized that he had picked up on something in her voice. "Indu, you don't sound well. Are you okay?"

In her heart she wanted to be honest about how much she missed him. But he seemed a world apart from her, not geographically but emotionally. She made her reply intentionally vague. "I'm okay. If anything, having more mental difficulty than physical." Wanting to change the subject, she asked what his plans were.

"I'll leave here in mid-April and fly to England. I'll stay there until after I retake my exam and then in July I can come for a visit when you have your holiday."

Indu felt immediate disappointment. She had hoped to see him well before July. She wondered how her heart could possibly tolerate another four months of not knowing the real direction of their relationship. With a certain assiduity she countered, "George, I don't automatically get a holiday in July. In the past, I've been taking leaves of absences in the summer so I could be with Guruji. But I have no idea if I can get one again this summer. I was actually thinking of resigning in the next few months."

"What's happened? Have you had a row with your boss?"

"Of course not. It's just we're going to be finishing a big project in June and it would be a good time to pull out."

"Did you think that you and I might be doing something then?"

"Well, you are in the back of my mind. But I have any number of considerations to make. For one, I might end up traveling to India with Guruji or relocating to New York. I'm just not sure where I'm going to be in July."

"Indu, I know we need to find out what there is between us but I had really wanted to wait until after the exam so I'd be free and without pressure and could possibly stay longer in the States without having commitments elsewhere."

"George, it sounds quite fine except I really don't know where I'll be or what I'll be doing then."

Possibly taken aback, he responded, "Did I mention in my last letter about being invited to do some sea theater during the summer in the Adriatic?"

"You did mention about your friends doing it. I suspected you might be thinking of joining them. I even wrote something about it in my letter. I guess we'll just have to wait and see how things work out."

"Indu, I'm just not ready to settle down, but you know that already. It will be awhile yet."

"Exactly how long is 'awhile'?"

After a short pause, he replied, "Well, I don't know. I guess until I meet the one I want to spend the rest of my life with."

Indu could only interpret that to mean that he hadn't. She accepted it for whatever it was worth. After all, if they were not to be together, the sooner she knew about it the better.

She decided to mention Mark's proposal. She had not intentionally planned to say anything about it. But she'd spoken of it in the letter and she was curious to know his reaction.

"George, it seems my life is moving in a strange direction recently. I tried to explain it in the letter. Should I give you a hint now?"

"Oh, yes do!" he replied with boyish eagerness. At that moment, she had wished he'd sounded more like a man, for what they were about to discuss was far beyond fun and games.

"I have another suitor, George." She said it simply and straightforwardly. His response came unnaturally quickly. "I'm, I'm very happy for you. Really very happy. It's a special time between two people, making a commitment for a lifetime." There was a pause, a silence, and he spoke again. "Well, I am sad. But no, I am happy, too. Please do give my love to him. I mean that."

Indu didn't mention that "the other guy" didn't even know he existed. She could tell he was trying to be magnanimous about it, just as she had been about his involvement with Alison.

Almost in the same breathe, George asked, "When does he want to marry?"

"A year ago," Indu replied, hoping her answer would convey that the matter was hardly decided. George picked right up on her meaning.

"Do you want to marry him?" he asked.

Now that was a tricky question for her to answer. If she answered honestly and said "no," then he would clearly wonder why she'd brought it up in the first place. And to say "yes" was simply not the case. She opted for the Fifth Amendment.

"George, for now, I'd like to refrain from answering."

"Well, that alone is an answer to me."

"What I want to do, George," she tried to explain, "is wait until I meet you again before saying what's in my heart. My heart is being pulled in two directions." Again, this was not altogether true, and she knew it. But how hard it was for her to communicate anything at such a great distance and with so many unknowns. A few accidental indiscretions seemed almost unavoidable. She continued by saying, "It is funny that now I'm in the same position that you were in with Alison. By the way, how is Alison?" She was still not sure how that relationship stood.

"I received a really lovely letter from her. She's living with a man in Italy who's involved in similar things as she is. She may be going to India soon. Sounded very clear-minded and friendly."

"That's really good news. I did like her a lot."

"Yes, well, I loved her a lot." Hearing him say it hit a sore point for Indu but again she accepted it.

"What will you do while you stay in England?" she asked, wanting to change the subject again.

"I'll try to get a job until the exam. But maybe I can come to Lawrence after all. Simply fly into London and then out again. Because of the kind of ticket I have, I have to return to London."

"Well, I have a big house. Not really a big house, but a house." She couldn't believe her ears that he was suggesting he might come after all. She tried to conceal her excitement. "Really, George, you should do whatever is best for you."

"What should I do after arriving in New York? Take a bus?"

"Goodness, flying is just as cheap."

"Yes, but I could see the country by bus."

"That's true, except buses often take highways and at least two days of hard travel."

"Okay, I'll fly. You've convinced me."

"Well, the faster you get here the better as far as I'm concerned."

"In that case, you just might be seeing me very soon."

"Good."

"The main problem I'm going to have is getting money out of the country. I'll have to buy some merchandise, dresses or something, and then resell them. Another alternative is simply to spend my money on phone bills so I can call you."

"That's an exceptional idea."

"Actually, it's hard to believe that I'm talking to you right now. Indu, do you think you know me?"

"On one level I do, and on another level I don't."

"That level you don't know is a very important part."

"That's probably true, but I doubt that I'll care for you any more or any less because of it." She intentionally avoided the word "love." Again, she changed the subject. "Who did you think was calling you?"

"It could have been any local friend or the butcher. They didn't tell me it was an international call. I can just see you now."

"You can! I'm lying in bed."

A surprised laugh came across the line. "Well, I'm leaning against a table wearing shorts and a shirt. I just bought these shorts in Merondera."

"What color is your shirt?"

"It's brown, blue and yellow. I'm looking out over a wide expanse of beautiful African terrain."

"It's still dark in Kansas, and cold with snow and I'm curled up under my heating blanket. Do you want to know what I'm wearing?"

"Of course I do."

"A peach nightie."

"Do you know that I keep your picture by my bed?" he asked.

"That's funny. Yours is right here by mine," she replied.

"And I keep all your letters in a drawer."

"I have every one of yours, too. George, how is your spirit and all?"

"Very good. But I'm not doing any yoga practice although my lifestyle still leans toward that philosophy. Are you surprised I'm not actually practicing?"

"No, not really. You've only recently started and it hasn't gotten under you skin."

"No, that's true, it hasn't. But I am practicing in a way, in an active way, like you described in your letter about milking the cows."

"Yes, that's important, too."

They had been talking almost an hour. She knew it was time for goodbyes although the very idea was emotionally brutal. They had connected again over thousands of miles and months of time, and even broken through the prideful barriers each had erected: his to defend his need for freedom without commitment and hers to hide her deep love for him. The very tone of his voice in the beginning of their talk had struck her as being cautious and full of ego. No doubt her tone had been taunting and belabored. But nothing could block the current of love that flowed between them. A karmic connection was there although she knew not the part it would play in either of their lives. With stoicism, she would often remind herself that unless George wanted the relationship, she would let go completely, as painful as that would be. From this conversation, though, it seemed she could hold onto her beloved for a while longer.

"We've been talking a long time, Indu. You're going to have a tremendous bill."

"Worth every penny. But listen, you'd better write, you bloody fool!"

"That's rather strong language coming from you."

"You're damn right, and I don't want you crumpling it up anymore."

"Well, I've been jotting things down as we've been talking so I can expand upon them in a letter. Otherwise, I'll forget specific points. In fact, I'll even start writing thoughts down while I wait for your letter to arrive. It should take it about ten days if you mail it today."

"Yes, I will."

"By the way, I'm now studying music from an African witch doctor."

"Are you learning anything else from him?" she asked, teasing.

"Yes, I'm learning a great deal from the man's nature and character. And one thing more. I'm also teaching juggling to the kids, and playing a lot of squash and badminton. Am generally feeling pretty healthy."

"No doubt your witchdoctor is helping your bohemian life."

"Well, don't you think you and I could both be into the same sorts of things?"

"Absolutely, only I lead my own bohemian life at the ashram."

With a gentle laugh he agreed, "We are alike in that sense."

"George, I hadn't really planned to mention anything about the marriage proposal to you."

"Of course you planned to."

"No, I didn't."

"Yes, you did."

"George, you're being unkind. I was half expecting you to come for a visit in May so there was no need to say anything. Then you said that you weren't coming until the middle of the summer and so that changed everything in my mind. Honestly, I didn't know what I would say. I only planned to talk ten minutes and then only to tell you a letter would be coming that would be a little strange. We could have a good row about it if only we were in the same country."

"They've actually offered me a permanent job here."

"Do you really want to stay?"

"I do like it here. Why don't you come down and teach here, too?"

"That part of Africa isn't the most popular place to be at the moment, politically and socially speaking."

"That's true. The discrimination is terrible, even from intelligent people. Indu, I'm really glad you called."

"I am, too."

"I'll be waiting for your letter."

"Take care of yourself, George."

"I'm sending you kissy-kissy and a big hug."

"The same is coming to you."

"So, after you hang up, what will you do next?"

"I'll wash my hair."

"What about the sunrise fire ceremony?"

"I haven't been doing the fire so much recently, but that is a good idea. I will do it this morning. I guess the reason I called was so that you could tell me what to do. Why didn't you tell me sooner?"

"I think I'll envision you taking your shower. It's easier than envisioning you doing the fire."

"And I'm envisioning you, out in the middle of Africa. Be well. You have my love."

"And you mine."

"Goodbye."

"Goodbye."

THIRTY

~

Before reading George's last letter, Indu admitted to me that her struggle was with herself, not with George. She was grappling with her own destiny and she worried that as intense a love as she had for George, her own wisdom might be aberrantly blinded by her passion. If the New Year's letter could discourage him from pursuing their relationship, then that would be the clearest signal that he was not to be part of her destiny. She knew she had a destiny to do something with the training that Guruji had given her. Only she didn't know what it was or with whom she was to do it.

Her outlook on life was serious and ethereal, much more so than most might be. But her explanation for this was simple. Her depressions had driven her down the path to know God. They had taken her to Guruji who had taught her how to meditate and in those devout moments, a bliss, an ecstasy had come that had transformed her heavy, forlorn and despairing spirit. She saw in those moments the greater picture of life, the blossoming that was possible if she nurtured the seeds that Guruji had planted. Her fear was that her personal, passionate desire would lock her in a union that would stifle that blossoming. But if George was her soulmate, then there was no danger. If he was her soulmate, then against all odds he would choose to be with her, no matter what she wrote or said or did.

In explaining this to me, she read a quote from Judith Thurman's biography of Isak Dinesen. Thurman cites Dinesen as saying to a friend that one of the perfect joys in life was "to be convinced one was fulfilling one's destiny."[24] But destiny is often misconstrued as simply a preordained plan when it is much more than that. Indu's own understanding of destiny had come from an ancient Sanskrit verse:

YATHĀ HYEKENA CHAKREṆA
NA RATHASYA GATIR BHAVET
EVAM PURUṢHAKĀREṆA
VINĀ DAIVAM NA SIDHYATI

It meant, "Destiny needs effort to come correctly." From Guruji, she also understood that no one could avoid their destiny. But human free will can choose to take a circuitous route toward its destined end, and in so doing only succeed in postponing final realization of God. Destiny has its weapon ready for those who wanted to take the less direct route, and that weapon is karma. By confronting karmas, one is brought a step closer to Godhood. "Our karmas will not leave us alone," Guruji had said. "The body is born to pay the karmic debt. When your karma is over, then your life begins. With the completion of personal karmas, then your body serves God's purpose."

It was in this light that Indu mailed her letter to George. There were to be no circuitous routes for her. If the karma was not beckoning for their union, if such an embrace would not bring them both a step closer to fulfilling their destinies, then she would cast aside her amorous feelings.

She waited six weeks for George's reply to come. When she read it, she knew it was time to let go, to sever the tie, to forsake him and cut the passion from her heart. Possibly this was their karma, that she should suffer tremendous pain in their parting. But if in so suffering she could make that fulfilling step, to pay that karmic debt, the cosmic tax, in order to reach her destiny with God, then she would choose to suffer it nobly.

She took one more sip of tea and then picked up the next air-mail envelope with blue and white stripes along the edges. From this one she pulled not only his letter but a travel brochure of Victoria Falls that he had also enclosed. I glanced at the brochure as she unfolded the thin onion skin pages of his letter and started to read.

ઈૅ * * * ૅ૩

The Letters

[George's Letter #5] Ruzawi School, Marondera, March 7

My dear Indu,

Well, today I received a large brown envelope from Corfu and among the Christmas cards was your letter from the 18th of December. What a lovely letter to receive, and despite your exhaustion you sounded cheerful and really looking forward to getting back home.

I have been rereading your most recent letter (February) and thinking a great deal about what you have said and what it reveals. I imagine that a certain amount of loneliness and desire to share your life with someone, and coping with your relationship with Mark, combined with a slight lack of energy was part of the cause of your feeling so low. How awful for you, Indu, and with so many thoughts and questions and tensions in your mind. However, the letter you wrote to me under those conditions has, I feel, brought me, in a much more realistic and down-to-earth sense, closer to understanding you, and for that I'm terribly glad. I feel I have a much better understanding of your ideas and beliefs and trains of thought that possibly I might not have been exposed to had you not been feeling depressed and felt it necessary to write.

My first reaction was that again I had been badly misunderstood (as I seem to be quite often), but I now feel that actually you understood me very well and that your letter was in fact a confirmation of that. Though I feel there are parts of the letter that swing back to a euphoric idealism that we both shared in England, I believe that that is indicative of some hesitancy in a commitment to your own beliefs and ideas about marriage. I believe that I have grown immensely due to those amazing experiences that I've called "euphoric idealism" and that is not to say that I don't consider them to be very dear in my heart but I recognize them to be a part of my spiritual adolescence. There is nothing worthless about those beautiful moments that we shared together and I will always treasure them; but to consider them as the basis for spending the rest of our lives together I think is naive. That is how I have always felt and my reticence about marriage, which I hope I conveyed in my letters, has borne that out. You are wrong in thinking that I am not yet able to accept, or am unwilling to receive "such a love as mine." Surely, Indu, I have shown you that I accept your love and I wonder how anyone is unable to accept or receive somebody's love. Love is divine and I do not believe one can escape from it, but I don't think you mean that I'm "not ready" for your love. I think you mean that the nature of your love for me as one of the ingredients for marriage is dissimilar to mine and it is a dissimilarity that I cannot reconcile. I am certain that this is due to a fundamental difference in our beliefs.

Your letter stunned me as I became aware of many differences between us that had previously remained undetected due to what I term our blissful euphorically idealistic relationship.

The first part of your letter is mainly concerned with marriage, the suitability of Mark and what you are looking for at this stage in your life. Are the grounds for your marriage to anyone going to be in terms of an almost "absolutely perfect match" and "I feel love could easily blossom?"

I passionately think of marriage in terms of a rock-solid foundation of love, trust, honesty and selflessness which is the only justifiable beginning on which to build a family. I'm sure you feel exactly the same, yet fatalism plays a large role in your life to the extent that, to my mind, it negates all those aspects of love. You see, Indu, I live and love my life by trying to follow God who illuminates new ground for me, not a God who tells that due to this, that or the other you are destined to a life with someone you don't even love. To my mind, that sort of fatalism can inhibit growth. I must go to bed now as it's becoming difficult to remain erudite and what I'm talking about is not the easiest thing to convey with accuracy anyway. So night night, love!

[George's Letter #5-continued] March 9

Commitment to a relationship can take many forms and often becomes a disguised acquisitiveness that is a perversion of love, a possessiveness that murders love. Too often I've heard and occasionally met couples who have married, and though there was fondness and attraction, what was lacking in true love was made up through technicality. I'm sure I've talked about those "technicalities" before, probably describing them as "do we like playing the same games together?" Although this is an important aspect in a relationship, I think it is secondary to love, honesty, trust and selflessness.

You speak very passionately about total involvement in a relationship and your own characteristic of doing just that and also of not wanting to be "in a relationship unless the other person is also involved totally."

"Mark called again today. Wants me to fly up to see him. Haven't mentioned about meeting you yet. Yet what can I say? 'Have met someone whom I haven't seen in five months and don't know when I'll see him again but if I don't marry him then you stand a really good chance.'"

How involved will you let Mark become, how involved can he get, when you don't tell him anything? Surely he can only become as committed to the relationship as you let him... "...unless the other person is also involved totally." Indu, you aren't letting him become totally involved. I remember you once saying that you hoped I would never treat you as I treated Alison. I don't defend myself, but I'm fortunate that I'm not being kept in the dark.

You know it also makes me wonder how easily someone might slip in between (someone like me?) your relationship and possible marriage to Mark in a few years' time. You know I can hardly believe that I'm writing this to you and that it's in reply to your letter. I really don't know what I feel. You've presented so many contradictions.

I don't think this is in any way the end of our relationship and I feel that the tone and contents of your letter were to a certain extent a result of feeling down. I only feel that my ideas and beliefs about marriage and relationships are right for me and I suppose I'm presumptuous enough to question your ideas on the subject simply because I'm on the receiving end of them and am bound to tell you what they make me think and feel.

[George's Letter #5-continued] March 10

It's terribly difficult to comment really, when we've done so little actual living together, or spending time together. I am inclined to think, in view of what you have written to me about relationships and commitment, that possibly your relationships have been quite ethereal. Certainly our relationship has been to some extent, and I wonder about the prudence and realism about founding a lifelong commitment on those grounds. But now I also understand fully well that you still give yourself up to a fatalism that prevents you from committing yourself to someone for the rest of your life. I do hope Mark knows that.

I suppose the reason I think it's all so mixed up is that I know you want to marry me but are willing to marry Mark as a sort of compromise. For your sake, Mark's, and all those other people whom it would affect, I implore you to think very carefully and realistically about what you are thinking. It would be too inconceivable to think that some of the reasons that you got married were that your family history is similar, Episcopal minister, etc., etc.

I must tell you about the sort of experiences I'm having out here as they are providing me with opportunities to test myself and my ability to love objectively.

Generally in Zimbabwe, the Europeans have lost the need to question and doubt their ideas and beliefs. I'm sure this is a result of having enjoyed complete mastery over the Africans and thus wallowing in authority. Incredible arrogance and complacency have been the result. Certainly at Ruzawi a respect and honoring of the old British school etiquette, chivalry, manners, etc., is of the utmost importance.

The incredible result is an intelligent person, a teacher after all, who couldn't be more polite and courteous and yet who doesn't scratch below the surface of any thought. Principles have been founded on a slightly military style of discipline, "toughen 'em up" sort of thing. Group conversation never goes further than social events, weather and sport, and when I'm with an individual and broach a different subject, such as questioning someone about who they are and why they do things, in other words, delving into the region of the human psyche, I come up against an indifference and disinterest.

I am rapidly coming to the conclusion that this attitude and indifference is a defense mechanism because were these people to question generally held beliefs, attitudes and actions, they would reveal some pretty unpleasant doctrines that form the basis of their insular European society. Sure, it's true of everyone. As you can doubtless imagine, living among such people is difficult but is an amazing test for objective love!

What it's brought home is how much I am looking for self-fulfillment in my relationship with all these people. Of course, one is always in need of a balance. But it's quite frightening, when there is no balance, to see how easy it is to become judgmental of others when our own needs are not being filled. It demands incredible compassion, understanding and selflessness in order to love objectively, and I find it very hard work.

It's funny how since I've been in Zimbabwe, life seems to be making me look at all aspects of love. Emotional love in our relationship and objective love with all the ex-Rhodesians. What a lot of learning!

Maybe you don't know what I'm doing here. My job is as catering manager which means that I feed everyone—plan menus, order food, supervise cooking and serving—and also buy all the housekeeping stuff—loo paper, polish, disinfectant, bleach, brushes, etc., etc., etc. You name it and somewhere it's in one of my stores. There are 216 boys between the ages of eight and thirteen and about twenty-five staff, so quite a quantity of mouths and food. Down here they've never heard of vegetarianism as it's meat every day, though I've got quite a few members of staff eating a breakfast of natural yogurt and bran flakes with fresh fruit. They're quite interested to hear me speak about diet and health, though yoga for them is about funny positions, and higher energy things go clean over their heads! (I went on a ten kilometer run yesterday with all the boys and I must admit, the mind-over-matter bit and mantra of "I am not this body" after about seven kilometers had not the slightest effect. I am still recovering!)

The headmaster also asked me if I would teach juggling, which you know, as I've just remembered I told you on the phone. I've done a show for the school on the occasion of its birthday and also one for the African village where all the workers live. That was by far the best as they've never seen anything like it and were absolutely spellbound. A squash club in Marondera has also asked for some help in raising money so we're planning a breakdance with "cabaret." There are two very good Kenyan breakdancers at the school where Jim lives who always help out so we'll do a combined show.

The school's half-term, five-day break was last week and I managed to do some shows in Harare. One was in a hotel disco and the other, a nightclub. Quite difficult, very good experience and I earned twenty dollars less than a month's salary.

The money was badly needed as I really splashed out and went and stayed in a lovely hotel near Victoria Falls. I only spent a couple of days there, much too short, but what an amazing place. Incredibly difficult to describe the awesome majesty of the falls. From the hotel, one is always aware of a thundering, and across the tops of the trees hangs a perpetual cloud of spray. The rainforest is wonderful, and depending on the direction of the wind you find yourself in seemingly driving rain. It's the most wonderful feeling standing near the edge, quite frightening in that you are so moved by the experience you feel like leaping over the edge just to become part of the magic. The spray has a strange quality about it, as seconds before, it's all part of a wall of water that hurdles down into the gorge and then becomes resurrected and falls gently upon your cheek. Quite wonderful.

[George's Letter #5-continued] March 14

Well, Indu, I think I ought to get this posted off to you now as you are probably wondering what's been going through my mind since receiving your letter. I feel very well and, despite the shortage of intellectual and spiritual inspiration, am quite happy. I hope you are now one hundred percent back to your normal self and not worrying too much about the future and what it might or might not hold in store for you. So, for the time being pip pip, as the English expression goes, and take care of yourself, my love.

Fondest love from George

THIRTY-ONE

~

Wanting to make the final break as quickly as possible, she phoned George the very day after receiving his letter. In that conversation, he only restated what he had already written: that her beliefs and ideas were different from his in regards to marriage; that their experiences together had been a euphoric, idealistic period, inadequate upon which to make any commitment; and labeling her views fatalistic, that he doubted she could ever make a lifelong commitment.

The karmic test was complete although it was not a question of passing or failing. The uncertainty had been merely which fork in the road to take for the most direct path to God.

If she was angry with George for reading her letter with his brain only and not his heart, she nonetheless forgave him the judgmental tone of his letter. She accepted it as the sign that their joining was not meant to be. This "fatalistic" view gave Indu her only solace.

೮ * * * ೮౩

I could feel how heartbreaking it must have been. If George had actually believed that she meant to break off their romantic involvement after the phone call, it was impossible to say. She had simply ended the conversation by saying, "It seems it would be the best thing for us to go our separate ways." With her heart in her throat, she wasn't sure how convincing she had really sounded, she admitted to me. But in her mind she had been absolutely sincere about it. She had removed his picture from her nightstand and collected all his letters in the large gray folder. With them she'd also kept mementos of their few days together: a small map of Cambridge, the note she had left for Shakti on her pillow in New Brighton when she and George had slipped off to the motel, the paper upon which she had written "Thursday, 11:00 – West Kensington tube station." Just bits of paper but the memories from them had brought tears to her eyes as she held them between her fingers before tucking them inside the folder. She would never have thought of parting with any of them but only wanted to seal them away in hopes that it would seal the pain from her heart.

Peering into the same gray folder now laying on the table before us, she withdrew a newspaper article which she had safely kept with George's letters, carefully folded into a small square. It had been given to her by Paul when she was in New Brighton. Somehow, in the course of her visit that weekend, Indu had mentioned the standing stone near Ickwell to him, as well as her curiosity regarding the prehistoric culture which had erected it. With a smile of a co-conspirator, he had produced from his files the clipping, one which he had extracted a year before from the newspaper. She unfolded it now to show me. It was entitled, "Have You Ever Heard a Stone Talking?" The subtitle read, "There's more mystery surrounding those prehistoric stone circles than were [sic] ever dreamt of by respectable scientists."

Remembering the heat felt in the palms of her hands as they hovered an inch above the hard stone surface, she was already a converted believer in their mystery. She assured me she would return to her story about George after she had read it to me. I could sense some revelation was coming. I wanted desperately to understand how her Guru's invitation to Denmark, her fascination with the stones and her passionate love affair with George were enigmatically tied together. With brimming curiosity, I listened to her articulate diction as she read this unusually titled newspaper article from the *Guardian* dated June 25, 1983:

At first sight the Rollrights in Oxfordshire seem ordinary enough, much like any other prehistoric circle. A ragged, jagged ring of limestone, flanked by a tumbledown dolmen and guarded by a solitary menhir—the Kingstone. Tourists note the empty beer cans, crumpled crisp bags, and re-markably little atmosphere. By day. But arrive there some chill, frost spangled sunrise at the turn of the year [or turn of the season] and it's a very different story. For then, if you are a bat, a "sensitive," or equipped with an ultrasound monitor, you will hear eerie, regular clicking emanating from the circle. It is the language of the stones.

What's more, they're all at it. From Lands End to the Western Isles, prehistoric sites chatter away to each other, the spheres, or no one in particular, in the grey equinoctial dawns.

We know because the archaeologists, scientists, dowsers, and mystics who make up the Dragon Project have finally started publishing their bizarre findings. And the talking stones are the almost tame preface to an uncanny tale of mystery and suspense. The story so far.

Six years ago a mixed bag of scientists and fringe investiga-tors got together to unravel the mystery of the stone circles. Don Robins, Ph.D., an inorganic chemist now researching at the Institute of Archaeology, became their scientific ad-viser. "Structures which took so much time and organised [sic] effort, involved advanced geometry and sophisticated alignments, must have meant a great deal to somebody," he says.

"They stretched the technology of the day to its limits—but what for? It doesn't make sense, either, to ignore the folk-lore...up and down the country you find the same tales of stones which dance or go down to the water to drink or have curative powers...there are stones which rock, lots of 'Tingle Stones', and stones which emit light beams...how-ever unlikely, there has to be something behind it all."

Thus the Dragon Project was hatched and called after the Chinese geomantic name for earth currents (the interaction of the earth's electromagnetic field with cosmic and solar radiation). Scientific and paranormal consultants were appointed and Paul Devereux, writer, photographer and editor of *The Leyhunter*, was made coordinator.

The scientists decided to study radioactivity and ultrasound. There are frequent reports of anomalous radiation levels at prehistoric sites. But ultrasound? It was a friend naturalist who put them on to that one. Returning home one daybreak after a totally sober stint of bat watching, he had been nonplussed to pick up ultrasonic signals from a standing stone. "That tip-off was our biggest single stroke of luck," says Robins.

The sensitives were to look for force fields, try to locate the position of the missing stones, and generally build up a picture of times past. Together the normal and paranormal inquirer would concentrate on one circle, in depth, and over a period of years. They chose the Rollrights. The Rollrights have everything. Magical origins (an uncouth warlord and his henchmen turned to stone by a perceptive witch), a propensity to wander about, to crush unwary strangers and cure childhood ailments. They were easily accessible from London and, most important, on private land and hence safe from interference from the DoE [Department of the Environment].

Just as well, too. Surely the most civil of civil servants could not have maintained a suitable sangfroid at those dawn watches. Imagine their reaction to muffled and hooded mystics picking their way through the high-tech gadgetry to paint pictures of the stone's auras or white robed priests at their nasty rituals. And all the while medics monitored the brain patterns of the dowsers who, in their turn, monitored the force patterns of the site. A zany amalgam of *General Hospital*, *Blithe Spirit*, and *Tomorrow's World*.

By sheer good luck, says Robins, they started work in October just as the ultrasonic pulsing is at its strongest. But when it came to the point, that grey dew-drenched pre-

dawn, he felt pretty silly and quite prepared to tell anyone who asked that he was an early tourist with an unusual transistor radio. Then, half an hour before sunrise,
the Kingstone suddenly sprang to life, emitting a regular
signal which was neither the rhythm of his heart, the rustle
of the undergrowth, nor some errant radio transmission.
It was a glorious moment. The signals lasted through the
dawn, gradually fading as the sun climbed up the sky.

Enthusiastic but wary, the scientists monitored control areas and other prehistoric sites. They devised increasingly
selective screening and finally ruled out all other sources.
The stones alone were responsible for the sound.

At the same time the geiger [sic] counter was discovering
strange levels of radioactivity in the circles, some higher
and some lower than the surrounding countryside. Some
of Paul Devereux's photographs showed strange effects
around the stones, and the dowsers, "two of the best in the
country," says Robbins, "found force fields inside the circle...seven concentric circles and lines radiating out from
their center."

When he began to realize the implications of the findings,
Robins felt a strong impulse to forget the whole thing. In
the end, he decided "to go for broke...press on to the point
where he had enough evidence to satisfy the demand of
scientific respectability, and prove that there was a genuine
scientific phenomenon at the circles."

This is what they found. At the times of the equinoxes—
March and October—the stones emit regular ultrasonic
signals. It happens around dawn whether or not the sun is
visible and quite independently of weather conditions. As
the year draws on towards the solstices, the signals fade
away.

But stranger by far, from time to time, the stones create an
ultrasonic barrier. A cone of silence on the hillside. "This

is the weirdest thing. You always have a background of ultrasound in the country—the movement of grasses, leaves rustling, even your own clothing. It all registers. But one morning, as we moved in and out of the circle monitoring the levels, suddenly we found that there was complete ultrasonic silence inside the circle. Our first thoughts were that it was an instrument malfunction. Then we walked through the gap in the stones and there was sound. Inside, silence—outside, normal background levels."

The geigers [*sic*] were busy, too. First they picked up occasional powerful radioactive flares from an area between the Kingstone and the circle. "Sometimes," says Paul Devereux, "it yielded more counts per minute than when the counter was placed less than a yard from a radioactive isotope." Then the readings showed that the level of radioactivity was always higher outside the circle than inside—often by a factor of two. Shielding again.

Finally the mystics were vindicated when three of Devereux's infrared photographs (checked out by an independent expert) showed a light mist around the Kingstone and a ray beaming heavenwards from its blunt crown.

No wonder that Robins, a respectable scientist with a reputation to consider, turned green at the implications. "What we seem to have found," he explains, "are refugees. The stones shield the interior of the circle from certain energy fields...we are not even certain which fields. They seem to exclude cosmic radiation, too, and that implies spherical shelter. It is as though the circles created holes in the landscape."

Researchers were sent to other sites for verification. In Cornwall, the Peaks, the mountains of Wales, and by the rivers of Ireland they got it.

"In the end we decided to come out from under the stones," says Robins. He published a bold account in *New Scien-*

tist, and Devereux wrote an equally restrained one in *Unexplained*. "Amazingly the archaeologists were not too aghast." There was no shock/horror response from the establishment. Scientists, he says, are more relaxed about the inexplicable these days.

What does it all mean? Devereux points out that the modern use of ultrasound to heal damaged tissue and improve seed germination may have some bearing on folk tales about healing powers and fertility bonuses. He also sees significant relationship between geological fault lines, the siting of the circles and electromagnetic radiation, even with the piezoelectric effects which look like UFOs.

But no matter how you press him, the cheery Dr. Robins is not prepared to hazard any guesses about the use to which our ancestors put the circles, even though he now has a new piece of corroborative evidence to add to the Dragon files.

Quite independently, a retired BBC engineer, Charles Brooker, had already done several electromagnetic scans of the Rollrights. Using a portable magnetometer he had found a seven ring spiral of magnetic intensity inside the circle. Prompted by Robin's article, he wrote a follow-up piece in *New Scientist*.

Now at this stage Robins had said nothing about the shielding power of the stones. Brooker, however, had come to the same conclusion by himself. "The Ancestors," he wrote, "knew exactly what they were doing…the stones form magnetic refuges—Stone Age Faraday Cages. Though why they should want magnetic refuges is another question." [25]

She looked at me and I looked at her. Trying to perceive the Milky Way from 42nd Street or Trafalgar Square would rival the feat I now had in forming a cohesive picture of what I had just heard. If a revelation had come, it had stunned my cognitive faculties and left me sitting puzzled and motionless.

Indu folded the article once again into its concise square. Clearly the research on the standing stones pleased the scientist in her. But the relevance of it was still shrouded in mystery, as she wanted it to be. By the sly smile on her face I could tell she was somewhat enjoying my perplexity.

Having brewed more tea, she suggested that we adjourn to the sitting room. Seated once again in our respective places, she promised that soon I would understand. In the end, her story would not just be about a personal romance, but a regal vindication of the powers of Nature, of love and of God.

She picked up her story on May 11, the day she had telephoned the ashram to inquire about her beloved teacher, the day she had heard his endearingly accented voice suggesting, "How about Denmark? Do you want to go?" The reason her mind had jumped immediately to George after talking to Guruji was simply because Denmark would put her that much closer to London and to the man she loved.

Her suffering heart had hardly been appeased by the six weeks which had passed since she'd made the decision for her and George to part ways. Her efforts to relinquish her love for him had failed miserably. From all he had written and said, she knew he should be in London studying for his exam. Still, she had held her emotions at bay and struggled to put any thoughts of reconciliation out of her mind. It was a battle she had fought many times already.

Four days after speaking with Guruji about Denmark, she was at the airport bidding farewell to a dear friend who was flying home to Japan, deathly ill with cancer. Her friend was but a woman of thirty-nine. The disease had been diagnosed in early April but her friend's condition had deteriorated rapidly. Indu had seen her off with prayers and a promise to write. Returning home, she had found herself sitting numbly in a high-back white swivel rocker. To be close to death, to see its shadow, had plunged her into renewed soul-searching queries about God's plan and life's purpose.

The Letters

℘ * * * ℃

Dazed and absorbed in thought, sitting in the rocker, she was only mechanically brought back to reality by the ringing of the phone. She heard the voice and was momentarily shaken. It was George. He was calling from London.

She carried the phone back to her chair. The emotional shock and the precise timing of his call triggered a flood of tears. She tried desperately to conceal the condition of her nerves. If her voice sounded shaky, he made no comment of it. The call lasted ten minutes. He said he was calling to say hello, was in fact studying for his exam, and planned to stay through the summer and fall with Oliver, hopefully finding work to make it profitable. After that, he was thinking of traveling.

All the while, Indu kept shaking with wonder that his call should come just days after her talk with Guruji and the prospect of Denmark before her. Would the same idea come to his mind as had come to hers regarding the trip and Denmark's proximity to London? She waited to say anything about it until he asked her plans.

"Oh, that sounds lovely. How lucky for you," was his reply.

She waited for something more to be said, for some hint of a desire to see her, but he said no more, except to wish her a happy journey. It was a blow to her heart, yet she had too much pride to suggest the possibility herself. Could it also have been pride that had held George back from mentioning anything about a reunion? Or had he been waiting for her to make the initial advance? Whatever the case, they both remained silent and their friendly exchange ended without a passionate word spoken. He wished her well and she wished him the same, and they bid each other farewell.

It seemed the decree had been signed that they should stay parted. On May 25, Indu received news that her friend had died of cancer that morning. To feel the loss of two dear friends, one a loss of life and the other a loss of love, which felt much like a death, left Indu boldly facing her own mortal destiny and grappling with the question of what to do with her life. She felt alone.

ℰ * * * ℭ

Fortunately, she said to me, it was at times like these that she knew to reflect back on what Guruji had taught her. Reading again from her notebook, it was this type of lesson from her Guru which was deeply consoling: "Our life is a dream. When it is in our favor then we don't mind. But when our dream is painful, then we want out. But it is not so easy. We must know God is within. We cannot find happiness outside ourselves. That outside happiness is only an illusion. True happiness is missing from our lives and that is what brings us pain. We can only remove the pain by finding true happiness which is beyond our dream life. It is union with the Absolute." He would continue, "God is our primary nature. Without worshiping that God, we cannot know who we are. I am not talking about religious God. I mean Absolute God because he is always with you. No church is needed in between."

Cradling these teachings in her mind, Indu had decided to throw herself into her spiritual practice, praying that divine guidance would come. She knew that it would, that a light would shine once again in her grief-clouded heart, giving her a glimpse of the meaning of it all. Even the quote from the movie *The Sound of Music,* spoken by Maria when still a novitiate, had helped give Indu a more humorous perspective: "When the Lord closes a door, somewhere He opens a window." She felt a door had been closed and she was watching for the window, and it did appear in an unusual way.

ℰ * * * ℭ

The first week of June, Indu received a call from Shakti who was making the travel arrangements for the Denmark trip. Shakti had only just heard that Indu was thinking of joining them and the deadline for the ticket booking was in three days. For Indu to make that deadline, she would have to rush a check of $1,100 to the ashram using express mail postal delivery. She did send the check that day, but by the third day Shakti had still not received it. Indu telephoned her that Saturday morning and was puzzled to hear of the check's disappearance. But she told Shakti not to worry, that she would arrange her own ticket.

Immediately she went to a travel agency to see what special rates she could get. Flights from Kansas City into Copenhagen were neither cheap, nor were they direct. She would have to fly out of Houston or New York. At that time, the best airfare for the distance was between Newark and London on several highly competitive carriers. The moment the agent gave her this information, Indu felt an inner jolt. Although other routes were possible, the agent was nonetheless suggesting that she could fly into London and then connect to Copenhagen using a European airline. The surge in her heart left every nerve tingling. She could see George again after all.

Before making any decision, she knew she must phone London. Her mind was racing. Had he not tried to reach out to her in May? Had he not wanted to reconnect with her? Had her own emotional state prevented her from recognizing his attempt to test the waters between them? The actual words spoken were possibly not as important as his effort to break the silence which had weighed heavily for six weeks. The only catch to booking the London flight was that she had to make the decision that day in order to meet the excursion fare restriction of three weeks' prior arrangement. The rate would otherwise jump substantially.

But George was not to be reached. He was gone for the weekend to a friend's wedding. It was Oliver who gave her this information. Indu was left in the awkward position of having to tell Oliver of her plans to fly through London and, George willing, a possible layover of several weeks. Delicately, she also had to ask him if she could make the imposition of staying at his flat. His reply, made in a most gentlemanly fashion, was that as far as he personally was concerned, he had no objection to her visit.

Indu booked the ticket and then wrote a letter to George explaining the circumstances.

ℰ℩ * * * ℭ℔

As she had all the others, she read this last letter to me.

June 19

Dear George,

Have turned in my letter of resignation to my boss. It's definitely time for me to move on. And so I'm off to Denmark. I've wondered what force might exist that would draw us back to the same country again, let alone the same city. I must admit your face does seem to keep popping into my mind and have found myself adding six hours to my time, wondering what you might be doing. But at the same time I have also felt something inside wanting to let go of you. A peaceful feeling comes just knowing that at least we did meet in this lifetime. Have thought a second meeting would be nice for both of us but hesitated during your phone call to even suggest that we try. But now it seems a chance has come for me to be in London.

It started with a call to Shakti this morning to see if she'd received my $1,100 check which I'd sent express mail to cover the Denmark ticket. I had assumed everything was set. But she told me not only had she not received the money but that making a late reservation would cost even more. Things began clicking in my head: could I possibly save money if I made my own arrangements, and if I was going to arrange it myself, then why not come through London? It was at this point that I tried to call you and instead got Oliver. Felt a little presumptuous planning to come to see you without even asking if you wanted to see me, particularly since you didn't mention it during your call. But in order to get the excursion fare, I had to purchase the ticket no later than three weeks in advance, which made the cut-off date today. The fares would be incredibly higher after that. So it left me in a bit of a predicament. All Oliver could guarantee was that you would be in London at least through August. So I went ahead and made the arrangements to come through London en route to Denmark and stay three weeks in London before returning to New York. Won't really ly know if ultimately I saved money or not until I compare notes with Shakti. But it seems beside the point right now. The die has been cast and I will be in London August 1st. Can possibly stay with Muniji in Hampstead if it is not convenient (or appropriate) for me to stay at Oliver's.

Have no idea how you're going to feel about this. If I've made a terrible gaffe in doing this, please forgive me now. Certainly don't feel you need to entertain me the three weeks I'm there. If vibes are not comfortable between us, I'll do a bit of sightseeing, check out a few more standing stones and then head back.

Will contact you again sometime between now and then.

Love, Indu

Indu then told me that the following week, Shakti did receive her express letter with apologies from the post office for its delay. Thanks to their guarantee of service, Indu had been able to receive a full postage refund. And she couldn't help feeling bemused that once again the mail officials had been under the hand of destiny.

PART III

~

RETURN TO LONDON

All perfection and every divine virtue are hidden within you.
Reveal them to the world.
Wisdom, too, is already within you. Let it shine forth.
Let the Lord's grace make you free.
Let your life be that of the rose;
in silence, it speaks the language of fragrance.

Excerpt of Message from Haidakhandi Babaji
www.babaji.net

Reprinted with permission.

THIRTY-TWO

~

Now in London, Indu sat in a broad, padded high-back chair with armrests, a much-needed cup of coffee before her on a square coffee table and a book in her lap. The book was Dostoyevsky's *The Idiot*. In the preface, she had been amazed to read that Dostoyevsky had rewritten his story eight times. She had not thought that a great writer would have such problems of indecision about what to do with his characters. It was the first of Dostoyevsky's works that she'd ever read and she was having trouble finding her way into the intricate lives of the Russian intelligentsia. But it was by no fault of the author's. She simply could barely keep her eyes open.

She had arrived in London that afternoon after parting from Guruji in Copenhagen. When she told Guruji of her plans to stay in London, he had said very simply, "Ah, so you are going in search of your future." He asked if it had anything to do with the fellow from Ickwell and she admitted that it did. He then wrote down something strange on a piece of paper, handing it to Indu without a word of explanation. She had silently accepted it, although puzzled by its meaning. He had written two words, one on top of the other, with an "X" in between them, $\underset{\text{Down}}{\overset{\text{Up}}{X}}$. The two words were "up" and "down" and the "X" seemed to imply what goes up must come down and vice versa. To what exactly it referred she wasn't sure, but she guessed it must have something to do with her relationship with George. Seeing her bewildered expression, he had simply said, "Watch."

෨ * * * ෬

I already knew that Guruji was not a Guru to disclose fortunes or predict events, although Indu suspected he could do both very well. But that was not his way. His devotees had to constantly think for themselves and meditate in order to understand the critical points of his teaching. Indu described it to me this way: "To tell a four year old that $4 \times 4 = 16$ would have very little meaning. But let that same child at the age of nine discover multiplication, and then tell them that $4 \times 4 = 16$ and they will agree with you without question. So it is with mysticism. If we do not have certain 'Knowledge,' then any amount of explanation will only act to confuse us further. This 'Knowledge,' however, is neither academic nor is it cerebral. It is beyond the mind and acquired only through dedicated practice of meditation. The Guru knows this and therefore does not needlessly bother with talk. He knows that when you have the 'Knowledge,' your heart will automatically grasp the truth. His great genius is in dangling the carrot to entice devotees to venture toward the world beyond the mind where the storehouse of 'Knowledge' exists."

The "up" and "down" and the criss-cross were carrots to Indu. She was meditating and watching and trying to understand.

ℰ ✻ ✻ ✻ ℭ

She gazed out the large picture windows at the rainy London day, at the umbrellas passing by, at the big black taxis that hovered outside the hotel door. She was sitting in the lounge of the Grosvenor Hotel waiting for George to meet her. She kept wondering what it would be like to see him again. She'd called him from the airport on her way through London to say she'd be back in ten days and had asked how he thought it would work out to spend some time together. He'd been affably agreeable to the plan and assured her there would be a place for her to stay at Oliver's. But she had detected something peculiar in his voice, a strain, a shortness in tone. Doubts had suddenly filled her mind as to whether she'd done the right thing in coming. But he had said he was looking forward to seeing her and had given her his work number so she could reach him as soon as she arrived back in town.

That short conversation with George as she'd passed through London had left her with mixed emotions that were impossible to sort out. She could not know anything until she saw him again. She had tried to forget the anxiety in her heart, wanting to enjoy the trip she had ahead of her with Guruji.

The trip was not solely to Denmark. The instigating force behind it had been an invitation for Guruji to attend the Second European Conference on Universal Brotherhood, which was being held for four days in Copenhagen. He would present the keynote speech. But prior to attending the conference, he had decided to take the group to see the midnight sun at the northern tip of Norway. It was a spectacle he himself had seen two or three times already from different Arctic points.

So from London she actually flew into Oslo. Having a seven hour layover at the airport, she took a bus into the city and explored. By chance she happened upon a boat tour of the Oslo Harbor. It was not terribly exciting but it passed the time pleasantly. Afterward, walking in a civic square, she admired the smooth, rounded curves of the statuary, one a sculpture of a woman in the nude with two children. They were healthy and happy in expression and Indu liked that. Another was a group of four people, each facing different directions but all holding hands. To her, it was a lovely symbol of unity.

The seven hours passed quickly and she was soon aboard a small propeller plane which would take her from Oslo up to the northern city of Tromsø. Its airport was but a tiny building. It was evening and someone from the group was supposed to be meeting her, but she saw no familiar face when she entered the terminal. Unconcerned, she collected her luggage, and having exchanged currency in Oslo, took a few krone out to call the hotel where they had planned to stay. No sooner had she placed the call when the airport terminal main door opened and in walked Uma and one other friend traveling with the group. She would have soon received surprising news over the phone since at the last minute they had changed lodging accommodations. She'd actually been quite dependent on their kind hearts and good memories to come and retrieve her. It was a lovely feeling having friends in what seemed the middle of nowhere.

The next morning, their group, a total of nine including Guruji, filled an even tinier propeller plane than the one she'd taken the day before. It carried them from Tromsø to Alta. At Alta, they boarded a bus for Honningsvåg where they would spend the next four days. Two of those days, they would travel to North Cape, a mere precipice forty-five minutes from the town. Honningsvåg was one of northern Norway's busiest harbors, handling amongst other things four to five thousand fishing trawlers a year. It was located on the island of Magerøya, a name meaning "meager island." It aptly described the tundra country which generally produced only mosses, lichens and shrubs. But for the reindeer this was ideal pasturage.

On the bus ride from Honningsvåg to North Cape, Indu saw those "fairytale" creatures for the first time. One even pranced down the road in front of the bus. The epitome of grace it wasn't, to the great amusement of all on board. Without horns they resembled ordinary deer, and Indu wondered how they'd ever been dubbed the emissaries of Santa Claus.

Leaving the bustling port behind, the bus carried them across the open tundra, a beautiful green-brown and predominantly barren expanse, following a winding road, one that would be hidden by snow and ice for nearly six months of the year. The road ended at the isolated, serene point of North Cape, located on the far side of the island. It was at this point that one could claim to be at the northernmost tip of Europe. From its high plateau looking across the waters of the Arctic Ocean, one had an unobscured view of the midnight sun, the sun that never set.

It was not to show them a thing of beauty that Guruji had brought them to this isolated place, of this Indu was certain. Oddly, on that first day, there was quite a throng of people, for the clear skies had guaranteed a spectacular display of color as the sun approached the cradle of the horizon. Their group sat together to meditate on the warmth of the sun at midnight. The angle of the earth being what it was to the sun, it was possible to gaze with open eyes directly at the solar disc without risking damage to the retina. It was *trāṭakam* on the sun.

Indu watched through squinted eyes, acutely aware of a sensation behind her eyes, somewhere in the middle of her brain. She believed a photo-optic sensor adapted the brain (and consequently the nervous system and behavior) to the natural light hours of an environment, an endogenous circadian rhythm-setter established on the movement of the sun, circadian because the rhythm was synchronized to the length of a single day. Harvard scientists had recently shown that a small region in the frontal lobe called the suprachiasmatic nuclei could be the site of the biological clock controlling sleep-wake cycles. The human circadian clocks were no joke. Many suffering from depression in the winter months were helped by using artificial light to lengthen their daylight hours. Something in the brain did respond directly to light. Indu didn't need to be told this; she felt it. She didn't know what was happening, but something in her brain was exploding as the solar waves shot directly through her eyes. The effect was beyond description and the imprint left in her mind's eye was brilliant.

ℰ﹡﹡﹡ℭ

But there was something more to watching this midnight sun. "We become so readily conditioned by our surroundings that it is part and parcel of daily existence to take things for granted, and for a predominant part of the world the sun's rising and setting is one such event," Indu told me, trying to elaborate on why Guruji had brought them to this spot on the earth. "But defying expectation, this sun did not set. It hovered teasingly low over the horizon, dipping nearer and nearer with its rays shooting out to create an ever-growing radiant "skyscape," holding still on the brink of its glory only to ascend back up into the sky, jovially casting long dark shadows in the wee hours of the morning. It was a joke well told."

The joke was on the senses. Indu had pondered if that was why Guruji had brought them. Their usual sense-perceived reality had the sun disappearing, and that was not going to happen inside the summer Arctic Circle. The sun wasn't what was moving anyway, but instead the earth itself. Still, the senses did not perceive this. They did not register a planet rotating on its axis, spinning in its orbit around this shining star. It was for Copernicus to stop the sun and move the earth, yet he was labeled a heretic for doing so. Man preferred to believe that the sun sank beyond the ocean and rose above the mountains, even if it was only an illusion. Was this what Guruji had wanted to show them, that depending solely on sense perception for knowledge would blind them to the real understanding of the universe? The answer had been before them, in the midnight sun.

Picking up her notebook, Indu said that in the same vein Guruji would ask, "What is the proof that today is Sunday? What is the proof that sugar is sweet? What is the proof that we are beyond body and mind? The answer is direct perception, direct experience. Is not the perception of light the proof of electricity? In exactly the same way, you are the proof of God." It was an analogy that boggled Indu's mind, but one she instinctively knew was true. She again read from the notebook in which she had recorded his comments. He had said in good humor, "Even a bad meal is better than a delightful meal given by description. To be satisfied you need direct experience." And that experience cannot come through the senses. It can come only through meditation. That was his point.

"How to know when God is with you?" he would say to them. "When the sun shines its light, other lights make no difference. Neither moon, nor electricity, nor candles, nothing is needed in the presence of the sun. When you feel God, you do not want to talk. When thinking mind stops, then God works. Do not believe it, feel it." It was a command that Indu desperately had wanted to follow, and Guruji was showing her how.

His talk had continued. "All sciences, arts, they are part of the sense-perceived universe. Our knowledge is nothing but memory. We are surrounded by manifestations. And Reality is beyond manifestation. Our whole life is movement in time and space and Reality is beyond time and space. God cannot be felt by the senses. Why do you feel shy to see God directly? God is always with you. Why do you not understand God? Because you want to see by means of your senses. You cannot see God with eyes. You cannot see your own soul. The only way to see God is to be still. You must get out of the mind to see God.

"Whenever there is 'I', there is no God. Whenever there is God, there is no 'I'. Where the sun shines, there is no night. Darkness and light do not exist simultaneously." Seeing the midnight sun brought these words of Guruji's vibrantly to her mind, she told me. He had brought them to a point that knew no darkness. Was it not an allegorical journey? Was not the real journey happening within? Must we not realize the eternal light so that we no longer experience darkness?

He liked to quote the Bible passage, "And the light shineth in darkness; and the darkness comprehended it not."* Guruji would challenge them, "Can darkness comprehend the presence of light? Can light comprehend darkness? They cannot know each other. So why write such a thing?" Silence would fill the room until he spoke again. "Darkness represents psychological darkness, which is the abode of the mind, and light represents spirit."

Again with a joking glint in his eye he would announce, "At the North Pole, you cannot know day and night." With the sun shining brightly down on them at two o'clock in the morning, it was incomprehensible to think of it as night. Only the absence of people and the closed shops told that it was. But Guruji's point had been this: "When you have day and night, then you are living the life of body and mind. When you go beyond, through meditation, then you live the life like at the summer North Pole, all the time light."

---

* John 1:5 (AV).

ഇ) * * * (ൃ

Having arrived back in London and sitting in a half-dazed state in the hotel lounge, ensconced in a corner where no one would notice her, Indu thought about the angle of the planet in respect to the sun. There could be no "midnight sun" without the tilting axis. The thought made her wonder back over the article on the "talking" stones. Why was it only at the equinoxes that the stones' ultrasonic clicking was at its peak? She envisioned the earth's orbit:

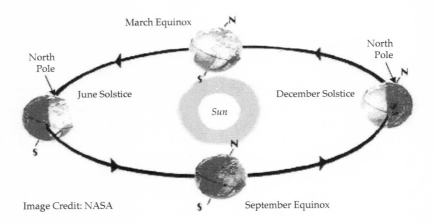

Image Credit: NASA

During the summer solstice, the North Pole was tipped entirely within the sun's range, which was why no matter how the earth rotated, darkness could never come. In the winter, the same area was tipped outside the sun's reach, which brought perpetual darkness. But at the equinoxes, when the hours of day and night were equal, the planet tilted neither toward nor away from the sun. Why did this period show the highest "chatter" among the stones? What had been prehistoric man's relationship to the sun? Had he discovered something about solar power which had eluded the modern mind? She decided firmly at that moment to do some investigating on the circles and standing stones while in London. For one thing, she would look up those reports in *New Scientist* to which the article had made reference.

A comment from Guruji came to her mind: "In prehistoric time, man was one. With the beginning of history, division started. The more civilized man became, the more disorganization crept in. Political leaders do not want to unite but divide." This was exactly the theme of his keynote speech made at the Copenhagen conference: we have lost the greater understanding of our real position on this planet, and only by regaining this understanding through meditation can peace and harmony be restored.

ॐ * * * ॐ

Indu had a copy of the speech and she asked if I wanted to read it. I did wonder what this teacher of hers would have to say at a universal brotherhood conference. According to Indu, Guruji had captured everyone's attention. I asked if she would read it aloud as she had the letters. Since it was quite long, she read these key excerpts:

> From the point of view of science, this is the age of electronics, nuclear energy and computers. From the psychological point of view, this is the age of anxiety, neurosis and psychosis. From the family and social point of view, this is the age of divorce and family disintegration. From the national and international point of view, this is the age of various pollutions, highjacking, piracy and airplane-shooting. From the point of view of religions, this is the age of confusion, lawlessness, disunity and complete chaos. From the academic point of view, this is the age of various degrees, diplomas and postgraduate degrees. Yet ignorance, egoism and lack of unity are growing among scholars like untouchability in India. From the economic point of view, this is the age of complete bankruptcy and devaluation.

There is no world economy, only national economy which depends on the exploitation of one nation by another.

In our modern history, we have the greatest boons of nature. We have motorcars, railways, buses, sputnik and satellites, missiles, airplanes, TVs and radios, walkie-talkies. Yet, unfortunately, we do not know how to walk on earth with our feet. We can talk on the telephone to every part of the earth, due to radio waves. Yet in spite of these luxuries, man is most unhappy, lost, confused and spiritually bankrupt.

Rāma and Kṛiṣhṇa were going and coming only by chariot, Buddha and Moses on foot, Jesus on a donkey. Mohammed was riding on a camel. Mahāvīra was naked, Guru Nānak had with him only holy books, Mahatma Gandhi had only eyeglasses, a stick, sandals, a loin cloth and an idol of three Chinese monkeys. Yet these divine and pious souls were so happy, because they had experienced the complete blossoming of Godhood within themselves.

God is eternal consciousness, existence and bliss. We forgot that God is our real soul and that we are his messengers, representatives and angels. In every soul God is hidden in the form of the root. Man is powerless and impotent without the blossoming of that Godhood. Everybody must have his own blossoming and incarnation of God in his own heart. This is the difference between a man and a computer. Otherwise computers work far better than men.

What is the cause of our energy crisis? What is the cause of our disunity? What is the cause of our disintegrity and downfall in spite of all material prosperity? The cause is our modern education. Jesus Christ, Buddha, Tulasīdāsa, Shankara, Rāma, Kṛiṣhṇa, Guru Nānak, Mahāvīra, Kabira, Mohammed, Moses, Zoroaster, Lao Tzu—they did not have Ph.D.s, but they were all enlightened souls. No matter how high skyscraper buildings may be, if their foundations are weak they are destined to fall. The highest progress is the sign of downfall if it is without foundation.

We have no knowledge of our own Self. We live the life of our body and mind. That is to say, we live by knowledge of information alone, and this knowledge comes from the outside as a burden, as a memory, and programs us like robots. We do not have the knowledge which originates from our meditative heart. We do not have our own knowledge.

Once upon a time the Viceroy, representative of the British Empire, visited Banaras Hindu University which was quite young at that time. The trees and plants were still young then and without blossoms. So to welcome this unique and distinguished guest, fruits and flowers were purchased from outside and tied onto the respective trees and plants. The Viceroy, His Majesty's representative, was very much pleased to see such a grand and pompous welcome with beautiful design, fruits and flowers. This is an unbelievable story, but it is true. It happened. To welcome the royal guest, the reception performance was so divinely and majestically performed that all Indian and world newspapers and radios were booming with praise.

However, after one week the whole university became intolerable with the stench of those rotten fruits and flowers. The Health Department had a serious task to disinfect and purify Banaras Hindu University to prevent the outbreak of infectious diseases as a result of those fruits and flowers tied onto foreign trees and plants. The trees and plants were true and real. The fruits and flowers were true and real as well. The mistake was that they were not growing naturally. They were unnaturally tied onto different trees and plants. Then if everything was true and real, what was the mistake? The mistake was that the fruits and flowers came from the outside and were foreign and unnatural to those trees.

The same fact is true of our modern *pandits*, priests, rabbis, mullas, maulavis, university scholars and religious leaders. The *pandits*, the scholars, the religious leaders are true and real. And all holy books are also true and real. But they have been tied by the thread of modern education to the foreign mind and brain. The *pandits* and religious leaders have no experience of those truths described by the Vedas, shāstras and holy books.

Our modern religious leaders, *pandits* and scholars are like moving libraries. Modern education is extremely excellent and beautiful, but its reality and beauty are like an uprooted tree, like plastic flowers. Modern *pandits* and religious leaders are "bunkum" in spiritual experience. Everybody acts like a great *pandit*, while everybody is bankrupt in the realm of the heart. They have no meditative heart.

The entire planet is shaking from nuclear weapons and various pollutions, especially mental pollution in the form of our cunningness, jealousy, hatred, intolerance, et cetera. Modern science has created a racecourse in the field of outer space journey. We have forgotten the fact that the inner space journey is more important than the outer space journey. Many countries are in the process of extinction, and many more may be annihilated in the future due to nuclear weapons. There is no answer. Therefore, we have to see God directly.

God is nearer to you than your own body and mind. This is the meaning of incarnation of God in human form. God is not missing, but he is misunderstood. Our inner Guru teaches us meditative life, and meditation teaches us that the mother of all thought and speech is silence. Silence speaks a million words, and a million words speak nothing but silence. We have forgotten this truth. Our thoughts and speech are like plastic trees. They are beautiful but lifeless, because they do not originate from our meditative heart. They are borrowed from others as information. Therefore, they cannot create East-West unity and harmony.

What is the difference between prayer and meditation? Through prayer we talk to God, and through silent meditation God talks to us in answer to our prayers. Prayer is like cooking a meal, and meditation is like eating, digesting and assimilating that meal. In the class when the teacher talks, the students listen, and when the students ask questions, the teacher listens silently. This is the law of expression and communication in the form of dialogue. We have forgotten to listen, to have a dialogue with God. At present we have only monologue, a one-way communication.

The mind cannot work without spirit, and spirit cannot work without the mind in the universe of relativity. And God cannot reveal his Godhood in relativity unless mind and spirit work together in harmony. The Western countries represent mind, and the Eastern countries represent spirit. Mind without spirit is blind, and spirit without mind is lame. If a lame man rides on the shoulders of a blind man with sure feet, then both can safely reach their destination.

The main cause of world tension, crisis and bankruptcy is East-West disunity, mutual distrust and hatred, division of spirit and mind. Any talk which unites humankind in harmony is divine virtue. Pollution and nuclear war are threatening the entire planet. Mutual conflicts, confusion, lawlessness, jealousy and hatred are swelling like the ebbs and tides of the ocean to annihilate our whole existence. Now we need the incarnation of God which can create unity between East and West. That incarnation has to take place in your meditative heart. The time and the increasing fear of planetary annihilation demand it. Therefore now we need unity and marriage of all sciences and religions.

In modern times due to extreme, unfavorable and destructive situations, we need the spirit of Mahatma Gandhi which can liberate us from the present state of crisis, law-lessness and anarchy and unite us in global togetherness. In conclusion, may this conference be a beacon light to wipe out all types of crisis and pollution and to create unity, harmony, peace and happiness on earth and in heaven.[26]

Indu said the speech had caused quite a stir. Reporters, who had been standing bored at the back of the huge forum, had rushed to the stage with their cameras within the first minute of the talk. Their report was shown on the national weekend news which was fortunately videotaped by an Indian devotee in Copenhagen. He had invited them all to his home to see it. Of the three-minute broadcast allocated to the four-day conference, half of it documented Guruji's presentation. Scanning him from head to foot, including a close-up shot of his blue track shoes under his orange robe, they identified him as a real East-West Guru. The camera had then panned the front row to show his Western devotees. For a split second, Indu had seen herself on the screen. She then described to me another unusual experience with Guruji.

೫ * * * ೞ

The following day being their last in Copenhagen, Guruji wanted to take everyone to the museum. There was a particular exhibit he wanted them to see, one which he had seen during a previous visit. It was that of a "talking" bone. At the front gate, however, they found the museum to be closed on Mondays. An attendant, whose attention was drawn to the nine people standing outside the gate, came over to kindly inform them of the official hours. Hearing Guruji's desire to see the "talking" bone, to everyone's surprise, he opened the gates. "Wasn't he the Guru shown on the news?" the attendant wanted to know. With the affirmation that he was the same, the man eagerly offered his services to give a private tour. It was unfortunate, however, that the "talking" bone exhibit had been dismantled due to reconstruction in that part of the museum.

After being recognized a second time that day by a restaurateur, it seemed they had become celebrities. In truth, they did make quite a spectacle. One smallish, lean, bearded Indian man in orange robes followed by eight in Western dress. Inconspicuous they weren't. Exactly what was behind the "talking" bone, Indu never found out. It was to remain a mystery, no doubt something else that Guruji wanted to use to show them the way beyond the sense-perceived universe.

THIRTY-THREE

~

It was almost four o'clock in the afternoon and Indu was still sitting in the Grosvenor Hotel lounge. George had said he'd meet her at a quarter before five in front of the "Left Luggage" counter at Victoria Station, which was directly adjacent to this stately hotel establishment, open since 1862. After arriving at Victoria, Indu had seen the hotel lobby entrance while standing inside the main station terminal. This inviting hotel portal had lured her into the lounge where she had waited for the hours to pass. Nervous anxiety fluttered through her stomach. Soon her eyes would meet his again. As she waited, so many thoughts whirled through her mind, including the movie scene from *Out of Africa* where Karen Blixen confided to a male friend about being in love with someone he knew. She had been seeking his advice. The man's response to the confessed passion was an apt warning for anyone romantically entangled. He recited what had been written on the edge of maps when the world was thought to be flat: "Beyond this place there be dragons."

Maybe that was the mystery, the allure of being in love, Indu thought. Somehow by its power, love could carry one to the "edge." But beyond this point, only the courageous dared to go. Indu had already set her course. She was ready to meet her dragon. In the movie, Karen also reflected that perhaps the earth was made round so we would not see too far down the road. It was true, Indu could not see far ahead, but the memory of her first meeting with George was still vivid. What was it that had bonded them so immediately?

୫୦ * * * ଓଷ

She digressed for a moment to say that she really had been fascinated reading scientific research done on the phenomenon of "falling in love." She explained some of it to me now. A Federal grant of $84,000 had surprisingly been awarded to two women psychologists studying romance. A not-too-impressed senator had peevishly declared that at the top of the things we don't want to know is why a man falls in love with a woman. But the derisive remarks had not stopped one psychologist at Johns Hopkins University from suggesting that love had a distinctive physiological basis, that inside the brain could be found "love pathways." Another psychologist had defined romantic passion as "the obsessive, all-consuming passion for another person that strikes seemingly from nowhere and makes life a hell of uncertainty, punctuated by brief moments of ecstasy." The psychologist had found that the goal of this kind of passion was frequently not sexual consummation as such, but simply emotional union with the other. [27]

Indu had laughed when reading this, given her prodigiously unsuccessful attempts with George. The scientists had kindly exonerated them for their failure, documenting that romantic love and sex were not unalterably linked. Sex, said they, was a bodily function—and love, a state of mind, one that Plato had described as "the greatest of heaven's blessings."

Science, however, was challenging love's divine origin. Indu had kept this article from *The New York Times* which gave the following prosaic report:

"It is superfluous to send chocolates to a loved one. Love is enough. Or rather, it produces the same response. Better to send chocolates to a rejected lover, since love lost may drain the body's store of a potent mood-altering chemical that chocolate has in rich supply. In love, 'chemistry' has always had a mystical connotation, but there is apparently a real laboratory-bench chemistry to love as well. [...] Love brings on a giddy response comparable to an amphetamine high. [...] And the crash that follows breakup is much like an amphetamine withdrawal. The reason for the similarity [...] is that the loving brain pours out its own chemical correlate to amphetamine—phenylethylamine—while the spurned or disillusioned brain halts production of the substance and immediately begins to suffer from its absence."[28]

Indu had a challenge for the scientists. It was all well and good to claim that a chemical similar to amphetamine was produced in the brain by emotions of love, but much like the question of the chicken and the egg, she wondered, could they claim which came first, the chemical or the love? Still unanswered was her question: What had triggered the immediate bond she'd felt when first seeing George? That mystery had not been solved in the laboratory.

In her personal sparring over this question, I was amazed by her collection of quotes and clippings which she had continued adding to the gray folder as the years went by. Even more impressive was the fervor with which she recollected them. She was indeed a woman of passion, and one with scientific and literary appreciation. In proof of the last observation, she warmly read quotes from Hemingway and Chekhov, who among other notable authors had cultivated a fascination for the heart's folly.

In a laconic dialogue of Hemingway's, two lovers express the happiness and despair incited by their love:

"… It's a lot of fun, too, to be in love."

"Do you think so?" her eyes looked flat again.

"I don't mean fun that way. In a way it's an enjoyable feeling."

"No," she said, "I think it's hell on earth."

"It's good to see each other."

"No. I don't think it is."

"Don't you want to?"

"I have to." [29]

In Chekhov's tale, the unsuspecting hero has finally fallen in love. "He remembered recent conversations in Moscow in which he himself had taken part—long discussions in which it was affirmed that one could live without love, that passionate love is a psychosis, that there is no such love, but merely a physical attraction between the sexes—and all that sort of thing. Recalling these conversations he ruefully thought that if anyone were to ask him now what love was, he would be at a loss for an answer." [30]

And so it was much the same for Indu as she awaited her reunion with George. She knew she had to see him, and she was at a total loss to understand why.

৪০ * * * ৫৪

She'd brushed her hair, put on fresh lipstick, and given herself a shrewd examination in the mirror of the hotel's ladies' room. Would he think she had changed? Would he have changed? She stood at the place where they were to meet, watching the crowd pass around her, wanting to spot him first, to see his eyes searching hers. Suddenly at a distance a well-dressed man walked into the station: tailored suit, medium height, dark hair.

"Oh my, could that be him?" With a sophistication, an assuredness in his gait, he disappeared around the corner. It was not. How could she have thought it was? A creeping concern shadowed her heart.

They'd written, they'd talked on the phone, they'd tried to span distance and time, but relatively speaking, they had been living in two separate worlds. These two worlds were about to come together, to merge, to exist as one. What had ever made her think it possible?

It was natural that she should be apprehensive. It was after all not logic but love that had brought her to stand where she was that very moment, in the middle of London, in the middle of Victoria Station, in front of "Left Luggage." And that love was far removed from any relative plane. The moment she had seen him in front of the brick archway, she had loved him. Where was the relativity?

જી * * * ૭૩

It was an exciting moment in her story, but again she paused to interject the real point she was trying to make. Reading from her notebook, she shared the following which Guruji had related:

"Someone had once asked Einstein, 'What's the meaning of relativity?'

"He had replied, 'I cannot tell. You have to know mathematics before I can tell. But suppose when you talk to your beloved, how do you pass your time?'

"The man answered, 'One night passes like one minute. I'm so happy. I'm angry with the sun rising in the morning.'

"Einstein then asked, 'Suppose you touch a hot plate, how will you pass that time?'

"The man responded, 'One second will seem like a year.'

"Einstein said, 'That is relativity.'

"Guruji gave us this definition: 'Relativity is time and space as our senses perceive it.' And as already evident, the senses will deceive us. No wonder the world can seem a crazy, mixed-up place. I'll tell you another one of Guruji's stories which drives this point home.

"A man was making a great sound in his mouth. Someone asked him, 'What are you doing to make so much sound?'

"The man said, 'I am chewing chickpeas raw.'

"The other man asked, 'Show me the chickpeas.'

"But the man said, 'Well, you see actually they are imaginary chickpeas.'

"The other man retorted, 'In that case, why don't you chew imaginary halva?'"

She said many would laugh, but all the while recognizing the reliance we have on our senses is just as ridiculous.

And she read the words of her Guru as he elaborated further: "Our problems are not real. If there is a chair hanging from the ceiling, then you can always pull it down. But if the chairs are imaginary, then how can you pull them down? It's like chewing imaginary chickpeas. Our problems are just like those imaginary chickpeas. We live in a fantasyland, the land of relativity, and this makes us neurotic. Do you know who the neurotic man is? He is one who builds castles in the air. And the psychotic is the man who lives in those castles. And the one who collects the rent is the psychiatrist.

"So what is the purpose of the body and mind? They are to enjoy the relative world, not to enjoy heaven. You cannot see God through your eyes or smell him with your nose. You cannot think God either. I will tell you another story. A man purchased a mantra for $150. After a short time, he decided to sell it second-hand for $125, just used but relatively still new."

Again more laughter would follow, but Indu knew that the absurdity was the very reflection of their lives. In truth, relativity was within time and space. Oneness with God, Reality, was beyond relativity. But how to reach this oneness? The job of the Guru was to help us find the answer.

From her notebook she also read this quote attributed to Houdini, "Limits of any kind are illusion," and Guruji had said, "Our illusions are relative." She easily extrapolated from this that beyond limits was beyond the senses, was beyond time and space, was beyond relativity, and that was where one would find oneness with God. And what was God but pure love?

ℰ * * * ℭ

Was her love for George pure and unconditional? She pondered on this as she stood waiting in the station. There was no easy answer to this question. She remembered Guruji's advice in Copenhagen—"Watch"—and she suddenly made the connection to something Guruji had once said, "To watch, you must be the witness. If we are acting with our senses then we cannot be the witness, because through sensory perception we become identified with the doing. We then become the agent, not the witness. The doer cannot be the witness. The doer is the one who suffers, mentally and physically. The witness never suffers."

Guruji's guidance was clear. She should go beyond language, beyond senses, beyond all activity of the ego, and watch. Only then would her love be pure and beyond relativity. The key word was desire, because the witness has no desire. If there was desire in her heart, desire to see, to hold, to love George, then most assuredly she was in the realm of relativity. That being the case, she sorely suspected a roller-coaster ride was about to begin, the "up" and the "down." She again saw in her mind's eye the two words written with the "X" in between.

If only she could remember to watch.

"Indu?" His voice was behind her. She turned around to see George.

"I didn't even hear you come up," she said. Her eyes were fixed on his. Was this the man she so adored? He looked tired and pale, although still characteristically handsome. She wondered if he was well. "How are you?" she asked.

"I'm doing quite fine. No complaints to speak of." He gave no indication that anything was amiss. She looked closely into his eyes again. Yes, the same feeling of recognition began vibrating in her heart, just as it had when he'd unobtrusively juggled past her at Ickwell. Then, he had been tan and radiantly healthy after juggling two hundred miles. Now, the toll of studying and working wore heavily on his appearance, as well as whatever strain he may have felt on seeing her again.

There was an awkward hesitation between them as they stood face to face looking at each other. Their separation had lasted for eleven months. The embrace which followed, however, revealed a deep passion surging in both of them. As much as she wanted to hide it and as desperately as he may have been trying to fight it, their attachment was as powerful as it had been a year ago. But they did not speak of it; they did not whisper endearing words to each other. After the moment had passed, judging by their outward behavior, one would have thought they were but ordinary friends.

He helped her collect her luggage and led the way toward the street exit. As they walked along, he asked her about the Denmark trip and she asked him about his job, and about his exam. She remembered the city blocks going by but she saw virtually nothing around her. All she knew was that George was next to her, a man who was in one sense almost a stranger and yet in another the very pulse of her existence. This dichotomy seemed as much a puzzle to him, the fact betrayed by a long sideways glance her way with darkly searching eyes. He had not meant for her to see it, but when their eyes met unexpectedly, he had quietly said, "I still can't believe you're here."

"I can't either." They had walked on in silence.

Oliver's flat was located about five blocks from the station. George finally stopped at a black wrought-iron fence. He motioned through its gate which opened down into a narrow cement L-shaped staircase. Cautious with her footing at the stairs' bend, she found herself standing in front of a high-gloss royal blue painted door guarded by a large clay pot filled with pink, red and white impatiens. George followed behind with her suitcase balanced on his head. He unlocked the door and they entered the flat. Turning immediately to the left, she walked down a long hallway, passing first a bedroom and then a bathroom, both off to the left. At the end of the hall was a sitting room beyond which lay the kitchen. It was sparsely furnished. Oliver had lived there for only six months. But it had a coziness. George set her bags down and went over to open French doors leading out to a private patio, the main advantage of having a basement flat. Before much time had passed, Oliver arrived home from work.

He welcomed her graciously. She felt an ease with him which she hadn't really noticed on their first meeting, the lunch in Berkeley Square. She presented him with two gifts, a package of orange hand-dipped candles from Copenhagen and a box of liqueur-filled chocolates which she'd bought at the duty-free shop in the airport. The big smile and hug that he gave her guaranteed their friendship.

There was no other special celebration of her arrival. The two men prepared dinner and then George commenced his ironing. It was as though he wanted to pretend that it was just an ordinary day. Indu sat watching him iron while they talked. She was keenly aware that he had a defensive reserve about him. He had let it slip for but a moment as they walked from the station, but a moment was long enough for her to see beyond it and, undaunted by it now, she could only wonder why he persisted in keeping it up. The truth came out that night as they curled up to share the small daybed in the sitting room.

There was another woman in his life at that moment, an involvement of six weeks, one he had not yet ended even after finding out about Indu's London visit. Indu had never been so physically close and yet so emotionally distant from anyone. It was hardly a romantic night, nor were the days that followed. The phone calls between the two lovers made her first week with him excruciatingly painful. Until seeing Indu again, it seems he had not known how he was going to handle her visit emotionally. It was a clear sign to Indu that he was not as sure about the feelings in his heart as she was of her own. Seeing himself as a bachelor in his prime, he had been preparing to balk at any harness leading to wedlock. But Indu held no harness in hand, only her love. Run as he might try, he could not deny the power it held over him, a power which would wreak havoc on his emotional certainty about anything during the weeks ahead. What he quickly realized was that no pretext of attachment to the other woman could be sustained. The brief alliance was terminated. Again the intensity of his inexplicable bond with Indu had pulled him away from yet another maiden.

She could hardly be angry with George for his philandering. They had made no commitment of fidelity. He must have doubted whether her encounter with Mark had been merely platonic. What was evident to both was the inescapable magnetic attraction of their souls. Deny it they could not, but dealing with it was another matter. And oppositely charged as magnets are, they can repel as well as attract, depending on which ends are paired. The very intensity of that magnetism was to set the erratic pace of the roller-coaster ride.

During her entire visit of seven weeks, extended an additional four over the original three planned, sharing that one twin bed, their romantic, intimate interludes numbered only three. This attested once again to the fact that theirs was not a physical infatuation. Although loving to snuggle next to him, she had to admit that night after night, half asleep and pinned between him and the wall, struggling to keep her share of the covers, was hardly conducive to restful sleep or romance. The accumulative exhaustion that crept up on both of them probably played a more significant role than either realized in the dynamics of their relationship. This was borne out by the fact that on the two weekends when Oliver was gone overnight, instead of relishing the privacy, they had collapsed on the two separate beds, obviously desperate to garner as much undisturbed sleep as possible.

George and Oliver would leave for work in the morning after juggling in and out of the bathroom for a hot bath and shave. Indu rarely bothered to get up until they were out the door. She would then dress and tidy the flat, after which she would head off to the libraries. She was determined to follow up on the promise she had made to herself to investigate the mystery of the prehistoric stones. The first step had been to trace the *New Scientist* articles. Making several inquiries, she had found them in the Science Reference Building of the British Library, located on Southampton Street.

ℴ * * * ℳ

She told me the essence of the articles was concerned with the existence of an "Earth energy." The authors supported their speculations with hard scientific data, ultrasonic intensity graphs and radioactivity charts. Although they admitted that "Earth energy" remained a mystical rather than mechanical concept, their data gave proof to anomalously high and anomalously low levels of several forms of radiation emitted by the stones. The fact that the emissions had cyclical variations argued against the existence of a fixed source of radioactivity. They questioned whether the activity they measured was due to radioactivity at all. Their equipment was not sensitive enough to distinguish between the radiation from a radioactive substance and other sources of electrons, called "exoelectrons." But they could give no explanation why such "exoelectrons" should be emitted at the ancient sites. Another mystery was the detection of ultrasonic pulsing, rapid and regular, recorded from a standing stone outside but near a stone circle. They wondered if the pulsing could be coming from stresses in a nearby fault, a well-documented phenomenon. But when they monitored the fault line, they found nothing distinguishable from background levels. Even next to a radio transmitter, they could not obtain the same regular pulsing as at the stone.[31]

Confronted with these mysteries, one scientist proposed that if there really was some significance to the location of the stone circles themselves, and if the significance was undetectable by the five senses, then the next parameter to check would be alterations in the magnetic field of the area. By measuring the fluctuations in the local magnetic field, they did delineate distinct lines of energy, which they called "ley lines," the most interesting point being that the lines converged on the geometric center of the stone circle they were examining. They further detected an unusual magnetic pattern inside the circle, a pattern in the form of a seven-ring spiral itself delineated by high and low magnetic areas. Another peculiarity was that the intensity of the field within the stone circle was significantly lower than that measured outside. It was as if the stones were shielding the area, as the "talking stone" article had described.

Stepping out of the strict scientific arena, the scientists had invited a "sensitive," someone with paranormal perception, to examine the site. She worked by reacting to tingling sensations in the hands and reported tingling exactly where the recording magnetometer had produced its blips on the chart. The perfect correlation between her feelings and the instrument showed that humans could have a magnetic sense, much like the homing instincts that many animals possess. Was it possible, they concluded, that mankind could be attuned to the earth's magnetic field and that the ancients knew exactly what they were doing when they formed stone circles to create a magnetic shield?[32]

Indu then reached for her notebook to read something from Guruji. "The Bible is telling a science," he had declared, "the science of the vibration of energy, not of theology. 'In the beginning was the Word'...* What do they mean by 'Word?' 'Word' is vibration of energy, vibration of light. We have the body of matter, the body of electricity, the body of mind, the body of understanding and the body of cosmic consciousness. Only one body dies. The other four do not die. You can feel the

---

* John 1:1 (AV).

body of pulsation, electricity, consciousness and cosmic consciousness. This is the ocean of radio waves."

There was a strikingly similar ring between the two, the scientific findings and the words of a mystic, both talking of energy, of electromagnetic waves. "We have forgotten how to go beyond time and space," Guruji had said. Indu wondered if the ancients had known how. This was the "science" that Guruji was teaching, how to go beyond. It was not natural time and space that he was concerned with but psychological time and space. It was the "psychic atom" he was trying to break, not the physical one. And when it breaks, what happens? He gave the hint: "Deep in the tiny atom of psyche lies hidden a tremendous force [...]."[33]

Another report came to Indu's mind concerning a religious relic. She asked if I knew about the Shroud of Turin. In a documentary on the life of Jesus, the narrator had described that the aura of a spiritual person expands twenty to thirty feet, creating a powerful radiation around the body. He had speculated that the radiation intensity around Jesus' body may have caused the imprint on the shroud. Where did that radiation come from? It was a paradigm of mysticism.

"Could one of the downfalls of modern civilization be the intolerance of the mystical?" Indu pondered with me. She again quoted Guruji: "Our religions have lost the mysticism in them and Truth cannot be told by any mind."

THIRTY-FOUR

~

In recounting to me certain episodes with George, Indu reflected on how she and George had had such little time together before finding themselves suddenly living side by side. She may have known some essence of his spirit, but it was true, there were facets of his nature as a man which were foreign to her. She wanted to know the man that he was just as she wanted him to know the intricacies of her own nature. But it was not easy for them. She had come without invitation and found another woman in his life. He was adrift, waiting for an exam mark and wondering what to do with the love that was between them. Inevitably, in trying to sort through their feelings and needs, with limited time, in limited space, there were moments when they appeared as two ships narrowly avoiding collision as they sailed past each other. That two people might disagree over certain matters is not unusual. But it was the intensity of their disagreements that surprised both Indu and George.

ℰ○ * * * ℂℬ

He asked her after one storm had passed, "Have you argued like this in other relationships?"

She thought a moment and then replied, "No."

"Well, I have," he said. "For some reason, I thought it would be different with you."

It was a myth she hardly wanted to perpetuate. By her "no," she had really meant that every encounter with him was special, no matter what emotion was shared. But just because she followed in the footsteps of a spiritual teacher, it didn't mean she wouldn't express her feelings in a manner appropriate to circumstances, and if it meant staunchly sticking to her guns over an issue about which she held firm beliefs, she would challenge the staunchest of opposition. In other words, she could be terribly hard-headed, of which she was quite aware.

But if his cool analytical exterior was blocking his heart from hearing hers, as she sometimes perceived it, she had no compunction about letting the waves ride high between them. She, in fact, wanted to see how they could bear the turbulence, knowing rough water could be at any bend in a marriage. What struck her was that George viewed their battles with regret whereas she viewed them as a necessary process for testing the practical as opposed to the ethereal bounds of their love. She never had any regrets, and after faring the worst, she always felt a greater understanding was gained. It was the last point to which George was sensitive. By his thinking, their thunderous upheavals in trying to reconcile seeming incongruities made him doubt how high a regard she could hold for him personally.

Their first stormy encounter occurred during her second week there. It was on a Saturday. Oliver and his girlfriend, Penny, and George and Indu decided to go on a picnic. The morning was bright and sunny, not that it was a guarantee that raindrops wouldn't descend in the next thirty minutes. But the warmth lured them out. They stopped at a delicatessen and purchased two French baguettes, several cheeses, a pâté, fruit, a cucumber, a bottle of wine and a bottle of sparkling water. Oliver packed it all into his knapsack. When he donned the pack, the bread stuck out on both sides, and everyone, including Oliver, enjoyed his comical appearance.

Weaving the Polo adeptly through the streets of London, George finally delivered them at the entrance of Kew Gardens, officially known as the Royal Botanic Gardens, among the most celebrated in the world. Started in 1759 by the mother of George III, they now covered three hundred acres. Since 1841 they had been open to the public.

Hungry, they located a sheltered picnic table and spread newspaper as a tablecloth. Their bounty before them, they tore the bread, broke the cheese, and filled and refilled the small glasses George had brought along for the occasion. It was a style of picnicking which to Indu was classically European. She sat absorbed in the novelty, *sans* potato chips, sandwiches and soft drinks.

The rain did come, but lasted only minutes and they felt not a drop under the shelter's protection. By the time they were finished, the sky was bright and blue again. They headed off to explore the majesty of the gardens, George serenading them on his *mbira*, an African "thumb piano" made of tuned metal slats set on a resonator and, as its name indicated, plucked with the thumbs. It was on this instrument that the witchdoctor had given George instruction. The lessons had paid off. Walking at his side, she was enchanted. It was unusually pleasing music, after an unusually delicious lunch, in an unusually beautiful garden.

The otherworldliness of it all transported her soul. Her body and mind seemed affected as well. She admitted to George after climbing a spiral staircase inside one of the domed Victorian greenhouses that her heart was virtually racing. He felt her pulse and suggested she sit down but she walked on in a daze. It was in this condition that she became aware of a presence. She would vehemently deny that she could see into the realm of the ethereal. But she would not deny that that realm could reveal itself to even the most ordinary person, in a vision, in a sound, in any number of ways.

Walking with George along an aesthetically winding path, she was silent as she bore witness to the ethereal visitor. It was a little girl of three, with dark curly hair, brown eyes and olive skin, adorned in a pink frilled dress. Indu was captivated. "Is this someone I know?" she wondered. "Is this someone I will know?" It occurred to her who it might be, her daughter with George, even now enjoying her parents' stroll through the park.

"What are you thinking?" George asked, possibly sensing her distraction. Indu's mesmerized, starry expression must have provoked the question. Or was he feeling an agitation, tantalized by the seraphic one?

Indu felt a sudden guarded hesitation. To tell of a mystical vision was inherently unwise. This she knew. Might not Joan of Arc have lived beyond her nineteen years if she'd not told of the voices? "But why should I fear ridicule at the hands of one loved so dearly?" she thought.

"Do you really want to know what was in my mind?" she asked George, hedging further before describing her vision.

"Of course, what's going on in that pretty head of yours?"

"George, I saw this little girl walking with us. I'm wondering if she might not be ours." His first thought was not that she was fanatic. His reaction took her by surprise.

"Our child? Well, there's no way she's mine. I have to tell you, Indu, I think the possibility is remote."

He wasn't about to question or deny what she had seen, but he waited not a second to refute that the child had anything to do with him. "George, what are you saying? You mean you don't think there's even the slightest possibility that we could have a child, that we could marry?"

"All I'm saying is that at this point in my life, I don't see marriage in the immanent future." What he grasped from her "vision" was that she was suddenly holding a "bridle." Indu felt his blunt denial of wedlock was too calculated. It was as if he had been lying in wait to dispel any ideas in her head about it.

Blunt as a bullet, his retort left her stunned. She didn't think she deserved such harsh treatment. It contradicted all the unspoken feelings that had passed between them since their meeting, and it made the whole point of her visit absurd.

"George, do you remember ever saying, 'I don't know how I can live without you?' That's what you said when we parted a year ago."

"I do remember and it was a silly thing to say."

"And the feelings we have for each other, are they silly, too?"

"No. They're perfectly normal feelings to exist between a man and a woman."

"And they mean nothing more to you?"

"Indu, I'm not denying what's between us. I'm only saying that right now I can't make any future plans based on these feelings."

"Then there's not much point of my staying, is there?" Indu meant every word. She would leave immediately. On the ride home, she didn't say a word. Oliver and Penny had no difficulty discerning that trouble was at hand, and upon arriving back at the flat, they quickly departed again for another engagement, or such was their excuse.

Indu's scheduled return flight was still a week away, but she'd decided in the car that she had enough money to spend a week at a hotel on the English Channel in Brighton, a hotel she had heard about before leaving the States. Still without a word to George, she left the flat to take a walk. She needed to think.

When she returned, she hardly expected to see George very near to tears. She was again stunned. Which was she to believe, his words or his deeply stricken face? But seeing tears in his eyes brought tears to her own, and her anger melted. It had not been her intention to back him into a corner of commitment, and he had not meant to repudiate the intensity of their love. The certainty of their future was not as important to her as the greatness of her passion for the man before her. Her ground-shaking silence was broken. Their first argument had passed. With great relief, they celebrated with dinner out.

Oddly, the second storm was similarly related. Sadly, it occurred just after their first intimate interlude. Even though they had slept side by side every night, they had refrained from intimacy until almost her third week. But the wisdom of it was obvious. The real dilemma confronting them was their deep attachment. Their passion for each other existed beyond physical desire, and the dilemma was what to do about it. George could give a litany of reasons why he was not ready for matrimony, but his love for Indu no doubt shook the tree of self-complacency under which he stood. Indu, on the other hand, was battling with her tradition-laden images of establishing home and family with the man she loved and with having to make an uneasy truce with time until she could figure out which direction karma and destiny were going. It was precarious for both of them and making love, they knew, would tempt to confound an already confused situation. But once caught in love's throes, there was nothing they could do but weather the emotional tempest that followed.

They lay close, his arm cradling her neck, their bodies warm and dewy. His eyes closed, she looked across his chest and admired as she often had the black curls of hair that adorned it. "Will I ever feel a greater peace, a deeper contentment that I feel right now after loving this man with my body and soul?" she wondered. The only complication in that moment was the imprudent absence of any barrier to pregnancy. George had not asked this time. Gazing at him, she pondered how he dared take such a risk, adamant as he was against making any commitment. The risk had been equal for her and yet for the first time, she felt at ease, thinking no greater blessing could come than a child from him. Such a child she would welcome with all her heart, but how sad for it to be brought into the world without both parents being equally joyful.

"George," she whispered.

"Mmmm," came a groggy response.

"You know, we really should think of using birth control next time."

His eyes popped open. "What do you mean? I took precaution. I withdrew in time."

"But George, there's always a chance sperm will make it out before. Everyone knows withdrawal is the most unreliable method of contraception. And this wasn't particularly one of the safest days for me."

"You didn't tell me it wasn't safe."

"You didn't ask, you know. It's only my eighth day, but it certainly isn't inconceivable that it could happen."

"You mean there's a chance you could become pregnant? My God!"

"I don't think I will be, George. I'm only saying we should keep something on hand for protection."

"I don't like to use anything. I've never used anything."

"Oh, that's great. You always leave the burden on the woman to do something, is that it? It's her problem. And what if she does get pregnant, some lady you're with? Then what did you plan to do?"

"Well, she wouldn't have the baby, that's for sure. Not if I had any say about it."

"So you just naturally assume that a woman will trot off and get an abortion. Well, that's jolly fine for you. Do you have any idea what kind of hell it is to have to go through something like that, physically, emotionally, mentally? How can you be so pragmatically cold-blooded? Didn't you even think about the pain you'd be inflicting on her? George, you knew I wasn't taking any precautions. You know I'm not on the pill. You know I didn't stop to insert anything, yet you went right ahead, never bothering even to ask. So what happens if I am pregnant?"

"Well, I can't marry you, Indu. I've made that as clear as I can."

"If I'm pregnant, I can tell you I'm not about to abort. And if you don't want it, I won't bother to tell you about it either."

"No, I'd want to know."

"That's too bad. You've just given up your rights to it."

With that, he exploded "Damn it all," and leaped out of bed, pulled on clothes, and stormed out of the flat.

It was two o'clock in the morning. Indu lay quiet and still, wondering how much of their argument Oliver had overheard. She hated the thought of having disturbed him in the middle of the night. What hurt her most was the unspoken implication from George that she would use pregnancy to trap him. It was her own fear of pregnancy which had made her speak about it in the first place. She couldn't deny that she would love a child from him, but it wouldn't be done like this. She had her standards and they didn't include blackmail to get a husband. Her blood began to boil at the thought. But after a few minutes another thought came.

"If only I can convince George that I'm not trying to press him, or trick him, or force him in any way. He must trust me that much or else there's no hope. He may have felt threatened and exploded because of it. Somehow we must come to trust each other and to hold each other's welfare even dearer than our own."

She got up and dressed and went out to wait on the steps for George to come home. She wanted to tell him those exact thoughts. She snuggled under a wool sweater against the cool air and waited for what seemed like a long time. Finally, she heard quick footsteps coming toward her. It was George. She hoped they could resolve everything then and there. But he didn't stop. He brushed past her, going down the stairs and into the flat.

She felt sadly alone. "How can he not want to work through this? He's feeling threatened and it's all for nothing. I only wanted to tell him that. I'm not looking to trap him. But if he wants to play silent, I can be silent, too. Let's see how far that gets us. Maybe time is what is needed anyway." She sat for another fifteen minutes in the cool night air trying hard to make sense of the situation. When she did go back inside, she found it ironic that her only choice was to climb over him and curl up on her side of the bed next to the wall. Sleep came quickly, though, for there was no more anger in her heart. She saw the problem. Real trust was missing. Either they came to terms with that, or else the relationship was finished.

The silence between them lasted two long days. Inwardly, she felt content to wait until George was ready to talk. "Why pressure the poor fellow further?" she thought. George was apparently doing a lot of thinking of his own, and late on the second night, he came to sit next to her on the bed. She was in her nightgown, ready to spend another silent night next to him.

"Indu, if you think I'm such a terrible, unfeeling human being, selfish and self-centered, then why do you bother to stay?" he asked in a quiet, sadly reserved tone.

"George, I don't think you're any of those things. I was only questioning what we were both doing taking such a risk. I love who you are, and that hasn't changed. And a part of love is accepting the other person's fears and anger. But more important than even that is trusting in the heart of the other. George, I do trust in your heart. I do. And you must trust in mine."

"God, Indu, I can get so confused sometimes, I feel like a little boy."

"George, I don't want to leave you, not unless you want me to."

"No. I want you to stay."

This had been a big one, and somehow they had come through it. But even so, nerves would be struck which would make flippant comments become volatile invectives. Indu might have regretted the next angry confrontation except for its touching outcome. She would have regretted it because it was an absurd argument over the purchase of a box of tissues.

George had chastised her, "Indu, you claim to be on such a tight budget and yet you go out and buy a box of tissues when loo paper would do just as well."

At first, Indu tried to make a joke of it. But George's critical tone finally broke her humor. "Look, this box cost forty-nine pence. A single roll of loo paper costs thirty pence. Now assuming one box provides the same number of blows for my nose as one roll, we're talking about a difference of twenty pence. That's hardly anything to make a federal case of. But if you're going to be that hard-nosed about it, I'd thank you not to use a single one. And if you're going to start adding up my pennies, let me tell you that when you run to that little market across the road to buy Imperial Soap, you're paying at least ten pence more than you would if you bought the soap at the grocery or a regular drug store. You don't know how much I've saved by carefully shopping. I'll also have you know I bought one of the cheapest boxes I could find." He had definitely offended her dignity to suggest she deny herself the luxury of a tissue. But even as she listened to herself, she couldn't believe what she was saying. She'd let anger get the better of her, and it was over something which should have remained a joke, a testy one perhaps, but nonetheless a joke. And to refuse him a single tissue could not have sounded more childish, and was itself an offense to her dignity.

But once it was said and done, and they'd had a moment to repent the silliness of their quarrel, George came up and took her by the shoulders. "We can both be goons sometimes, can't we?" he said with tender affection.

Still feeling defensive, she replied, "But George, you started it, for goodness' sake. And so much fuss over just pennies."

"I know, I know. Let's not start again," he said cajolingly, her pouting eyes showing her remorse. He looked at her squarely and intently appealed, "Don't you know when you're unhappy, I'm unhappy?" The olive branch was passed.

Indu gave him a resigned smile, but his words moved her more deeply than he would ever know. In retrospect, she could see that he must have had concern for the expense she was paying to be with him. His own financial situation being unsteady as it was, he was in no position to offer much support. That anxiety could have put him on the defensive and made his words sound sharper than intended.

෨ * * * ෫

Before giving me another example of how tenuous the dynamic could be between them, Indu noted that it is the underlying psychology that weaves its way into every human interaction that can disrupt the verbal message. Yet at the moment of exchange, differentiating the silent, psychological message from the spoken one is a task trained professionals find challenging. Even for the one speaking, it is not always easy to avoid evasive rationalizing and aloofness, especially when hidden fears and inner turmoil are present. Mixed messages are notorious for fueling frustrations in relationships. As hard as they were both trying to be clear and open with each other, Indu and George had had their share of turmoil trying to sort through each other's jargon to find the hidden feelings behind the words.

෨ * * * ෫

George sat on the bed and sententiously informed her, "I'm afraid you're going to feel left out this weekend. I'm going to be spending it with my father. He's in London for the week on business."

Half in jest, she responded, "I think I am going to feel excluded if you're not going to introduce me to your father."

Standing up, stolid resolution in his eyes, he tossed back the words, "Well, you can just work on it today."

Chalk was now on their toes, for they were standing far too close to the line separating jest from jab. George was out the door of the flat before Indu could dust off the proverbial chalk. She was not so much angry as hurt. Taking a pen and notepad, she began writing, mainly to have an outlet for the feelings that were welling up inside of her.

℘ * * * ℭ

Indu never gave this letter to George, although she'd saved it in the same gray folder with all the other letters to him. She showed it to me now. It had served its purpose to help her work through her feelings and see more clearly behind George's serrated jocosity. She had written:

Dear George,

I desperately want to express something but am having difficulty even knowing where to start. But if I don't say something now when the moment is at hand, the hurt feelings I have will be harbored inside only to resurface at another time in possibly a totally irrelevant way.

I keep wondering if the situation were reversed whether you would not feel the same as I do now; you staying with me under somewhat precarious circumstances and I turning to you and saying, "Well, my dear, I'm afraid you're going to be on your own this weekend because I'm going to be spending it exclusively with a family member/relative/ friend whom I haven't seen in a long time."

And you say half jokingly, "Gosh, I am going to feel left out."

And I reply in the same half-joking voice, "You'll just have to deal with the anxiety you have about being excluded and come to terms with it by yourself."

I can't help feeling that you're the one who has the anxiety about me meeting your father. Instead of acknowledging it, you've chosen to make glib remarks and try to find excuses to avoid the whole encounter. And if I should eventually meet your father, then what should you say my name is? When you only know me by one name, it seems a bit of a funny question. But I'm not totally unsympathetic to your predicament since I know that with the name "Indu" needs to come some kind of explanation: spiritual path, Guru, devotion. It can be a bit much on the first meeting. I think we need to discuss this together instead of you totally shutting me out, which is what I feel. I can't imagine leaving you out of any gathering I would have with a family member or relative, particularly if it were my parents.

Why are you so embarrassed to introduce a woman you love to your father? This same question entered my head when you hesitated to have me meet your work colleagues. It seems the woman you love is almost an invasion into a certain part of your life which you want to keep private.

We talked about having respect for each other's differences in dealing with things and I do have respect for your preference that I not meet your father at this time. I only wish you could have expressed it in such a way that would not have left me feeling third person out.

I remember you saying that you know you're negligent at times in responding with a note to thank someone for in-

viting you for a lovely weekend/holiday/occasion. But because of their great love for you, you feel they can forgive
your transgressions and must know anyway that you are
grateful and appreciative. Love is forgiving, but at the same
time it needs careful nurturing and protection. It needs to
be treated like a baby, because in expressing love, a very
vulnerable side of the heart/body/soul is exposed. Please
don't make the wrong assumption that because I love you,
my heart can tolerate any action on your part. My love
wants to understand, to help, to make amends, but it cannot tolerate insensitivity. My heart cringes at mistreatment
by your hand, even if it's unintentional. The moment I felt
slighted this morning, I immediately felt my energy pulling away from you. Again it seems we've gotten out of tune
with each other.

I respect most sincerely your desire to keep this weekend,
the first you've had with your father in many months, separate from events in your personal life. I can only wish that
a little more care for my feelings could have been given.

Love, Indu

&) * * * C8

When he returned an hour later after doing some shopping,
she put the question to him directly. Was he feeling shy about
introducing a lady friend to his father, especially one with a
strange name and unusual background? He admitted there
was some truth to her suspicion. She suggested a compromise,
that he could introduce her as Elizabeth. At least that might
help eliminate any heavy discussion of religion or beliefs. Just
as he was feeling comfortable with the idea, the phone rang. It
was his father.

As she listened to their conversation, she was ready to
swear that his father was psychic. He was calling to confirm the afternoon meeting with his son and in the ensu-
ing discussion actually inquired if there was a girlfriend

in praesenti. Upon hearing that one did exist, he had immediately suggested his son should bring her along. The problem was solved. They had steered through troubled water yet again.

THIRTY-FIVE

~

Indu continued to ponder the source of her connection to George. In what past era had their souls met previously? Had they clashed so frequently then—had they loved as intensely?

"Why am I so utterly convinced that dying does not separate us from the one we love? [...] We're no more separated by death than we're separated by life! [...] We shall forever return to the arms of those we love, whether our parting be overnight or overdeath."[34] These words of Richard Bach's had also landed in her notebook and for Indu they gave the quintessential answer to the question of why she'd had to see George again. Her "undying" love from some time long ago had requisitioned it. It was the only explanation which she felt could resolve their connection. It was firmly based on the belief in transmigration of the soul, wherein a former incarnation can have a determining influence on the next, the purpose of the cyclical process being to propel one toward the goal of final liberation or God realization, when the individual soul merges with the Absolute.

"But isn't this what happens at death anyway?" I asked her.

"What is death?" She brightly countered my question. "Listen to this," she said, having pulled from her file yet another *New York Times* article. It was entitled "Where Uncertainty Is King and Paradox Shares Throne," a compelling title for an article reviewing recent scientific studies on entrapment of atoms. She read:

> As atoms in a trap get colder and colder and slower and slower, so the [Bose-Einstein condensation] theory goes,

they will spontaneously collapse into the same quantum state. In a way, they will all merge into one another. [...]

A physicist says they collapse into the same spatial wave function. In a sense, that means these thousands or millions of atoms are all in the same place, except that the notion of place has lost its meaning.

A golden and notorious principle of quantum mechanics is Werner Heisenberg's uncertainty principle, which dictates, among other things, that a particle's velocity and position can never be precisely measured together. These two pieces of knowledge sit at opposite ends of a seesaw. When the precision of one measurement rises, that of the other must fall.

If an atom becomes very slow, the uncertainty about its velocity becomes very small. [The velocity of any slow-moving object can hardly raise much question.] So the uncertainty about its position grows. [That is the paradox.] The atom can be anywhere in a large piece of space. And for some purposes that means the atom is everywhere in that large piece of space. [...]

As the notions of place and size get fuzzy, so does the even more fundamental notion of identity, especially when Bose-Einstein condensation takes place. When atoms start to merge, they start to be the same in more ways than one.[35]

We can do research on atoms, Indu had continued, but how to do research on the quantum nature of the soul, quantum being an individual unit of energy? If atoms can be anywhere and everywhere, if their very identity can become fuzzy, if they can merge into one another, why can't the soul do the same, merge into a greater oneness, and must there be death for this to happen?

"You can doubt the presence of God, but you cannot doubt the presence of matter and energy," Indu read Guruji's statement from her notebook. It was one he made often as he reminded them that by means of the mind there was an exchange going on between the two: "thought" being matter, and "no thought" transforming matter into pure energy.

Guruji's approach was very scientific. It was ironic that the scientists had to admit that the fundamental state of matter involved paradoxes and "uncertainty principles." How then can we expect easy answers to the deeper questions of life and death, of transmigration, of the reality of the soul? If quantum physics is baffling, how to make sense of quantum metaphysics? Referencing the article she had just read, Indu summed it up by saying that even Einstein, one of the greatest quantum theorists, was so unnerved by the paradoxes of "hard reality giving way to fuzzy probability" and "uncertainty replacing certainty" that he exclaimed, "In that case, I would rather be a cobbler, or even an employee in a gaming house, than a physicist!"[36]

So what of the question of death?

"I suppose," Indu admitted, "we won't know until we're there."

But opening files, she pulled out this quote from Hemingway: "I tried to breathe but my breath would not come and I felt myself rush bodily out of myself and out and out and out and all the time bodily in the wind. I went out swiftly, all of myself, and I knew I was dead and that it had all been a mistake to think that you just died. Then I floated, and instead of going on I felt myself slide back."[37]

She had a wonderful quote from Guruji in which he had further added to the paradoxes of life and death by saying, "We die and are reborn until we come to understand who we are. We start from where we get up... An ignorant man understands, 'I am the body, I am the mind.' A wise man understands, 'I have a body, I have a mind.' We are here to know who we are. We are going up and up. But it is a long journey. Deeper than the ocean. You cannot cross the ocean by swimming. You must take a jet, and that jet is meditation on 'Who am I?' Then you will find you are beyond body and mind. Meditation is like death. In both you have to leave behind body and mind."

Indu and I agreed that the picture of existence was not a simple one. So it was not surprising that in trying to understand her connection to George, she'd had to accept the uncertainty of her future with him, and the paradox that anger, frustration and confusion could coexist with love, compatibility and a desire to be together.

ℰ෪ * * * ℭℬ

Indu's meeting with George's father could not have been a more congenial encounter. Oddly, she felt no timidity as she and George stood outside a massive oak door which would give them entry into an exclusive London dwelling. George pressed a button and moments later the buzzer sounded on the electronically locked door, ushering them to the other side. His father was awaiting their entrance at the door of flat Number One. Five minutes after the introductions, George's father and Indu had sized each other up, both with an equally critical eye, and Indu hoped that each had found good cause for mutual respect.

He was an older man, sixty-ish, distinguished in appearance. Indu could go as far as to say that she even felt a strange affinity with him, but one possibly fostered by the striking resemblance that he bore to her deceased grandfather. Seeing the ease in rapport between the two, glowing signs of relief streamed from George as he realized that his slightly overbearing father actually liked his girlfriend. Indu was eager to shine as bright a light as possible on George, now faced with paternal scrutiny. When his father asked skeptically if she thought George had passed his exam this second time around, she replied without hesitation that she was sure he had. Her certainty surprised his father, although he accepted it as a sign of her loving faith in his son's ability. In truth, instinct told her that George had passed. How she knew it, she didn't know.

Their father-son relationship was indeed one fraught with the traditional tensions—father clearly wanting son to be a success but at a loss on how to encourage him, and son silently insisting that he would accomplish plenty in his own time and in his own way. But it was a tug-of-war on friendly ground and Indu tried not to interfere with their sparring. In all, over the week, their meetings numbered three: that first tea-time chat, a subsequent father's treat-out-to-dinner, and a morning coffee on the day of his departure. Mr. Acroilus bid farewell to Indu with a kiss on each cheek, European-style, but delivered with genuine sincerity.

That week marked the beginning of a blossoming for George and Indu, triggered by no one event but emerging as a growing acknowledgement of the trust that they could have in each other. It was in this period that they would again play witness to the mystery and perplexity of the standing stones.

Seeing her devouring book after book concerned with the prehistoric wonders, George arranged a weekend trip to the farm of close family friends, a farm southwest of London in Wiltshire. It was close to the Avebury stone circle and to Stonehenge, with Salisbury only slightly further beyond. But before going south, they headed north on a sentimental journey back to the solitary stone at Ickwell, where by destiny's hand, their lives had been brought together by a single embrace.

One might have imagined that they would repeat, almost ritualistically, that walk through the rose garden, over the iron gate and down the narrow, winding path, stealthily approaching the stone hand in hand, moving their hands together over the cold stone surface to feel once again its thermal presence, sitting tranquilly between the bubbling spring and their three-foot enigma to reflect philosophically on the unbelievably convoluted course of the past year. That they did not follow this exact scenario was partly because they had not come alone. By invitation, Oliver and Penny had joined them for the outing. Oliver had heard stories of Ickwell and had been interested to see the seventeenth-century retreat. George and Indu were glad to have their company. They needed that tie to the present. There was something unsettling for them in reminiscing about their first meeting. Too many questions were still unanswered and too many painful moments had been part of their struggle to come to terms with the love that bonded them.

Yet they were drawn to return to the site. It was part of the mystery between them.

Driving under the brick archway into the quadrangle, Indu could feel her heart gripped by the phantom of time. Everything looked exactly the same. And who should be the first to greet them as they stepped from the car but Gretchen. She also looked exactly the same. She remembered George immediately but only slowly recognized Indu's face. George made no attempt to explain how it was that one of the American devotees from last year's intensive was now standing by his side, and being her same guardedly noncommittal self, Gretchen asked no questions.

The welcome complete, they headed to the rose garden with their picnic. The roses were beautifully in bloom, just as they had been the summer before. As they ate, Indu sat pondering. This was not going to be as simple as she had thought. The emotional impact of those first ten days was being compounded by the haunting familiarity of a place unchanged. But she and George had changed. Between them they had practically traversed the world, been in jobs and left them, renounced their own connection and re-established it. They were hardly the same two people. But the past and the future were united at that moment by the changeless face of uncertainty. They had been uncertain in the beginning as to the direction their lives would take, they were still uncertain as to how their destinies would intertwine, and once again, future projection led only to the abode of uncertainty. And the bridge for this time traveler was none other than their love, a love which it seemed had spanned an eternity.

Indu suddenly felt the need to be alone, to integrate the time-warp into some kind of psychological sense. It was this need to get firmly grounded in the present that led her to excuse herself, if no objections were raised, to go ahead to the stone. It was with relief that George nodded in approval. He had not been unaware of the crosscurrents tormenting the raft of their love, turning it in the direction from whence it had come and then back to face the approaching bend in the river of life, causing it to lurch and spin and advance with excruciating slowness. For Indu, the crosscurrents subsided for the time being as she parted from the group.

Carrying George's pullover, tenderly presented for her to sit upon should the ground near the stone be damp, Indu traversed the iron gate and forged down the obscure little path leading to the stone. George had known she wanted to sit near its radiant warmth. But the winding path stopped in the middle of overgrown brush. There was no clear sign as to the direction of the stone. This untended field was not the same. At least, she thought, it had evolved, grown and developed, just as she had. But where to find the stone?

She headed further to the left for some distance. Then something stopped her. No... Back up. She felt bemused as she followed the inner command. Is it this way? Her mind wasn't sure but she felt compelled. She turned back, cut across the taller grasses and abruptly hit the hidden dirt path. Ahead she saw the tree. The stone would be just beyond.

It was there, standing silently and serenely as it had twelve months before, leaning magisterially toward the round pool of water. As though in a dance, she approached it with slow rhythmic steps, moving in a half circle around it. She didn't know why she'd stopped to pick flowers on the way but these she laid without ceremony at its base. She stepped back from it again. With every fiber of curiosity vibrating, she quietly studied it. Why was it not just another stone? What was its secret? Wanting to document its existence, its size, its tilt, its square top, its relation to the spring, she continued her examination through the lens of her camera with the same reverence as that of an archaeologist viewing an excavation. Could she capture on film its mystery, its mystique? At least she could capture the memory, for she knew she might never return.

Placing George's sweater on the ground next to it, she sat down facing the water, the stone just inches from her back. She wanted to face the same direction in which it was leaning, to feel it leaning in toward her. She could feel it. She closed her eyes. There was silence. A soft rain began to fall but she didn't move. She heard Guruji's words: "Sabbath means the time we go beyond the six senses, the sixth sense being the thinking mind. God created the universe in six days. This means we operate using our six senses but we are not the senses. We are beyond. We should feel this on the Sabbath. Sabbath is not a day. It is the inner silence which goes beyond the six senses." Indu tried to go deeply into this silence.

The drizzling rain stopped. She now heard voices. Through the grasses she could see George, Oliver and Penny. Her Sabbath was over. She stood up as they came along the dirt path under the tree. George immediately asked if she'd felt the heat. She'd been so mesmerized by the stone that she'd forgotten to check.

Penny stood estranged from the group as the three moved their hands through the space surrounding the stone, palms open. Her level of excitement hardly increased with their exclaims of "Feel it here" and "Definitely at the top!" Her strict Catholic upbringing did not allow for any pagan endowment of powers to the stones. Whether by their cajoling or her own curiosity, she brought her reluctant palm to hover tentatively in the air by the vertical rock. She tried one spot and then another but denied feeling anything. She quickly withdrew her hands. Seeing Penny's distraught apprehension over the whole subject of mystical "hot spots" and natural "energy," Indu withdrew hers as well. It didn't matter that Penny couldn't feel it. What was more amazing was that Oliver could.

$\wp$ * * * $\wp$

The only difference between Oliver and Penny, Indu commented to me, was that Oliver had been receptive to the idea from the very beginning. It had been at that moment that Indu felt she had grasped the missing link in the modern mind. It was the lack of receptivity. Was it this lack which caused a block in perception and therefore in cognizance of mystical phenomena, phenomena not just of a physical but also of a metaphysical nature? Was this why Guruji had repeated hundreds of times to "feel, feel, feel" in order to fine-tune her inner reception, reception beyond the six senses?

She read another quote to me where Guruji had claimed, "You cannot see God through the eyes, or smell him with the nose. You cannot think God either. The whole universe is within you. To find this out, you must leave the universe of manifestation. Smoke is the manifestation of fire. Logically you can say where there is smoke there is fire. But the mind can go no further because the mind is also part of manifestation. We must go to 'see' the fire directly."

To "see" directly, one had to feel. It was a paradox. Belief alone would not bring the wisdom.

୫ * * * ଓ

Indu was ready to ponder the receptiveness of the prehistoric mind as she sat there by the stone, a mind possibly possessing an instinctive knowledge of the mystical sciences related to the planet, to the surrounding cosmic influences and perhaps to the human mind itself. But she was pulled back to the moment. The others were ready to leave.

The hour was getting late and the skies hinted at more rain. But she did not want to go without having at least a few minutes alone with George by the stone. Oliver and Penny obliged and agreed to meet them back at the car. Taking George's hand, Indu led him to the same spot where they had sat talking all those hours.

He settled into his old position by the stone, next to her. "I was hoping we'd have at least some time alone here," he said.

For a moment, neither spoke. She took his hand in hers again. "There's so much, George, I want to say to you now. There's so much. But I feel at a loss for words. I didn't have this trouble a year ago, did I?"

"Well," George laughed, "I must say you hardly needed encouragement to keep up your end of the conversation. I was amazed and I kept thinking, 'There's so much I could learn from this woman.' And you went on and on, and I didn't want you to stop."

"But now there's no time and..." Her voice trailed off pensively. "I think we need to talk like that again, George."

"You mean you want me to sit and listen to you talk for six hours again!"

"You know exactly what I mean—to abandon time, and inhibitions."

"I'm not inhibited."

"But we are guarded. We're guarded in what we say, afraid to presume too much about the future. Look how many arguments we've had. I know that's also part of getting to know each other but I'd like for us to find a way to do it without getting angry. I want to know what your joys and hopes and desires are. Don't you see what we've been doing, George? We've been skirting anything to do with the future because we don't know how we fit into each other's lives yet. When have we sat and just talked an evening away, just the two of us?"

George gave a strained, resigned smile. The answer was not once since she had arrived. But he didn't need to say it. They both knew.

With watery eyes she said, "What if we hadn't talked then? You know we wouldn't be here now." There was a sadness in his eyes when she looked into them. The truth was painful. The unknown future was frightening for both of them. If they didn't confront it soon, their relationship would not have long to last.

Their few minutes were up. They stood up and held each other closely, tightly, silently. The stone was their witness. Come what may, they would always know they had loved deeply, deeper than either had ever known before. Soon after this day, they made love for the second time. While still snugly embraced between her thighs, in a breathless whisper, he professed, "It's never, never been like this before." She had also never experienced such passionate lovemaking. To embrace the body of one so loved, to move as one, to breathe as one, it was to glimpse the heavens. It was a merging, a total surrendering, losing all feeling of separateness. It was a union beyond imagination, beyond the mind, beyond the self. It was glorious.

There were many happy moments during the days that preceded their trip to the Wiltshire farm: going as a couple to meet his friends, seeing an American film on bawdy Leicester Square, watching him juggle for two hours at a juggler's workshop in a gymnasium near the Savoy Hotel. There was also the day he received the letter about his exam. It listed all the names of those tested. There were twelve. Only George had passed.

On the following Sunday evening, they went to Westminster Abbey. Nine hundred years ago, the Abbey had been a Benedictine Monastery. Now, situated across from the Houses of Parliament, it was an architectural masterpiece, the setting for every coronation since 1066. Dedicated to regular worship and to the celebration of great events in the life of England, it could be called neither a cathedral nor a parish church.

80 * * * 03

As described in one brochure which Indu still had and was happy to show me, "Westminster Abbey is a 'royal peculiar' under the jurisdiction of a Dean and Chapter, subject only to the Sovereign." Within its walls were buried five kings and four queens, as well as Geoffrey Chaucer.

It was an inspiring landmark, but Indu and George had not been concerned with its historical import. They had been there for Evensong, the evening service. Kneeling side by side, she had looked over at George after the prayers ended and had seen him with hands still folded and head bent down.

Unforgettable tears had filled her eyes. This was the man she loved, a man who would truly pray, pray even when the service card bearing the order for the choral Evensong said it was time to sing.

Far from being heavily indoctrinated in Christian liturgy, Indu had followed the service as best as she could. She had listened to the reading of Psalm 34, then to the story of Jonah from the Old Testament and the story of St. Paul reaching Rome from the New Testament. Next an anthem had been sung, the first line of which was from Isaiah Chapter 26, verse 3: "Thou wilt keep him in perfect peace, whose mind is stayed on thee: because he trusteth in thee." The congregation had risen and gone on to sing two more hymns, but Indu had no longer followed. Their voices had grown fainter and fainter as she'd gazed at the words of the anthem. She'd felt suddenly transported back to Norway and the midnight sun.

She handed me the Evensong leaflet from that evening service which listed the hymns that were sung. The words that had transported her were the following:

Thou wilt keep him in perfect peace, whose mind is stayed on Thee.
The darkness is no darkness with Thee, but the night is as clear as day:
The darkness and light to Thee are both alike.

God is light, and in Him is no darkness at all.
O let my soul live, and it shall praise Thee.
For Thine is the Kingdom, the power and the glory for
evermore.

S.S. Wesley (1810-1876)

She had seen the time when the "night was as clear as day." It
had been so because the sun had not set. If she had not seen
it with her own eyes, the words themselves would have been
a paradox, "night as clear as day." But having broken the paradox, the meaning behind the words stood out brilliantly. It
was the same metaphor, she said, that often came from Guruji's
lips: "The I-AM is shining like the sun."

It was just as the anthem had praised: "God is light, and in
Him is no darkness at all." That light, that "I-AM" can be seen,
but not with the physical eyes. It is within our reach, but not
with the physical hand. The light is within. We are that light.
As she told me this, she reached for her notebook to read a Bible passage that Guruji often referenced: "[...] Believe me that I
AM in the Father, and the Father in me [...]."*

The memory of standing in the Abbey next to George had
stirred Indu deeply. "I suddenly felt the power of the midnight
sun, the power of the anthem, the power of Guruji's words, the
power of Jesus' words. They had all pointed to the same thing,"
she enthusiastically reiterated for me. "The 'sun' is within, the
'light' is within, God is within. We are not separate from the
eternally shining spirit, the inner shining light."

---

* John 14:10-11 (AV).

THIRTY-SIX

~

The sign read, "Constructed for unknown semi-religious purposes between 2450-2200 B.C."

Indu stood staring at it. "How can something be semi-religious?" she wondered. "Either it's religious or it's not. Or are they trying to say that the stone circle was used partly for religious purposes and partly for some other function?"

"How really naive we are," Indu mused while standing in front of the museum glass case which exhibited artifacts found within the Avebury stone circle. George had brought her once again to the standing stones.

ℰ * * * ℭ

Somewhere in antiquity, the purpose of the standing stones was hidden from modern knowledge, and as Indu saw it, modern man was none too pleased to be left in the dark. Using twentieth century technology, scientists, archaeologists and mystics alike had tried to unlock the stones' secrets, a product of their effort being a mass of literature on the prehistoric phenomenon. Having immersed herself in their studies, pouring over book after book, what Indu had concluded was that the builders of the stone structures had had an extraordinarily special and mysterious relationship to the planet and the cosmos.

Indu knew her viewpoint contradicted the popular conception that prehistoric Britons were half a step up from cavemen. It was true that the basis of their life in 2500 B.C. was a rudimentary form of agriculture and that people had lived in primitive conditions. "But we like to flatter ourselves," Indu commented to me, "by thinking that we are smarter and better endowed than they were."

She recollected that it was this idea which had been beautifully expressed by Isak Dinesen. She read the Dinesen quote from her notebook: "We of the present day, who love our machines, cannot quite imagine how people in the old days could live without them. [...] And if we had not found them there ready for our use, we should have had to do without them. Still we must imagine, since they have been made at all, that there was a time when the hearts of humanity cried out for these things, and when a deeply felt want was relieved when they were made."[38]

She shared with me what her research had uncovered. Avebury was cited as the largest stone circle of the British Isles, covering nearly twenty-eight and a half acres. Uniquely surrounding it was a ditch and a bank, but hardly of childish proportions. Archaeologists had estimated that the bank itself contained 150,000 tons of chalk rubble laboriously excavated from the ditch. When finished, the height of the bank had been twenty-one feet, although time and erosion had lowered it to a present-day height of sixteen and a half feet. What was peculiar was that the ditch, which had all the appearances of a medieval moat, was inside the bank perimeter, not on the outside as one might expect a defensive moat to be. Furthermore, intentional gaps had been left in the bank and ditch when the earthwork was built, thus dividing the circle into four quadrants.

The number of sarsen stones inside the circular ditch had at one time been approximately one hundred, the average weight being fifteen tons but some weighing well over fifty. Outside the ditch, from the south and west entrances, avenues of standing stones had formerly run for distances of over one and a half miles using more than four hundred stone markers. In its construction, then, more than five hundred stones, some of enormous mass, had been dragged an estimated one to two miles and carefully erected, and approximately 3,950,000 cubic feet of chalk had been carried and hoisted bucket after bucket. It was an unbelievable feat considering that there had been no pulleys or wheels and that tools had been made of wood and stone and bone, the shoulder blades of oxen and horses being used for digging.

"What could have been going through their minds?" Indu had pondered at the time. Quite clearly, an effort which had required such a staggering number of man-hours to complete could not have been conceived haphazardly, she was sure. Adding to the mystery were two other features of Avebury. One was the fact that although none of the stones were hand-shaped, two notable shapes were selected: stones with thin and straight sides and stones shaped like diamonds. Many of the diamond ones, even one weighing forty tons, had been carefully tilted up and set into the ground on their point. The second unusual feature was that inside the large circle of standing stones, two smaller circles had been constructed, each originally composed of thirty stones, and inside one of these had existed a fourth circle of about twelve stones.

There was no direct evidence whether the earthwork, stone circles and avenues were planned and executed as one project or whether they were divided into separate and successive phases of construction, but it was believed that they were built during the late Neolithic period, around 2500 B.C. Sadly, the centuries had not been kind to the ancient site. Only twenty-seven sarsen stones were left in the inner circles and even fewer in the outer avenues. In fact, most of those presently standing had actually been discovered toppled over and buried. A massive effort in the 1930s was made to re-erect those stones and to mark with concrete pyramids the positions of the other stones found broken and buried right at the site.

As one scientist had noted, "By the 14th century, however, it is clear that stones were being deliberately pulled down and buried, possibly at fairly regular intervals, so that the Church could demonstrate to each succeeding generation of inhabitants its abhorrence of pagan practices which may still have survived from an earlier time."[39]

Indu knew there had to be something significant behind these "pagan practices." Why had leading scientists carried magnetometers and ultrasonic detection equipment to a prehistoric site and stood vigilant at the crack of dawn waiting for anomalous recordings? She read to me this statement that acknowledged the obvious: "Our planet, our solar system, our cosmos, interrelate in ways that are subtle to our hard and superficial culture, but which may have been more apparent to our ancient ancestors."[40]

The subtleties detected at the ancient sites included electromagnetic phenomena, or earth currents, currents undetected by our culture of steel and concrete. According to the scientific data, although ancient man may not have academically understood the concept of electromagnetism, he nonetheless knew of its power. But how did he discover it? One answer Indu found was ingeniously proposed by Paul Devereux, the same scientist mentioned in the "talking stone" article. His theory was that prehistoric man had sited discoids hovering above the ground, discoids we have cleverly called UFOs.

Not to discount the existence of extraterrestrials, Devereux submitted that the mysterious lights seen in the sky could actually be explained as unidentified atmospheric phenomenon, UAPs instead of UFOs. The atmospheric phenomenon was hypothesized as being the product of the interaction between the earth's physical body, the surrounding atmosphere, and ambient cosmic and terrestrial forces. Indu read the theory presented in Devereux's book: "It is the discoid form of rotating dipolar magnetic fields that produces the traditional UFO form within our atmosphere [...] a contracting and rotating mass of air, the rotation producing ionization and therefore, ultimately, the production of light. The areas where air has the optimum ionic properties for this mechanism are rural, mountainous, and coastal regions."[41] Certainly the prehistoric Salisbury Plain had been rural and its position spanning inland thirty miles from the coast of the English Channel may have given it a coastal milieu. But other conditions could also have prevailed which may have enhanced the electromagnetic displays for ancient man.

Devereux had continued in his explanation: "Mankind lives on a thin shell beneath which 'mammoth forces' operate [...]. During the strain of seismic unrest, pressure on rock crystals in a large area produces electrical fields through a modification of the piezo-electrical effect. These pre-fracture electrical fields can reach values of several thousand volts per meter—intensities capable of ionizing the local area into visible luminosities."[42] The fact that many stone circles were situated near geological faults was well documented.

Another well-documented fact was the preponderance of astronomical alignments—alignments with the sun and the moon that were established in the positions of the stones themselves. Although astronomical alignments did seem present at Avebury, its near destruction rendered the evidence inconclusive. But at Stonehenge, one of the best preserved stone circles, the orientation of the central axis on the point of the rising sun at midsummer solstice could not be refuted. Stonehenge also had stone alignments for sunrise at winter solstice and at the fall and spring equinoxes. It was at the equinoxes when the sun rose exactly due east and set exactly due west.

But why would Neolithic man have wanted to know about the solstice and equinox? The tilt of the earth's axis was what caused the sun to rise at different points on the horizon. If the planetary axis was perpendicular to its orbit around the sun, then the sun would always be seen to rise due east and set due west no matter where one was on the planet. Day would be exactly the same length throughout the year. There would be no seasons except for slight temperature changes caused by the earth's varying distance from the sun. But that was not the case. Only in September and March was the tilt of the earth neither toward nor away from the sun, and that accounted for the precise east-west positioning and for night equaling day.

Indu doubted that Neolithic man had endeavored to take any glory away from Copernicus by proving that the earth had an axis and orbit; nor did she think he had been trying to formalize a calendar system to facilitate sowing and reaping. If his astronomical calculations had been solely for the latter purpose, then why would he have bothered observing the moon, whose cycle was far from annual but repeated only once every 18.6 years? But observe it he had. The Heel Stone of Stonehenge, a thirty-five-ton stone standing alone just east of the henge, had been found to mark exactly the moonrise at the midpoint of the lunar cycle. Other stone alignments marked the northernmost and southernmost moonrise and moonset at both the major and minor standstills, events that occurred only once in the 18.6 years.

No one can deny that to make such observations would have required a high level of organization and intellectual sophistication. But why make lunar observations in the first place? Indu read about one scientist's studies on tidal phenomena which he stated "are quite complicated when studied in detail." But quite simply tides rise and fall twice every twenty-four hours. Each day high tide is a little later than the day before. Tides are not always the same height. The rise and fall can be twice over what it is at other times. And he concluded that the moon's responsibility for the tides is a connection so obvious that ancient man should have been aware: "The connection between the tides and the moon could have stimulated interest in tracking its celestial movement."[43] Indu believed early man had been aware, aware of much more than modern man had ever wanted to concede. Oddly, Stonehenge stood directly over a blind spring, an affinity often repeated at other Neolithic sites as well. Sites with blind springs could have had a preponderance of unidentified atmospheric phenomena since running water was a great generator of negative ions.

Solar activity, lunar phase and cosmic radiation all are known to affect processes in water, reaching the water molecule by alterations in the earth's magnetic field. The human body, also heavily composed of water and surrounded by its own magnetic field, could also be susceptible to the same cosmic forces as the planet. If equipment can actually measure the tidal effect in a cup of coffee, how about the man holding the cup? Could he also have ebbs and flows in synch with gravitational and electromagnetic influences? Don't words "lunacy" and "lunatic"—*luna* being Latin for moon—suggest that something in man is affected? Indu was definitely on a roll with this. All of these ideas she had been mulling over for quite some time.

Soon to return to her story, she asked for me to indulge her just a few more minutes so she could continue hypothesizing on what those ancient ones had really been up to. Assuming ancient man did witness the electromagnetic illuminations of UFO infamy in areas near faults and blind springs, why had he made such enormous effort to mark these sites and to encode lunar and solar positions into those structures? Indu found the words of some alternative archaeologists to come closest to solving the riddle. They suggested that there could have been a prehistoric science: "the existence in prehistoric times of an active science of spiritual physics, whereby functions of the mind and body were integrated with currents in the earth and powers from the cosmos."[44] It was a loaded proposition, but if true, it was no wonder that the standing stones' purpose had eluded the rocket man's comprehension. The windows of technologically-oriented perception had long been closed to any "pagan practices" of spiritual physics. Those same windows had been suspiciously cracked open by the discovery of the "talking stones."

What that group of Rollright scientists had suspected was that the standing stones and stone circles were situated at places of power, places where an optimum confluence of cosmic factors, subterranean water and geological conditions existed which helped to maximize energy storage and transduction occurring naturally in the stones. And somehow, along with all these factors, the groundplan geometry was equally critical, although as of yet the scientists had not grasped the logic behind it, if logic indeed could ever decipher it. For the stones and earthworks were created as symbols, and as one scientist had put it, these symbols had to "transmit an entire constellation of meanings through a specially selected (or constructed) physical form. A true symbol was able to tolerate variety and even contradiction in messages it received and radiated because, before the Age of Logic, [...] contradiction and paradox were accepted, and acknowledged to be embedded in the nature of things."[45]

The question was whether the modern, rational, intellectual mind would ever be able to comprehend the prehistoric symbols, constructed with phenomenal effort over hundreds of years, and possibly devoted to a geophysic mysticism. To do this modern man would have to come to terms with contradictions and paradoxes, a prospect that had left even Einstein wishing to be a cobbler. Indu saw that the stone monuments left technological man trying to push square large blocks into square small holes, and triangular large ones into triangular small ones. Prehistoric shapes were simply not going to fit into the restricted, narrow slots of our modern perception boxes. Our perception would have to be broadened to ever understand.

Paul Devereux had taken a giant step in that direction when he stated, "There is a spiritual reality beyond time and space; there is a mental reality composed of many levels existing 'between' the spiritual and material realms which dips in and out of our reality; and there is the physical world where energy hits 'rock bottom' and appears deceptively as solid matter which seems to obey reliable laws—until one looks too closely. These are not separate worlds but, rather, one continuum."[46]

Was this the message the ancients had tried to leave? If it was, then it was no wonder that ultrasonic devices in the hands of a few rather enlightened researchers had suddenly made the scientists quake in their boots. Who was ever going to believe their findings?

Carefully tempering their speculations, what they presented was sound evidence on the transduction effects occurring in the stones. At Rollright, they wired a stone to a special camera which was a device to induce an electrical current into the stone. They obtained a norm against which to measure fluctuations in frequency or amplitude of the current, fluctuations which would have to be caused by an extraneous energy or force working on or within the stone. An oscilloscope was wired to register such changes. All was normal until the sun broke the horizon, causing an increase in the electrical field as seen by the oscilloscope. It proved that energy was coming from somewhere and passing through the stone. The effect was recorded only at dawn. Little change occurred during the daylight hours. They stated that one possible explanation could be that a highly conducive material was buried in the rock strata. If this were the case, then a normally dormant rock could become electrically charged, generating a large electromagnetic field around it during an increase in solar activity.

Indu showed me the diagram so I would understand. The experiment at Rollright was none other than a test of the Hall Effect. The Hall Effect was a well-known physical phenomenon produced when a current, passed through a slab of material located in a magnetic field, caused a voltage to appear between the sides of the slab. If the current was held constant, the voltage could only be altered by changes in the magnetic field. It would seem that the rays of the dawning sun could produce such changes.

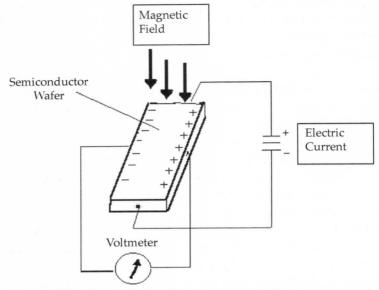

[*Ken Hatton & Harold Fennel,* The Hall Effect *(paper presented for the First SUNYIT Applied Mathmatics Project Contest at the SUNY Institute of Technology, Utica, NY.) www. math.sunyit.edu/projects.* Reprinted with permission.]

The Hall Effect, first discovered in 1879, had taught scientists how substances conducted electricity. Interestingly enough, the current-magnetism-voltage effect was not as obvious in metals as it was in semiconductors, substances which could conduct electricity but with much less facility than metals, hence their name. However, a prominent electrical property of semiconductors was a sensitivity to light. For this reason they were often used in photoelectric cells and solar batteries. Semiconductors used in technology were usually small crystals.

"You see," Indu said to me, "This is the key." Many of the stones that the ancients had selected and transported over a great distance were sarsen. The term was derived from Saracen, meaning "heathen." Saxons had applied the term *saresyn* to pagans or heathens. The geological formations associated with paganism also acquired the appellation, meaning "heathen stone." These "heathen stones" were sandstone, a stone which contained predominantly subangular quartz crystal grains cemented together with silica. The coarse, sugary-looking stones were in effect semiconductors. As explained by Devereux, the electromagnetic energizing of electrons in such semiconductors could occur only within narrowly defined parameters. If the input energy was too great or too small, the electrons would not be properly excited. The radiation that satisfied all the criterion was microwave radiation. At sunrise, the microwave region was maximized. Indu read to me the hypothesis of Robins, the other scientist mentioned in the "talking stone" article: "Microwave radiation from the sun at dawn could possibly energize the stones, causing populations of trapped electrons within them to vibrate. [...] These electrons form an equilibrium population in that they are continually being formed and trapped while others are escaping from their lattice traps and migrating through the stone. At any given time, therefore, a stone will contain a small but definite drifting potential and in a standing stone, it is reasonable to expect this current to drift to earth. [...] Some of the energy [radiation] produced by vibration of electrons in their lattice traps could possibly be transduced through the lattice structure of the stone into pressure waves such as ultrasound. According to this view, the ultrasonics would be a side-effect of an electromagnetic process occurring within the megaliths."[47]

The evidence of the ultrasound pulses provided credence to the theory that ancient sites were chosen to either absorb energy or transmit it, being as they were natural capacitor systems. The fact that many ancient sites were built in alignment with others, possibly concentrating the energizing effect, only added to the suspicions that something extraordinary might have been going on in ancient Britain.

The alignments of the sites were the ley lines. Indu realized that the studies of Michael Faraday, the father of electromagnetism, could actually show how the leys might have worked. Faraday had taken a powerful dipolar magnet, a magnet with a north and south pole, and suspended a string of straight pins from it, one magically hanging from the other. Once again she showed me a diagram:

The phenomenon was called induction, where the power of the magnet could act over a considerable distance. The space around a magnet in which the effect could be felt was called the magnetic field and it extended in all three dimensions. A two-dimensional illustration of the field could be seen by sprinkling iron filings around a magnetic bar. The filings would fall naturally into a pattern of lines. Michael Faraday had called this pattern "lines of force." For Faraday, the concept of lines of force was a powerful tool in working out the qualitative theory of magnetic fields. Was it inconceivable that, like the straight row of pins dangling from the magnet, there was an induction effect occurring along the leys which connected the electromagnetic energies of the ancient sites, thus establishing a channel of energy?

Still, what did it all mean? Indu had thought about the strong presence of quartz at the ancient sites. The puzzle was far from solved but experience with quartz crystals as a healing tool gave Indu suspicions of her own. She'd made a transcript from an audio recording of a lecture given at Guruji's ashram in New York by a well-known healer, and she read to me the following from it:

> Quartz crystals have piezoelectric properties. What this means is that tension or pressure applied to a crystal can induce an electrical potential. The crystals are electrically alive. This gives them the power to increase the electromagnetic field surrounding the body. The crystal itself grows in a precise manner, in a spiral. The spiral, so often noticed in sacred geometry, creates an energizing effect. This causes the earth energy to be transformed into a higher vibration called bioenergy. An interesting fact is that the genetic map itself is encoded in the spirals of the DNA molecule.

> If you touch a crystal, your bioenergy will be increased drastically, the effect of which can be measured by Kirlian photography, by electrical measurements along the

acupuncture meridians, or by measurements of body temperature changes and blood chemistry changes. Why does it work? Because the body generates negative ions. Any living object generates negative ions. Any naturally formed object generates negative ions. Crystals increase negative ion generation of the body. The crystal itself, however, is not a great negative ion generator, but it is a transformer. In electronics, that is what crystals are used for, to transform a wave form into electricity and electricity into a wave. Our bodies transform energy. If you touch a television that has a fuzzy picture due to poor reception, the picture will suddenly get better. We act as antennae, causing a greater energizing effect in the crystals of the television's electrical circuit board, therefore transforming energy more efficiently.

What crystals can do is to transform the electromagnetic field of the earth into bioenergy. Bioenergy may then be transformed into thought energy and then transmitted. This is called telepathy. Energy is a form of vibration. Crystals can help you gain control of the movement of energy, but often it requires you to change your reality. Crystals give us power to get into the mental computer. They move the brainwaves into alpha, the first step of relaxation; they balance the energies of the body to help one handle stress; they make one calmer and more relaxed, allowing more light to emanate from the body. When you expand your consciousness, you connect to the world in a different way. The physical body can hold us back. The crystal helps to break through the blocked energy. In this way, crystals can take us beyond our limitations.[48]

Indu wondered if the ancients had known of a science which set human habitat and activity into harmony with the visible and invisible world. This science, if indeed it had existed, had quite clearly run into conflict with the dawning of the Bronze Age and industrialization. The sacred harmony would slowly have been destroyed; the geophysic properties of the earth would slowly have been forgotten.

Indu read one last quote on the subject which put it quite succinctly. Paul Devereux had written, "Anyone with any grasp of what consciousness is [...] realizes that it inhabits the body and is not dependent on it."[49] All of this research brought Indu to the conclusion that if the ancients had understood this, if they had understood how to use electromagnetism to promote out-of-body experiences, to break through the physical and mental limitations, then they were the true worshipers of spirit and their stone legacies were indeed temples of the most extraordinary kind.

THIRTY-SEVEN

~

"Indu?" It was George. "How long do you plan to stand in front of that glass case? You looked like you were a thousand miles away." Pondering the real purpose of these stone circles, Indu had not been a thousand miles but four thousand years away. Back in the present, she was ready to join George and Rebecca, the daughter of the Freeth family who had been close friends with George's sister. "And here I thought you'd be pulling my arm to get to the stones, not me pulling yours." It was George's final teasing mutter as they exited the museum to begin their hike around the four and a half acre stone ring of Avebury.

Indu and George had arrived the evening before at the Freeth farm located in Wiltshire just a few miles from Avebury. The farm had been in the Freeth family for almost two hundred years. There was a central courtyard with a brick house on one side and a long barn and storage shed on the other. Chicken and turkey coops were at the far end of the enclosure, where aromas and feathers would be least disturbing. But it was not solely a poultry farm. They also owned a large acreage for harvesting straw.

After getting past the front door without letting even one of the eight Labradors in behind them, George and Indu had been welcomed into the "dining" room, laid with authentic flagstone worn smooth from ages of use. George had immediately warned her that sitting in this room could be hazardous since at any time the dogs could break in, or a stray chicken could tiptoe through, or there was the goat which liked to visit. No, they'd gotten rid of the goat. Just as well. At that moment, the room was without dog, chicken or goat, and the cat was out. But still, there were the two big bird cages in the middle of the room, with feathers and birdseed scattered around. These were the cozy homes of two cockatoos, a mated pair. In addition to the cages and the round dining table by the windows, the room had a row of china cupboards and a large, six-burner, wrought-iron stove. The room's heat came exclusively from it. A modern gas cooker was in the kitchen, but the old stove was still used for warming dishes and toasting bread.

But more enchanting than the farmhouse were the Freeths themselves. Mrs. Freeth was a woman in her late fifties, a magistrate in the local community, a strong woman with gray hair swept up into a bun. Her husband was twenty years her senior. Silver haired, he squinted through his silver wire-rimmed glasses and rarely missed anything happening in the room. Besides Rebecca, they had a son, Jason, who also worked on the farm.

That evening, they all sat around the dinner table together. Having been informed in advance that Indu was not a meat eater, Mrs. Freeth had prepared a frying-pan-sized omelet stuffed with black olives. Indu had never eaten any omelet more delicious. There were also home-grown runner beans. The others enjoyed a roast. But when dinner was over and the dishes were cleared, there was no movement to leave the table. Cookies and coffee came and went and everyone stayed sitting and talking. The only serious moment was when Mrs. Freeth, seated next to Indu, scooted her chair back from the table and leaned Indu's way. The question was not meant for anyone else's ears but George overheard her ask, "So, what about Jesus?"

It was asked directly and sincerely. Probably in trying to explain her unusual name, George had told of Indu's study of Eastern philosophy. Indu understood. Mrs. Freeth was not interested in any religious discussion. She only wanted to know, did Indu accept the teachings of Jesus? With the same directness and sincerity, Indu met the eyes of this lovely gray-haired woman and nodded "yes," making an affirmative sound, "Mmm hmmm," in her throat. It was all the answer needed.

Mrs. Freeth smiled. After a moment's silence, she said, "That's good." Something great had been communicated. They were of kindred heart. George seemed relieved that the exchange, such as it was, appeared so mutually agreeable and that by all outward signs, Mrs. Freeth approved of Indu. In his eyes, the enjoyability of the entire weekend had just been guaranteed. He almost bubbled with boyish exuberance the rest of the night. Jokes and silly stories were told. To top off the night, George serenaded the cockatoos with his ocarina. One of the birds was particularly wooed. It fluffed its feathers and began a slow seductive dance, shifting from one foot to the other, all the while bobbing its head. Even Mr. Freeth couldn't keep from chuckling.

While the dishes were being washed in the kitchen, Mr. Freeth motioned for Indu to follow him. "I want to show you something," he said as he led her out the front door into the pitch darkness of the night. They had met only hours before, but there was a comfortable ease between them. She followed him behind the house, passing the well-lit windows of the dining room, taking his broad, calloused hand as they went through a rickety wooden gate. He brought her to stand just beyond the low hanging branches of an enormous tree and pointed up to the sky. There was a radiant full moon surrounded by a galaxy of stars.

"Isn't it beautiful," he said. They stood almost two minutes, silently side by side, admiring. Such glories of nature could not be seen in London, where the summer night sky always held an orange incandescent cast reflected from the city street lights.

To admire was one thing, but to track its 18.6 year cycle, to mark its rise and fall and even its eclipses was another matter entirely. Indu couldn't keep from pondering over the motives of Neolithic man. No sooner had the thought crossed her mind than Mr. Freeth took a step toward the gate. "I suppose we should head back in before they miss us," he said. Indu took his arm and together they walked around and into the house.

Their cold, flushed cheeks gave them away and they were met by raised eyebrows. They confessed nothing and only smiled mischievously. Seeing her in cahoots with the old man brought a wondrous grin to George's face. All was well.

For propriety's sake, separate bedrooms had been arranged, which Indu and George accepted naturally and without comment. Saying a hearty goodnight, the elder Freeths had retired, leaving the youngsters to put themselves to bed. Indu had stepped into George's room on the way to the bathroom and happened to be present as he slid under the covers. With a whoop, he suddenly leapt back out again. She was dumfounded as to what was wrong. George reached under the covers and withdrew a lobster, a metal one, complete with movable joints and wiggling tail.

"She does it to me every time. I'm damn stupid not to check before I get into any bed in this house. And you'd better check yours. There's no guarantee she's going to exempt you."

"Who? Rebecca?"

"Rebecca! No. It's Mrs. Freeth. She's got one devilish sense of humor. You really have to be on your guard around her or she'll getcha. That's what I like about being here, never a dull moment." Once back in her room, Indu cautiously pulled back the covers and peered beneath. Nothing was there.

Early the next morning, they set off for Avebury. Rebecca came along for the fun and to offer her assistance as a guide. Naturally, she had seen it many times, having grown up in its prehistoric shadow. They parked the car and stepped into the village museum to get some historical background before making the tour.

Although having done extensive reading, Indu had also been curious to see if the museum could shed any new light on the facts she had already collected. Obviously it couldn't, seeing as "semi-religious purposes" was the extent of its historical out-look. Now, she was about to make her own assessment.

Walking down the village road of Avebury, they began their hike at the northern entrance of the circle, as was popularly suggested. Looking ahead, Indu could see the stones. They were there, one following another, odd shaped and lonely. Her heart ached. She wanted to tell them that she did understand, that she did know of their greatness, although she was just a beginner. She was just beginning to grasp the unusual power of crystals, the mystery of electromagnetism, the essence of the spirit world. A small Indian man had been trying to teach her.

She moved around each one with unobtrusive open palms. She wanted to be receptive, to feel their energy, to feel their warmth. George checked the first few with her, too, out of curiosity. The hot spots were there. But he did not feel compelled to check them all, particularly with Rebecca watching. He didn't mind being an eccentric but he dared not go overboard. Indu, on the other hand, had already been acknowledged and accepted as a bona fide eccentric, so nothing seemed unusual about her waving her hands around the stones, at least not to Rebecca and George. No doubt the tourists looked suspiciously at her now and then as they casually walked from one stone to an-other. Oddly, no one asked what she was doing. An eccentric is often left in peace. Even George and Rebecca seemed to stay several stones ahead of her or else were roving about on top of the huge chalk bank. But Indu didn't mind. She was not going to miss her chance to test the power of the stones.

It was a beautiful day, sunny with a blue sky. Part of the four and a half acres had been fenced off as pasture land and the sight of grazing cows, peaceful and serene, was idyllic. Indu felt full and happy to be in such a lovely place. It was a moment which she knew would soon become vivid memory, as would Stonehenge and Salisbury, which would come the following day.

She felt a tinge of sadness as she approached the ring's end. It was not a sadness that the end had come. But as she looked back over her shoulder upon leaving the site, she again saw the last few stones, standing erect, noble and alone. Their aloneness seemed only to add to their mystery. What made her sad was that so few people in this millennium had ever tried to understand.

That evening her experimental results came in. She was flying sky-high. Literally, she could barely feel the floor with her feet. She felt flooded with joy and overcome by the sense of an inner awakening, much like after a deep meditation. She tried to tell George, and at the same time was curious to know if he wasn't energized, too. She wanted to enjoy the discovery with him, the excitement. He admitted he felt quite good but he stepped back and withdrew. There was a light in Indu's eyes which he had never seen before, or if he had seen it at Ickwell it had only appeared as a reflection from her teacher. Now she was radiating something and it more than bemused him. Who was she anyway, and what had she done? Indu saw the quizzical cloud hovering before his eyes and decided to control her enthusiasm, as difficult as it might be. "Some things simply cannot be explained in words, or shared with another. There are times we must be islands unto ourselves, with only God, or Nature or the divine as our witness," she had thought. She went back downstairs with him and acted as though nothing had happened. But inside, she continued to shake with joy.

At dinner there was another omelet before her and more fresh vegetables from the garden which she devoured hungrily. An apple crisp was served for dessert with coffee, but again there was no movement to leave the table. During the course of the meal, George had demonstrated his talent at blowing peas, throwing his head back, puckering his lips and popping one out of his mouth with a stream of air so forceful that the pea hovered above his lips until he ran out of breath. It had delighted Mrs. Freeth to no end, who immediately had had to try it herself, sending peas flying through the air right and left. Dared into it, Indu, more timid than Mrs. Freeth, sent the peas rolling down both cheeks. It was a matter of lifting the round ball dead center from the lips with a powerful enough blast and Indu defended her attempt saying it was too hard to concentrate with all the laughter.

The mood went from ridiculous to even more ridiculous as Mrs. Freeth carried on after dinner with ten choruses of "Lloyd George knew my father/Father knew Lloyd George. Lloyd George knew my father/Father knew Lloyd George," to the tune of "Onward Christian Soldiers." What was funny was not what she was singing but how she sang it. It put Indu in stitches. This was followed by George's demonstration of stomach rolling, which he could do quite well. Feigning shyness at first, he had held a towel up in front so only Mrs. Freeth could see.

Grabbing for it, Mrs. Freeth had cried, "Take it away, George. Take it away."

"I can't show this to the 'apple of my eye,'" George had protested. "What will she think?" But Mrs. Freeth had won out and Indu had responded with enthusiastic applause. Seeing as no one else had anything more to show off or tell, a motion was made to start the "winking game." Mrs. Freeth insisted that everyone at the table had to play, including her husband, who complained he wasn't any good. The game began by drawing ballots. All were blank except one. The person with the marked ballot was the "winker," or "killer" as was the game term. The "killer" had to be very crafty to keep his or her role secret. The objective was to wink "dead" as many people in the circle as possible without being discovered, all the while feigning innocence. Each watched the other closely to try to catch the "killer" in action. But when winked at, one was obligated to declare, "I'm dead," thereafter silenced from identifying the winker, but then becoming part of the conspiracy. For over an hour they sat eyeing each other suspiciously, "killing" and being "killed." The extraordinary fun was being the winker and not getting caught, building the suspense with everyone waiting and then, with a fast twitch of the eye, silencing another. What amazed Indu was that fifty years of age spanned the table and yet all were eager to play round after round, each hoping to get the "killer" ballot. Exhaustion finally stopped them.

The elders retired and Rebecca, Jason and his girlfriend, George and Indu all collapsed in the living room to watch television. During a commercial, George took the bench at their piano and revealed another hidden talent. He played a touch of something classical, but he did it beautifully. Now Indu was the one who stood back from him in quizzical wonder. Who was this man she loved, who could blow peas, and roll his stomach after a full dinner, and yield a rolling refrain from a piano, and who also had such lovely family friends?

The next morning she and George met in the bathroom. It was a large bathroom with a window that overlooked the courtyard and fixtures that looked a century old. Indu stood gazing out the window as George hopped into the tub. It was another beautiful day, with a clear blue sky, although the climatic capriciousness of the British Isles could make any pleasure outing a gamble. This fact, however, made Indu stand in even greater admiration of the rising sun and the warmth it beamed down on her face. That day they would head even further south to Stonehenge and Salisbury.

She heard George muttering something behind her. "Did you say something?"

"I outsmarted her last night."

"You did? What does that mean?" Indu asked.

"There was another surprise waiting for me under the covers. This time it was an old bellows."

"So you remembered to look first," Indu laughed. "Funny, there's not been anything in mine."

"She's just being nice to you. Wait until the next visit."

Indu liked the sound of that. It meant that he had in his mind that there would be a next time. For someone as reticent about the future as he was, the comment was a bold one. She hoped with all her heart that it would be true. She turned to the sink for the usual morning routine. It felt so natural having him there while she stuck a toothbrush in her mouth, and with her contacts freshly in place, she watched from the corner of her eye as he shook the water off his arms and legs before stepping from the tub, totally uninhibited as he flung the towel this way and that. Could he have any idea how dearly she regarded him?

They were soon off to Stonehenge, a picnic lunch of sandwiches, fruit and gooey cookies from Rebecca packed in a plastic box. Rebecca could not come on this trip since a business acquaintance had called that morning needing help with some horses. She was known in the area to be quite a good horsewoman, and George and Indu had both encouraged her to take care of business. George knew the roads well anyway. He looped them through the small town of Devizes where one of the best Neolithic collections of artifacts was exhibited, but the small museum was unfortunately closed on Sundays. Driving along the A344 for a short distance, the stone megaliths suddenly loomed ahead. The road actually passed just yards from the Heel Stone.

They parked the car, paid the admission fee and walked through the pedestrian underground which passed beneath the road. As they emerged from the tunnel, Indu's eyes were mesmerized by the stones, the upright sarsens standing sixteen feet tall, many weighing fifty tons. They had been transported from the Marlborough Downs twenty miles north, the same area where those of Avebury had come from. Several of those now standing were still connected by lintels, flat stones resting horizontally on top of the tall uprights. Indu was immediately amazed at the refinement of the site compared to the more natural appearing Avebury. The enormous height of the stones was not the only striking difference. Stonehenge exhibited an unbelievable precision. The massive rectangular, flat-sided slabs had been set into the ground at depths that allowed the tops of all the uprights to be on the same horizontal plane. But before erection, each upright had also been tapered toward the top to give a slight convex outline, a technique in Greek architecture called "entasis." The resulting effect was the cancellation of perspective upon close viewing. This gave them the optical illusion of being straight-sided all the way up, instead of narrower at the top. The question was why such great pains had been taken to shape the stones. Was it only to give an appearance of increased height?

Furthermore, "Stone Age" man had jointed the uprights to the lintels, although it was not easily visible. Indu, however, had read that hollow mortice holes on the underside of the lintels fitted over tenons projecting from the tops of the uprights. The lintels themselves were also interlocked by vertical tongues and grooves. These were not joints of masons, however, but the joints of carpenters, as Neolithic man imitated the methods learned with timber.

As Indu approached the stone circle, she could see that the henge and the area immediately surrounding had been roped off. Visitors were no longer permitted to walk among the stones without special permission. The number of tourists had so drastically increased in the past decade that the Department of the Environment had feared for the preservation of what had been recognized as one of the most profound historical sites in existence. Profundity aside, it was one that was captivating the fascination of more and more people. Other prehistoric sites had yet to win such popularity. But if the rise in sincere inquisition prevailed, their time would come in the future.

Indu had mixed emotions about the ropes. In one sense she was glad that precautions were being taken to preserve the site. Obviously, thousands of trampling feet year after year would have to leave an indelible mark. Still, she was saddened that she would not be able to conduct the same experiment that she had done at Avebury. She would simply not be allowed close enough to "feel" the stones. Only if permission was granted following a written request would she be allowed inside the stone ring.

She stopped to read the signs that bordered the walk approaching the henge. They told of the henge's construction, a feat encompassing over a thousand years, involving three separate stages, the first of which had begun in 3100 B.C. The uprights and lintels had actually not been erected until around 2000 B.C. Other minor changes in the stones' formation had been made until 1550 B.C. The last alteration at the site involved the Avenue, a processional earthwork demarcated by low-lying parallel mounds. Originally built between 2500 and 2000 B.C., the Avenue was extended in 1100 B.C. to the River Avon near West Amesbury. This suggested that Stonehenge, to which the Avenue led, was still in use at that date, and probably for some time afterward, a total of almost seventeen centuries.

ℰ * * * ℭ

She told me that the beauty of this most famous stone circle had taken her breath away, although at a glance anyone could see that the past three thousand years had been devastating, leaving only a faint semblance of what had once been. A disclaimer on the last sign relieved the onus of ignorance from the mind of modern-day man. Indu had carefully written it down and read it to me now. It said: "We shall never know what religious beliefs Stonehenge represents, or what forms of worship or ceremonies took place within it. These are questions, like many others concerning prehistoric sites, for which the evidence provides no real answers, either because it is not there, or because it is completely ambiguous."

"Thus absolved from stupidity," Indu said to me, "tourists are free to admire the colossal efforts of prehistoric man."

ℰ * * * ℭ

Indu could not take her eyes off of it. She and George stayed for two hours, walking from one end of the ropes to the other and back again, pausing twice to sit and stare. Indu blessed George a hundred times over for his patient tolerance of her seeming idolization of the stones. She felt she could not get enough of them, an insatiability compounded by the fact that only long-range viewing was permitted. Indu had some idea of why Neolithic man had built it, but how they had done it still remained tantalizingly obscure to her, as it did for everyone. She was glad at least that modern man could not absolve himself of all ignorance. The evidence was there, ancient man had done it, fifty-ton stones carried twenty miles and without wheel or pulley. It was a sight to behold.

Not wanting to test George's patience, Indu finally consented to continue on to Salisbury, but not until garnering a picture of her and George standing side by side in front of the henge, taken by an amiable tourist. It was a gut feeling, but a strong one, that somehow she, George and the stones were all connected. It seemed mysteriously fitting that they should stand together again.

The city of Salisbury was only eight miles away. Indu and George drove straight to the cathedral, whose Chapter House was in direct alignment with the Stonehenge ley.

ℰ) * * * ℭ

To further clarify that "leys" were the "lines" of electromagnetic energy running through the landscape, Indu read to me the definition originally forged by Alfred Watkins in his 1925 book *The Old Straight Track*: "a network of lines, standing out like glowing wires across the country, intersecting the sites of churches, old stones and ancient sites." In other words, they linked areas of sanctity. Leys were not a concept unanimously accepted. But when confronted by scoffing orthodox archaeologists, the ley proponents felt justified in humorously citing the Columbus principle: people had laughed at Christopher

Columbus after he reported the finding of a new continent. The world was never without its skeptics.

Indu went on to give me a little more historical background. Salisbury Cathedral had been built 2,000 years after Bronze-Aged man had become disinterested in Stonehenge. The cathedral was first begun at one site in 1075 A.D. and then moved to its present site in 1220 A.D. and consecrated in 1258 A.D. It had already seen 725 years of active worship. In one book, Indu told me she had read that somewhere over a portal was inscribed, "May the burdens of those weighing heavy of the heart be lifted." It was a prayer for all humanity. Visitors were further encouraged in the cathedral brochure: "If you wish to sit quietly, to think, to pray or just to rest, please use the Trinity Chapel beyond the High Altar, or the Morning Chapel on the north side of the Quire or the Chapel of St. Michael in the South Transept." I glanced at this brochure as she continued her story.

℘ * * * ℘

Upon entering, Indu and George did just that—they found places to sit and pray. Indu chose to sit quietly in a wooden chair in the Trinity Chapel, located at the far end of the cathedral. In front of her in brilliant shades of blue and accents of red, orange, green and amber were a peaked row of tall, arched stained-glass windows. The stained-glass design was abstract, clearly dating it to be from the fairly recent past, but it still possessed a majesty befitting the hallowed hall it embellished. Indu found it entrancing. After a short period of silent meditation, she got up to find George.

Seeing no signs of him in the vicinity, she suspected he had also found a quiet place to sit and wondered if she could attune their spirits and find him. All sensors out, she began walking slowly. She looked to the right and to the left and on passing a doorway leading into a centrally located section, she peeked around the corner and saw George. Whether she really had "tuned in," it amused her greatly how easy it had been. George sat alone in a pew, hands folded in his lap, eyes closed. She stood a moment looking at him. The nobility of his spirit tugged heavily at her heart, just as it had when she had first seen him. He was never one to claim piety, however, and would in fact be the first to give verse to his sinful ways. But for Indu, even during their most trying times, his pureness of heart was ever-present. It was only his bombastic, analytical mind that could confound her, not to say that she was without her own stubborn shortcomings.

Alerted to her presence, he took a deep prayerful breath and then joined her. Together they went to view the Magna Carta on permanent display in the cathedral's Chapter House. It was one of four original surviving copies. Two others were housed in the British Library in London and the third in the Lincoln Cathedral. The Latin document had been sealed in 1215 by King John at Runneymede upon the insistent demands of the barons. It laid down what the barons considered to be the recognized and fundamental principles of a government and bound king and barons alike to maintain them. Its main provisions were that no man should be punished without fair trial, that ancient liberties should generally be preserved and that no unusual demands should be made by an overlord to his vassal without the sanction of the great council of the realm.

It was a document held in high esteem by both British and Americans, its basic principles having been incorporated into the Constitution of the United States. Protected in its glass case, it was proof that the written word had great power to alter the affairs of mankind. Looking at the minutely scribbled Latin letters, Indu couldn't help wondering if preliterate man had really been in need of such a piece of paper. Could they have carried on seventeen centuries of construction at one site if there had not been a unity and peaceful bond amongst them? She even went as far as to speculate that literacy itself had somehow made necessary the stipulations of laws and individual rights. At some point, humanity had lost the sense of unity.

Back at the car, George announced he would like to be married at the Cathedral. It seemed a lovely idea, but one unquestionably requiring connections in high places. Surprisingly, he had one. It was Jim, his school chaplain-mentor. Jim had belonged to a parish in the Diocese, and had even given several sermons at the Cathedral. She found it touching that a young man should have in mind the place of his impending marriage. She wondered whether he also had in mind the woman with whom he would embark on the conjugal journey. She decided not to press the issue and he said no more about it.

They arrived back at the farm in time to help Rebecca and her uncle load a flatbed truck with bales of straw. After that would come dinner and then a hurried departure so they could make it back to London before midnight. Consuming a third omelet, Indu doubted she had eaten so many eggs in the span of any three days before. But she astutely watched as it was being prepared and committed to memory the fact that Mrs. Freeth submitted the frying pan and beaten egg to the heat of the broiler before stuffing and folding. When Indu informed George of the trick, Mrs. Freeth interjected that she had a frying pan for George, if he wanted one to take back. It was agreed since it was something Oliver was without.

A bag with the frying pan was presented as hugs and kisses were generously exchanged in farewell. The next morning before George and Oliver left for work, the pan was pulled from its wrapper and found to be a rusting relic with a bulging envelope sitting in the middle. It was another one of her jokes. And knowing its originator, George suspiciously held the envelope up to the window for careful scrutiny. The bulge had a tail, no doubt something caught by the cat. Tossing it triumphantly back into the frying pan, he departed for work.

ဆ * * * ၛ

That morning Indu had written to the Freeths to thank them for their generous hospitality. As usual, she had kept a copy of her note which read: "We had a nice two-hour drive back

Sunday night, chatting all the way about the weekend. George said that a stay with the Freeths was about the best cure for anyone who took themselves (or just about anything) too seriously. I couldn't agree more. I haven't laughed so much in a long time. Really did enjoy being at your home—dogs, parrots and all! Don't think I've eaten so well (all those home-grown veggies) or so much since I've been in England. But do you know, Mrs. Freeth, that both George and Oliver went off this morning leaving your mysteriously bulging envelope on the kitchen table, left carefully unopened after holding it up to the window to see that the blob had a tail, leaving me to dispose of it or put up with the smell! They are dear fellows! Still not sure how much longer I'll be able to stay in London, but do hope sometime I'll see you again."

THIRTY-EIGHT

~

The question of how much longer to remain in London under the given circumstances was one frequently preying on Indu's mind. She had already stayed longer than originally planned. To leave before establishing a clear direction in her relationship with George, however, did not seem to be advisable either. For her own peace of mind, she needed to know what hope, if any, existed for a future with this man whom she loved.

She knew he loved her too, but he had never once seriously said, "I want you to be in my life," and the absence of such a statement left the doors of uncertainty open, and vulnerably so. He had suggested that she could stay in London until November and then travel with him across Canada to the Pacific Islands and then on to Australia. There he planned to spend an indeterminate amount of time as a scuba diver, assisting his sister in research for her master's degree in reef and marine ecology. Indu was heartened that the invitation had been made but disheartened that it was not followed by an avowal, "Come with me because I want you with me." Instead, the unspoken message received was, "This is what I'm doing and come along if you please."

Yet, they loved each other. They loved because they had to love, they were destined to love. As the weeks passed, however, a realization slowly dawned that an emotional commitment from him was not likely to be forthcoming at any imminent date. Without a permanent job or permanent address, he was not a bastion of stability ready to don the matrimonial ring. And without a commitment, Indu could see no wisdom in making a life-rending sacrifice to follow in tow the man she loved. She began to sense the crossroad that lay ahead of them, and her only hope was that at their inevitable parting they could at least agree to bring the roads of their lives together again in the not-too-distant future. A foreboding which weighed heavily on her heart was that the crossroad would make a sudden appearance.

Fortunately, they both had the courage to talk about a pending separation, a separation which would require them to make some resolve in their relationship. Either they would decide to maintain close contact via post and phone with a future meeting planned or they would draw the line and say that together they could go no further.

"What do you think will happen?" George asked her one night as they were curled up next to each other.

"I don't know what's going to happen between us. I don't know what's best. It's extremely difficult to carry on a long-distance relationship. We already know that. Yet, obviously, it's not the time to set a wedding date."

"Good grief. The very thought gives me the shudders."

"What?" Indu said with a pretense of indignation. "You know you were the first to bring the topic up."

"You mean a year ago? Yes, but I was naively out of my head," he said, defending himself against his own words.

"You were sweetly out of your head, but I warn you, I'm going to stop believing anything you say if you keep changing your mind about things."

"I don't change my mind about things," he said with his usual stubbornness. "I'm only being cautious."

"Yes, I can see that. But back to your original question about us... I think the answer is going to come in the eleventh hour. I think out of the blue we will know whether we should stay together or not."

It felt good that they could be honest with each other but the subject brought a sadness to them both. It was another foreboding sign. Granted, one could argue that if only she would commit to stay with him, he would probably be able to commit also. From her viewpoint, the argument was hardly a healthy psychological move. If mutuality was missing, then the resulting imbalance in commitment could make living together intolerable.

George might have seen it a little differently. The very suggestion that she would leave him was in effect forcing his hand, pressuring him to make a decision in order to alter her plans. What he may have been wanting was for her to alter them herself as a true demonstration of her unmitigated love. Neither was wrong in their feelings, but their inner confusion over the situation was mounting daily.

One evening George blurted out, "I think it was a good decision for you not to agree to go to Australia." It took Indu by surprise. She was sitting at the kitchen table and he had his back to her while he sharpened some knives.

"Doesn't he realize," she thought, "that I'd go in a second if he would only say he wanted me with him? It's not because I don't want to. Can't he see that? Honorably I cannot go unless he acknowledges there is a future in our relationship." Pride and tact kept her from saying anything. She did not want to sound as if begging a proposal.

At another time he asked if she couldn't at least stay until the first of October when his mother would come to London. The suggestion astonished her and itself seemed full of contradiction, although she really did want to meet his mother. Still, what was the point of such a meeting if there was no future for them?

He might have countered, "Can't you see it's too difficult for me to say the words you want me to say. Can't you see I'm trying to show you what's really in my heart?"

But she couldn't see it. Blinded as she was by her own emotional turmoil, she couldn't see his difficulty in saying, "I love you; please stay."

As the date approached for the annual International Juggling Convention, the strain between them was only exacerbated. The convention was being held in Brussels. George had unflinchingly announced that he would attend. Again, there was the hanging question of what she should do. Her heart wanted to go with him. But George, with seeming careful intention, had maintained an ambiguous stance in her regard. Before his departure, sitting across from her at the kitchen table, he asked, "Well, have you brushed up on your French?" His eyes were wide and questioning. They were asking, "Are you coming?"

But for Indu it was nothing but Australia in a smaller version. She had taken the initiative to come and see him in London. Could he really expect her to tag along after him everywhere he went?

"George, I'm not going to go to Brussels. I've got work to do here researching more on the standing stones. And maybe we need time apart to think, to decide what we ought to do." Without protest or emotional display, he accepted her decision silently.

That night they made love almost as a desperate attempt to express what they had failed to put into words. They truly did want to be with each other. It was a passionate embrace. It should have erased all ambiguity in their actions and words. They dearly loved each other. The aftermath, however, was strangely an unhappy one, leaving both feeling awkward and uneasy. "How can you love me so intensely and choose to leave me?' or "Why aren't you asking me to be part of your life?" These were the cries from their hearts, unspoken and unanswered.

The next evening, she went to see him off at the bus. He suddenly asked if she'd still be in London when he got back. She looked at him with a bewildered smile. The very thought had actually crossed her mind, to simply disappear silently, foregoing any tortuous farewell. Had he sensed that she might do it? Looking into his dark brown eyes, she knew she could not. She would wait for his return. "No, I will still be here."

A flood of emotion broke from them both, and they held each other tightly. "I wish so much that you were coming, too." His words were spoken quickly, as though escaping from some closely guarded place. How desperately she had wanted to hear those words, and now they came too late.

"If only he had said them the night before," she had thought. She would have had a packed bag with her that very minute. How different things might have been if she had gone with him. She had always wondered if it might not have become the turning point in their relationship. It would forever be unknown.

Four days passed and George returned, arriving back at the flat at one o'clock in the morning after hitching a ride with another Londoner from the convention. Indu was half asleep when she heard him quietly enter the flat and push open the door to the sitting room. He dropped his bags and came over to sit on the edge of the bed beside her. As she took his hand she felt a quivering joy at the very sight of him again. She had missed him. While he was gone she had realized there was so much they needed to talk about. A great part of their difficulty had been caused by what she perceived as a clear lack of communication. Why had he not told her sooner that he really wanted her to go to Brussels? Why had pride and principle barred her from expressing her heart to him? Many topics had been brought up only to be left on the cliff's edge untouched or unclarified, left to teeter precariously, adding to the instability of any topic remotely related.

One such example was their discussion on the need to feel complete in a relationship. George had voiced the opinion that completeness was a product of two people successfully joining their lives together. It rang similarly to the adage, "We're not whole until we meet our better half." But the idea that one needed another before feeling complete was but the fuel which propelled many to bounce from one unsuccessful relationship to another, in Indu's eyes. Her view was that no one could make life complete for another. Expecting any individual to fulfill such a demand was as practical as carrying a bomb around in one's pocket. Eternally looming on the horizon would be danger that the other would cease to fulfill what was needed. For Indu, completeness was not an external acquisition but an internal realization. She and George had dropped the subject without resolution but it was still on Indu's mind and she knew it was one that they needed to probe more deeply.

Yet, inwardly she was torn. If heart-to-heart talks over a period of another few weeks did not bring a clarity to their intentions toward each other, then she would have to make the heart-crushing decision to either accept the state of non-commitment or to return to her life in the States. But her decision already seemed a foregone conclusion. While George was gone, she had begun inquiring into seat availability on flights departing in the forthcoming two weeks. Economy class was fully booked well in advance, but cancellations were not uncommon. She was advised to call daily. At dinner one evening, she told Oliver that there was a possibility she might be leaving soon. She deemed it appropriate to tell him for two reasons: one being he was the host and it seemed the considerate thing to do, and two, and probably more important, she suspected he might pass word onto George. Coming indirectly, she hoped it would encourage George to look even more closely at his feelings and come to some decision of his own.

To stay without resolution would have been an affront to her own dignity and sense of integrity. To leave without one would also doom the relationship. The question was what to do. Studies with her teacher had trained her to recognize an endogenous signal, a warning sign triggered by serious disequilibrium in herself. As much as she loved George, she could not let their relationship erode her own psychic and emotional balance. At all costs, she had to be true to herself. She would not depend on him to give meaning to her life. He in fact could not.

୫୦ * * * ୯୫

Indu had very much identified with Gail Sheehy's book *Passages*. It was one with which I was also quite familiar. Sheehy had written on the need to balance "both individuality and mutuality,"[50] something Indu knew was essential in any relationship. The words gave expression to intuitive feelings which had already emerged from her own spiritual practice. "Each of us travels alone," she read aloud to me. "To reach the clearing beyond, we must stay with the weightless journey through uncertainty." She quoted Sheehy further: "The crux of it is to see, to feel, and finally to *know* that none of us can aspire to fulfillment through someone else."[51]

Indu elaborated with her own ideas. "It is at the end of that journey of uncertainty that the oneness within ourselves can be discovered," she said to me. "It exists. We know it exists for we have glimpsed it during two seemingly opposite encounters. Opposite, that is, unless one has studied tantra." She paused, wanting to make sure I understood. I nodded that I did. "So you see. We have felt that oneness in our intimate sexual embraces with a beloved and in any devoted worship."

She then read to me another quote from Sheehy: "In the ecstasy of sexual union we come closest to recapturing the feeling of fusion [...] a state of timeless harmony reminiscent of that original state when self and other seemed as one."[52] When she looked up from her paper, I saw a face with the most earnest expression.

"Do you know there is a Sanskrit mantra which says the same thing?" she asked me. "It even describes that sense of uncertainty when we have lost that feeling of fusion. Guruji has said it covers relationships both between two lovers and between God and the devotee."

Solemnly she recited it for me:

YŪYAM VAYAM VAYAM YŪYAM
ITYĀSĪN MATIR ĀVAYOH
KIM JĀTAM ADHUNĀ YENA
YŪYAM YŪYAM VAYAM VAYAM

"It means: 'You are me and I am you. This was our contract, our understanding. Now what has happened, that you are now you and I am now me?' It is lamenting that we have lost the unity within ourselves. When that feeling is lost, then we feel disconnected from everyone and foremost from God." Then with a grin, she admitted, "I've just remembered a parable that Guruji would tell if ever someone questioned the existence of a divine presence. Do you want to hear it?" Of course I did.

"There was a father and son. The son believed in God and the father did not.

The father challenged the son, 'If there is a God, then prove His existence.'

The son remained silent. The father thought he had shown his son that a man of reason does not believe in an ultimate authority and he had departed only to return a few days later to find an exquisite oil painting sitting on a chair in the middle of his son's apartment. He exclaimed, 'What a work of art! Who did it?'

The son replied, 'Nobody.'

Disconcerted by the preposterous answer, he protested, 'But that's impossible. Paint cannot simply arrange itself on a canvas.'

The son countered, 'Couldn't it have happen by chance?'

'Don't be absurd,' the father retorted.

'So you're saying,' the son asked, 'that logically some outside presence had to be involved to create this work of art?'

'I have said it,' the father responded. 'Paint doesn't just appear on a canvas.'

'Yet, you claim,' said the son, 'that by chance the universe has appeared; that a creation much greater than this oil painting can come into existence without the orchestration of a commanding force?'''

The parable was well worth the moment's digression. But now, taking a deep breath, Indu commenced with the final episode of her story, a tale of a relationship epitomized by the unbelievable, the improbable, the mystical.

෨ * * * ෫

Two nights after George's return, as they were sitting alone at the kitchen table, Indu decided it was time to broach the need for serious discussion. She did not intend that they should stay up all night seeking a resolution. What she had in mind was simply to present the crucial necessity to explore ambiguities between them, and anticipating George's question of "What ambiguities do you mean?" she had mentally prepared four questions. They were questions meant to exemplify that their communication had fallen way short and that this was what was making the navigation of troubled waters between them so difficult.

Earlier that evening, George had gone off somewhat hesitantly to the Tuesday evening jugglers' workshop, one which would be attracting many from the International Convention. Indu had encouraged him to go, feeling it was important that they each pursue their individual interests. She was thankful he came home invigorated and in high spirits. Being in a clear frame of mind herself, it seemed as good a time as any to talk. Also, presuming George had been alerted to her possible departure plans, she did not want to let too many days go by before explaining what her real feelings were behind her decision. She loved him. She did not want to go. But she could not be untrue to herself. The very necessity for such an explanation also exemplified the sadly barren field between them which they had both let evolve for fear of confronting the future, a fear which was undermining the psychological and emotional needs of both.

"George," she began. "You know while you were gone, I did a lot of thinking."

"I did, too," he said.

"At least we're off to a good start," Indu thought.

She continued. "What I realized was that there were many things that were unclear for me. I think that if sometime soon we could talk about them it would be helpful for both of us."

"Okay. It's already pretty late tonight and tomorrow evening I'm meeting my dad." Indu knew his father was back in London. "How about we do it Thursday evening?"

Indu agreed. "All right. Let's do it then."

Getting up from the table, almost nervously, he asked without directly facing her, "What sort of things were unclear?"

It was as she had foreseen. But she hesitated. If he wasn't wanting to get into a heavy discussion that night, it seemed more prudent to save her questions for Thursday. "Oh, they were just particular points from previous discussions."

"For example, like what?"

She could see he was not to be eluded. But thinking it was a good sign that he wanted to know, she decided to present the questions, not as separate entities, but as one glowing example of the desire she had to understand his thinking, his needs, his wants. And in so doing, she would set the stage to present her own desires, hopes and needs.

ℰ) * * * Cℬ

Indu interjected, reading to me one more quote from Sheehy. Surviving as a couple was just as Sheehy had described: the "most delicate and enigmatic balancing act of all: the art of giving to another while still maintaining a lively sense of self. Or, to put it another way, the capacity for intimacy." [53]

ℰ) * * * Cℬ

Preparing to answer his question, Indu hoped she and George could find the right balance. She began, "Well, for example, I was wondering what you meant by saying you thought I'd made the right decision to not go to Australia. I was also wondering what you meant by feeling complete with someone. And if our relationship goes only as far as this visit, then what difference does it make if I leave in one week or three? Which reminds me of the time you suggested I stay through until November. What were you thinking then?"

She had been wrong about the balance.

His immediate response left her stunned.

"What is it that you want from me? What is it that you expect me to say?" Having spun around to face her, he then bolted from the kitchen, swinging the door closed behind him.

She sat without moving. It amazed her that she had not foreseen the threat that the very questions themselves would pose. The final inning had been played, bringing home the glaring reality of how far out of reach they were from each other. It was time to go home.

After several minutes passed, she went into the sitting room. George was on the bed, lying on his back with his arm swung across his forehead. She sat down next to him and said the words she had dreaded ever having to say. The eleventh hour had come. "I guess it's time for me to go." She swallowed hard, trying to fight back tears that wanted to fall with each blink.

Without moving his arm from his eyes, he spoke not with anger, but with a voice of a man torn between emotion and pride. "Yes, it's probably for the best. It's probably for the best."

Neither one could say any more. Closing her eyes, Indu felt a pain welling in her chest. It brought with it a gush of tears and she buried her head in her hands. She had never before cried in such anguish. Although fully anticipating that a separation was likely, nothing could have prepared her for the shock that the end had come for them. In the darkness behind her closed eyes, aware that her shoulders were shaking uncontrollably with each sob, a numbness pulled part of her consciously away. "I cannot believe that in my whole life, I have never felt such an overpowering pain, an anguish that torments every nerve. This is what it is to suffer. It is amazing to feel it, to be human."

The thoughts did not subdue the torrents of emotion but only made her shoulders shake with even deeper sobs. Finally dropping her hands, she looked over at George to see his eyes upon her, looking pathetically helpless, wet with his own tears. She leaned toward him and he took her in his arms and they kissed with a passion, not of reuniting but of final farewell.

Thirty-six hours later she was on a flight back across the Atlantic, having secured a seat for immediate departure. The pain had not stopped. She could eat nothing, feel nothing, think nothing. With headphones over her ears, she tuned to some music, trying to find a distraction. The voice of Elvis came across, singing "Memories." The tears were back. The memories of her time with George would always be with her. Would she ever be able to hear a love song and not think of him?

The six-hour flight seemed an eternity, but by the evening's end, she was once again sitting on the floor before her teacher at the same ashram in New York where she had come at seventeen. She looked absolutely composed, if not almost serene. The pain was not gone. It had only gone deeper within, to hide itself from the eyes of others. But one pair of eyes did see it.

ℰℴ * * * ℂℬ

She picked up her notebook one more time. "After the silent meditation, Guruji began to speak. I recorded verbatim his words. This is what he said: 'Body, mind and senses are for going out. They are not for God. God is your real home. You don't need a body to see God; you don't need the Vedas, or the Bible, or science or law or anything. Only I-AM is needed. You will always feel something or other is missing while in time and space. When you are with God, then you will feel nothing is missing. When we have union with God, then even our sickness can be a cause of our Enlightenment. Our problem is our disconnection from God. Our problem is not poverty, or lack of success, or accident. We are lost, disconnected. Do you know the cause of suffering? You can feel it when there is disunity in an intimate relationship.'"

There was a heightened intensity as she spoke. "He looked directly at me as his pen pounded down on the paper in front of him. He continued looking at me saying, 'Not an ordinary relationship but an intimate one.' My eyes were held by his and my breathing practically stopped. I felt any movement would make me miss the words that were to follow. 'Disunity with the divine Light will cause the greatest suffering. Our separation from our divine Self, from God, should feel just as painful as our separation and disunity from a beloved intimate friend.'"

Indu had sat in front of Guruji in disbelief as these words had penetrated her mind. She told me, "I sat there and thought, 'I see why I had to meet George, so I could deeply feel what Guruji has been telling us.'"

She continued. "It all sank in at once, that in time and space, we think we are limited by the bounds of a physical body and we believe, *yūyam yūyam, vayam vayam*—'I am me and you are you.' In effect, the mind/body paradigm acts to keep the individual self separate from the divine Self, and this separation creates all of our suffering. The paradox is that this sense of duality is an illusion which we take to be real, and our unity with God happens only when this illusion vanishes."

She had already had glimpses of being "beyond" this paradigm, so she knew the truth of what Guruji was saying. But how to make the illusion of time and space vanish for good? Guruji was showing her the way. The heartache she felt in her separation from George was what she should feel in her separation from the divine. She was startled to find herself asking, "Do I feel this same anguish and longing for God?" She knew the answer would lead to something mystically beyond the limits of the body and mind. It would lead her to her "real home"—just as Guruji had always been saying. Her story was finished.

All that she told me that afternoon about the teachings of her Master, I recount here for those who have known that "longing" for love, to inspire them on their spiritual path. But I couldn't help wonder what had become of George. When I asked her, she gave me a half smile and mysteriously replied, "That's another story."

EPILOGUE

~

All plannings of the body and mind which are without the consent of "I-Am" (the Self) lead our life toward destruction. Our whole life is then running towards Disneyworld, where everything is artificial. When we meditate on the sense of "I-Am," then the mind evaporates.

This mind is not real. There is no such thing as "my mind," "his mind" or "her mind." As the ocean of air is undivided, although our lungs create the feeling of division, so the ocean of mind and consciousness is undivided, although the psychosomatic machine presents the sensation of division. As there is no separate air in us, so also there is no separate mind or consciousness in us.

This truth you will know by yourself automatically, without reading any holy book. [...] You will know the whole truth [...] if you meditate on "I-Am" above the body and mind.[54]

Shri Brahmananda Sarasavati
Excerpt from his essay, "The Most Powerful Man," 1986

Do George and Indu really part forever? I worked on this manuscript twenty-five years ago and at that time, I did not know what lay ahead in my future and so this seemed the best place to end the story. In fact, writing was no doubt cathartic to healing my broken heart. As explained in the preface, this is an autobiographical account of the twists and turns of my spiritual growth and the amazing Guru who guided my way.

I recently found this entry in my notes made on the day when the manuscript's first draft was completed. I was once again back in London and it was August 18, 1987, at 2:24 a.m.: "The book is finished. Wrote a total of 117 pages since arriving in London. Adding to that the pages written here in 1985 [when staying with 'George' after Copenhagen] and calculating its percentage against the total number of pages, it came out that twenty-five percent of the book was written here in 'Oliver's' flat —possibly the most important twenty-five percent, the beginning and the end. Have realized I could not have finished it any place else—[…] what the walls spoke, the memories they brought back. 'Oliver' was definitely a part of the book's destiny, of my destiny. We do have a uniquely unusual friendship.

"Tomorrow, August 19, marks the anniversary of meeting 'George.' Three years ago to that day he came into my life. Who would have imagined that three years from that point a book over the relationship would be complete with thirty-eight chapters. Yet, at that time I felt something unusual, the drive to write down the events in careful detail. Those notes were invaluable in recapturing the mysticism and romance of those first three weeks.

"Am happy—not excessively but quietly. I knew this day would eventually come. God bless Guruji for encouraging me that I would finish it. 'Oliver' is not here tonight. He had to stay over at the hotel [where he worked]. It's nice to be here alone—although [...] no doubt we will celebrate!"

Three months after that I wrote the following, a hypothetical letter to "George" asking for permission to use his letters: "I have printed your letters [in the book] not because now they are any less dear to me but because they are beautifully written. Please do not think I am exploiting anything that we have shared. If after reading the book you do not think they serve a noble purpose, then I will leave them out and do something else. What was happening between us was special. We were two people searching for God, searching for the right path and wondering if we should do it together. I simply could not find the right words to express those feelings that would be better than our letters. I did have my reservations in doing it because they were meant just for you and me to read. But the story [*The Standing Stone: The Challenge of the Master*] is about the journey to God, and the letters show that it is no easy journey, with the rational and intuitive minds battling away, sometimes logically and sometimes illogically. Before you decide anything, please read Part III." And he did, of course, grant his permission.

Why it was that years passed before publishing, I really cannot say. I have always felt that the book had its own destiny. My sister, upon reading this manuscript a couple of years ago and knowing what transpired in my life, felt I should reveal a little more of what happened between myself and "George." My editor also encouraged me to write just a few words about the outcome of the love story. What I could write is another volume of chapters. I ask the reader's forgiveness for not revealing more here, except to say that the romance does not end after my return to the States. "George" and I eventually meet again in Kenya, a trip planned only after Guruji asked me a key question at a pivotal time, about eighteen months after that heart-breaking departure from London. I was working on the book while traveling in the group with Guruji in Florida. Guruji emerged from his room late one evening, posed the question and gave me an unusual task to help me find the answer.

Epilogue

For now, I simply leave the reader with "George's" words, "So love is eternal after all." I hope someday to continue the story, because it will allow me to tell more of the mystical work of a Master.

Margaret Dillsaver, September 2, 2012
Ananda Ashram, Monroe, New York

GLOSSARY OF TERMS

These simple definitions are to help readers unfamiliar with Eastern philosophy gain a reasonable understanding of these concepts to enhance their enjoyment of the story. All the words are Sanskrit, or directly derived from Sanskrit, except where stated otherwise. (The diacritical marks, the lines and dots over or under a letter, are derived from a standard system of transliteration, the lines indicating long vowels, the dots a certain positioning of the tongue for proper pronunciation).

ashram – A place for spiritual training or renewal, where a peaceful atmosphere is cultivated.

Bhagavad Gītā – *Bhagavad* refers to "the Lord" and *Gītā* literally means "song." A religious scripture, or divine song, that contains the teachings of non-dualism and yoga philosophy, in the form of a dialogue between Lord Kṛishṇa and Arjuna, Kṛishṇa's greatest devotee. The *Gītā* is included as part of the epic *Mahābhārata*.

Buddha – Often referring to Gautama Buddha, an enlightened Master who taught universal truths, living in about the sixth century B.C. His teachings form the basis of Buddhist tradition.

chakra – Literally meaning "wheel." The chakras are the seven major astral or energy centers in the spine and brain, each with unique attributes.

dhyāna – Described by Patanjali in the *Yoga Sūtras* as one of the eight limbs (or steps) of yoga; meaning meditation or continuous concentration. Explained by Shri Brahmananda Sarasvati in the *Fundamentals of Yoga* as "autosuggestion."

Gāyatrī Mantra – A highly revered mantra, a Vedic Sanskrit verse meaning: "We meditate on the effulgent glory of the divine Light; may this Light inspire our understanding."

ghee – (Hindi) Clarified butter, used in Indian cuisine and also in the Vedic fire ceremony.

Gītā – Literally means "song." Refers to the *Bhagavad Gītā*.

Guru – *Ru* means "remover," and *gu* means "darkness or ignorance." A teacher, especially a spiritual teacher who undertakes to guide disciples to God realization.

Harih Om – A Sanskrit expression invoking supreme consciousness.

haṭha yoga – *Ha* symbolizes the sun; *ṭha* symbolizes the moon. Together they represent a system that helps restore the harmonious balance in the body and mind through practice of postures, breathing techniques and cleansing techniques.

jī – In Hindi, a suffix reflecting respect, as in Gurujī.

karma – Means "action." Also, cause and effect of our actions, whether from our current or past lives. Karma Yoga is work or activity offered without attachment to the fruits of our labor.

kikoi – (Swahili) A piece of cotton cloth with colored bands worn wrapped around the body. [not related to Eastern philosophy, but mentioned in the book.]

Kṛiṣhṇa – Lord Kṛiṣhṇa, honored as a manifestation of God on earth in India in prehistoric times. The *Mahābhārata*, a great epic poem, contains stories of his life. The *Bhagavad Gītā* summarizes Lord Kṛiṣhṇa's teachings.

kuṇḍalinī – Means "coiled energy." In yoga, it refers to concentrated energy that can move up the spine helping to lead the meditator to the highest realization. *Kuṇḍalinī* Yoga includes those practices which help awaken this energy coiled in a dormant state at the base of the spine.

Mahābhārata – A Sanskrit epic of unparalleled proportion, which among many other topics contains philosophical and devotional discussion on the "goals of life." Eighteen chapters of the *Mahābhārata* constitute the *Bhagavad Gītā.*

mālā – Literally means "garland." More commonly a set of beads, usually 108 in number, worn for spiritual purposes around the neck or used to count the repetitions of a mantra.

mantra – *Man* means "mind" and *tra* signifies "protection." A mantra is a sacred word or phrase that when repeated verbally or mentally helps still the mind.

mūlādhāra – The first chakra, or energy center, positioned at the base of the spine.

nādam – Referring to the inner sound current, the "unstruck" sound, the sound of silence; cosmic music, the music that is uncreated and uncaused.

Nāda Yoga – the practice of using the inner sound current as a means to move beyond identity with the body and mind.

neti – A yogic cleansing practice of the nasal passageway using warm salt water or, in oil neti, almond or sesame oil, which has the added benefit of stimulating the brain.

Om – The mystical sacred syllable designating the supreme; the symbol for the inner (or cosmic) sound and vibration.

pandit – The same as "pundit" or scholar.

Patanjali – Author of the *Yoga Sūtras,* the great classical text at the root of the School of Yoga in Indian philosophy.

prāṇa – Energy or life force, also breath. When this energy flow is balanced and strong, then health prevails. When *prāṇa* is weak or disturbed, psychological and physical distress may occur.

pūjā – Literally means "worship." Religious prayers, songs and rituals performed with devotional attention to honor or worship the divine.

sādhanā – Spiritual practice, the foundation for liberation; effort made to understand ourselves so we can achieve the purpose of life, connecting our consciousness to the infinite within.

sañsāra – Refers to the "world of constant changes" dominated by the body/mind perceptions; the cyclic existence of birth, death and rebirth, the illusion from which one is liberated after enlightenment.

Sanskrit – Ancient Indian language, the language of the "science of vibration." The language of early sacred texts, such as the Vedas, Upanishads, *Yoga Sūtras* of Patanjali and *Bhagavad Gītā*. It is related to all Indo-European languages. Sanskrit mantras are used to facilitate spiritual awakening.

satsang – *Sat* means "truth," also "those who follow the truth"; *sanga* means "company." Keeping company with those people assembled for the purpose of contemplating spiritual truths, especially by means of meditation.

shāntih – Literally means "peace," often chanted three times after chanting *Om*.

Shri – Used in India as a title of respect.

svādhiṣṭhāna – The second chakra, or energy center, positioned at the sacrum of the spine.

tantra – A conscious method for liberation, originating in India, focused on total union of the individual soul with the supreme consciousness, by expanding one's understanding of the depth of the mind and becoming master of it. Tantra Yoga is the practice of this method and includes a heightened awareness during sexual union.

trāṭakam – A meditation technique of gazing one-pointedly at an object. Gazing steadily with the eyes is recommended in yoga scripture as a powerful method for focusing life force energy and developing concentration. It can awaken psychic powers that are dormant in everyone.

Vedas – *Veda* means "knowledge." The most ancient of the sacred scriptures of India, containing spiritual knowledge encompassing all aspects of life.

yoga – Literally means "union"; the root *yuj* means to "yoke" or "unite." Yoga is the pathway to union or oneness with God.

Yoga Sūtras of Patanjali – *Sūtra* means "thread." Written by Patanjali, a Sanskrit treatise on yoga with four chapters explaining the practice that enables an aspirant to be God-realized. The *Sūtras* give the points and techniques for the meditative discipline of liberation.

yogi – One who practices yoga; one spiritually attuned to the higher states of consciousness; one who renounces mundane attachments and selflessly works to help others.

ENDNOTES

PREFACE

1   Deepak Chopra, *The Third Jesus: The Christ We Cannot Ignore*, Harmony Books, an imprint of the Crown Publishing Group, a division of Random House, Inc. Reprinted with permission.

2   'Osho,' with permission of the OSHO International Foundation, www.osho.com.

3   Dolano "Who Am I?" Opening lecture to "Intensive Satsang," Pune, India, November 9, 2007, private audio recording. Quote from transcript reprinted with kind permission. *See* www.dolano.com *or* www.myspace.com/dolanosatsang *or* friendsofdolano.org *for information on joining an Intensive Satsang with Dolano.*

PART I – CHAPTER ONE

4   Rammurti S. Mishra, M.D., *Fundamentals of Yoga: A Handbook of Theory, Practice and Application* (New York: Julian Press, 1959), 62. Currently available as: Ramamurti S. Mishra, M.D. (Shri Brahmananda Sarasvati), *Fundamentals of Yoga: A Handbook of Theory, Practice and Application* (Monroe: Baba Bhagavandas Publication Trust, 2002). Distributed by the Trust and Ananda Ashram, Monroe, NY. Chapter Five reprinted with permission. [Author's Note: "Rammurti" is another spelling of "Ramamurti" used by Dr. Mishra in his earlier published works. I reference Ramamurti S. Mishra in my book as author of this seminal work, *Fundamentals of Yoga*.] www.ashramstore.com

5   Ibid., 58-62.

6   Ramamurti S. Mishra, M.D., *Healing Through Yoga Sutras Chanting*, Ananda Ashram, 1982, cassette. Currently available as: Shri Brahmananda Sarasvati (Ramamurti S. Mishra, M.D.) *The Yoga Sutras of Patanjali: Healing Through Chanting*, Baba Bhagavandas Publication Trust, 2010, set of 2 compact discs. Also available as DVD. Excerpt of transcript reprinted with permission. www. ashramstore.com

7   From the New York Times, Harold M. Schmeck, Jr., "Schizophrenia Focus Shifts to Dramatic Changes in Brain," March 18 © 1986 The New York Times. All rights reserved. Used by permission and protected by the Copyright Laws of the United States. The printing, copying, redistribution, or retransmission of this Content without expression written permission is prohibited. www.nytimes.com

8   Shri Brahmananda Sarasvati (Ramamurti S. Mishra), *Mantra, Music, and Meditation with Shri Brahmananda Sarasvati and Students,* Ananda Ashram, 1985, cassette. Excerpt of transcript reprinted with permission.

PART I – CHAPTER THREE

9   Fyodor Dostoyevsky, *The Brothers Karamazov,* trans. Constance Garnett, The Modern Library, an imprint of Random House, Inc.

10   Isak Dinesen, *Shadows on the Grass,* Random House, Inc. Reprinted with permission.

11   Isak Dinesen, *Out of Africa and Shadows on the Grass,* Vintage Books, a division of Random House, Inc. Reprinted with permission.

PART I – CHAPTER FOUR

12   Paul Devereux, *Earth Lights* (Northamptonshire: Turnstone Press Limited, 1982), 94. Reprinted with kind permission of Mr. Paul Devereux.

PART I – CHAPTER SIX

13   From the author's personal notebooks, handwritten during a guided meditation given by Shri Brahmananda Sarasvati (Guruji) at Ananda Ashram on January 31, 1987. Guruji kindly tolerated the author's note-taking during his programs.

PART I – CHAPTER NINE

14   Shri Brahmananda Sarasvati (Ramamurti S. Mishra, M.D.), *Meditation on Your Electrical Body, Read by Joan Suval*, Ananda Ashram, 1986, cassette. Currently available as: *Blue Sky Meditations of Shri Brahmananda Sarasvati, Read by Joan Suval*, Baba Bhagavandas Publication Trust, 2004, set of 6 compact discs. Transcript adapted with permission from the Baba Bhagavandas Publication Trust. www.ashramstore.com

PART I – CHAPTER TEN

15   From the author's personal notebooks, handwritten during talks given by Shri Brahmananda Sarasvati (Guruji) at Ananda Ashram between November & December, 1986.

PART I – CHAPTER FIFTEEN

16   Richard Bach, *The Bridge Across Forever*. Copyright © 1984 by HarperCollins Publishers. Reprinted with permission.

PART II – CHAPTER TWENTY-SIX

17   A Monk of the Eastern Church, *Orthodox Spirituality: An Outline of the Orthodox Ascetical and Mystical Tradition* (Crestwood: St. Vladimir's Seminary Press, 1978), 27-28. Reprinted with kind permission of St. Vladimir's Seminary Press.

18   Shri Ramamurti (Ramamurti S. Mishra, M.D.) *Holistic Health and Healing Through Chanting Yoga Sutras of Patanjali* (Monroe: ICSA Press Ananda Ashram, 1982), 7. Currently avail-

able as: Shri Brahmananda Sarasvati (Ramamurti S. Mishra, M.D.), *The Yoga Sutras of Patanjali: Sanskrit Text with Translation* (Monroe: Baba Bhagavandas Publication Trust, 2010). Reprinted with permission. www.ashramstore.com

PART II – CHAPTER TWENTY-EIGHT

19   Roy Eugene Davis, *The Bhagavad Gita: God's Revealing Word* (Lakemont: CSA Press, 1968), 55-56. Reprinted with kind permission of Mr. Roy Eugene Davis. www.csa-davis.org

20   Ibid., 64-65.

21   Ibid., 70.

22   Reprinted with the permission of Touchstone, a Division of Simon & Schuster, Inc., from *SAINT FRANCIS* by Nikos Kazantzakis. Translation by P. A. Bien. Copyright © 1962 by Simon & Schuster, Inc. All rights reserved. *Separate permission obtained from Kazantzakis Publication Ltd., Foreign Rights Department, for markets outside North America.*

PART II – CHAPTER TWENTY-NINE

23   Pir Vilayat Inayat Khan, "A Double Wedding," *New Age Contact*, Vol. 8, April 1974, 14. Reprinted with kind permission of the Sufi Order International. www.sufiorder.org

PART II – CHAPTER THIRTY

24   Judith Thurman, *Isak Dinesen: The Life of a Storyteller* (New York: St. Martin's Press, 1982), 351. Reprinted with permission.

PART II – CHAPTER THIRTY-ONE

25   Susan Thomas, "Have You Ever Heard a Stone Talking?" *The Guardian*, June 25, 1983. Copyright Guardian News & Media Ltd 1983. Reprinted with permission. www.guardian.co.uk

ENDNOTES

PART III – CHAPTER THIRTY-TWO

26   Shri Brahmananda Sarasvati (Ramamurti S. Mishra, M.D.), excerpted from "Keynote Speech," delivered at Second European Conference on Universal Brotherhood, Copenhagen, Denmark, July 1985. Copyright by Baba Bhagavandas Publication Trust 1993, unpublished. An adaptation of the speech currently available as: Shri Brahmananda Sarasvati (Ramamurti S. Mishra, M.D.), "Why Are We Assembled Here?" *The Universal Search for Peace* (Monroe: Baba Bhagavandas Publication Trust, 2002). Reprinted with permission. www.ashramstore.com

PART III – CHAPTER THIRTY-THREE

27   From Newsweek, Jerry Adler with John Carey, "The Science of Love," February 25 (c) 1980 The Newsweek/Daily Beast Company LLC. All rights reserved. Used by permission and protected by the Copyright Laws of the United States. The printing, copying, redistribution, or retransmission of the Material without express written permission is prohibited. www.newsweek.com

28   From the New York Times, Dava Sobel, "Three Current Studies: In Pursuit of Love Defining Love Obsession," January 22 © 1980 The New York Times. All rights reserved. Used by permission and protected by the Copyright Laws of the United States. The printing, copying, redistribution, or retransmission of this Content without expression written permission is prohibited. www.nytimes.com

29   Reprinted with the permission of Scribner, a Division of Simon & Schuster, Inc., from *THE SUN ALSO RISES* by Ernest Hemingway. Copyright © 1926 by Charles Scribner's Sons; copyright renewed © 1954 by Ernest Hemingway. All rights reserved. *Separate permission obtained for print format throughout the UK and Commonwealth excluding Canada: from* The Sun Also Rises *by Ernest Hemingway, published by Jonathan Cape. Used by permission of The Random House Group Limited.*

30   Anton Chekhov, "Three Years," in *Anton Chekhov: Selected Stories,* translation by Ann Dunnigan. Copyright © 1960 by New American Library, an imprint of Penguin Group (USA). Reprinted with permission.

31   Copyright 1982, Reed Business Information - UK. Don Robbins, "The Dragon Project and the Talking Stones," *New Scientist,* Vol. 96, October 21, 1982, 166-170. All Rights Reserved. Distributed by Tribune Media Services. Used with permission. www.tmsinternational.com

32   Copyright 1983, Reed Business Information - UK. Charles Brooker, "Magnetism and the Standing Stones," *New Scientist,* Vol. 97, January 13, 1983, 105. All Rights Reserved. Distributed by Tribune Media Services. Used with permission. www.tmsinternational.com

33   Rammurti S. Mishra, M.D., "Acknowledgements," *Textbook of Yoga Psychology: A New Translation and Interpretation of Patanjali's Yoga Sutras for Meaningful Application in all Modern Psychologic Disciplines* (New York: Julian Press, Inc. 1963). Currently available as: Ramamurti S. Mishra, M.D. (Shri Brahmananda Sarasvati), *Textbook of Yoga Psychology: A Definitive Translation and Interpretation of the Yoga Sūtras of Patanjali* (Monroe: Baba Bhagavandas Publication Trust, 1997). Author's note: The concept of "psychic atom" is further developed in the essay of Dr. Mishra (Shri Brahmananda Sarasvati), "World of Energy," published in *Highlights from Five Decades: Selected Writings* (Monroe: Baba Bhagavandas Publication Trust, 2005), 67. Reprinted with permission. www.ashramstore.com

PART III – CHAPTER THIRTY-FIVE

34   Bach, *The Bridge Across Forever.* Reprinted with permission of HarperCollins Publishers.

35   From the New York Times, "Where Uncertainty Is King and Paradox Shares Throne," July 13 © 1986 The New York Times. All rights reserved. Used by permission and protected

36   Ibid.

37   Reprinted with the permission of Scribner, a Division of Simon & Schuster, Inc., from *A FAREWELL TO ARMS* by Ernest Hemingway. Copyright © 1929 by Charles Scribner's Sons. Copyright renewed © 1957 by Ernest Hemingway. All rights reserved. *Separate permission obtained for print format throughout the UK and Commonwealth excluding Canada: from* A Farewell to Arms *by Ernest Hemingway, published by Jonathan Cape. Used by permission of The Random House Group Limited.*

PART III – CHAPTER THIRTY-SIX

38   Dinesen, *Out of Africa and Shadows on the Grass*. Reprinted with permission of Random House, Inc.

39   John Green and R.J.C. Atkinson, *The Prehistoric Temples of Stonehenge and Avebury: A Pitkin Pictorial Guide and Souvenir Book* (London: Pitkin Pictorials Ltd., 1980), 24. Reprinted with permission of The History Press. www.thehistorypress.co.uk

40   From *The Ley Hunter's Companion* by Paul Devereux and Ian Thomson. © 1979 Thames & Hudson Ltd., London. Reprinted by kind permission of Thames & Hudson. www.thamesandhudson.com

41   Devereux, *Earth Lights*, 68. Reprinted with kind permission of Mr. Paul Devereux.

42   Ibid., 71.

43   John Edwin Wood, *Sun, Moon and Standing Stones* (Oxford: Oxford University Press, 1978), 185-186. By permission of Oxford University Press. www.oup.com.

44   Paul Screeton, *Quicksilver Heritage: The Mystic Leys, Their Legacy of Ancient Wisdom,* Thorsons Publishers Limited, Wellingborough, 1974, 14. Reprinted with kind permission of Mr. Paul Screeton.

45   From *The Avebury Cycle* by Michael Dames. © 1977 Thames & Hudson Ltd., London. Reprinted by kind permission of Thames & Hudson. www.thamesandhudson.com

46   Devereux, *Earth Lights*, 66. Reprinted with kind permission of Mr. Paul Devereux.

47   Ibid., 144-146.

48   DaEl Walker, "Crystal Healing," Introductory talk for weekend workshop at Ananda Ashram, Monroe, New York, October 18, 1985, private audio recording. Reprinted by kind permission of Mr. DaEl Walker.

49   Devereux, *Earth Lights*, 84. Reprinted with kind permission of Mr. Paul Devereux.

PART III – CHAPTER THIRTY-EIGHT

50   Gail Sheehy, *Passages: Predictable Crises of Adult Life.* Copyright © 1974 by E.P. Dutton & Co., an imprint of the Penguin Group (USA) Inc. Reprinted with permission. www.us.penguingroup.com

51   Ibid.

52   Ibid.

53   Ibid.

EPILOGUE

54   Shri Brahmananda Sarasvati, "The Most Powerful Man," written in 1986, © 2001 by Baba Bhagavandas Publication Trust,

ENDNOTES

Ananda Ashram, Monroe, New York. Reprinted with permission.

AUTHOR'S BIOGRAPHY

Margaret Dillsaver's introduction to her Guru, Ramamurti S. Mishra, M.D. (known later in his life as Shri Brahmananda Sarasvati), founder of Ananda Ashram in Monroe, New York, was at age seven when her mother first read to her from his book, *Fundamentals of Yoga*. To her young mind, "Dr. Mishra" had the answer to any and all problems. Given her serious nature, however, examination of the deep existential questions of life led her into depression when she was seventeen years old. Fortunately, her mother decided the best solution was to drop her off at the ashram, in hopes she would find relief from her malaise. She thus met her Guru in 1974 and the course of her life changed forever. At first a frequent visitor to the ashram, she moved there in 1985 and was very lucky to have an intense period of study with him before his passing in 1993. She continues to live and work at the ashram.